Miles

0	200	400	600

CALCUTTA

MAHRATTA
CONFEDERATION

jndia
1799-1803

BATTLES & SIEGES

Seringapatam	4 May 1799
Ammednuggur	12 Aug 1803
✗ Assaye	23 Sept 1803
✗ Argaum	29 Nov 1803
Gawilghur	15 Dec 1803

RAS

CEYLON

KEN LEWIS

SHARPE'S FORTRESS

By the same author

The Sharpe novels
(in chronological order)

SHARPE'S TIGER
Richard Sharpe and the Siege of Seringapatam, 1799

SHARPE'S TRIUMPH
Richard Sharpe and the Battle of Assaye, September 1803

SHARPE'S RIFLES
Richard Sharpe and the French Invasion of Galicia, January 1809

SHARPE'S EAGLE
Richard Sharpe and the Talavera Campaign, July 1809

SHARPE'S GOLD
Richard Sharpe and the Destruction of Almeida, August 1810

SHARPE'S BATTLE
Richard Sharpe and the Battle of Fuentes de Oñoro, May 1811

SHARPE'S COMPANY
Richard Sharpe and the Siege of Badajoz,
January to April 1812

SHARPE'S SWORD
Richard Sharpe and the Salamanca Campaign,
June and July 1812

SHARPE'S ENEMY
Richard Sharpe and the Defence of Portugal, Christmas 1812

SHARPE'S HONOUR
Richard Sharpe and the Vitoria Campaign,
February to June 1813

SHARPE'S REGIMENT
Richard Sharpe and the Invasion of France,
June to November 1813

SHARPE'S SIEGE
Richard Sharpe and the Winter Campaign, 1814

SHARPE'S REVENGE
Richard Sharpe and the Peace of 1814

SHARPE'S WATERLOO
Richard Sharpe and the Waterloo Campaign,
15 June to 18 June 1815

SHARPE'S DEVIL
Richard Sharpe and the Emperor, 1820–21

The Starbuck Chronicles

REBEL
COPPERHEAD
BATTLE FLAG
THE BLOODY GROUND

SHARPE'S FORTRESS

Richard Sharpe and
the Siege of Gawilghur,
December 1803

BERNARD CORNWELL

LONDON NEW YORK SYDNEY TORONTO

This edition published 1999
by BCA
By arrangement with HarperCollins*Publishers*

CN 7818

Copyright © Bernard Cornwell 1999

The Author asserts the moral right to
be identified as the author of this work

Maps by Ken Lewis

Set in Postscript Monotype Baskerville and Linotype Meridien by
Rowland Phototypesetting Ltd, Bury St Edmunds, Suffolk

Printed and bound in Great Britain by
Mackays of Chatham plc, Chatham, Kent

Sharpe's Fortress is for
Christine Clarke,
with many thanks

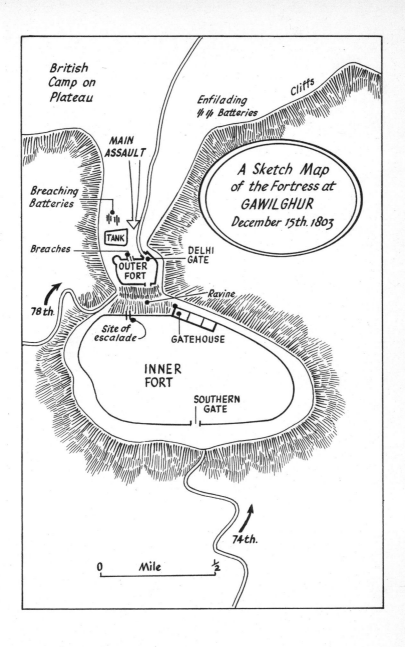

British
Camp on
Plateau

Cliffs

Enfilading
Batteries

MAIN
ASSAULT

A Sketch Map
of the Fortress at
GAWILGHUR
December 15th. 1803

Breaching
Batteries

TANK

Breaches

DELHI
GATE

OUTER
FORT

Ravine

78 th.

Site of
escalade

GATEHOUSE

INNER
FORT

SOUTHERN
GATE

74th.

0   Mile   ½

CHAPTER 1

Richard Sharpe wanted to be a good officer. He truly did. He wanted it above all other things, but somehow it was just too difficult, like trying to light a tinderbox in a rain-filled wind. Either the men disliked him, or they ignored him, or they were over-familiar and he was unsure how to cope with any of the three attitudes, while the battalion's other officers plain disapproved of him. You can put a racing saddle on a carthorse, Captain Urquhart had said one night in the ragged tent which passed for the officers' mess, but that don't make the beast quick. He had not been talking about Sharpe, not directly, but all the other officers glanced at him.

The battalion had stopped in the middle of nowhere. It was hot as hell and no wind alleviated the sodden heat. They were surrounded by tall crops that hid everything except the sky. A cannon fired somewhere to the north, but Sharpe had no way of knowing whether it was a British gun or an enemy cannon.

A dry ditch ran through the tall crops and the men of the company sat on the ditch lip as they waited for orders. One or two lay back and slept with their mouths wide open while Sergeant Colquhoun leafed though his tattered Bible. The Sergeant was short-sighted, so had to hold the book very close to his nose from which drops of sweat fell onto the pages. Usually the Sergeant read quietly, mouthing the words and sometimes frowning when he came across a difficult name, but today he was just slowly turning the pages with a wetted finger.

'Looking for inspiration, Sergeant?' Sharpe asked.

'I am not, sir,' Colquhoun answered respectfully, but somehow managed to convey that the question was still impertinent. He dabbed a finger on his tongue and carefully turned another page.

So much for that bloody conversation, Sharpe thought. Somewhere

9

ahead, beyond the tall plants that grew higher than a man, another cannon fired. The discharge was muffled by the thick stems. A horse neighed, but Sharpe could not see the beast. He could see nothing through the high crops.

'Are you going to read us a story, Sergeant?' Corporal McCallum asked. He spoke in English instead of Gaelic, which meant that he wanted Sharpe to hear.

'I am not, John. I am not.'

'Go on, Sergeant,' McCallum said. 'Read us one of those dirty tales about tits.'

The men laughed, glancing at Sharpe to see if he was offended. One of the sleeping men jerked awake and looked about him, startled, then muttered a curse, slapped at a fly and lay back. The other soldiers of the company dangled their boots towards the ditch's crazed mud bed that was decorated with a filigree of dried green scum. A dead lizard lay in one of the dry fissures. Sharpe wondered how the carrion birds had missed it.

'The laughter of fools, John McCallum,' Sergeant Colquhoun said, 'is like the crackling of thorns under the pot.'

'Away with you, Sergeant!' McCallum said. 'I heard it in the kirk once, when I was a wee kid, all about a woman whose tits were like bunches of grapes.' McCallum twisted to look at Sharpe. 'Have you ever seen tits like grapes, Mister Sharpe?'

'I never met your mother, Corporal,' Sharpe said.

The men laughed again. McCallum scowled. Sergeant Colquhoun lowered his Bible and peered at the Corporal. 'The Song of Solomon, John McCallum,' Colquhoun said, 'likens a woman's bosom to clusters of grapes, and I have no doubt it refers to the garments that modest women wore in the Holy Land. Perhaps their bodices possessed balls of knotted wool as decoration? I cannot see it is a matter for your merriment.' Another cannon fired, and this time a round shot whipped through the tall plants close to the ditch. The stems twitched violently, discharging a cloud of dust and small birds into the cloudless sky. The birds flew about in panic for a few seconds, then returned to the swaying seedheads.

'I knew a woman who had lumpy tits,' Private Hollister said. He was a dark-jawed, violent man who spoke rarely. 'Lumpy like a coal sack, they were.' He frowned at the memory, then shook his head. 'She died.'

'This conversation is not seemly,' Colquhoun said quietly, and the men shrugged and fell silent.

Sharpe wanted to ask the Sergeant about the clusters of grapes, but he knew such an enquiry would only cause ribaldry among the men and, as an officer, Sharpe could not risk being made to look a fool. All the same, it sounded odd to him. Why would anyone say a woman had tits like a bunch of grapes? Grapes made him think of grapeshot and he wondered if the bastards up ahead were equipped with canister. Well, of course they were, but there was no point in wasting canister on a field of bulrushes. Were they bulrushes? It seemed a strange thing for a farmer to grow, but India was full of oddities. There were naked sods who claimed to be holy men, snake-charmers who whistled up hooded horrors, dancing bears draped in tinkling bells, and contortionists draped in bugger all, a right bloody circus. And the clowns ahead would have canister. They would wait till they saw the redcoats, then load up the tin cans that burst like duckshot from the gun barrels. For what we are about to receive among the bulrushes, Sharpe thought, may the Lord make us truly thankful.

'I've found it,' Colquhoun said gravely.

'Found what?' Sharpe asked.

'I was fairly sure in my mind, sir, that the good book mentioned millet. And so it does. Ezekiel, the fourth chapter and the ninth verse.' The Sergeant held the book close to his eyes, squinting at the text. He had a round face, afflicted with wens, like a suet pudding studded with currants. '"Take thou also unto thee wheat, and barley,"' he read laboriously, '"and beans, and lentils, and millet, and fitches, and put them in one vessel, and make thee bread thereof."' Colquhoun carefully closed his Bible, wrapped it in a scrap of tarred canvas and stowed it in his pouch. 'It pleases me, sir,' he explained, 'if I can find everyday things in the scriptures. I like to see things, sir, and imagine my Lord and Saviour seeing the selfsame things.'

'But why millet?' Sharpe asked.

'These crops, sir,' Colquhoun said, pointing to the tall stems that surrounded them, 'are millet. The natives call it *jowari*, but our name is millet.' He cuffed the sweat from his face with his sleeve. The red dye of his coat had faded to a dull purple. 'This, of course,' he went on, 'is pearl millet, but I doubt the scriptures mention pearl millet. Not specifically.'

11

'Millet, eh?' Sharpe said. So the tall plants were not bulrushes, after all. They looked like bulrushes, except they were taller. Nine or ten feet high. 'Must be a bastard to harvest,' he said, but got no response. Sergeant Colquhoun always tried to ignore swear words.

'What are fitches?' McCallum asked.

'A crop grown in the Holy Land,' Colquhoun answered. He plainly did not know.

'Sounds like a disease, Sergeant,' McCallum said. 'A bad dose of the fitches. Leads to a course of mercury.' One or two men sniggered at the reference to syphilis, but Colquhoun ignored the levity.

'Do you grow millet in Scotland?' Sharpe asked the Sergeant.

'Not that I am aware of, sir,' Colquhoun said ponderously, after reflecting on the question for a few seconds, 'though I daresay it might be found in the Lowlands. They grow strange things there. English things.' He turned pointedly away.

And sod you too, Sharpe thought. And where the hell was Captain Urquhart? Where the hell was anybody for that matter? The battalion had marched long before dawn, and at midday they had expected to make camp, but then came a rumour that the enemy was waiting ahead and so General Sir Arthur Wellesley had ordered the baggage to be piled and the advance to continue. The King's 74th had plunged into the millet, then ten minutes later the battalion was ordered to halt beside the dry ditch while Captain Urquhart rode ahead to speak with the battalion commander, and Sharpe had been left to sweat and wait with the company.

Where he had damn all to do except sweat. Damn all. It was a good company, and it did not need Sharpe. Urquhart ran it well, Colquhoun was a magnificent sergeant, the men were as content as soldiers ever were, and the last thing the company needed was a brand new officer, an Englishman at that, who, just two months before, had been a sergeant.

The men were talking in Gaelic and Sharpe, as ever, wondered if they were discussing him. Probably not. Most likely they were talking about the dancing girls in Ferdapoor, where there had been no mere clusters of grapes, but bloody great naked melons. It had been some sort of festival and the battalion had marched one way and the half-naked girls had writhed in the opposite direction and Sergeant Colquhoun had blushed as scarlet as an unfaded coat and shouted at the men to keep their eyes front. Which had been a pointless order, when a score of undressed *bibbis* were bobbling down the highway with silver bells tied to their wrists and even the officers were staring at them like starving men seeing a plate of roast beef. And if the men were not discussing women, they were probably grumbling about all the marching they had done in the last weeks, criss-crossing the Mahratta countryside under a blazing sun without sight or smell of the enemy. But whatever they were talking about they were making damn sure that Ensign Richard Sharpe was left out.

Which was fair enough, Sharpe reckoned. He had marched in the ranks long enough to know that you did not talk to officers, not unless you were spoken to or unless you were a slick-bellied crawling bastard looking for favours. Officers were different, except Sharpe did not feel different. He just felt excluded. I should have stayed a sergeant, he thought. He had increasingly thought that in the last few weeks, wishing he was back in the Seringapatam armoury with Major Stokes. That had been the life! And Simone Joubert, the Frenchwoman who had clung to Sharpe after the battle at Assaye, had gone back to Seringapatam to wait for him. Better to be there as a sergeant, he reckoned, than here as an unwanted officer.

No guns had fired for a while. Perhaps the enemy had packed up and gone? Perhaps they had hitched their painted cannon to their ox teams, stowed the canister in its limbers and buggered off northwards? In which case it would be a quick about-turn, back to the village where the baggage was stored, then another awkward evening in the officers' mess. Lieutenant Cahill would watch Sharpe like a hawk, adding tuppence to Sharpe's mess bill for every glass of wine, and Sharpe, as the junior officer, would have to propose the loyal toast and pretend not to see when half the bastards wafted their mugs over their canteens. King over the water. Toasting a dead Stuart pretender to the throne who had died in Roman exile. Jacobites who pretended George III was not the proper King. Not that any of them were truly disloyal, and the secret gesture of passing the wine over the water was not even a real secret, but rather was intended to goad Sharpe into English indignation. Except Sharpe did not give a fig. Old King Cole could have been King of Britain for all Sharpe cared.

Colquhoun suddenly barked orders in Gaelic and the men picked up their muskets, jumped into the irrigation ditch where they formed into four ranks and began trudging northwards. Sharpe, taken by surprise, meekly followed. He supposed he should have asked Colquhoun what was happening, but he did not like to display ignorance, and then he saw that the rest of the battalion was also marching, so plainly Colquhoun had decided number six company should advance as well. The Sergeant had made no pretence of asking Sharpe for permission to move. Why should he? Even if Sharpe did give an order the men automatically looked for Colquhoun's nod before they obeyed. That was how the company worked; Urquhart commanded, Colquhoun came next, and Ensign Sharpe tagged along like one of the scruffy dogs adopted by the men.

Captain Urquhart spurred his horse back down the ditch. 'Well done, Sergeant,' he told Colquhoun, who ignored the praise. The Captain turned the horse, its hooves breaking through the ditch's crust to churn up clots of dried mud. 'The rascals are waiting ahead,' Urquhart told Sharpe.

'I thought they might have gone,' Sharpe said.

'They're formed and ready,' Urquhart said, 'formed and ready.' The Captain was a fine-looking man with a stern face, straight back and steady nerve. The men trusted him. In other days Sharpe would have been proud to serve a man like Urquhart, but the Captain seemed irritated by Sharpe's presence. 'We'll be wheeling to the right soon,' Urquhart called to Colquhoun, 'forming line on the right in two ranks.'

'Aye, sir.'

Urquhart glanced up at the sky. 'Three hours of daylight left?' he guessed. 'Enough to do the job. You'll take the left files, Ensign.'

'Yes, sir,' Sharpe said, and knew that he would have nothing to do there. The men understood their duty, the corporals would close the files and Sharpe would simply walk behind them like a dog tied to a cart.

There was a sudden crash of guns as a whole battery of enemy cannon opened fire. Sharpe heard the round shots whipping through the millet, but none of the missiles came near the 74th. The battalion's pipers had started playing and the men picked up their feet and hefted their muskets in preparation for the grim work ahead. Two more guns fired, and this time Sharpe saw a wisp of smoke above the seedheads and he knew that a shell had gone overhead. The smoke trail from the burning fuse wavered in the windless heat as Sharpe waited for the explosion, but none sounded.

'Cut his fuse too long,' Urquhart said. His horse was nervous, or perhaps it disliked the treacherous footing in the bottom of the ditch. Urquhart spurred the horse up the bank where it trampled the millet. 'What is this stuff?' he asked Sharpe. 'Maize?'

'Colquhoun says it's millet,' Sharpe said, 'pearl millet.'

Urquhart grunted, then kicked his horse on towards the front of the company. Sharpe cuffed sweat from his eyes. He wore an officer's red tail coat with the white facings of the 74th. The coat had belonged to a Lieutenant Blaine who had died at Assaye and Sharpe had purchased the coat for a shilling in the auction of dead officers' effects, then he had clumsily sewn up the bullet hole in the left breast, but no amount of scrubbing had rid the coat of Blaine's blood which stained the faded red weave black. He wore his old trousers, the ones issued to him when he was a sergeant, red leather riding boots that he had taken from an Arab corpse in Ahmednuggur, and a tasselled red officer's sash that he had pulled off a corpse at Assaye. For a sword he wore a light cavalry sabre, the same weapon he had used to save Wellesley's life at the battle of Assaye. He did not like the sabre much. It was clumsy, and the curved blade was never where you thought it was. You struck with the sword, and just when you thought it would bite home, you found that the blade still had six inches to travel. The other officers carried claymores, big, straight-bladed, heavy and lethal, and Sharpe should have equipped himself with one, but he had baulked at the auction prices.

He could have bought every claymore in the auction if he had wished, but he had not wanted to give the impression of being wealthy. Which he was. But a man like Sharpe was not supposed to have money. He was up from the ranks, a common soldier, gutter-born and gutter-bred, but he had hacked down a half-dozen men to save Wellesley's life and the General had rewarded Sergeant Sharpe by making him into an officer, and Ensign Sharpe was too canny to let his new battalion know that he possessed a king's fortune. A dead king's fortune: the jewels he had taken from the Tippoo Sultan in the blood and smoke-stinking Water Gate at Seringapatam.

Would he be more popular if it was known he was rich? He doubted it. Wealth did not give respectability, not unless it was inherited.

Besides, it was not poverty that excluded Sharpe from both the officers' mess and the ranks alike, but rather that he was a stranger. The 74th had taken a beating at Assaye. Not an officer had been left unwounded, and companies that had paraded seventy or eighty strong before the battle now had only forty to fifty men. The battalion had been ripped through hell and back, and its survivors now clung to each other. Sharpe might have been at Assaye, he might even have distinguished himself on the battlefield, but he had not been through the murderous ordeal of the 74th and so he was an outsider.

'Line to the right!' Sergeant Colquhoun shouted, and the company wheeled right and shook itself into a line of two ranks. The ditch had emerged from the millet to join a wide, dry riverbed, and Sharpe looked northwards to see a rill of dirty white gunsmoke on the horizon. Mahratta guns. But a long way away. Now that the battalion was free of the tall crops Sharpe could just detect a small wind. It was not strong enough to cool the heat, but it would waft the gunsmoke slowly away.

'Halt!' Urquhart called. 'Face front!'

The enemy cannon might be far off, but it seemed that the battalion would march straight up the riverbed into the mouths of those guns. But at least the 74th was not alone. The 78th, another Highland battalion, was on their right, and on either side of those two Scottish battalions were long lines of Madrassi sepoys.

Urquhart rode back to Sharpe. 'Stevenson's joined.' The Captain spoke loud enough for the rest of the company to hear. Urquhart was encouraging them by letting them know that the two small British armies had combined. General Wellesley commanded both, but for most of the time he split his forces into two parts, the smaller under Colonel Stevenson, but today the two small parts had combined so that twelve thousand infantry could attack together. But against how many? Sharpe could not see the Mahratta army beyond their guns, but doubtless the bastards were there in force.

'Which means the 94th's off to our left somewhere,' Urquhart added loudly, and some of the men muttered their approval of the news. The 94th was another Scottish regiment, so today there were three Scottish battalions attacking the Mahrattas. Three Scottish and ten sepoy battalions, and most of the Scots reckoned that they could have done the job by themselves. Sharpe reckoned they could too. They may not have liked him much, but he knew they were good soldiers. Tough bastards. He sometimes tried to imagine what it must be like for the Mahrattas to fight against the Scots. Hell, he guessed. Absolute hell. 'The thing is,' Colonel McCandless had once told Sharpe, 'it takes twice as much to kill a Scot as it does to finish off an Englishman.'

Poor McCandless. He had been finished off, shot in the dying moments of Assaye. Any of the enemy might have killed the Colonel, but Sharpe had convinced himself that the traitorous Englishman, William Dodd, had fired the fatal shot. And Dodd was still free, still fighting for the Mahrattas, and Sharpe had sworn over McCandless's grave that he would take vengeance on the Scotsman's behalf. He had made the oath as he had dug the Colonel's grave, getting blisters as he had hacked into the dry soil. McCandless had been a good friend to Sharpe and now, with the Colonel deep buried so that no bird or beast could feast on his corpse, Sharpe felt friendless in this army.

'Guns!' A shout sounded behind the 74th. 'Make way!'

Two batteries of six-pounder galloper guns were being hauled up the dry riverbed to form an artillery line ahead of the infantry. The guns were called gallopers because they were light and were usually hauled by horses, but now they were all harnessed to teams of ten oxen so they plodded rather than galloped. The oxen had painted horns and some had bells about their necks. The heavy guns were all back on the road somewhere, so far back that they would probably be too late to join this day's party.

The land was more open now. There were a few patches of tall millet ahead, but off to the east there were arable fields and Sharpe watched as the guns headed for that dry grassland. The enemy was watching too, and the first round shots bounced on the grass and ricocheted over the British guns.

'A few minutes before the gunners bother themselves with us, I fancy,' Urquhart said, then kicked his right foot out of its stirrup and slid down beside Sharpe. 'Jock!' He called a soldier. 'Hold onto my horse, will you?' The soldier led the horse off to a patch of grass, and Urquhart jerked his head, inviting Sharpe to follow him out of the company's earshot. The Captain seemed embarrassed, as was Sharpe, who was not accustomed to such intimacy with Urquhart. 'D'you use a cigar, Sharpe?' the Captain asked.

'Sometimes, sir.'

'Here.' Urquhart offered Sharpe a roughly rolled cigar, then struck a light in his tinderbox. He lit his own cigar first, then held the box with its flickering flame to Sharpe. 'The Major tells me a new draft has arrived in Madras.'

'That's good, sir.'

'It won't restore our strength, of course, but it'll help,' Urquhart said. He was not looking at Sharpe, but staring at the British guns that steadily advanced across the grassland. There were only a dozen of the cannon, far fewer than the Mahratta guns. A shell exploded by one of the ox teams, blasting the beasts with smoke and scraps of turf, and Sharpe expected to see the gun stop as the dying beasts tangled the traces, but the oxen trudged on, miraculously unhurt by the shell's violence. 'If they advance too far,' Urquhart murmured, 'they'll become so much scrap metal. Are you happy here, Sharpe?'

'Happy, sir?' Sharpe was taken aback by the sudden question.

Urquhart frowned as if he found Sharpe's response unhelpful. 'Happy,' he said again, 'content?'

'Not sure a soldier's meant to be happy, sir.'

'Not true, not true,' Urquhart said disapprovingly. He was as tall as Sharpe. Rumour said that Urquhart was a very rich man, but the only sign of it was his uniform which was cut very elegantly in contrast to Sharpe's shabby coat. Urquhart rarely smiled, which made it difficult to be easy in his company. Sharpe wondered why the Captain had sought this conversation, which seemed untypical of the unbending Urquhart. Perhaps he was nervous about the imminent battle? It seemed unlikely to Sharpe after Urquhart had endured the cauldron of fire at Assaye, but he could think of no other explanation. 'A fellow should be content in his work,' Urquhart said with a flourish of his cigar, 'and if he ain't, it's probably a sign that he's in the wrong line of business.'

'Don't have much work to do, sir,' Sharpe said, wishing he did not sound so surly.

'Don't suppose you do,' Urquhart said slowly. 'I do see your meaning. Indeed I do.' He shuffled his feet in the dust. 'Company runs itself, I suppose. Colquhoun's a good fellow, and Sergeant Craig's showing well, don't you think?'

'Yes, sir.' Sharpe knew he did not need to call Urquhart 'sir' all the time, but old habits died hard.

'They're both good Calvinists, you see,' Urquhart said. 'Makes 'em trustworthy.'

'Yes, sir,' Sharpe said. He was not exactly sure what a Calvinist was, and he was not going to ask. Maybe it was the same as a freemason, and there were plenty of those in the 74th's mess, though Sharpe again did not really know what they were. He just knew he was not one of them.

'Thing is, Sharpe,' Urquhart went on, though he did not look at Sharpe as he spoke, 'you're sitting on a fortune, if you follow me.'

'A fortune, sir?' Sharpe asked with some alarm. Had Urquhart somehow smelt out Sharpe's hoard of emeralds, rubies, diamonds and sapphires?

'You're an ensign,' Urquhart explained, 'and if you ain't happy you can always sell your commission. Plenty of fine fellows in Scotland who'll pay you for the rank. Even some fellows here. I gather the Scotch Brigade has some gentlemen rankers.'

So Urquhart was not nervous about the coming fight, but rather about Sharpe's reaction to this conversation. The Captain wanted to be rid of Sharpe, and the realization made Sharpe even more awkward. He had wanted to be made an officer so badly, and already he wished he had never dreamed of the promotion. What had he expected? To be slapped on the back and welcomed like a long-lost brother? To be given a company of troops? Urquhart was watching him expectantly, waiting for a response, but Sharpe said nothing.

'Four hundred pounds, Sharpe,' Urquhart said. 'That's the official rate for an ensign's commission, but between you and me you can squeeze at least another fifty. Maybe even a hundred! And in guineas. But if you do sell to a ranker here, then make damn sure his note is good.'

Sharpe said nothing. Were there really gentlemen rankers in the 94th? Such men could afford to be officers, and had an officer's breeding, but until a commission was vacant they served in the ranks, yet ate in the mess. They were neither fish nor fowl. Like Sharpe himself. And any one of them would snap at the chance to buy a commission in the 74th. But Sharpe hardly needed the money. He possessed a fortune already, and if he wanted to leave the army then all he needed to do was resign his commission and walk away. Walk away a rich man.

'Of course,' Urquhart went on, oblivious of Sharpe's thoughts, 'if the note's written on a decent army agent then you won't have any worries. Most of our fellows use John Borrey in Edinburgh, so if you see one of his notes then you can place full trust in it. Borrey's an honest fellow. Another Calvinist, you see.'

'And a freemason, sir?' Sharpe asked. He was not really sure why he asked, but the question just got blurted out. He supposed he wanted to know if it was the same thing as a Calvinist.

'I really couldn't say.' Urquhart frowned at Sharpe and his voice became colder. 'The point is, Sharpe, he's trustworthy.'

Four hundred and fifty guineas, Sharpe thought. It was not to be spat on. It was another small fortune to add to his jewels, and he felt the temptation to accept Urquhart's advice. He was never going to be welome in the 74th, and with his plunder he could set himself up in England.

'Coins on the barrel-head,' Urquhart said. 'Think on it, Sharpe, think on it. Jock, my horse!'

Sharpe threw away the cigar. His mouth was dry with dust and the smoke was harsh, but as Urquhart mounted his horse he saw the scarcely smoked cigar lying on the ground and gave Sharpe an unfriendly look. For a second it seemed as if the Captain might say something, then he pulled on the reins and spurred away. Bugger it, Sharpe thought. Can't do a thing right these days.

The Mahratta cannon had got the range of the British galloper guns now and one of their round shot landed plumb on a carriage. One wheel splintered, tipping the six-pounder gun onto its side. The gunners leaped off the limber, but before they could detach the spare wheel, the ox team bolted. They dragged the broken gun back towards the sepoys, leaving a vast plume of dust where the axle boss dragged through the dry soil. The gunners ran to head the oxen off, but then a second team panicked. The beasts had their painted horns down and were galloping away from the bombardment. The Mahratta guns were firing fast now. A round shot slashed into another gun team, spurting ox blood bright into the sky. The enemy guns were big brutes, and with a much longer range than the small British six-pounders. A pair of shells exploded behind the panicked oxen, driving them even faster towards the sepoy battalions on the right of Wellesley's line. The limbers were bouncing frantically on the uneven ground and every lurch sent shot tumbling or powder spilling. Sharpe saw General Wellesley turn his horse towards the sepoys. He was doubtless shouting at them to open ranks and so allow the bolting oxen to pass through the line, but instead, quite suddenly, the men themselves turned and ran. 'Jesus!' Sharpe said aloud, earning himself a reproving look from Sergeant Colquhoun.

Two battalions of the sepoys were fleeing. Sharpe saw the General riding among the fugitives, and he imagined Wellesley shouting at the frightened men to stop and re-form, but instead they kept running towards the millet. They had been panicked by the oxen and by the weight of enemy shot that beat the dry grassland with dust and smoke. The men vanished in the high stalks, leaving nothing behind but a scatter of embarrassed officers and, astonishingly, the two panicked gun teams which had inexplicably stopped short of the millet and now waited patiently for the gunners to catch them.

'Sit yourselves down!' Urquhart called to his men, and the company squatted in the dry riverbed. One man took a stump of clay pipe from his pouch and lit it with a tinderbox. The tobacco smoke drifted slowly in the small wind. A few men drank from their canteens, but most were hoarding their water against the dryness that would come when they bit into their cartridges. Sharpe glanced behind, hoping to see the *puckalees* who brought the battalion water, but there was no sign of them. When he turned back to the north he saw that some enemy cavalry had appeared on the crest, their tall lances making a spiky thicket against the sky. Doubtless the enemy horsemen were tempted to attack the broken British line and so stampede more of the nervous sepoys, but a squadron of British cavalry emerged from a wood with their sabres drawn to threaten the flank of the enemy horsemen. Neither side charged, but instead they just watched each other. The 74th's pipers had ceased their playing. The remaining British galloper guns were deploying now, facing up the long gentle slope to where the enemy cannon lined the horizon. 'Are all the muskets loaded?' Urquhart asked Colquhoun.

'They'd better be, sir, or I'll want to know why.'

Urquhart dismounted. He had a dozen full canteens of water tied to his saddle and he unstrung six of them and gave them to the company. 'Share it out,' he ordered, and Sharpe wished he had thought to bring some extra water himself. One man cupped some water in his hands and let his dog lap it up. The dog then sat and scratched its fleas while its master lay back and tipped his shako over his eyes.

What the enemy should do, Sharpe thought, is throw their infantry forward. All of it. Send a massive attack across the skyline and down towards the millet. Flood the riverbed with a horde of screaming warriors who could add to the panic and so snatch victory.

But the skyline stayed empty except for the guns and the stalled enemy lancers.

And so the redcoats waited.

Colonel William Dodd, commanding officer of Dodd's Cobras, spurred his horse to the skyline from where he stared down the slope to see the British force in disarray. It looked to him as though two or more battalions had fled in panic, leaving a gaping hole on the right of the redcoat line. He turned his horse and kicked it to where the Mahratta warlord waited under his banners. Dodd forced his horse through the aides until he reached Prince Manu Bappoo. 'Throw everything forward, sahib,' he advised Bappoo, 'now!'

Manu Bappoo showed no sign of having heard Dodd. The Mahratta commander was a tall and lean man with a long, scarred face and a short black beard. He wore yellow robes, had a silver helmet with a long horse-tail plume, and carried a drawn sword that he claimed to have taken in single combat from a British cavalry officer. Dodd doubted the claim, for the sword was of no pattern that he recognized, but he was not willing to challenge Bappoo directly on the matter. Bappoo was not like most of the Mahratta leaders that Dodd knew. Bappoo might be a prince and the younger brother of the cowardly Rajah of Berar, but he was also a fighter.

'Attack now!' Dodd insisted. Much earlier in the day he had advised against fighting the British at all, but now it seemed that his advice had been wrong, for the British assault had dissolved in panic long before it reached musket range. 'Attack with everything we've got, sahib,' Dodd urged Bappoo.

'If I throw everything forward, Colonel Dodd,' Bappoo said in his oddly sibilant voice, 'then my guns will have to cease fire. Let the British walk into the cannon fire, then we shall release the infantry.' Bappoo had lost his front teeth to a lance thrust, and hissed his words so that, to Dodd, he sounded like a snake. He even looked reptilian.

Maybe it was his hooded eyes, or perhaps it was just his air of silent menace. But at least he could fight. Bappoo's brother, the Rajah of Berar, had fled before the battle at Assaye, but Bappoo, who had not been present at Assaye, was no coward. Indeed, he could bite like a serpent.

'The British walked into the cannon fire at Assaye,' Dodd growled, 'and there were fewer of them and we had more guns, but still they won.'

Bappoo patted his horse which had shied away from the sound of a nearby cannon. It was a big, black Arab stallion, and its saddle was encrusted with silver. Both horse and saddle had been gifts from an Arabian sheik whose tribesmen sailed to India to serve in Bappoo's own regiment. They were mercenaries from the pitiless desert who called themselves the Lions of Allah and they were reckoned to be the most savage regiment in all India. The Lions of Allah were arrayed behind Bappoo: a phalanx of dark-faced, white-robed warriors armed with muskets and long, curved scimitars. 'You truly think we should fight them in front of our guns?' Bappoo asked Dodd.

'Muskets will kill more of them than cannon will,' Dodd said. One of the things he liked about Bappoo was that the man was willing to listen to advice. 'Meet them halfway, sahib, thin the bastards out with musket fire, then pull back to let the guns finish them with canister. Better still, sahib, put the guns on the flank to rake them.'

'Too late to do that,' Bappoo said.

'Aye, well. Mebbe.' Dodd sniffed. Why the Indians stubbornly insisted on putting guns in front of infantry, he did not know. Daft idea, it was, but they would do it. He kept telling them to put their cannon between the regiments, so that the gunners could slant their fire across the face of the infantry, but Indian commanders reckoned that the sight of guns directly in front heartened their men. 'But put some infantry out front, sahib,' he urged.

Bappoo thought about Dodd's proposal. He did not much like the Englishman who was a tall, ungainly and sullen man with long yellow teeth and a sarcastic manner, but Bappoo suspected his advice was good. The Prince had never fought the British before, but he was aware that they were somehow different from the other enemies he had slaughtered on a score of battlefields across western India. There was, he understood, a stolid indifference to death in those red ranks

23

that let them march calmly into the fiercest cannonade. He had not seen it happen, but he had heard about it from enough men to credit the reports. Even so he found it hard to abandon the tried and tested methods of battle. It would seem unnatural to advance his infantry in front of the guns, and so render the artillery useless. He had thirty-eight cannon, all of them heavier than anything the British had yet deployed, and his gunners were as well trained as any in the world. Thirty-eight heavy cannon could make a fine slaughter of advancing infantry, yet if what Dodd said was true, then the red-coated ranks would stoically endure the punishment and keep coming. Except some had already run, which suggested they were nervous, so perhaps this was the day when the gods would finally turn against the British. 'I saw two eagles this morning,' Bappoo told Dodd, 'outlined against the sun.'

So bloody what? Dodd thought. The Indians were great ones for auguries, forever staring into pots of oil or consulting holy men or worrying about the errant fall of a trembling leaf, but there was no better augury for victory than the sight of an enemy running away before they even reached the fight. 'I assume the eagles mean victory?' Dodd asked politely.

'They do,' Bappoo agreed. And the augury suggested the victory would be his whatever tactics he used, which inclined him against trying anything new. Besides, though Prince Manu Bappoo had never fought the British, nor had the British ever faced the Lions of Allah in battle. And the numbers were in Bappoo's favour. He was barring the British advance with forty thousand men, while the redcoats were not even a third of that number. 'We shall wait,' Bappoo decided, 'and let the enemy get closer.' He would crush them with cannon fire first, then with musketry. 'Perhaps I shall release the Lions of Allah when the British are closer, Colonel,' he said to pacify Dodd.

'One regiment won't do it,' Dodd said, 'not even your Arabs, sahib. Throw every man forward. The whole line.'

'Maybe,' Bappoo said vaguely, though he had no intention of advancing all his infantry in front of the precious guns. He had no need to. The vision of eagles had persuaded him that he would see victory, and he believed the gunners would make that victory. He imagined dead red-coated bodies among the crops. He would avenge Assaye and prove that redcoats could die like any other enemy. 'To your men, Colonel Dodd,' he said sternly.

Dodd wheeled his horse and spurred towards the right of the line where his Cobras waited in four ranks. It was a fine regiment, splendidly trained, which Dodd had extricated from the siege of Ahmednuggur and then from the panicked chaos of the defeat at Assaye. Two disasters, yet Dodd's men had never flinched. The regiment had been a part of Scindia's army, but after Assaye the Cobras had retreated with the Rajah of Berar's infantry, and Prince Manu Bappoo, summoned from the north country to take command of Berar's shattered forces, had persuaded Dodd to change his allegiance from Scindia to the Rajah of Berar. Dodd would have changed allegiance anyway, for the dispirited Scindia was seeking to make peace with the British, but Bappoo had added the inducement of gold, silver and a promotion to colonel. Dodd's men, mercenaries all, did not care which master they served so long as his purse was deep.

Gopal, Dodd's second-in-command, greeted the Colonel's return with a rueful look. 'He won't advance?'

'He wants the guns to do the work.'

Gopal heard the doubt in Dodd's voice. 'And they won't?'

'They didn't at Assaye,' Dodd said sourly. 'Damn it! We shouldn't be fighting them here at all! Never give redcoats open ground. We should be making the bastards climb walls or cross rivers.' Dodd was nervous of defeat, and he had cause to be for the British had put a price on his head. That price was now seven hundred guineas, nearly six thousand rupees, and all of it promised in gold to whoever delivered William Dodd's body, dead or alive, to the East India Company. Dodd had been a lieutenant in the Company's army, but he had encouraged his men to murder a goldsmith and, faced with prosecution, Dodd had deserted and taken over a hundred sepoys with him. That had been enough to put a price on his head, but the price rose after Dodd and his treacherous sepoys murdered the Company's garrison at Chasalgaon. Now Dodd's body was worth a fortune and William Dodd understood greed well enough to be fearful. If Bappoo's army collapsed today as the Mahratta army had disintegrated at Assaye, then Dodd would be a fugitive on an open plain dominated by enemy cavalry. 'We should fight them in the hills,' he said grimly.

'Then we should fight them at Gawilghur,' Gopal said.

'Gawilghur?' Dodd asked.

'It is the greatest of all the Mahratta fortresses, sahib. Not all the armies of Europe could take Gawilghur.' Gopal saw that Dodd was sceptical of the claim. 'Not all the armies of the world could take it, sahib,' he added earnestly. 'It stands on cliffs that touch the sky, and from its walls men are reduced to the size of lice.'

'There's a way in, though,' Dodd said, 'there's always a way in.'

'There is, sahib, but the way into Gawilghur is across a neck of high rock that leads only to an outer fortress. A man might fight his way through those outer walls, but then he will come to a deep ravine and find the real stronghold lies on the ravine's far side. There are more walls, more guns, a narrow path, and vast gates barring the way!' Gopal sighed. 'I saw it once, years ago, and prayed I would never have to fight an enemy who had taken refuge there.'

Dodd said nothing. He was staring down the gentle slope to where the red-coated infantry waited. Every few seconds a puff of dust showed where a round shot struck the ground.

'If things go badly today,' Gopal said quietly, 'then we shall go to Gawilghur and there we shall be safe. The British can follow us, but they cannot reach us. They will break themselves on Gawilghur's rocks while we take our rest at the edge of the fortress's lakes. We shall be in the sky, and they will die beneath us like dogs.'

If Gopal was right then not all the king's horses nor all the king's men could touch William Dodd at Gawilghur. But first he had to reach the fortress, and maybe it would not even be necessary, for Prince Manu Bappoo might yet beat the redcoats here. Bappoo believed there was no infantry in India that could stand against his Arab mercenaries.

Away on the plain Dodd could see that the two battalions that had fled into the tall crops were now being brought back into the line. In a moment, he knew, that line would start forward again. 'Tell our guns to hold their fire,' he ordered Gopal. Dodd's Cobras possessed five small cannon of their own, designed to give the regiment close support. Dodd's guns were not in front of his white-coated men, but away on the right flank from where they could lash a murderous slanting fire across the face of the advancing enemy. 'Load with canister,' he ordered, 'and wait till they're close.' The important thing was to win, but if fate decreed otherwise, then Dodd must live to fight again at a place where a man could not be beaten.

At Gawilghur.

*　　*　　*

The British line at last advanced. From east to west it stretched for three miles, snaking in and out of millet fields, through pastureland and across the wide, dry riverbed. The centre of the line was an array of thirteen red-coated infantry battalions, three of them Scottish and the rest sepoys, while two regiments of cavalry advanced on the left flank and four on the right. Beyond the regular cavalry were two masses of mercenary horsemen who had allied themselves to the British in hope of loot. Drums beat and pipes played. The colours hung above the shakos. A great swathe of crops was trodden flat as the cumbersome line marched north. The British guns opened fire, their small six-pound missiles aimed at the Mahratta guns.

Those Mahratta guns fired constantly. Sharpe, walking behind the left flank of number six company, watched one particular gun which stood just beside a bright clump of flags on the enemy-held skyline. He slowly counted to sixty in his head, then counted it again, and worked out that the gun had managed five shots in two minutes. He could not be certain just how many guns were on the horizon, for the great cloud of powder smoke hid them, but he tried to count the muzzle flashes that appeared as momentary bright flames amidst the grey-white vapour and, as best he could guess, he reckoned there were nearly forty cannon there. Forty times five was what? Two hundred. So a hundred shots a minute were being fired, and each shot, if properly aimed, might kill two men, one in the front rank and one behind. Once the attack was close, of course, the bastards would switch to canister and then every shot could pluck a dozen men out of the line, but for now, as the redcoats silently trudged forward, the enemy was sending round shot down the gentle slope. A good many of these missed. Some screamed overhead and a few bounced over the line, but the enemy gunners were good, and they were lowering their cannon barrels so that the round shot struck the ground well ahead of the redcoat line and, by the time the missile reached the target, it had bounced a dozen times and so struck at waist height or below. Grazing, the gunners called it, and it took skill. If the first graze was too close to the gun then the ball would lose its momentum and do nothing but raise jeers from the redcoats as it rolled to a harmless stop, while if the first graze was too close to the attacking line then the ball would bounce clean over the redcoats. The skill was to skim the ball low enough to be certain of a hit, and all along the line the round shots were taking their toll. Men were plucked back with shattered hips and legs. Sharpe passed one spent cannonball that was sticky with blood and thick with flies, lying twenty paces from the man it had eviscerated. 'Close up!' the sergeants shouted, and the file-closers tugged men to fill the gaps. The British guns were firing into the enemy smoke cloud, but their shots seemed to have no effect, and so the guns were ordered farther forward. The ox teams were brought up, the guns were attached to the limbers, and the six-pounders trundled on up the slope.

'Like ninepins.' Ensign Venables had appeared at Sharpe's side. Roderick Venables was sixteen years old and attached to number seven company. He had been the battalion's most junior officer till Sharpe joined, and Venables had taken it on himself to be a tutor to Sharpe in how officers should behave. 'They're bowling us over like ninepins, eh, Richard?'

Before Sharpe could reply a half-dozen men of number six company threw themselves aside as a cannonball bounced hard and low towards them. It whipped harmlessly through the gap they had made. The men laughed at having evaded it, then Sergeant Colquhoun ordered them back into their two ranks.

'Aren't you supposed to be on the left of your company?' Sharpe asked Venables.

'You're still thinking like a sergeant, Richard,' Venables said. 'Pig-ears doesn't mind where I am.' Pig-ears was Captain Lomax, who had earned his nickname not because of any peculiarity about his ears, but because he had a passion for crisply fried pig-ears. Lomax was easy-going, unlike Urquhart who liked everything done strictly according to regulations. 'Besides,' Venables went on, 'there's damn all to do. The lads know their business.'

'Waste of time being an ensign,' Sharpe said.

'Nonsense! An ensign is merely a colonel in the making,' Venables said. 'Our duty, Richard, is to be decorative and stay alive long enough to be promoted. But no one expects us to be useful! Good God! A junior officer being useful? That'll be the day.' Venables gave a hoot of laughter. He was a bumptious, vain youth, but one of the few officers in the 74th who offered Sharpe companionship. 'Did you hear a new draft has come to Madras?' he asked.

'Urquhart told me.'

'Fresh men. New officers. You won't be junior any more.'

Sharpe shook his head. 'Depends on the date the new men were commissioned, doesn't it?'

'Suppose it does. Quite right. And they must have sailed from Britain long before you got the jump up, eh? So you'll still be the mess baby. Bad luck, old fellow.'

Old fellow? Quite right, Sharpe thought. He was old. Probably ten years older than Venables, though Sharpe was not exactly sure for no one had ever bothered to note down his birth date. Ensigns were youths and Sharpe was a man.

'Whoah!' Venables shouted in delight and Sharpe looked up to see that a round shot had struck the edge of an irrigation canal and bounced vertically upwards in a shower of soil. 'Pig-ears says he once saw two cannonballs collide in mid-air,' Venables said. 'Well, he didn't actually see it, of course, but he heard it. He says they suddenly appeared in the sky. Bang! Then flopped down.'

'They'd have shattered and broken up,' Sharpe said.

'Not according to Pig-ears,' Venables insisted. 'He says they flattened each other.' A shell exploded ahead of the company, whistling scraps of iron casing overhead. No one was hurt and the files stepped round the smoking fragments. Venables stooped and plucked up a scrap, juggling it because of the heat. 'Like to have keepsakes,' he explained, slipping the piece of iron into a pouch. 'I'll send it home for my sisters. Why don't our guns stop and fire?'

'Still too far away,' Sharpe said. The advancing line still had half a mile to go and, while the six-pounders could fire at that distance, the gunners must have decided to get really close so that their shots could not miss. Get close, that was what Colonel McCandless had always told Sharpe. It was the secret of battle. Get close before you start slaughtering.

A round shot struck a file in seven company. It was on its first graze, still travelling at blistering speed, and the two men of the file were whipped backwards in a spray of mingling blood. 'Jesus,' Venables said in awe. 'Jesus!' The corpses were mixed together, a jumble of splintered bones, tangled entrails and broken weapons. A corporal, one of the file-closers, stooped to extricate the men's pouches and haversacks from the scattered offal. 'Two more names in the church porch,' Venables remarked. 'Who were they, Corporal?'

'The McFadden brothers, sir.' The Corporal had to shout to be heard over the roar of the Mahratta guns.

29

'Poor bastards,' Venables said. 'Still, there are six more. A fecund lady, Rosie McFadden.'

Sharpe wondered what fecund meant, then decided he could guess. Venables, for all his air of carelessness, was looking slightly pale as though the sight of the churned corpses had sickened him. This was his first battle, for he had been sick with the Malabar Itch during Assaye, but the Ensign was forever explaining that he could not be upset by the sight of blood because, from his earliest days, he had assisted his father who was an Edinburgh surgeon, but now he suddenly turned aside, bent over and vomited. Sharpe kept stolidly walking. Some of the men turned at the sound of Venables's retching.

'Eyes front!' Sharpe snarled.

Sergeant Colquhoun gave Sharpe a resentful look. The Sergeant believed that any order that did not come from himself or from Captain Urquhart was an unnecessary order.

Venables caught up with Sharpe. 'Something I ate.'

'India does that,' Sharpe said sympathetically.

'Not to you.'

'Not yet,' Sharpe said and wished he was carrying a musket so he could touch the wooden stock for luck.

Captain Urquhart sheered his horse leftwards. 'To your company, Mister Venables.'

Venables scuttled away and Urquhart rode back to the company's right flank without acknowledging Sharpe's presence. Major Swinton, who commanded the battalion while Colonel Wallace had responsibility for the brigade, galloped his horse behind the ranks. The hooves thudded heavily on the dry earth. 'All well?' Swinton called to Urquhart.

'All well.'

'Good man!' Swinton spurred on.

The sound of the enemy guns was constant now, like thunder that did not end. A thunder that pummelled the ears and almost drowned out the skirl of the pipers. Earth fountained where round shot struck. Sharpe, glancing to his left, could see a scatter of bodies lying in the wake of the long line. There was a village there. How the hell had he walked straight past a village without even seeing it? It was not much of a place, just a huddle of reed-thatched hovels with a few patchwork gardens protected by cactus-thorn hedges, but he had still walked clean past without noticing its existence. He could see no one there. The villagers had too much sense. They would have packed their few pots and pans and buggered off as soon as the first soldier appeared near their fields. A Mahratta round shot smacked into one of the hovels, scattering reed and dry timber, and leaving the sad roof sagging.

Sharpe looked the other way and saw enemy cavalry advancing in the distance, then he glimpsed the blue and yellow uniforms of the British 19th Dragoons trotting to meet them. The late-afternoon sunlight glittered on drawn sabres. He thought he heard a trumpet call, but maybe he imagined it over the hammering of the guns. The horsemen vanished behind a stand of trees. A cannonball screamed overhead, a shell exploded to his left, then the 74th's Light Company edged inwards to give an ox team room to pass back southwards. The British cannon had been dragged well ahead of the attacking line where they had now been turned and deployed. Gunners rammed home shot, pushed priming quills into touch-holes, stood back. The sound of the guns crashed across the field, blotting the immediate view with grey-white smoke and filling the air with the nauseous stench of rotted eggs.

The drummers beat on, timing the long march north. For the moment it was a battle of artillerymen, the puny British six-pounders firing into the smoke cloud where the bigger Mahratta guns pounded at the advancing redcoats. Sweat trickled down Sharpe's belly, it stung his eyes and it dripped from his nose. Flies buzzed by his face. He pulled the sabre free and found that its handle was slippery with perspiration, so he wiped it and his right hand on the hem of his red coat. He suddenly wanted to piss badly, but this was not the time to stop and unbutton breeches. Hold it, he told himself, till the bastards are beaten. Or piss in your pants, he told himself, because in this heat no one would know it from sweat and it would dry quickly enough. Might smell, though. Better to wait. And if any of the men knew he had pissed his pants he would never live it down. Pisspants Sharpe. A ball thumped overhead, so close that its passage rocked Sharpe's shako. A fragment of something whirred to his left. A man was on the ground, vomiting blood. A dog barked as another tugged blue guts from an opened belly. The beast had both paws on the corpse to give its tug purchase. A file-closer kicked the dog away, but as soon as the man was gone the dog ran back to the body. Sharpe wished he could have a good wash. He knew he was lousy, but then everyone was lousy.

31

Even General Wellesley was probably lousy. Sharpe looked eastwards and saw the General spurring up behind the kilted 78th. Sharpe had been Wellesley's orderly at Assaye and as a result he knew all the staff officers who rode behind the General. They had been much friendlier than the 74th's officers, but then they had not been expected to treat Sharpe as an equal.

Bugger it, he thought. Maybe he should take Urquhart's advice. Go home, take the cash, buy an inn and hang the sabre over the serving hatch. Would Simone Joubert go to England with him? She might like running an inn. The Buggered Dream, he could call it, and he would charge army officers twice the real price for any drink.

The Mahratta guns suddenly went silent, at least those that were directly ahead of the 74th, and the change in the battle's noise made Sharpe peer ahead into the smoke cloud that hung over the crest just a quarter-mile away. More smoke wreathed the 74th, but that was from the British guns. The enemy gun smoke was clearing, carried northwards on the small wind, but there was nothing there to show why the guns at the centre of the Mahratta line had ceased fire. Perhaps the buggers had run out of ammunition. Some hope, he thought, some bloody hope. Or perhaps they were all reloading with canister to give the approaching redcoats a rajah's welcome.

God, but he needed a piss and so he stopped, tucked the sabre into his armpit, then fumbled with his buttons. One came away. He swore, stooped to pick it up, then stood and emptied his bladder onto the dry ground. Then Urquhart was wheeling his horse. 'Must you do that now, Mister Sharpe?' he asked irritably.

Yes, sir, three bladders full, sir, and damn your bloody eyes, sir. 'Sorry, sir,' Sharpe said instead. So maybe proper officers didn't piss? He sensed the company was laughing at him and he ran to catch up, fiddling with his buttons. Still there was no gunfire from the Mahratta centre. Why not? But then a cannon on one of the enemy flanks fired slantwise across the field and the ball grazed right through number six company, ripping a front rank man's feet off and slashing a man behind through the knees. Another soldier was limping, his leg deeply pierced by a splinter from his neighbour's bone. Corporal McCallum, one of the file-closers, tugged men into the gap while a piper ran across to bandage the wounded men. The injured would be left where they fell until after the battle when, if they still lived, they would be carried to the surgeons. And if they survived the knives and saws they would be shipped home, good for nothing except to be a burden on the parish. Or maybe the Scots did not have parishes; Sharpe was not sure, but he was certain the buggers had workhouses. Everyone had workhouses and paupers' graveyards. Better to be buried out here in the black earth of enemy India than condemned to the charity of a workhouse.

Then he saw why the guns in the centre of the Mahratta line had ceased fire. The gaps between the guns were suddenly filled with men running forward. Men in long robes and headdresses. They streamed between the gaps, then joined together ahead of the guns beneath long green banners that trailed from silver-topped poles. Arabs, Sharpe thought. He had seen some at Ahmednuggur, but most of those had been dead. He remembered Sevajee, the Mahratta who fought alongside Colonel McCandless, saying that the Arab mercenaries were the best of all the enemy troops.

Now there was a horde of desert warriors coming straight for the 74th and their kilted neighbours.

The Arabs came in a loose formation. Their guns had decorated stocks that glinted in the sunlight, while curved swords were scabbarded at their waists. They came almost jauntily, as though they had utter confidence in their ability. How many were there? A thousand? Sharpe reckoned at least a thousand. Their officers were on horseback. They did not advance in ranks and files, but in a mass, and some, the bravest men, ran ahead as if eager to start the killing. The great robed mass was chanting a shrill war cry, while in its centre drummers were beating huge instruments that pulsed a belly-thumping beat across the field. Sharpe watched the nearest British gun load with canister. The green banners were being waved from side to side so that the silk trails snaked over the warriors' heads. Something was written on the banners, but it was in no script that Sharpe recognized.

'74th!' Major Swinton called. 'Halt!'

The 78th had also halted. The two Highland battalions, both under strength after their losses at Assaye, were taking the full brunt of the Arab charge. The rest of the battlefield seemed to melt away. All Sharpe could see was the robed men coming so eagerly towards him.

'Make ready!' Swinton called.

'Make ready!' Urquhart echoed.

'Make ready!' Sergeant Colquhoun shouted. The men raised their muskets chest high and pulled back the heavy hammers.

Sharpe pushed into the gap between number six company and its left-hand neighbour, number seven. He wished he had a musket. The sabre felt flimsy.

'Present!' Swinton called.

'Present!' Colquhoun echoed, and the muskets went into the men's shoulders. Heads bowed to peer down the barrels' lengths.

'You'll fire low, boys,' Urquhart said from behind the line, 'you'll fire low. To your place, Mister Sharpe.'

Bugger it, Sharpe thought, another bloody mistake. He stepped back behind the company where he was supposed to make sure no one tried to run.

The Arabs were close. Less than a hundred paces to go now. Some had their swords drawn. The air, miraculously smoke-free, was filled with their blood-chilling war cry which was a weird ululating sound. Not far now, not far at all. The Scotsmen's muskets were angled slightly down. The kick drove the barrels upwards, and untrained troops, not ready for the heavy recoil, usually fired high. But this volley would be lethal.

'Wait, boys, wait,' Pig-ears called to number seven company. Ensign Venables slashed at weeds with his claymore. He looked nervous.

Urquhart had drawn a pistol. He dragged the cock back, and his horse's ears flicked back as the pistol's spring clicked.

Arab faces screamed hatred. Their great drums were thumping. The redcoat line, just two ranks deep, looked frail in front of the savage charge.

Major Swinton took a deep breath. Sharpe edged towards the gap again. Bugger it, he wanted to be in the front line where he could kill. It was too nerve-racking behind the line.

'74th!' Swinton shouted, then he paused. Men's fingers curled about their triggers.

Let them get close, Swinton was thinking, let them get close.

Then kill them.

Prince Manu Bappoo's brother, the Rajah of Berar, was not at the village of Argaum where the Lions of Allah now charged to destroy the heart of the British attack. The Rajah did not like battle. He liked the idea of conquest, he loved to see prisoners paraded and he craved the loot that filled his storehouses, but he had no belly for fighting.

Manu Bappoo had no such qualms. He was thirty-five years old, he had fought since he was fifteen, and all he asked was the chance to go on fighting for another twenty or forty years. He considered himself a true Mahratta; a pirate, a rogue, a thief in armour, a looter, a pestilence, a successor to the generations of Mahrattas who had dominated western India by pouring from their hill fastnesses to terrorize the plump princedoms and luxurious kingdoms in the plains. A quick sword, a fast horse and a wealthy victim, what more could a man want? And so Bappoo had ridden deep and far to bring plunder and ransom back to the small land of Berar.

But now all the Mahratta lands were threatened. One British army was conquering their northern territory, and another was here in the south. It was this southern redcoat force that had broken the troops of Scindia and Berar at Assaye, and the Rajah of Berar had summoned his brother to bring his Lions of Allah to claw and kill the invader. This was not a task for horsemen, the Rajah had warned Bappoo, but for infantry. It was a task for the Arabs.

But Bappoo knew this was a task for horsemen. His Arabs would win, of that he was sure, but they could only break the enemy on the immediate battlefield. He had thought to let the British advance right up to his cannon, then release the Arabs, but a whim, an intimation of triumph, had decided him to advance the Arabs beyond the guns. Let the Lions of Allah loose on the enemy's centre and, when that centre was broken, the rest of the British line would scatter and run in panic, and that was when the Mahratta horsemen would have their slaughter. It was already early evening, and the sun was sinking in the reddened west, but the sky was cloudless and Bappoo was anticipating the joys of a moonlit hunt across the flat Deccan Plain. 'We shall gallop through blood,' he said aloud, then led his aides towards his army's right flank so that he could charge past his Arabs when they had finished their fight. He would let his victorious Lions of Allah pillage the enemy's camp while he led his horsemen on a wild victorious gallop through the moon-touched darkness.

And the British would run. They would run like goats from the tiger. But the tiger was clever. He had only kept a small number of horsemen with the army, a mere fifteen thousand, while the greater

35

part of his cavalry had been sent southwards to raid the enemy's long supply roads. The British would flee straight into those men's sabres.

Bappoo trotted his horse just behind the right flank of the Lions of Allah. The British guns were firing canister and Bappoo saw how the ground beside his Arabs was being flecked by the blasts of shot, and he saw the robed men fall, but he saw how the others did not hesitate, but hurried on towards the pitifully thin line of redcoats. The Arabs were screaming defiance, the guns were hammering, and Bappoo's soul soared with the music. There was nothing finer in life, he thought, than this sensation of imminent victory. It was like a drug that fired the mind with noble visions.

He might have spared a moment's thought and wondered why the British did not use their muskets. They were holding their fire, waiting until every shot could kill, but the Prince was not worrying about such trifles. In his dreams he was scattering a broken army, slashing at them with his *tulwar*, carving a bloody path south. A fast sword, a quick horse and a broken enemy. It was the Mahratta paradise, and the Lions of Allah were opening its gates so that this night Manu Bappoo, Prince, warrior and dreamer, could ride into legend.

CHAPTER 2

'Fire!' Swinton shouted.

The two Highland regiments fired together, close to a thousand muskets flaming to make an instant hedge of thick smoke in front of the battalions. The Arabs vanished behind the smoke as the redcoats reloaded. Men bit into the grease-coated cartridges, tugged ramrods that they whirled in the air before rattling them down into the barrels. The churning smoke began to thin, revealing small fires where the musket wadding burned in the dry grass.

'Platoon fire!' Major Swinton shouted. 'From the flanks!'

'Light Company!' Captain Peters called on the left flank. 'First platoon, fire!'

'Kill them! Your mothers are watching!' Colonel Harness shouted. The Colonel of the 78th was mad as a hatter and half delirious with a fever, but he had insisted on advancing behind his kilted Highlanders. He was being carried in a palanquin and, as the platoon fire began, he struggled from the litter to join the battle, his only weapon a broken riding crop. He had been recently bled, and a stained bandage trailed from a coat sleeve. 'Give them a flogging, you dogs! Give them a flogging.'

The two battalions fired in half companies now, each half company firing two or three seconds after the neighbouring platoon so that the volleys rolled in from the outer wings of each battalion, met in the centre and then started again at the flanks. Clockwork fire, Sharpe called it, and it was the result of hours of tedious practice. Beyond the battalions' flanks the six-pounders bucked back with each shot, their wheels jarring up from the turf as the canisters ripped apart at the muzzles. Wide swathes of burning grass lay under the cannon smoke. The gunners were working in shirtsleeves, swabbing, ramming, then ducking aside as the guns pitched back again. Only the gun commanders, most of them sergeants, seemed to look at the enemy, and then only when they were checking the alignment of the cannon. The other gunners fetched shot and powder, sometimes heaved on a handspike or pushed on the wheels as the gun was relaid, then swabbed and loaded again. 'Water!' a corporal shouted, holding up a bucket to show that the swabbing water was gone.

'Fire low! Don't waste your powder!' Major Swinton called as he pushed his horse into the gap between the centre companies. He peered at the enemy through the smoke. Behind him, next to the 74th's twin flags, General Wellesley and his aides also stared at the Arabs beyond the smoke clouds. Colonel Wallace, the brigade commander, trotted his horse to the battalion's flank. He called something to Sharpe as he went by, but his words were lost in the welter of gunfire, then his horse half spun as a bullet struck its haunch. Wallace steadied the beast, looked back at the wound, but the horse did not seem badly hurt. Colonel Harness was thrashing one of the native palanquin bearers who had been trying to push the Colonel back into the curtained vehicle. One of Wellesley's aides rode back to quieten the Colonel and to persuade him to go southwards.

'Steady now!' Sergeant Colquhoun shouted. 'Aim low!'

The Arab charge had been checked, but not defeated. The first volley must have hit the attackers cruelly hard for Sharpe could see a line of bodies lying on the turf. The bodies looked red and white, blood against robes, but behind that twitching heap the Arabs were firing back to make their own ragged cloud of musket smoke. They fired haphazardly, untrained in platoon volleys, but they reloaded swiftly and their bullets were striking home. Sharpe heard the butcher's sound of metal hitting meat, saw men hurled backwards, saw some fall. The file-closers hauled the dead out of the line and tugged the living closer together. 'Close up! Close up!' The pipes played on, adding their defiant music to the noise of the guns. Private Hollister was hit in the head and Sharpe saw a cloud of white flour drift away from the man's powdered hair as his hat fell off. Then blood soaked the whitened hair and Hollister fell back with glassy eyes.

'One platoon, fire!' Sergeant Colquhoun shouted. He was so short-sighted that he could barely see the enemy, but it hardly mattered. No one could see much in the smoke, and all that was needed was a steady nerve and Colquhoun was not a man to panic.

'Two platoon, fire!' Urquhart shouted.

'Christ Jesus!' a man called close to Sharpe. He reeled backwards, his musket falling, then he twisted and dropped to his knees. 'Oh God, oh God, oh God,' he moaned, clutching at his throat. Sharpe could see no wound there, but then he saw blood seeping down the man's grey trousers. The dying man looked up at Sharpe, tears showed at his eyes, then he pitched forward.

Sharpe picked up the fallen musket, then turned the man over to unstrap the cartridge box. The man was dead, or so near as to make no difference.

'Flint,' a front rank man called. 'I need a flint!'

Sergeant Colquhoun elbowed through the ranks, holding out a spare flint. 'And where's your own spare flint, John Hammond?'

'Christ knows, Sergeant.'

'Then ask Him, for you're on a charge.'

A man swore as a bullet tore up his left arm. He backed out of the ranks, the arm hanging useless and dripping blood.

Sharpe pushed into the gap between the companies, put the musket to his shoulder and fired. The kick slammed into his shoulder, but it felt good. Something to do at last. He dropped the butt, fished a cartridge from the pouch and bit off the top, tasting the salt in the gunpowder. He rammed, fired again, loaded again. A bullet made an odd fluttering noise as it went past his ear, then another whined overhead. He waited for the rolling volley to come down the battalion's face, then fired with the other men of six company's first platoon. Drop the butt, new cartridge, bite, prime, pour, ram, ramrod back in the hoops, gun up, butt into the bruised shoulder and haul back the dog-head, Sharpe did it as efficiently as any other man, but he had been trained to it. That was the difference, he thought grimly. He was trained, but no one trained the officers. They had bugger all to do, so why train them? Ensign Venables was right, the only duty of a junior officer was to stay alive, but Sharpe could not resist a fight. Besides, it felt better to stand in the ranks and fire into the enemy's smoke than stand behind the company and do nothing.

The Arabs were fighting well. Damned well. Sharpe could not remember any other enemy who had stood and taken so much concentrated platoon fire. Indeed, the robed men were trying to advance, but they were checked by the ragged heap of bodies that had been their front ranks. How many damned ranks had they? A dozen? He watched a green flag fall, then the banner was picked up and waved in the air. Their big drums still beat, making a menacing sound to match the redcoats' pipers. The Arab guns had unnaturally long barrels that spewed dirty smoke and licking tongues of flame. Another bullet whipped close enough to Sharpe to bat his face with a gust of warm air. He fired again, then a hand seized his coat collar and dragged him violently backwards.

'Your place, Ensign Sharpe,' Captain Urquhart said vehemently, 'is here! Behind the line!' The Captain was mounted and his horse had inadvertently stepped back as Urquhart seized Sharpe's collar, and the weight of the horse had made the Captain's tug far more violent than he had intended. 'You're not a private any longer,' he said, steadying Sharpe who had almost been pulled off his feet.

'Of course, sir,' Sharpe said, and he did not meet Urquhart's gaze, but stared bitterly ahead. He was blushing, knowing he had been reprimanded in front of the men. Damn it to hell, he thought.

'Prepare to charge!' Major Swinton called.

'Prepare to charge!' Captain Urquhart echoed, spurring his horse away from Sharpe.

The Scotsmen pulled out their bayonets and twisted them onto the lugs of their musket barrels.

'Empty your guns!' Swinton called, and those men who were still loaded raised their muskets and fired a last volley.

'74th!' Swinton shouted. 'Forward! I want to hear some pipes! Let me hear pipes!'

'Go on, Swinton, go on!' Wallace shouted. There was no need to encourage the battalion forward, for it was going willingly, but the Colonel was excited. He drew his claymore and pushed his horse into the rear rank of number seven company. 'Onto them, lads! Onto them!' The redcoats marched forward, trampling through the scatter of little fires started by their musket wadding.

The Arabs seemed astonished that the redcoats were advancing. Some drew their own bayonets, while others pulled long curved swords from scabbards.

'They won't stand!' Wellesley shouted. 'They won't stand.'

'They bloody well will,' a man grunted.

'Go on!' Swinton shouted. 'Go on!' And the 74th, released to the kill, ran the last few yards and jumped up onto the heaps of dead before slashing home with their bayonets. Off to the right the 78th were also charging home. The British cannon gave a last violent blast of canister, then fell silent as the Scots blocked the gunners' aim.

Some of the Arabs wanted to fight, others wanted to retreat, but the charge had taken them by surprise and the rearward ranks were still not aware of the danger and so pressed forward, forcing the reluctant men at the front onto the Scottish bayonets. The Highlanders screamed as they killed. Sharpe still held the unloaded musket as he closed up on the rear rank. He had no bayonet and was wondering whether he should draw his sabre when a tall Arab suddenly hacked down a front rank man with a scimitar, then pushed forward to slash with the reddened blade at the second man in the file. Sharpe reversed the musket, swung it by the barrel and hammered the heavy stock down onto the swordsman's head. The Arab sank down and a bayonet struck into his spine so that he twisted like a speared eel. Sharpe hit him on the head again, kicked him for good measure, then shoved on. Men were shouting, screaming, stabbing, spitting, and, right in the face of number six company, a knot of robed men were slashing with scimitars as though they could defeat the 74th by themselves. Urquhart pushed his horse up against the rear rank and fired his pistol. One of the Arabs was plucked back and the others stepped away at last, all except one short man who screamed in fury and slashed with his long curved blade. The front rank parted to let the scimitar cut the air between two files, then the second rank also split apart to allow the short man to come screaming through on his own, with only Sharpe in front.

'He's only a lad!' a Scottish voice shouted in warning as the ranks closed again.

It was not a short man at all, but a boy. Maybe only twelve or thirteen years old, Sharpe guessed as he fended off the scimitar with the musket barrel. The boy thought he could win the battle single-handed and leaped at Sharpe, who parried the sword and stepped back to show he did not want to fight. 'Put it down, lad,' he said.

The boy spat, leaped and cut again. Sharpe parried a third time, then reversed the musket and slammed its stock into the side of the boy's head. For a second the lad stared at Sharpe with an astonished look, then he crumpled to the turf.

'They're breaking!' Wellesley shouted from somewhere close by. 'They're breaking!'

Colonel Wallace was in the front rank now, slicing down with his claymore. He hacked like a farmer, blow after blow. He had lost his cocked hat and his bald pate gleamed in the late sunlight. There was blood on his horse's flank, and more blood spattered on the white turnbacks of his coat tails. Then the pressure of the enemy collapsed and the horse twisted into the gap and Wallace spurred it on. 'Come on, boys! Come on!' A man stooped to rescue Wallace's cocked hat. Its plumes were blood-soaked.

The Arabs were fleeing. 'Go!' Swinton shouted. 'Go! Keep 'em running! Go!'

A man paused to search a corpse's robes and Sergeant Colquhoun dragged the man up and pushed him on. The file-closers were making sure none of the enemy bodies left behind the Scottish advance were dangerous. They kicked swords and muskets out of injured men's hands, prodded apparently unwounded bodies with bayonets and killed any man who showed a spark of fight. Two pipers were playing their ferocious music, driving the Scots up the gentle slope where the big Arab drums had been abandoned. Man after man speared the drum-skins with bayonets as they passed.

'Forward on! Forward on!' Urquhart bellowed as though he were on a hunting field.

'To the guns!' Wellesley called.

'Keep going!' Sharpe bellowed at some laggards. 'Go on, you bastards, go on!'

The enemy gun line was at the crest of the low rise, but the Mahratta gunners dared not fire because the remnants of the Lions of Allah were between them and the redcoats. The gunners hesitated for a few seconds, then decided the day was lost and fled.

'Take the guns!' Wellesley called.

Colonel Wallace spurred among the fleeing enemy, striking down with the claymore, then reined in beside a gaudily painted eighteen-pounder. 'Come on, lads! Come on! To me!'

The Scotsmen reached the guns. Most had reddened bayonets, all had sweat streaks striping their powder-blackened faces. Some began rifling the limbers where gunners stored food and valuables.

'Load!' Urquhart called. 'Load!'

'Form ranks!' Sergeant Colquhoun shouted. He ran forward and tugged men away from the limbers. 'Leave the carts alone, boys! Form ranks! Smartly now!'

Sharpe, for the first time, could see down the long reverse slope. Three hundred paces away were more infantry, a great long line of it massed in a dozen ranks, and beyond that were some walled gardens and the roofs of a village. The shadows were very long for the sun was blazing just above the horizon. The Arabs were running towards the stationary infantry.

'Where are the galloper guns?' Wallace roared, and an aide spurred back down the slope to fetch the gunners.

'Give them a volley, Swinton!' Wellesley called.

The range was very long for a musket, but Swinton hammered the battalion's fire down the slope, and maybe it was that volley, or perhaps it was the sight of the defeated Arabs that panicked the great mass of infantry. For a few seconds they stood under their big bright flags and then, like sand struck by a flood, they dissolved into a rabble.

Cavalry trumpets blared. British and sepoy horsemen charged forward with sabres, while the irregular horse, those mercenaries who had attached themselves to the British for the chance of loot, lowered their lances and raked back their spurs.

It was a cavalryman's paradise, a broken enemy with nowhere to hide. Some Mahrattas sought shelter in the village, but most ran past it, throwing down their weapons as the terrible horsemen streamed into the fleeing horde with sabres and lances slicing and thrusting.

'*Puckalees!*' Urquhart shouted, standing in his stirrups to look for the men and boys who brought water to the troops. There was none in sight and the 74th was parched, the men's thirst made acute by the saltpetre in the gunpowder which had fouled their mouths. 'Where the . . . ?' Urquhart swore, then frowned at Sharpe. 'Mister Sharpe? I'll trouble you to find our *puckalees.*'

'Yes, sir,' Sharpe said, not bothering to hide his disappointment at the order. He had hoped to find some loot when the 74th searched the village, but instead he was to be a fetcher of water. He threw down the musket and walked back through the groaning, slow-moving litter of dead and dying men. Dogs were scavenging among the bodies.

'Forward now!' Wellesley called behind Sharpe, and the whole long line of British infantrymen advanced under their flags towards the

43

village. The cavalry was already far beyond the houses, killing with abandon and driving the fugitives ever farther northwards.

Sharpe walked on southwards. He suspected the *puckalees* were still back with the baggage, which would mean a three-mile walk and, by the time he had found them, the battalion would have slaked its thirst from the wells in the village. Bugger it, he thought. Even when they gave him a job it was a useless errand.

A shout made him look to his right where a score of native cavalrymen were slicing apart the robes of the dead Arabs in search of coins and trinkets. The scavengers were Mahrattas who had sold their services to the British and Sharpe guessed that the horsemen had not joined the pursuit for fear of being mistaken for the defeated enemy. One of the Arabs had only been feigning death and now, despite being hugely outnumbered, defied his enemies with a pistol that he dragged from beneath his robe. The taunting cavalrymen had made a ring and the Arab kept twisting around to find that his tormentor had skipped away before he could aim the small gun.

The Arab was a short man, then he turned again and Sharpe saw the bruised, bloody face and recognized the child who had charged the 74th so bravely. The boy was doomed, for the ring of cavalrymen was slowly closing for the kill. One of the Mahrattas would probably die, or at least be horribly injured by the pistol ball, but that was part of the game. The boy had one shot, they had twenty. A man prodded the boy in the back with a lance point, making him whip round, but the man with the lance had stepped fast back and another man slapped the boy's headdress with a *tulwar*. The other cavalrymen laughed.

Sharpe reckoned the boy deserved better. He was a kid, nothing more, but brave as a tiger, and so he crossed to the cavalrymen. 'Let him be!' he called.

The boy turned towards Sharpe. If he recognized that the British officer was trying to save his life he showed no sign of gratitude; instead he lifted the pistol so that its barrel pointed at Sharpe's face. The cavalrymen, reckoning this was even better sport, urged him to shoot and one of them approached the boy with a raised *tulwar*, but did not strike. He would let the boy shoot Sharpe, then kill him. 'Let him be,' Sharpe said. 'Stand back!' The Mahrattas grinned, but did not move. Sharpe could take the single bullet, then they would tear the boy into sabre-shredded scraps of meat.

44

The boy took a step towards Sharpe. 'Don't be a bloody fool, lad,' Sharpe said. The boy obviously did not speak English, but Sharpe's tone was soothing. It made no difference. The lad's hand was shaking and he looked frightened, but defiance had been bred into his bone. He knew he would die, but he would take an enemy soul with him and so he nerved himself to die well. 'Put the gun down,' Sharpe said softly. He was wishing he had not intervened now. The kid was just distraught enough and mad enough to fire, and Sharpe knew he could do nothing about it except run away and thus expose himself to the jeers of the Mahrattas. He was close enough now to see the scratches on the pistol's blackened muzzle where the rammer had scraped the metal. 'Don't be a bloody fool, boy,' he said again. Still the boy pointed the pistol. Sharpe knew he should turn and run, but instead he took another pace forward. Just one more and he reckoned he would be close enough to swat the gun aside.

Then the boy shouted something in Arabic, something about Allah, and pulled the trigger.

The hammer did not move. The boy looked startled, then pulled the trigger again.

Sharpe began laughing. The expression of woe on the child's face was so sudden, and so unfeigned, that Sharpe could only laugh. The boy looked as if he was about to cry.

The Mahratta behind the boy swung his *tulwar*. He reckoned he could slice clean through the boy's grubby headdress and decapitate him, but Sharpe had taken the extra step and now seized the boy's hand and tugged him into his belly. The sword hissed an inch behind the boy's neck. 'I said to leave him alone!' Sharpe said. 'Or do you want to fight me instead?'

'None of us,' a calm voice said behind Sharpe, 'wants to fight Ensign Sharpe.'

Sharpe turned. One of the horsemen was still mounted, and it was this man who had spoken. He was dressed in a tattered European uniform jacket of green cloth hung with small silver chains, and he had a lean scarred face with a nose as hooked as Sir Arthur Wellesley's. He now grinned down at Sharpe.

'Syud Sevajee,' Sharpe said.

'I never did congratulate you on your promotion,' Sevajee said, and leaned down to offer Sharpe his hand.

Sharpe shook it. 'It was McCandless's doing,' he said.

'No,' Sevajee disagreed, 'it was yours.' Sevajee, who led this band of horsemen, waved his men away from Sharpe, then looked down at the boy who struggled in Sharpe's grip. 'You really want to save that little wretch's life?'

'Why not?'

'A tiger cub plays like a kitten,' Sevajee said, 'but it still grows into a tiger and one day it eats you.'

'This one's no kitten,' Sharpe said, thumping the boy on the ear to stop his struggles.

Sevajee spoke in quick Arabic and the boy went quiet. 'I told him you saved his life,' Sevajee explained to Sharpe, 'and that he is now beholden to you.' Sevajee spoke to the boy again who, after a shy look at Sharpe, answered. 'His name's Ahmed,' Sevajee said, 'and I told him you were a great English lord who commands the lives and deaths of a thousand men.'

'You told him what?'

'I told him you'd beat him bloody if he disobeys you,' Sevajee said, looking at his men who, denied their entertainment, had gone back to looting the dead. 'You like being an officer?' he asked Sharpe.

'I hate it.'

Sevajee smiled, revealing red-stained teeth. 'McCandless thought you would, but didn't know how to curb your ambition.' Sevajee slid down from his saddle. 'I am sorry McCandless died,' the Indian said.

'Me too.'

'You know who killed him?'

'I reckon it was Dodd.'

Sevajee nodded. 'Me too.' Syud Sevajee was a high-born Mahratta, the eldest son of one of the Rajah of Berar's warlords, but a rival in the Rajah's service had murdered his father, and Sevajee had been seeking revenge ever since. If that revenge meant marching with the enemy British, then that was a small price to pay for family pride. Sevajee had ridden with Colonel McCandless when the Scotsman had pursued Dodd, and thus he had met Sharpe. 'Beny Singh was not with the enemy today,' he told Sharpe.

Sharpe had to think for a few seconds before remembering that Beny Singh was the man who had poisoned Sevajee's father. 'How do you know?'

'His banner wasn't among the Mahratta flags. Today we faced Manu Bappoo, the Rajah's brother. He's a better man than the Rajah, but he refuses to take the throne for himself. He's also a better soldier than the rest, but not good enough, it seems. Dodd was there.'

'He was?'

'He got away.' Sevajee turned and gazed northwards. 'And I know where they're going.'

'Where?'

'To Gawilghur,' Sevajee said softly, 'to the sky fort.'

'Gawilghur?'

'I grew up there.' Sevajee spoke softly, still gazing at the hazed northern horizon. 'My father was killadar of Gawilghur. It was a post of honour, Sharpe, for it is our greatest stronghold. It is the fortress in the sky, the impregnable refuge, the place that has never fallen to our enemies, and Beny Singh is now its killadar. Somehow we shall have to get inside, you and I. And I shall kill Singh and you will kill Dodd.'

'That's why I'm here,' Sharpe said.

'No.' Sevajee gave Sharpe a sour glance. 'You're here, Ensign, because you British are greedy.' He looked at the Arab boy and asked a question. There was a brief conversation, then Sevajee looked at Sharpe again. 'I have told him he is to be your servant, and that you will beat him to death if he steals from you.'

'I wouldn't do that!' Sharpe protested.

'I would,' Sevajee said, 'and he believes you would, but it still won't stop him thieving from you. Better to kill him now.' He grinned, then hauled himself into his saddle. 'I shall look for you at Gawilghur, Mister Sharpe.'

'I shall look for you,' Sharpe said.

Sevajee spurred away and Sharpe crouched to look at his new servant. Ahmed was as thin as a half-drowned cat. He wore dirty robes and a tattered headdress secured by a loop of frayed rope that was stained with blood, evidently where Sharpe's blow with the musket had caught him during the battle. But he had bright eyes and a defiant face, and though his voice had not yet broken he was braver than many full-grown men. Sharpe unslung his canteen and pushed it into the boy's hand, first taking away the broken pistol that he tossed away. 'Drink up, you little bugger,' Sharpe said, 'then come for a walk.'

The boy glanced up the hill, but his army was long gone. It had vanished into the evening beyond the crest and was now being pursued by vengeful cavalry. He said something in Arabic, drank what remained of Sharpe's water, then offered a grudging nod of thanks.

So Sharpe had a servant, a battle had been won, and now he walked south in search of *puckalees*.

Colonel William Dodd watched the Lions of Allah break, and spat with disgust. It had been foolish to fight here in the first place and now the foolery was turning to disaster. 'Jemadar!' he called.

'Sahib?'

'We'll form square. Put our guns in the centre. And the baggage.'

'Families, sahib?'

'Families too.' Dodd watched Manu Bappoo and his aides galloping back from the British advance. The gunners had already fled, which meant that the Mahrattas' heavy cannon would all be captured, every last piece of it. Dodd was tempted to abandon his regiment's small battery of five-pounders which were about as much use as pea-shooters, but a soldier's pride persuaded him to drag the guns from the field. Bappoo might lose all his guns, but it would be a cold day in hell before William Dodd gave up artillery to an enemy.

His Cobras were on the Mahratta right flank and there, for the moment, they were out of the way of the British advance. If the rest of the Mahratta infantry remained firm and fought, then Dodd would stay with them, but he saw that the defeat of the Arabs had demoralized Bappoo's army. The ranks began to dissolve, the first fugitives began to run north and Dodd knew this army was lost. First Assaye, now this. A goddamn disaster! He turned his horse and smiled at his white-jacketed men. 'You haven't lost a battle!' he shouted to them. 'You haven't even fought today, so you've lost no pride! But you'll have to fight now! If you don't, if you break ranks, you'll die. If you fight, you'll live! Jemadar! March!'

The Cobras would now attempt one of the most difficult of all feats of soldiering, a fighting withdrawal. They marched in a loose square, the centre of which gradually filled with their women and children. Some other infantry tried to join the families, but Dodd snarled at his men to beat them away. 'Fire if they won't go!' he shouted. The last thing he wanted was for his men to be infected by panic.

Dodd trailed the square. He heard cavalry trumpets and he twisted in his saddle to see a mass of irregular light horsemen come over the crest. 'Halt!' he shouted. 'Close ranks! Charge bayonets!'

The white-jacketed Cobras sealed the loose square tight. Dodd pushed through the face of the square and turned his horse to watch the cavalrymen approach. He doubted they would come close, not when there were easier pickings to the east and, sure enough, as soon as the leading horsemen saw that the square was waiting with levelled muskets, they sheered away.

Dodd holstered his pistol. 'March on, Jemadar!'

Twice more Dodd had to halt and form ranks, but both times the threatening horsemen were scared away by the calm discipline of his white-coated soldiers. The red-coated infantry was not pursuing. They had reached the village of Argaum and were content to stay there, leaving the pursuit to the horsemen, and those horsemen chased after the broken rabble that flooded northwards, but none chose to die by charging Dodd's formed ranks.

Dodd inclined to the west, angling away from the pursuers. By nightfall he was confident enough to form the battalion into a column of companies, and by midnight, under a clear moon, he could no longer even hear the British trumpets. He knew that men would still be dying, ridden down by cavalry and pierced by lances or slashed by sabres, but Dodd had got clean away. His men were tired, but they were safe in a dark countryside of millet fields, drought-emptied irrigation ditches and scattered villages where dogs barked frantically when they caught the scent of the marching column.

Dodd did not trouble the villagers. He had sufficient food, and earlier in the night they had found an irrigation tank that had yielded enough water for men and beasts. 'Do you know where we are, Jemadar?' he asked.

'No, sahib.' Gopal grinned, his teeth showing white in the darkness.

'Nor do I. But I know where we're going.'

'Where, sahib?'

'To Gawilghur, Gopal. To Gawilghur.'

'Then we must march north, sahib.' Gopal pointed to the mountains that showed as a dark line against the northern stars. 'It is there, sahib.'

Dodd was marching to the fortress that had never known defeat. To the impregnable fastness on the cliff. To Gawilghur.

*　　*　　*

49

Dawn came to the millet fields. Ragged-winged birds flopped down beside corpses. The smell of death was already rank, and would only grow worse as the sun rose to become a furnace in a cloudless sky. Bugles called reveille, and the picquets who had guarded the sleeping army around Argaum cleared their muskets by loosing off shots. The gunfire startled birds up from corpses and made the feasting dogs growl among the human dead.

Regiments dug graves for their own dead. There were few enough to bury, for no more than fifty redcoats had died, but there were hundreds of Mahratta and Arab corpses, and the lascars who did the army's fetching and carrying began the task of gathering the bodies. Some enemies still lived, though barely, and the luckiest of those were despatched with a blow of a mattock before their robes were rifled. The unlucky were taken to the surgeons' tents.

The enemy's captured guns were inspected, and a dozen selected as suitable for British service. They were all well made, forged in Agra by French-trained gunsmiths, but some were the wrong calibre and a few were so overdecorated with writhing gods and goddesses that no self-respecting gunner could abide them. The twenty-six rejected guns would be double-shotted and exploded. 'A dangerous business,' Lieutenant Colonel William Wallace remarked to Sharpe.

'Indeed, sir.'

'You saw the accident at Assaye?' Wallace asked. The Colonel took off his cocked hat and fanned his face. The hat's white plumes were still stained with blood that had dried black.

'I heard it, sir. Didn't see it,' Sharpe said. The accident had occurred after the battle of Assaye when the enemy's captured cannon were being destroyed and one monstrous piece, a great siege gun, had exploded prematurely, killing two engineers.

'Leaves us short of good engineers,' Wallace remarked, 'and we'll need them if we're going to Gawilghur.'

'Gawilghur, sir?'

'A ghastly fortress, Sharpe, quite ghastly.' The Colonel turned and pointed north. 'Only about twenty miles away, and if the Mahrattas have any sense that's where they'll be heading.' Wallace sighed. 'I've never seen the place, so maybe it isn't as bad as they say, but I remember poor McCandless describing it as a brute. A real brute.

Like Stirling Castle, he said, only much larger and the cliff's twenty times higher.'

Sharpe had never seen Stirling Castle, so had no real idea what the Colonel meant. He said nothing. He had been idling the morning away when Wallace sent for him, and now he and the Colonel were walking through the battle's litter. The Arab boy followed a dozen paces behind. 'Yours, is he?' Wallace asked.

'Think so, sir. Sort of picked him up yesterday.'

'You need a servant, don't you? Urquhart tells me you don't have one.'

So Urquhart had been discussing Sharpe with the Colonel. No good could come of that, Sharpe thought. Urquhart had been nagging Sharpe to find a servant, implying that Sharpe's clothes were in need of cleaning and pressing, which they were, but as he only owned the clothes he wore, he could not really see the point in being too finicky. 'I hadn't really thought what to do with the lad, sir,' Sharpe admitted.

Wallace turned and spoke to the boy in an Indian language, and Ahmed stared up at the Colonel and nodded solemnly as though he understood what had been said. Perhaps he did, though Sharpe did not. 'I've told him he's to serve you properly,' Wallace said, 'and that you'll pay him properly.' The Colonel seemed to disapprove of Ahmed, or maybe he just disapproved of everything to do with Sharpe, though he was doing his best to be friendly. It had been Wallace who had given Sharpe the commission in the 74th, and Wallace had been a close friend of Colonel McCandless, so Sharpe supposed that the balding Colonel was, in his way, an ally. Even so, Sharpe felt awkward in the Scotsman's company. He wondered if he would ever feel relaxed among officers. 'How's that woman of yours, Sharpe?' Wallace asked cheerfully.

'My woman, sir?' Sharpe asked, blushing.

'The Frenchwoman, can't recall her name. Took quite a shine to you, didn't she?'

'Simone, sir? She's in Seringapatam, sir. Seemed the best place for her, sir.'

'Quite, quite.'

Simone Joubert had been widowed at Assaye where her husband, who had served Scindia, had died. She had been Sharpe's lover and, after the battle, she had stayed with him. Where else, she asked, was she to go? But Wellesley had forbidden his officers to take their wives on the campaign, and though Simone was not Sharpe's wife, she was white, and so she had agreed to go to Seringapatam and there wait for him. She had carried a letter of introduction to Major Stokes, Sharpe's friend who ran the armoury, and Sharpe had given her some of the Tippoo's jewels so that she could find servants and live comfortably. He sometimes worried he had given her too many of the precious stones, but consoled himself that Simone would keep the surplus safe till he returned.

'So are you happy, Sharpe?' Wallace asked bluffly.

'Yes, sir,' Sharpe said bleakly.

'Keeping busy?'

'Not really, sir.'

'Difficult, isn't it?' Wallace said vaguely. He had stopped to watch the gunners loading one of the captured cannon, a great brute that looked to take a ball of twenty or more pounds. The barrel had been cast with an intricate pattern of lotus flowers and dancing girls, then painted with garish colours. The gunners had charged the gaudy barrel with a double load of powder and now they rammed two cannonballs down the blackened gullet. An engineer had brought some wedges and a gunner sergeant pushed one down the barrel, then hammered it home with the rammer so that the ball would jam when the gun was fired. The engineer took a ball of fuse from his pocket, pushed one end into the touch-hole, then backed away, uncoiling the pale line. 'Best if we give them some space,' Wallace said, gesturing that they should walk south a small way. 'Don't want to be beheaded by a scrap of gun, eh?'

'No, sir.'

'Very difficult,' Wallace said, picking up his previous thought. 'Coming up from the ranks? Admirable, Sharpe, admirable, but difficult, yes?'

'I suppose so, sir,' Sharpe said unhelpfully.

Wallace sighed, as though he was finding the conversation unexpectedly hard going. 'Urquhart tells me you seem' – the Colonel paused, looking for the tactful word – 'unhappy?'

'Takes time, sir.'

'Of course, of course. These things do. Quite.' The Colonel wiped a hand over his bald pate, then rammed his sweat-stained hat back into place. 'I remember when I joined. Years ago now, of course, and I was only a little chap. Didn't know what was going on! They said turn left, then turned right. Damned odd, I thought. I was arse over elbow for months, I can tell you.' The Colonel's voice tailed away. 'Damned hot,' he said after a while. 'Damned hot. Ever heard of the 95th, Sharpe?'

'95th, sir? Another Scottish regiment?'

'Lord, no. The 95th Rifles. They're a new regiment. Couple of years old. Used to be called the Experimental Corps of Riflemen!' Wallace hooted with laughter at the clumsy name. 'But a friend of mine is busy with the rascals. Willie Stewart, he's called. The Honourable William Stewart. Capital fellow! But Willie's got some damned odd ideas. His fellows wear green coats. Green! And he tells me his riflemen ain't as rigid as he seems to think we are.' Wallace smiled to show he had made some kind of joke. 'Thing is, Sharpe, I wondered if you wouldn't be better suited to Stewart's outfit? His idea, you should understand. He wrote wondering if I had any bright young officers who could carry some experience of India to Shorncliffe. I was going to write back and say we do precious little skirmishing here, and it's skirmishing that Willie's rogues are being trained to do, but then I thought of you, Sharpe.'

Sharpe said nothing. Whichever way you wrapped it up, he was being dismissed from the 74th, though he supposed it was kind of Wallace to make the 95th sound like an interesting sort of regiment. Sharpe guessed they were the usual shambles of a hastily raised wartime battalion, staffed by the leavings of other regiments and composed of gutter rogues discarded by every other recruiting sergeant. The very fact they wore green coats sounded bad, as though the army could not be bothered to waste good red cloth on them. They would probably dissolve in panicked chaos in their first battle.

'I've written to Willie about you,' Wallace went on, 'and I know he'll have a place for you.' Meaning, Sharpe thought, that the Honourable William Stewart owed Wallace a favour. 'And our problem, frankly,' Wallace continued, 'is that a new draft has reached Madras. Weren't expecting it till spring, but they're here now, so we'll be back to strength in a month or so.' Wallace paused, evidently wondering if he had softened the blow sufficiently. 'And the fact is, Sharpe,' he resumed after a while, 'that Scottish regiments are more like, well, families!

Families, that's it, just it. My mother always said so, and she was a pretty shrewd judge of these things. Like families! More so, I think, than English regiments, don't you think?'

'Yes, sir,' Sharpe said, trying to hide his misery.

'But I can't let you go while there's a war on,' Wallace continued heartily. The Colonel had turned to watch the cannon again. The engineer had finished unwinding his fuse and the gunners now shouted at everyone within earshot to stand away. 'I do enjoy this,' the Colonel said warmly. 'Nothing like a bit of gratuitous destruction to set the juices flowing, eh?'

The engineer stooped to the fuse with his tinderbox. Sharpe saw him strike the flint then blow the charred linen into flame. There was a pause, then he put the fuse end into the small fire and the smoke fizzed up.

The fuse burned fast, the smoke and sparks snaking through the dry grass and starting small fires, then the red hot trail streaked up the back of the gun and down into the touch-hole.

For a heartbeat nothing happened, then the whole gun just seemed to disintegrate. The charge had tried to propel the double shot up the wedged barrel, but the resistance was just big enough to restrict the explosion. The touch-hole shot out first, the shaped piece of metal tearing out a chunk of the upper breach, then the whole rear of the painted barrel split apart in smoke, flame and whistling lumps of jagged metal. The forward part of the barrel, jaggedly torn off, dropped to the grass as the gun's wheels were splayed out. The gunners cheered. 'One less Mahratta gun,' Wallace said. Ahmed was grinning broadly. 'Did you know Mackay?' Wallace asked Sharpe.

'No, sir.'

'Captain Mackay. Hugh Mackay. East India Company officer. Fourth Native Cavalry. Very good fellow indeed, Sharpe. I knew his father well. Point is, though, that young Hugh was put in charge of the bullock train before Assaye. And he did a very good job! Very good. But he insisted on joining his troopers in the battle. Disobeyed orders, d'you see? Wellesley was adamant that Mackay must stay with his bullocks, but young Hugh wanted to be on the dance floor, and quite right too, except that the poor devil was killed. Cut in half by a cannonball!' Wallace sounded shocked, as though such a thing was an outrage. 'It's left the bullock train without a guiding hand, Sharpe.'

Christ, Sharpe thought, but he was to be made bullock master!

'Not fair to say they don't have a guiding hand,' Wallace continued, 'because they do, but the new fellow don't have any experience with bullocks. Torrance, he's called, and I'm sure he's a good fellow, but things are likely to get a bit more sprightly from now on. Going deeper into enemy territory, see? And there are still lots of their damned horsemen at large, and Torrance says he needs a deputy officer. Someone to help him. Thought you might be just the fellow for the job, Sharpe.' Wallace smiled as though he was granting Sharpe a huge favour.

'Don't know anything about bullocks, sir,' Sharpe said doggedly.

'I'm sure you don't! Who does? And there are dromedaries, and elephants. A regular menagerie, eh? But the experience, Sharpe, will do you good. Think of it as another string to your bow.'

Sharpe knew a further protest would do no good, so he nodded. 'Yes, sir,' he said.

'Good! Good! Splendid.' Wallace could not hide his relief. 'It won't be for long, Sharpe. Scindia's already suing for peace, and the Rajah of Berar's bound to follow. We may not even have to fight at Gawilghur, if that's where the rogues do take refuge. So go and help Torrance, then you can set a course for England, eh? Become a Greenjacket!'

So Ensign Sharpe had failed. Failed utterly. He had been an officer for two months and now he was being booted out of a regiment. Sent to the bullocks and the dromedaries, whatever the hell they were, and after that to the green-coated dregs of the army. Bloody hell fire, he thought, bloody hell fire.

The British and their allied cavalry rode all night, and in the dawn they briefly rested, watered their horses, then hauled themselves into their saddles and rode again. They rode till their horses were reeling with tiredness and white with sweat, and only then did they give up the savage pursuit of the Mahratta fugitives. Their sabre arms were weary, their blades blunted and their appetites slaked. The night had been a wild hunt of victory, a slaughter under the moon that had left the plain reeking with blood, and the sun brought more killing and wide-winged vultures that flapped down to the feast.

The pursuit ended close to a sudden range of hills that marked the northern limit of the Deccan Plain. The hills were steep and thickly wooded, no place for cavalry, and above the hills reared great cliffs, dizzyingly high cliffs that stretched from the eastern to the western horizon like the nightmare ramparts of a tribe of giants. In places there were deep re-entrants cut into the great cliff and some of the British pursuers, gaping at the vast wall of rock that barred their path, supposed that the wooded clefts would provide a path up to the cliff's summit, though none could see how anyone could reach the highland if an enemy chose to defend it.

Between two of the deep re-entrants a great promontory of rock jutted from the cliff face like the prow of a monstrous stone ship. The summit of the jutting rock was two thousand feet above the horsemen on the plain, and one of them, scrubbing blood from his sabre blade with a handful of grass, glanced up at the high peak and saw a tiny puff of whiteness drifting from its crest. He thought it a small cloud, but then he heard a faint bang of gunfire, and a second later a round shot dropped vertically into a nearby patch of millet. His captain pulled out a telescope and trained it high into the sky. He stared for a long time, then gave a low whistle.

'What is it, sir?'

'It's a fortress,' the Captain said. He could just see black stone walls, shrunken by distance, poised above the grey-white rock. 'It's hell in the bloody sky,' he said grimly, 'that's what it is. It's Gawilghur.'

More guns fired from the fortress, but they were so high in the air that their shots lost all their forward momentum long before they reached the ground. The balls fell like nightmare rain and the Captain shouted at his men to lead their horses out of range. 'Their final refuge,' he said, then laughed, 'but it's nothing to do with us, boys! The infantry will have to deal with that big bastard.'

The cavalrymen slowly moved southwards. Some of their horses had lost shoes, which meant they had to be walked home, but their night's work was well done. They had ravaged a broken army, and now the infantry must cope with the Mahrattas' final refuge.

A sergeant shouted from the right flank and the Captain turned westwards to see a column of enemy infantry appearing from a grove of trees just over a mile away. The white-coated battalion still possessed their artillery, but they showed no sign of wanting a fight. A crowd of civilians and several companies of fugitive Mahrattas had joined the regiment which was heading for a road that twisted into the hills

56

beneath the fort, then zigzagged its way up the face of the rock promontory. If that road was the only way into the fort, the cavalry Captain thought, then God help the redcoats who had to attack Gawilghur. He stared at the infantry through his telescope. The white-coated troops were showing small interest in the British cavalry, but it still seemed prudent to quicken his pace southwards.

A moment later and the cavalry was hidden behind millet fields. The Captain turned a last time and gazed again at the fortress on the soaring cliffs. It seemed to touch the sky, so high it stood above all India. 'Bastard of a place,' the Captain said wonderingly, then turned and left. He had done his job, and now the infantry must climb to the clouds to do theirs.

Colonel William Dodd watched the blue-coated cavalrymen walk their tired horses southwards until they vanished beyond a field of standing millet. The subadar in charge of the regiment's small cannon had wanted to unlimber and open fire on the horsemen, but Dodd had refused his permission. There would have been no point in attacking, for by the time the guns were loaded the cavalrymen would have walked out of range. He watched a last salvo of round shot plummet to earth from the fort's high guns. Those cannon were of little use, Dodd thought, except to overawe people on the plain.

It took Dodd's regiment over seven hours to climb to the fort of Gawilghur, and by the time he reached the summit Dodd's lungs were burning, his muscles aching and his uniform soaked with sweat. He had walked every step of the way, refusing to ride his horse, for the beast was tired and, besides, if he expected his men to walk up the long road, then he would walk it as well. He was a tall, sallow-faced man with a harsh voice and an awkward manner, but William Dodd knew how to earn his men's admiration. They saw that he walked when he could have ridden, and so they did not complain as the steep climb sapped their breath and stole their strength. The regiment's families, its baggage and its battery of cannon were still far below on the twisting, treacherous track that, in its last few miles, was little more than a ledge hacked from the cliff.

Dodd formed his Cobras into four ranks as they approached Gawilghur's southern entrance where the great metal-studded gates were being swung open in welcome. 'March smartly now!' Dodd called to his men. 'You've nothing to be ashamed of! You lost no battle!' He pulled himself up into his saddle and drew his gold-hilted sword to salute the flag of Berar that flapped above the high gate-tower. Then he touched his heels to the mare's flanks and led his undefeated men into the tower's long entrance tunnel.

He emerged into the afternoon sun to find himself staring at a small town that was built within the stronghold's ramparts and on the summit of Gawilghur's promontory. The alleys of the town were crammed with soldiers, most of them Mahratta cavalrymen who had fled in front of the British pursuit, but, twisting in his saddle, Dodd saw some infantry of Gawilghur's garrison standing on the firestep. He also saw Manu Bappoo who had outridden the British pursuit and now gestured to Dodd from the gate-tower's turret.

Dodd told one of his men to hold his horse, then climbed the black walls to the top firestep of the tower where he stopped in awed astonishment at the view. It was like standing at the edge of the world. The plain was so far beneath and the southern horizon so far away that there was nothing in front of his eyes but endless sky. This, Dodd thought, was a god's view of earth. The eagle's view. He leaned over the parapet and saw his guns struggling up the narrow road. They would not reach the fort till long after nightfall.

'You were right, Colonel,' Manu Bappoo said ruefully.

Dodd straightened to look at the Mahratta prince. 'It's dangerous to fight the British in open fields,' he said, 'but here . . . ?' Dodd gestured at the approach road. 'Here they will die, sahib.'

'The fort's main entrance,' Bappoo said in his sibilant voice, 'is on the other side. To the north.'

Dodd turned and gazed across the roof of the central palace. He could see little of the great fortress's northern defences, though a long way away he could see another tower like the one on which he now stood. 'Is the main entrance as difficult to approach as this one?' he asked.

'No, but it isn't easy. The enemy has to approach along a narrow strip of rock, then fight through the Outer Fort. After that comes a ravine, and then the Inner Fort. I want you to guard the inner gate.'

Dodd looked suspiciously at Bappoo. 'Not the Outer Fort?' Dodd reckoned his Cobras should guard the place where the British would attack. That way the British would be defeated.

'The Outer Fort is a trap,' Bappoo explained. He looked tired, but the defeat at Argaum had not destroyed his spirit, merely sharpened his appetite for revenge. 'If the British capture the Outer Fort they will think they have won. They won't know that an even worse barrier waits beyond the ravine. That barrier has to be held. I don't care if the Outer Fort falls, but we must hold the Inner. That means our best troops must be there.'

'It will be held,' Dodd said.

Bappoo turned and stared southwards. Somewhere in the heat-hazed distance the British forces were readying to march on Gawilghur. 'I thought we could stop them at Argaum,' he admitted softly.

Dodd, who had advised against fighting at Argaum, said nothing.

'But here,' Bappoo went on, 'they will be stopped.'

Here, Dodd thought, they would have to be stopped. He had deserted from the East India Company's army because he faced trial and execution, but also because he believed he could make a fortune as a mercenary serving the Mahrattas. So far he had endured three defeats, and each time he had led his men safe out of the disaster, but from Gawilghur there would be no escape. The British would block every approach, so the British must be stopped. They must fail in this high place, and so they would, Dodd consoled himself. For nothing imaginable could take this fort. He was on the world's edge, lifted into the sky, and for the redcoats it would be like scaling the very heights of heaven.

So here, at last, deep inside India, the redcoats would be beaten.

Six cavalrymen in the blue and yellow coats of the 19th Light Dragoons waited outside the house where Captain Torrance was said to be billeted. They were under the command of a long-legged sergeant who was lounging on a bench beside the door. The Sergeant glanced up as Sharpe approached. 'I hope you don't want anything useful out of the bastards,' he said acidly, then saw that the shabby-uniformed Sharpe, despite wearing a pack like any common soldier, also had a sash and a sabre. He scrambled to his feet. 'Sorry, sir.'

Sharpe waved him back down onto the bench. 'Useful?' he asked.

'Horseshoes, sir, that's all we bleeding want. Horseshoes! Supposed to be four thousand in store, but can they find them?' The Sergeant spat. 'Tells me they're lost! I'm to go to the *bhinjarries* and buy them!

I'm supposed to tell my captain that? So now we have to sit here till Captain Torrance gets back. Maybe he knows where they are. That monkey in there' – he jerked his thumb at the house's front door – 'doesn't know a bloody thing.'

Sharpe pushed open the door to find himself in a large room where a half-dozen men argued with a harried clerk. The clerk, an Indian, sat behind a table covered with curling ledgers. 'Captain Torrance is ill!' the clerk snapped at Sharpe without waiting to discover the newcomer's business. 'And take that dirty Arab boy outside,' the clerk added, jerking his chin at Ahmed who, armed with a musket he had taken from a corpse on the battlefield, had followed Sharpe into the house.

'Muskets!' A man tried to attract the clerk's attention.

'Horseshoes!' an East India Company lieutenant shouted.

'Buckets,' a gunner said.

'Come back tomorrow,' the clerk said. 'Tomorrow!'

'You said that yesterday,' the gunner said, 'and I'm back.'

'Where's Captain Torrance?' Sharpe asked.

'He's ill,' the clerk said disapprovingly, as though Sharpe had risked the Captain's fragile health even by asking the question. 'He cannot be disturbed. And why is that boy here? He is an Arab!'

'Because I told him to be here,' Sharpe said. He walked round the table and stared down at the ledgers. 'What a bleeding mess!'

'Sahib!' The clerk had now realized Sharpe was an officer. 'Other side of the table, sahib, please, sahib! There is a system here, sahib. I stay this side of the table and you remain on the other. Please, sahib.'

'What's your name?' Sharpe asked.

The clerk seemed affronted at the question. 'I am Captain Torrance's assistant,' he said grandly.

'And Torrance is ill?'

'The Captain is very sick.'

'So who's in charge?'

'I am,' the clerk said.

'Not any longer,' Sharpe said. He looked up at the East India Company lieutenant. 'What did you want?'

'Horseshoes.'

'So where are the bleeding horseshoes?' Sharpe asked the clerk.

'I have explained, sahib, I have explained,' the clerk said. He was a middle-aged man with a lugubrious face and pudgy ink-stained fingers that now hastily tried to close all the ledgers so that Sharpe could not read them. 'Now please, sahib, join the queue.'

'Where are the horseshoes?' Sharpe insisted, leaning closer to the sweating clerk.

'This office is closed!' the clerk shouted. 'Closed till tomorrow! All business will be conducted tomorrow. Captain Torrance's orders!'

'Ahmed!' Sharpe said. 'Shoot the bugger.'

Ahmed spoke no English, but the clerk did not know that. He held his hands out. 'I am closing the office! Work cannot be done like this! I shall complain to Captain Torrance! There will be trouble! Big trouble!' The clerk glanced at a door that led to the inner part of the house.

'Is that where Torrance is?' Sharpe asked, gesturing at the door.

'No, sahib, and you cannot go in there. The Captain is sick.'

Sharpe went to the door and pushed it open. The clerk yelped a protest, but Sharpe ignored him. A muslin screen hung on the other side of the door and entangled Sharpe as he pushed into the room where a sailor's hammock hung from the beams. The room seemed empty, but then a whimper made him look into a shadowed corner. A young woman crouched there. She was dressed in a sari, but she looked European to Sharpe. She had been sewing gold braid onto the outer seams of a pair of breeches, but now stared in wide-eyed fright at the intruder. 'Who are you, Ma'am?' Sharpe asked.

The woman shook her head. She had very black hair and very white skin. Her terror was palpable. 'Is Captain Torrance here?' Sharpe asked.

'No,' she whispered.

'He's sick, is that right?'

'If he says so, sir,' she said softly. Her London accent confirmed that she was English.

'I ain't going to hurt you, love,' Sharpe said, for fear was making her tremble. 'Are you Mrs Torrance?'

'No!'

'So you work for him?'

'Yes, sir.'

'And you don't know where he is?'

'No, sir,' she said softly, looking up at Sharpe with huge eyes. She was lying, he reckoned, but he guessed she had good reason to lie, perhaps fearing Torrance's punishment if she told the truth. He considered soothing the truth out of her, but reckoned it might take too long. He wondered who she was. She was pretty, despite her terror, and he guessed she was Torrance's *bibbi*. Lucky Torrance, he thought ruefully. 'I'm sorry to have disturbed you, Ma'am,' he said, then he negotiated the muslin curtain back into the front room.

The clerk shook his head fiercely. 'You should not have gone in there, sahib! That is private quarters! Private! I shall be forced to tell Captain Torrance.'

Sharpe took hold of the clerk's chair and tipped it, forcing the man off. The men waiting in the room gave a cheer. Sharpe ignored them, sat on the chair himself and pulled the tangle of ledgers towards him. 'I don't care what you tell Captain Torrance,' he said, 'so long as you tell me about the horseshoes first.'

'They are lost!' the clerk protested.

'How were they lost?' Sharpe asked.

The clerk shrugged. 'Things get lost,' he said. Sweat was pouring down his plump face as he tentatively tried to tug some of the ledgers away from Sharpe, but he recoiled from the look on the Ensign's face. 'Things get lost,' the clerk said again weakly. 'It is the nature of things to get lost.'

'Muskets?' Sharpe asked.

'Lost,' the clerk admitted.

'Buckets?'

'Lost,' the clerk said.

'Paperwork,' Sharpe said.

The clerk frowned. 'Paperwork, sahib?'

'If something's lost,' Sharpe said patiently, 'there's a record. This is the bloody army. You can't have a piss without someone making a note of it. So show me the records of what's been lost.'

The clerk sighed and pulled one of the big ledgers open. 'Here, sahib,' he said, pointing an inky finger. 'One barrel of horseshoes, see? Being carried on an ox from Jamkandhi, lost in the Godavery on November 12th.'

'How many horseshoes in a barrel?' Sharpe asked.

'A hundred and twenty.' The long-legged cavalry Sergeant had come into the office and now leaned against the doorpost.

'And there are supposed to be four thousand horseshoes in store?' Sharpe asked.

'Here!' The clerk turned a page. 'Another barrel, see?'

Sharpe peered at the ill-written entry. 'Lost in the Godavery,' he read aloud.

'And here.' The clerk stabbed his finger again.

'Stolen,' Sharpe read. A drop of sweat landed on the page as the clerk turned it back. 'So who stole it?'

'The enemy, sahib,' the clerk said. 'Their horsemen are everywhere.'

'Their bloody horsemen run if you so much as look at them,' the tall cavalry Sergeant said sourly. 'They couldn't steal an egg from a chicken.'

'The convoys are ambushed, sahib,' the clerk insisted, 'and things are stolen.'

Sharpe pushed the clerk's hand away and turned the pages back, looking for the date when the battle had been fought at Assaye. He found it, and discovered a different handwriting had been used for the previous entries. He guessed Captain Mackay must have kept the ledger himself, and in Mackay's neat entries there were far fewer annotations reading 'stolen' or 'lost'. Mackay had marked eight cannonballs as being lost in a river crossing and two barrels of powder had been marked down as stolen, but in the weeks since Assaye no fewer than sixty-eight oxen had lost their burdens to either accidents or thieves. More tellingly, each of those oxen had been carrying a scarce commodity. The army would not miss a load of round shot, but it would suffer grievously when its last reserve of horseshoes was gone. 'Whose handwriting is this?' Sharpe had turned to the most recent page.

'Mine, sahib.' The clerk was looking frightened.

'How do you know when something is stolen?'

The clerk shrugged. 'The Captain tells me. Or the Sergeant tells me.'

'The Sergeant?'

'He isn't here,' the clerk said. 'He's bringing a convoy of oxen north.'

'What's the Sergeant's name?' Sharpe asked, for he could find no record in the ledger.

'Hakeswill,' the cavalry Sergeant said laconically. 'He's the bugger we usually deal with, on account of Captain Torrance always being ill.'

'Bloody hell,' Sharpe said, and pushed the chair back. Hakeswill! Obadiah bloody Hakeswill! 'Why wasn't he sent back to his regiment?' Sharpe asked. 'He isn't supposed to be here at all!'

'He knows the system,' the clerk explained. 'Captain Torrance wanted him to stay, sahib.'

And no bloody wonder, Sharpe thought. Hakeswill had worked himself into the army's most profitable billet! He was milking the cow, but making sure it was the clerk's handwriting in the ledger. No flies on Obadiah. 'How does the system work?' he asked the clerk.

'Chitties,' the clerk said.

'Chitties?'

'An ox driver is given a chitty, sahib, and when he has delivered his load the chitty is signed and brought here. Then he is paid. No chitty, no money. It is the rule, sahib. No chitty, no money.'

'And no bloody horseshoes either,' put in the lean Sergeant of the 19th.

'And Sergeant Hakeswill pays the money?' Sharpe asked.

'If he is here, sahib,' the clerk said.

'That doesn't get me my damned horseshoes,' the Company Lieutenant protested.

'Or my buckets,' the gunner put in.

'The *bhinjarries* have all the essentials,' the clerk insisted. He made shooing gestures. 'Go and see the *bhinjarries*! They have necessaries! This office is closed till tomorrow.'

'But where did the *bhinjarries* get their necessaries, eh? Answer me that?' Sharpe demanded, but the clerk merely shrugged. The *bhinjarries* were merchants who travelled with the army, contributing their own vast herds of pack oxen and carts. They sold food, liquor, women and luxuries, and now, it seemed, they were offering military supplies as well, which meant that the army would be paying for things that were normally issued free, and doubtless, if bloody Hakeswill had a finger in the pot, things which had been stolen from the army in the first place. 'Where do I go for horseshoes?' Sharpe asked the clerk.

The clerk was reluctant to answer, but he finally spread his hands and suggested Sharpe ask in the merchants' encampment. 'Someone will tell you, sahib.'

'You tell me,' Sharpe said.

'I don't know!'

'So how do you know they have horseshoes?'

'I hear these things!' the clerk protested.

Sharpe stood and bullied the clerk back against the wall. 'You do more than hear things,' he said, leaning his forearm against the clerk's neck, 'you know things. So you bloody well tell me, or I'll have my Arab boy chop off your goolies for his breakfast. He's a hungry little bugger.'

The clerk fought for breath against the pressure of Sharpe's arm. 'Naig.' He offered the name plaintively when Sharpe relaxed his arm.

'Naig?' Sharpe asked. The name rang a distant bell. A long-ago bell. Naig? Then he remembered a merchant of that name who had followed the army to Seringapatam. 'Naig?' Sharpe asked again. 'A fellow with green tents?'

'The very one, sahib.' The clerk nodded. 'But I did not tell you this thing! These gentlemen are witnesses, I did not tell you!'

'He runs a brothel!' Sharpe said, remembering, and he remembered too how Naig had been a friend to Sergeant Obadiah Hakeswill four years before. Sharpe had been a private then and Hakeswill had trumped up charges that had fetched Sharpe a flogging. 'Nasty Naig' had been the man's nickname, and back then he had sold pale-skinned whores who travelled in green-curtained wagons. 'Right!' Sharpe said. 'This office is closed!' The gunner protested and the cavalry Sergeant looked disappointed. 'We're going to see Naig,' Sharpe announced.

'No!' the clerk said too loud.

'No?' Sharpe asked.

'He will be angry, sahib.'

'Why should he be angry?' Sharpe demanded. 'I'm a customer, ain't I? He's got horseshoes, and we want horseshoes. He should be delighted to see us.'

'He must be treated with respect, sahib,' the clerk said nervously. 'He is a powerful man, Naig. You have money for him?'

'I just want to look at his horseshoes,' Sharpe said, 'and if they're army issue then I'll ram one of them down his bloody throat.'

The clerk shook his head. 'He has guards, sahib. He has *jettis*!'

'I think I might let you go on your own,' the East India Company Lieutenant said, backing away.

'*Jettis?*' The light dragoon Sergeant asked.

'Strongmen,' Sharpe explained. 'Big buggers who kill you by wringing your neck like a chicken.' He turned back to the clerk. 'Where did Naig get his *jettis*? From Seringapatam?'

'Yes, sahib.'

'I killed enough of the buggers,' Sharpe said, 'so I don't mind killing a few more. Are you coming?' he asked the cavalry Sergeant.

'Why not?' The man grinned.

'Anyone else?' Sharpe asked, but no one else seemed to want a fight that afternoon.

'Please, sahib,' the clerk said weakly.

Sharpe ignored him and, followed by Ahmed and the cavalryman, went back into the sunlight. 'What's your name?' Sharpe asked the Sergeant.

'Lockhart, sir. Eli Lockhart.'

'I'm Dick Sharpe, Eli, and you don't have to call me "sir", I'm not a proper bleeding officer. I was made up at Assaye, and I wish the buggers had left me a sergeant now. They sent me to be a bloody bullock driver, because I'm not fit for anything else.' He looked at Lockhart's six troopers who were still waiting. 'What are they doing here?'

'Didn't expect me to carry the bloody horseshoes myself, did you?' Lockhart said, then gestured at the troopers. 'Come on, boys. We're going to have a scrap.'

'Who said anything about a scrap?' Sharpe asked.

'He's got horseshoes,' Lockhart explained, 'but we don't have money. So there's only one way to get them off him.'

'True,' Sharpe said, and grinned.

Lockhart suddenly looked oddly shy. 'Was you in the Captain's quarters, sir?'

'Yes, why?'

The tough-looking Sergeant was actually blushing now. 'You didn't see a woman there, did you, sir?'

'Dark-haired girl. Pretty?'

'That's her.'

'Who is she?'

'Torrance's servant. A widow. He brought her and her husband out from England, but the fellow died and left her on her own. Torrance won't let her go.'

66

'And you'd like to take her off his hands, is that it?'

'I've only ever seen her at a distance,' the Sergeant admitted. 'Torrance was in another regiment, one of the Madrassi's, but we camped together often enough.'

'She's still there,' Sharpe said drily, 'still alive.'

'He keeps her close, he does,' Lockhart said, then kicked a dog out of his path. The eight men had left the village and entered the sprawling encampment where the merchants with their herds, wagons and families were camped. Great white oxen with painted horns were hobbled by pegs, and children scurried among the beasts collecting their dung which they slapped into cakes that would be dried for fuel. 'So tell me about these *jettis*,' Lockhart asked.

'Like circus strongmen,' Sharpe said, 'only it's some kind of religious thing. Don't ask me. None of it makes bleeding sense to me. Got muscles like mountains, they have, but they're slow. I killed four of the buggers at Seringapatam.'

'And you know Hakeswill?'

'I know bloody Hakeswill. Recruited me, he did, and he's been persecuting me ever since. He shouldn't even be with this army, he's supposed to be with the Havercakes down south, but he came up here with a warrant to arrest me. That didn't work, so he's just stayed, hasn't he? And he's working the bleeding system! You can wager your last shilling that he's the bastard who supplies Naig, and splits the profit.' Sharpe stopped to look for green tents. 'How come you don't carry your own spare horseshoes?'

'We do. But when they've gone you have to get more from the supplies. That's how the system's supposed to work. And yesterday's pursuit left half the hooves wrecked. We need shoes.'

Sharpe had seen a cluster of faded green tents. 'That's where the bastard is,' he said, then looked at Lockhart. 'This could get nasty.'

Lockhart grinned. He was as tall as Sharpe and had a face that looked as though it had survived a lifetime of tavern brawls. 'Come this far, ain't I?'

'Is that thing loaded?' Sharpe nodded at the pistol at Lockhart's belt. A sabre also hung there, just like the one at Sharpe's hip.

'It will be.' Lockhart drew the pistol and Sharpe turned to Ahmed and mimed the actions of loading the musket. Ahmed grinned and pointed to the lock, indicating that his weapon was already charged.

'How many of the buggers will be waiting for us?' Lockhart asked.

'A dozen?' Sharpe guessed.

Lockhart glanced back at his six men. 'We can deal with a dozen buggers.'

'Right,' Sharpe said, 'so let's bloody well make some trouble.' He grinned, because for the first time since he had become an officer he was enjoying himself.

Which meant someone was about to get a thumping.

CHAPTER 3

Major General Sir Arthur Wellesley rode northwards among a caval-
cade of officers whose horses kicked up a wide trail of dust that lingered
in the air long after the horsemen had passed. Two troops of East
India Company cavalry provided the General's escort. Manu Bappoo's
army might have been trounced and its survivors sent skeltering back
into Gawilghur, but the Deccan Plain was still infested with Mahratta
cavalry ready to pounce on supply convoys, wood-cutting parties or
the grass-cutters who supplied the army's animals with fodder and so
the two troops rode with sabres drawn. Wellesley set a fast pace,
revelling in the freedom to ride in the long open country. 'Did you
visit Colonel Stevenson this morning?' he called back to an aide.

'I did, sir, and he's no better than he was.'

'But he can get about?'

'On his elephant, sir.'

Wellesley grunted. Stevenson was the commander of his smaller
army, but the old Colonel was ailing. So was Harness, the commander
of one of Wellesley's two brigades, but there was no point in asking
about Harness. It was not just physical disease that assaulted Harness,
for the Scotsman's wits were gone as well. The doctors claimed it was
the heat that had desiccated his brains, but Wellesley doubted the
diagnosis. Heat and rum, maybe, but not the heat alone, though he
did not doubt that India's climate was bad for a European's health.
Few men lived long without falling prey to some wasting fever, and
Wellesley was thinking it was time he left himself. Time to go back
home before his health was abraded and, more important, before his
existence was forgotten in London. French armies were unsettling all
Europe and it could not be long before London despatched an army
to fight the old foe, and Wellesley wanted to be a part of it. He was

in his middle thirties and he had a reputation to make, but first he had to finish off the Mahrattas, and that meant taking Gawilghur, and to that end he was now riding towards the great rampart of cliffs that sealed off the plain's northern edge.

An hour's ride brought him to the summit of a small rise which offered a view northwards. The plain looked dun, starved of water by the failed monsoon, though here and there patches of millet grew tall. In a good year, Wellesley guessed, the millet would cover the plain from horizon to horizon, a sea of grain bounded by the Gawilghur cliffs. He dismounted on the small knoll and took out a telescope that he settled on his horse's saddle. It was a brand new glass, a gift from the merchants of Madras to mark Wellesley's pacification of Mysore. Trade now moved freely on India's eastern flank, and the telescope, which had been specially ordered from Matthew Berge of London, was a generous token of the merchants' esteem, but Wellesley could not get used to it. The shape of the eyepiece was less concave than the one he was used to, and after a moment he snapped the new telescope shut and pulled out his old glass which, though lower powered, was more comfortable. He stared for a long time, gazing at the fort which crowned the rock promontory. The black stone of the fortress walls looked particularly sinister, even in the sunlight. 'Good God,' the General muttered after a while. Fail up there, he thought, and there would be no point in going home. He could go to London with some victories under his belt, and men would respect him even if the victories had not been against the French, but go with a defeat and they would despise him. Gawilghur, he thought sourly, had the look of a career-breaker.

Colonel Wallace, Wellesley's healthy brigade commander, had also dismounted and was inspecting the fortress through his own glass. 'Devil of a place, Sir Arthur,' Wallace said.

'How high is it, Blackiston?' Wellesley called to one of his aides, an engineer.

'I took a triangulation yesterday, sir,' Blackiston said, 'and discovered the fortress walls are eighteen hundred feet above the plain.'

'Is there water up there?' Colonel Butters, the chief engineer, asked.

'We hear there is, sir,' Blackiston said. 'There are tanks in the fort; huge things like lakes.'

'But the water level must be low this year?' Butters suggested.

'I doubt it's low enough, sir,' Blackiston murmured, knowing that Butters had been hoping that thirst might defeat the garrison.

'And the rascals will have food, no doubt,' Wellesley commented.

'Doubtless,' Wallace agreed drily.

'Which means they'll have to be prised out,' the General said, then bent to the glass again and lowered the lens to look at the foothills below the bluff. Just south of the fort was a conical hill that rose almost halfway up the flank of the great promontory. 'Can we get guns on that near hill?' he asked.

There was a pause while the other officers decided which hill he was referring to. Colonel Butters flinched. 'We can get them up there, sir, but I doubt they'll have the elevation to reach the fort.'

'You'll get nothing bigger than a twelve-pounder up there,' Wallace said dubiously, then slid the telescope's view up the bluff to the walls. 'And you'll need bigger shot than twelve-pounders to break down that wall.'

'Sir Arthur!' The warning call came from the officer commanding the East India Company cavalry who was pointing to where a group of Mahratta horsemen had appeared in the south. They had evidently been following the lingering dust cloud left by the General's party and, though the approaching horsemen only numbered about twenty men, the sepoy cavalry wheeled to face them and spread into a line.

'It's all right,' Wellesley called, 'they're ours. I asked them to meet us here.' He had inspected the approaching horsemen through his telescope and now, waving the sepoy cavalry back, he walked to greet the *silladars*. 'Syud Sevajee,' Wellesley acknowledged the man in the shabby green and silver coat who led the cavalrymen, 'thank you for coming.'

Syud Sevajee nodded brusquely at Wellesley, then stared up at Gawilghur. 'You think you can get in?'

'I think we must,' Wellesley said.

'No one ever has,' Sevajee said with a sly smile.

Wellesley returned the smile, but slowly, as if accepting the implied challenge, and then, as Sevajee slid down from his saddle, the General turned to Wallace. 'You've met Syud Sevajee, Wallace?'

'I've not had that pleasure, sir.'

Wellesley made the introduction, then added that Syud Sevajee's father had been one of the Rajah of Berar's generals.

'But is no longer?' Wallace asked Sevajee.

'Beny Singh murdered him,' Sevajee said grimly, 'so I fight with you, Colonel, to gain my chance to kill Beny Singh. And Beny Singh now commands that fortress.' He nodded towards the distant promontory.

'So how do we get inside?' Wellesley asked.

The officers gathered around Sevajee as the Indian drew his *tulwar* and used its tip to draw a figure eight in the dust. He tapped the lower circle of the eight, which he had drawn far larger than the upper. 'That's what you're looking at,' he said, 'the Inner Fort. And there are only two entrances. There's a road that climbs up from the plain and goes to the Southern Gate.' He drew a squiggly line that tailed away from the bottom of the figure eight. 'But that road is impossible. You will climb straight into their guns. A child with a pile of rocks could keep an army from climbing that road. The only possible route into the Inner Fort is through the main entrance.' He scratched a brief line across the junction of the two circles.

'Which will not be easy?' Wellesley asked drily.

Sevajee offered the General a grim smile. 'The main entrance is a long corridor, barred by four gates and flanked by high walls. But even to reach it, Sir Arthur, you will have to take the Outer Fort.' He tapped the small upper circle of the figure eight.

Wellesley nodded. 'And that, too, is difficult?'

'Again, two entrances,' Sevajee said. 'One is a road that climbs from the plain. You can't see it from here, but it twists up the hills to the west and it comes to the fort here.' He tapped the waist of the figure eight. 'It's an easier climb than the southern road, but for the last mile of the journey your men will be under the guns of the Outer Fort. And the final half-mile, General, is steep.' He stressed the last word. 'On one side of the road is a cliff, and on the other is a precipice, and the guns of the Outer Fort can fire straight down that half-mile of road.'

Colonel Butters shook his head in gloomy contemplation of Sevajee's news. 'How come you know all this?' he asked.

'I grew up in Gawilghur,' Sevajee said. 'My father, before he was murdered, was killadar of the fortress.'

'He knows,' Wellesley said curtly. 'And the main entrance of the Outer Fort?'

'That,' Sevajee said, 'is the fortress's weakest point.' He scratched a line that pierced the uppermost curve of the small circle. 'It's the only level approach to the fortress, but it's very narrow. On one side' – he tapped the eastern flank of the line – 'the ground falls steeply away. On the other side is a reservoir tank. So to reach the fort you must risk a narrow neck of land that is swept by two ramparts of guns, one above the other.'

'Two walls?' Wallace asked.

'Set on a steep hill,' Sevajee said, nodding. 'You must fight uphill across both walls. There is an entrance, but it's like the Inner Fort's entrance: a series of gates with a narrow passage leading from one to the other, and men above you on both sides hurling down rocks and round shot.'

'And once we've captured the Outer Fort,' Wellesley asked, 'what then?'

Sevajee offered a wolfish smile. 'Then your troubles are just beginning, Sir Arthur.' He scuffed out the diagram he had made in the dust and scratched another, this one showing two circles, one large and one small, with a space between them. 'The two forts are not connected. They are separated here' – he tapped the space between the circles with his *tulwar* – 'and that is a ravine. A deep ravine. So once you have the Outer Fort, you still have to assault the Inner Fort, and its defences will be untouched. It has a wall which stands at the top of the ravine's cliff, and that is where your enemy will be taking refuge; inside the wall of the Inner Fort. My father reckoned no enemy could ever capture Gawilghur's Inner Fort. If all India should fall, he said, then its heart would still beat at Gawilghur.'

Wellesley walked a few paces north to stare at the high promontory. 'How big is the garrison?'

'Normally,' Sevajee said, 'about a thousand men, but now? It could be six or seven times that many. There is room inside for a whole army.'

And if the fort did not fall, Wellesley thought, then the Mahrattas would take heart. They would gather a new army and, in the new year, raid southwards again. There would be no peace in western India till Gawilghur fell. 'Major Blackiston?'

'Sir?'

'You'll make an exploration of the plateau.' The General turned to

Sevajee. 'Will you escort Major Blackiston up into the hills? I want sketches, Blackiston, of the neck of land leading to the main entrance. I want you to tell me where we can place breaching batteries. I need to know how we can get guns up to the tops of the hills, and I need to know it all within two days.'

'Two days?' Blackiston sounded appalled.

'We don't want the rascals to take root up there, do we? Speed, Blackiston, speed! Can you leave now?' This question was directed at Sevajee.

'I can,' Sevajee answered.

Wellesley waved Blackiston on his way. 'Two days, Major! I want you back tomorrow evening!'

Colonel Butters frowned at the far hills. 'You're taking the army to the top?'

'Half the army,' Wellesley said, 'the other half will stay on the plain.' He would need to hold Gawilghur between his redcoats like a nut, and hope that when he squeezed it was the nut, and not the nutcracker, that broke. He pulled himself back into the saddle, then waited as the other officers mounted. Then he turned his mare and started back towards the camp. 'It'll be up to the engineers to get us onto the heights,' he said, 'then a week's hard carrying to lift the ammunition to the batteries.' The thought of that job made the General frown. 'What's the problem with the bullock train?' he demanded of Butters. 'I'm hearing complaints. Over two thousand muskets stolen from convoys, and Huddlestone tells me there are no spare horseshoes; that can't be right!'

'Torrance says that bandits have been active, sir,' Butters said. 'And I gather there have been accidents,' he added lamely.

'Who's Torrance?' Wellesley asked.

'Company man, sir, a captain. He took over poor Mackay's duties.'

'I could surmise all that for myself,' the General said acidly. 'Who is he?'

Butters blushed at the reproof. 'His father's a canon at Wells, I think. Or maybe Salisbury? But more to the point, sir, he has an uncle in Leadenhall Street.'

Wellesley grunted. An uncle in Leadenhall Street meant that Torrance had a patron who was senior in the East India Company, someone to wield the influence that a clergyman father might not have. 'Is he as good as Mackay?'

Butters, a heavy-set man who rode his horse badly, shrugged. 'He was recommended by Huddlestone.'

'Which means Huddlestone wanted to be rid of him,' Wellesley snapped.

'I'm sure he's doing his best,' Butters said defensively. 'Though he did ask me for an assistant, but I had to turn him down. I've no one to spare. I'm short of engineers already, sir, as you well know.'

'I've sent for more,' Wellesley said.

Wallace intervened. 'I gave Torrance one of my ensigns, Sir Arthur.'

'You can spare an ensign, Wallace?'

'Sharpe, sir.'

'Ah.' Wellesley grimaced. 'Never does work out, does it? You lift a man from the ranks and you do him no favours.'

'He might be happier in an English regiment,' Wallace said, 'so I'm recommending he exchanges into the Rifles.'

'You mean they're not particular?' Wellesley asked, then scowled. 'How the devil are we to fight a war without horseshoes?' He kicked back at the mare, angry at the predicament. 'My God, Butters, but your Captain Torrance must do his job!' Wellesley, better than anyone, knew that he would never take Gawilghur if the supply train failed.

And Gawilghur had never been taken.

Dear God, Wellesley thought, but how was it ever to be done?

'Big buggers,' Sergeant Eli Lockhart murmured as they neared the two green tents. The cavalryman was speaking of the guards who lolled in chairs outside Naig's tents. There were four in view, and two of them had bare, oiled chests that bulged with unnatural muscle. Their hair was never cut, but was instead coiled around their heads. They were keeping guard outside the larger of the tents, the one Sharpe guessed was Naig's brothel. The other tent might have been the merchant's living quarters, but its entrance was tightly laced, so Sharpe could not glimpse inside.

'The two greasy fellows are the *jettis*,' Sharpe said.

'Big as bloody beeves, they are,' Lockhart said. 'Do they really wring your neck?'

'Back to front,' Sharpe said. 'Or else they drive a nail into your

75

skull with their bare hand.' He swerved aside to go past the tents. It was not that he feared to pick a fight with Naig's guards, indeed he expected a scrap, but there was no point in going bald-headed into battle. A bit of cleverness would not go amiss. 'I'm being canny,' he explained to Lockhart, then turned to make sure that Ahmed was keeping up. The boy was holding Sharpe's pack as well as his musket.

The four guards, all of them armed with firelocks and *tulwars*, watched the British soldiers walk out of sight. 'They didn't like the look of us,' Lockhart said.

'Mangy buggers, they are,' Sharpe said. He was glancing about the encampment and saw what he wanted just a few paces away. It was some straw, and near it was a smouldering campfire, and he screwed a handful of the straw stalks into a spill that he lit and carried to the rear of the smaller tent. He pushed the flaming spill into a fold of the canvas. A child watched, wide-eyed. 'If you say anything,' Sharpe told the half-naked child, 'I'll screw your head off back to front.' The child, who did not understand a word, grinned broadly.

'You're not really supposed to be doing this, are you?' Lockhart asked.

'No,' Sharpe said. Lockhart grinned, but said nothing. Instead he just watched as the flames licked at the faded green canvas which, for a moment or two, resisted the fire. The material blackened, but did not burn, then suddenly it burst into fire that licked greedily up the tent's high side. 'That'll wake 'em up,' Sharpe said.

'What now?' Lockhart asked, watching the flame sear up the tent's side.

'We rescue what's inside, of course.' Sharpe drew his sabre. 'Come on, lads!' He ran back to the front of the tent. 'Fire!' he shouted. 'Fire! Fetch water! Fire!'

The four guards stared uncomprehendingly at the Englishman, then leaped to their feet as Sharpe slashed at the laces of the small tent's doorway. One of them called a protest to Sharpe.

'Fire!' Lockhart bellowed at the guards who, still unsure of what was happening, did not try to stop Sharpe. Then one of them saw the smoke billowing over the ridge of the tent. He yelled a warning into the larger tent as his companions suddenly moved to pull the Englishman away from the tent's entrance.

'Hold them off!' Sharpe called, and Lockhart's six troopers closed on the three men. Sharpe slashed at the lacing, hacking down through the tough rope as the troopers thumped into the guards. Someone swore, there was a grunt as a fist landed, then a yelp as a trooper's boot slammed into a *jetti*'s groin. Sharpe sawed through the last knot, then pushed through the loosened tent flaps. 'Jesus!' He stopped, staring at the boxes and barrels and crates that were stacked in the tent's smoky gloom.

Lockhart had followed him inside. 'Doesn't even bother to hide the stuff properly, does he?' the Sergeant said in amazement, then crossed to a barrel and pointed to a 19 that had been cut into one of the staves. 'That's our mark! The bugger's got half our supplies!' He looked up at the flames that were now eating away the tent roof. 'We'll lose the bloody lot if we don't watch it.'

'Cut the tent ropes,' Sharpe suggested, 'and push it all down.'

The two men ran outside and slashed at the guy ropes with their sabres, but more of Naig's men were coming from the larger tent now. 'Watch your back, Eli!' Sharpe called, then turned and sliced the curved blade towards a *jetti*'s face. The man stepped back, and Sharpe followed up hard, slashing again, driving the huge man farther back. 'Now bugger off!' he shouted at the vast brute. 'There's a bloody fire! Fire!'

Lockhart had put his attacker on the ground and was now stamping on his face with a spurred boot. The troopers were coming to help and Sharpe let them deal with Naig's men while he cut through the last of the guy ropes, then ran back into the tent and heaved on the nearest pole. The air inside the tent was choking with swirling smoke, but at last the whole heavy array of canvas sagged towards the fire, lifting the canvas wall behind Sharpe into the air.

'Sahib!' Ahmed's shrill voice shouted and Sharpe turned to see a man aiming a musket at him. The lifting tent flap was exposing Sharpe, but he was too far away to rush the man, then Ahmed fired his own musket and the man shuddered, turned to look at the boy, then winced as the pain in his shoulder struck home. He dropped the gun and clapped a hand onto the wound. The sound of the shot startled the other guards and some reached for their own muskets, but Sharpe ran at them and used his sabre to beat the guns down. 'There's a bloody fire!' he shouted into their faces. 'A fire! You want everything to burn?' They did not understand him, but some realized that the fire threatened

77

their master's supplies and so ran to haul the half-collapsed burning canvas away from the wooden crates.

'But who started the fire?' a voice said behind Sharpe, and he turned to see a tall, fat Indian dressed in a green robe that was embroidered with looping fish and long-legged water-birds. The fat man was holding a half-naked child by the hand, the same small boy who had watched Sharpe push the burning straw into a crease of the canvas. 'British officers,' the fat man said, 'have a deal of freedom in this country, but does that mean they can destroy an honest man's property?'

'Are you Naig?' Sharpe asked.

The fat man waved to his guards so that they gathered behind him. The tent had been dragged clear of the crates and was burning itself out harmlessly. The green-robed man now had sixteen or seventeen men with him, four of them *jettis* and all of them armed, while Sharpe had Lockhart and his battered troopers and one defiant child who was reloading a musket as tall as himself. 'I will give you my name,' the fat man said unpleasantly, 'when you tell me yours.'

'Sharpe. Ensign Sharpe.'

'A mere ensign!' The fat man raised his eyebrows. 'I thought ensigns were children, like this young man.' He patted the half-naked boy's head. 'I am Naig.'

'So perhaps you can tell me,' Sharpe said, 'why that tent was stuffed full of our supplies?'

'Your supplies!' Naig laughed. 'They are my goods, Ensign Sharpe. Perhaps some of them are stored in old boxes that once belonged to your army, but what of that? I buy the boxes from the quartermaster's department.'

'Lying bastard,' Sergeant Lockhart growled. He had prised open the barrel with the number 19 incised on its side and now flourished a horseshoe. 'Ours!' he said.

Naig seemed about to order his guards to finish off Sharpe's small band, but then he glanced to his right and saw that two British officers had come from the larger tent. The presence of the two, both captains, meant that Naig could not just drive Sharpe away, for now there were witnesses. Naig might take on an ensign and a few troopers, but captains carried too much authority. One of the captains, who wore the red coat of the Scotch Brigade, crossed to Sharpe. 'Trouble?' he asked. His revels had plainly been interrupted, for his trousers were still unbuttoned and his sword and sash were slung across one shoulder.

'This bastard, sir, has been pilfering our supplies.' Sharpe jerked his thumb at Naig then nodded towards the crates. 'It's all marked as stolen in the supply ledgers, but I'll wager it's all there. Buckets, muskets, horseshoes.'

The Captain glanced at Naig, then crossed to the crates. 'Open that one,' he ordered, and Lockhart obediently stooped to the box and levered up its nailed lid with his sabre.

'I have been storing these boxes,' Naig explained. He turned to the second captain, an extraordinarily elegant cavalryman in Company uniform, and he pleaded with him in an Indian language. The Company Captain turned away and Naig went back to the Scotsman. The merchant was in trouble now, and he knew it. 'I was asked to store the boxes!' he shouted at the Scotsman.

But the infantry Captain was staring down into the opened crate where ten brand new muskets lay in their wooden cradles. He stooped for one of the muskets and peered at the lock. Just forward of the hammer and behind the pan was an engraved crown with the letters GR beneath it, while behind the hammer the word Tower was engraved. 'Ours,' the Scotsman said flatly.

'I bought them.' Naig was sweating now.

'I thought you said you were storing them?' the Scotsman said. 'Now you say you bought them. Which is it?'

'My brother and I bought the guns from *silladars*,' Naig said.

'We don't sell these Tower muskets,' the Captain said, hefting the gun that was still coated with grease.

Naig shrugged. 'They must have been captured from the supply convoys. Please, sahib, take them. I want no trouble. How was I to know they were stolen?' He turned and pleaded again with the Company cavalry Captain who was a tall, lean man with a long face, but the cavalryman turned and walked a short distance away. A crowd had collected now and watched the drama silently, and Sharpe, looking along their faces, suspected there was not much sympathy for Naig. Nor, Sharpe thought, was there much hope for the fat man. Naig had been playing a dangerous game, but with such utter confidence that he had not even bothered to conceal the stolen supplies. At the very least he could have thrown away the government issue boxes and tried to file the lock markings off the muskets, but Naig must have believed he had powerful friends who would protect him. The cavalryman seemed to be one of those friends, for Naig had followed him and was hissing in his ear, but the cavalryman merely pushed the Indian away, then turned to Sharpe. 'Hang him,' he said curtly.

'Hang him?' Sharpe asked in puzzlement.

'It's the penalty for theft, ain't it?' the cavalryman insisted.

Sharpe looked to the Scottish Captain, who nodded uncertainly. 'That's what the General said,' the Scotsman confirmed.

'I'd like to know how he got the supplies, sir,' Sharpe said.

'You'll give the fat bastard time to concoct a story?' the cavalryman demanded. He had an arrogance that annoyed Sharpe, but everything about the cavalryman irritated Sharpe. The man was a dandy. He wore tall, spurred boots that sheathed his calves and knees in soft, polished leather. His white breeches were skin tight, his waistcoat had gold buttons, while his red tail coat was clean, uncreased and edged with gold braid. He wore a frilled stock, a red silk sash was draped across his right shoulder and secured at his left hip by a knot of golden braid, his sabre was scabbarded in red leather, while his cocked hat was plumed with a lavishly curled feather that had been dyed pale green. The clothes had cost a fortune, and clearly his servants must spend hours on keeping their master so beautifully dressed. He looked askance at Sharpe, a slight wrinkle of his nostrils suggesting that he found Sharpe's appearance distressing. The cavalryman's face suggested he was a clever man, but also that he despised those who were less clever than himself. 'I don't suppose Sir Arthur will be vastly pleased when he hears that you let the fellow live, Ensign,' he said acidly. 'Swift and certain justice, ain't that the penalty for theft? Hang the fat beast.'

'That is what the standing orders say,' the Scotch Brigade Captain agreed, 'but does it apply to civilians?'

'He should have a trial!' Sharpe protested, not because he was so committed to Naig's right to a hearing, but because he feared the whole episode was getting out of hand. He had thought to find the supplies, maybe have a mill with Naig's guards, but no one was supposed to die. Naig deserved a good kicking, but death?

'Standing orders apply to anyone within the picquet lines,' the cavalry Captain averred confidently. 'So for God's sake get on with it! Dangle the bastard!' He was sweating, and Sharpe sensed that the elegant cavalryman was not quite so confident as he appeared.

'Bugger a trial,' Sergeant Lockhart said happily. 'I'll hang the bastard.' He snapped at his troopers to fetch a nearby ox cart. Naig had tried to retreat to the protection of his guards, but the cavalry Captain had drawn a pistol that he now held close to Naig's head as the grinning troopers trundled the empty ox cart into the open space in front of the pilfered supplies.

Sharpe crossed to the tall cavalryman. 'Shouldn't we talk to him, sir?'

'My dear fellow, have you ever tried to get the truth out of an Indian?' the Captain asked. 'They swear by a thousand gaudy gods that they'll tell the truth, then lie like a rug! Be quiet!' Naig had begun to protest and the cavalryman rammed the pistol into the Indian's mouth, breaking a tooth and gashing Naig's gum. 'Another damned word, Naig, and I'll castrate you before I hang you.' The cavalryman glanced at Sharpe, who was frowning. 'Are you squeamish, Ensign?'

'Don't seem right, sir. I mean I agree he deserves to be hung, but shouldn't we talk to him first?'

'If you like conversation so much,' the cavalryman drawled, 'institute a Philosophical Society. Then you can enjoy all the hot air you like. Sergeant?' This last was to Lockhart. 'Take the bastard off my hands, will you?'

'Pleasure, sir.' Lockhart seized Naig and shoved him towards the cart. One of the cavalry troopers had cut a length of guy rope from the burnt remnants of the tent and he now tied one end to the tip of the single shaft that protruded from the front of the ox cart. He made a loop in the rope's end.

Naig screamed and tried to pull away. Some of his guards started forward, but then a hard voice ordered them back and Sharpe turned to see that a tall, thin Indian in a black and green striped robe had come from the larger tent. The newcomer, who looked to be in his forties, walked with a limp. He crossed to the cavalry Captain and spoke quietly, and Sharpe saw the cavalryman shake his head vehemently, then shrug as if to suggest that he was powerless. Then the Captain gestured to Sharpe and the tall Indian gave the Ensign a look of such malevolence that Sharpe instinctively put his hand on his sabre's hilt. Lockhart had pulled the noose over Naig's head. 'Are you sure, sir?' he asked the cavalry Captain.

'Of course I'm sure, Sergeant,' the cavalryman said angrily. 'Just get on with it.'

'Sir?' Sharpe appealed to the Scots Captain, who frowned uncertainly, then turned and walked away as though he wanted nothing more to do with the affair. The tall Indian in the striped robe spat into the dust, then limped back to the tent.

Lockhart ordered his troopers to the back of the cart. Naig was attempting to pull the noose free of his neck, but Lockhart slapped his hands down. 'Now, boys!' he shouted.

The troopers reached up and hauled down on the backboard so that the cart tipped like a seesaw on its single axle and, as the troopers pulled down, so the shaft rose into the air. The rope stretched and tightened. Naig screamed, then the cavalryman jumped up to sit on the cart's back and the shaft jerked higher still and the scream was abruptly choked off. Naig was dangling now, his feet kicking wildly under the lavishly embroidered robe. None of the crowd moved, none protested.

Naig's face was bulging and his hands were scrabbling uselessly at the noose which was tight about his neck. The cavalry officer watched with a small smile. 'A pity,' he said in his elegant voice. 'The wretched man ran the best brothel I ever found.'

'We're not killing his girls, sir,' Sharpe said.

'That's true, Ensign, but will their next owner treat them as well?' The cavalryman turned to the big tent's entrance and took off his plumed hat to salute a group of sari-clad girls who now watched wide-eyed as their employer did the gallows dance. 'I saw Nancy Merrick hang in Madras,' the cavalryman said, 'and she did the jig for thirty-seven minutes! Thirty-seven! I'd wagered on sixteen, so lost rather a lot of tin. Don't think I can watch Naig dance for half an hour. It's too damned hot. Sergeant? Help his soul to perdition, will you?'

Lockhart crouched beneath the dying man and caught hold of his heels. Then he tugged down hard, swearing when Naig pissed on him. He tugged again, and at last the body went still. 'Do you see what happens when you steal from us?' the cavalry Captain shouted at the crowd, then repeated the words in an Indian language. 'If you steal from us, you will die!' Again he translated his words, then gave Sharpe a crooked grin. 'But only, of course, if you're stupid enough to be caught, and I didn't think Naig was stupid at all. Rather the reverse. Just how did you happen to discover the supplies, Ensign?'

'Tent was on fire, sir,' Sharpe said woodenly. 'Me and Sergeant Lockhart decided to rescue whatever was inside.'

'How very public-spirited of you.' The Captain gave Sharpe a long, speculative look, then turned back to Lockhart. 'Is he dead, Sergeant?'

'Near as makes no difference, sir,' Lockhart called back.

'Use your pistol to make sure,' the Captain ordered, then sighed. 'A shame,' he said. 'I rather liked Naig. He was a rogue, of course, but rogues are so much more amusing than honest men.' He watched as Lockhart lowered the shaft, then stooped over the prostrate body and put a bullet into its skull. 'I suppose I'll have to find some carts to fetch these supplies back where they belong,' the Captain said.

'I'll do that, sir,' Sharpe said.

'You will?' The Captain seemed astonished to discover such willingness. 'Why on earth would you want to do that, Ensign?'

'It's my job, sir,' Sharpe said. 'I'm Captain Torrance's assistant.'

'You poor benighted bastard,' the Captain said pityingly.

'Poor, sir? Why?'

'Because I'm Captain Torrance. Good day to you, Ensign.' Torrance turned on his heel and walked away through the crowd.

'Bastard,' Sharpe said, for he had suddenly understood why Torrance had been so keen to hang Naig.

He spat after the departed Captain, then went to find some bullocks and carts. The army had its supplies back, but Sharpe had made a new enemy. As if Hakeswill were not enough, he now had Torrance as well.

The palace in Gawilghur was a sprawling one-storey building that stood on the highest point within the Inner Fort. To its north was a garden that curled about the largest of the fortress's lakes. The lake was a tank, a reservoir, but its banks had been planted with flowering trees, and a flight of steps led from the palace to a small stone pavilion on the lake's northern shore. The pavilion had an arched ceiling on which the reflections of the lake's small waves should have rippled, but the season had been so dry that the lake had shrunk and the water level was some eight or nine feet lower than usual. The water and the exposed banks were rimed with a green, foul-smelling scum, but Beny

Singh, the Killadar of Gawilghur, had arranged for spices to be burned in low, flat braziers so that the dozen men inside the pavilion were not too offended by the lake's stench.

'If only the Rajah was here,' Beny Singh said, 'we should know what to do.' Beny Singh was a short, plump man with a curling moustache and nervous eyes. He was the fortress commander, but he was a courtier by avocation, not a soldier, and he had always regarded his command of the great fortress as a licence to make his fortune rather than to fight the Rajah's enemies.

Prince Manu Bappoo was not surprised that his brother had chosen not to come to Gawilghur, but had instead fled farther into the hills. The Rajah was like Beny Singh, he had no belly for a fight, but Bappoo had watched the first British troops creep across the plain beneath the fort's high walls and he welcomed their coming. 'We don't need my brother here to know what we must do,' he said. 'We fight.' The other men, all commanders of the various troops that had taken refuge in Gawilghur, voiced their agreement.

'The British cannot be stopped by walls,' Beny Singh said. He was cradling a small white lap dog which had eyes as wide and frightened as its master's.

'They can, and they will,' Bappoo insisted.

Singh shook his head. 'Were they stopped at Seringapatam? At Ahmednuggur? They crossed those city walls as though they had wings! They are – what is the word your Arabs use? – *djinns*!' He looked about the gathered council and saw no one who would support him. 'They must have the *djinns* on their side,' he added weakly.

'So what would you do?' Bappoo asked.

'Treat with them,' Beny Singh said. 'Ask for *cowle*.'

'*Cowle*?' It was Colonel Dodd who intervened, speaking in his crude, newly learned Marathi. 'I'll tell you what terms Wellesley will offer you. None! He'll march you away as a prisoner, he'll slight these walls and take away the Rajah's treasures.'

'There are no treasures here,' Beny Singh said, but no one believed him. He was soothing the little dog which had been frightened by the Englishman's harsh voice.

'And he'll give your women to his men as playthings,' Dodd added nastily.

Beny Singh shuddered. His wife, his concubines and his children were all in the palace, and they were all dear to him. He pampered them, worshipped them and adored them. 'Perhaps I should remove my people from the fort?' he suggested hesitantly. 'I could take them to Multai? The British will never reach Multai.'

'You'd run away?' Dodd asked in his harsh voice. 'You bloody won't!' He spoke those three words in English, but everyone understood what they meant. He leaned forward. 'If you run away,' he said, 'the garrison loses heart. The rest of the soldiers can't take their women away, so why should you? We fight them here, and we stop them here. Stop them dead!' He stood and walked to the pavilion's edge where he spat onto the green-scummed bank before turning back to Beny Singh. 'Your women are safe here, Killadar. I could hold this fortress from now till the world's end with just a hundred men.'

'The British are *djinns*,' Beny Singh whispered. The dog in his arms was shivering.

'They are not *djinns*,' Dodd snapped. 'There are no demons! They don't exist!'

'Winged *djinns*,' Beny Singh said in almost a whimper, 'invisible *djinns*! In the air!'

Dodd spat again. 'Bloody hell,' he said in English, then turned fast towards Beny Singh. 'I'm an English demon. Me! Understand? I'm a *djinn*, and if you take your women away I'll follow you and I'll come to them at night and fill them with black bile.' He bared his yellowed teeth and the Killadar shuddered. The white dog barked shrilly.

Manu Bappoo waved Dodd back to his seat. Dodd was the only European officer left in his forces and, though Bappoo was glad to have the Englishman's services, there were times when Colonel Dodd could be tiresome. 'If there are *djinns*,' Bappoo told Singh, 'they will be on our side.' He waited while the Killadar soothed the frightened dog, then he leaned forward. 'Tell me,' he demanded of Beny Singh, 'can the British take the fortress by using the roads up the hill?'

Beny Singh thought about those two steep winding roads that twisted up the hill beneath Gawilghur's walls. No man could survive those climbs, not if the defenders were raining round shot and rocks down the precipitous slopes. 'No,' he admitted.

'So they can only come one way. Only one way! Across the land bridge. And my men will guard the Outer Fort, and Colonel Dodd's men will defend the Inner Fort.'

'And no one,' Dodd said harshly, 'no one will get past my Cobras.' He still resented that his well-trained, white-coated soldiers were not defending the Outer Fort, but he had accepted Manu Bappoo's argument that the important thing was to hold the Inner Fort. If, by some chance, the British did capture the Outer Fort, they would never fight past Dodd's men. 'My men,' Dodd growled, 'have never been defeated. They never will be.'

Manu Bappoo smiled at the nervous Beny Singh. 'You see, Killadar, you will die here of old age.'

'Or of too many women,' another man put in, provoking laughter.

A cannon sounded from the Outer Fort's northern ramparts, followed a few seconds later by another. No one knew what might have caused the firing and so the dozen men followed Manu Bappoo as he left the pavilion and walked towards the Inner Fort's northern ramparts. Silver-furred monkeys chattered at the soldiers from the high branches.

Arab guards stood at the gate of the Rajah's garden. They were posted to stop any common soldiers of the garrison going to the paths beside the tank where the Killadar's women liked to stroll in the cool of the evening. A hundred paces beyond the garden gate was a steep-sided rock pit, about twice as deep as a man stood high, and Dodd paused to look down into its shadowed depths. The sides had been chiselled smooth by stone-workers so that nothing could climb up from the floor that was littered with white bones. 'The Traitor's Hole,' Bappoo said, as he paused beside Dodd, 'but the bones are from baby monkeys.'

'But they do eat men?' Dodd asked, intrigued by the shadowed blackness at the foot of the hole.

'They kill men,' Bappoo said, 'but don't eat them. They're not big enough.'

'I can't see any,' Dodd said, disappointed, then suddenly a sinuous shadow writhed swiftly between two crevices. 'There!' he said happily. 'Don't they grow big enough to eat men?'

'Most years they escape,' Bappoo said. 'The monsoon floods the pit and the snakes swim to the top and wriggle out. Then we must find new ones. This year we've been saved the trouble. These snakes will grow bigger than usual.'

Beny Singh waited a few paces away, clutching his small dog as though he feared Dodd would throw it down to the snakes. 'There's a bastard who ought to be fed to the snakes,' Dodd said to Bappoo, nodding towards the Killadar.

'My brother likes him,' Bappoo said mildly, touching Dodd's arm to indicate that they should walk on. 'They share tastes.'

'Such as?'

'Women, music, luxury. We really do not need him here.'

Dodd shook his head. 'If you let him go, sahib, then half the damned garrison will want to run away. And if you let the women go, what will the men fight for? Besides, do you really think there's any danger?'

'None,' Bappoo admitted. He had led the officers up a steep rock stairway to a natural bastion where a vast iron gun was trained across the chasm towards the distant cliffs of the high plateau. From here the far cliffs were almost a mile away, but Dodd could just see a group of horsemen clustered at the chasm's edge. It was those horsemen, all in native robes, who had prompted the Outer Fort's gunners to open fire, but the gunners, seeing their shots fall well short of the target, had given up. Dodd drew out his telescope, trained it, and saw a man in the uniform of the Royal Engineers sitting on the ground a few paces from his companions. The engineer was sketching. The horsemen were all Indians. Dodd lowered the telescope and looked at the huge iron gun. 'Is it loaded?' he asked the gunners.

'Yes, sahib.'

'A *haideri* apiece if you can kill the man in the dark uniform. The one sitting at the cliff's edge.'

The gunners laughed. Their gun was over twenty feet long and its wrought-iron barrel was cast with decorations that had been painted green, white and red. A pile of round shot, each over a foot in diameter, stood beside the massive carriage that was made from giant baulks of teak. The gun captain fussed over his aim, shouting at his men to lever the vast carriage a thumb's width to the right, then a finger's breadth back, until at last he was satisfied. He squinted along the barrel for a second, waved the officers who had followed Bappoo to move away from the great gun, then leaned over the breach to dab his glowing portfire onto the gun's touch-hole.

The reed glowed and smoked for a second as the fire dashed down to the charge, then the vast cannon crashed back, the teak runners sliding up the timber ramp that formed the lower half of the carriage.

Smoke jetted out into the chasm as a hundred startled birds flapped from their nests on the rock faces and circled in the warm air.

Dodd had been standing to one side, watching the engineer through his glass. For a second he actually saw the great round shot as a flicker of grey in the lower right quadrant of his lens, then he saw a boulder close to the engineer shatter into scraps. The engineer fell sideways, his sketch pad falling, but then he picked himself up and scrambled up the slope to where his horse was being guarded by the cavalrymen.

Dodd took a single gold coin from his pouch and tossed it to the gunner. 'You missed,' he said, 'but it was damned fine shooting.'

'Thank you, sahib.'

A whimper made Dodd turn. Beny Singh had handed his dog to a servant and was staring through an ivory-barrelled telescope at the enemy horsemen. 'What is it?' Bappoo asked him.

'Syud Sevajee,' Singh said in a small voice.

'Who's Syud Sevajee?' Dodd asked.

Bappoo grinned. 'His father was once killadar here, but he died. Was it poison?' he asked Beny Singh.

'He just died,' Singh said. 'He just died!'

'Murdered, probably,' Bappoo said with amusement, 'and Beny Singh became killadar and took the dead man's daughter as his concubine.'

Dodd turned to see the enemy horsemen vanishing among the trees beyond the far cliff. 'Come for revenge, has he? You still want to leave?' he demanded of Beny Singh. 'Because that fellow will be waiting for you. He'll track you through the hills, Killadar, and slit your throat in the night's darkness.'

'We shall stay here and fight,' Beny Singh declared, retrieving the dog from his servant.

'Fight and win,' Dodd said, and he imagined the British breaching batteries on that far cliff, and he imagined the slaughter that would be made among the crews by this one vast gun. And there were fifty other heavy guns waiting to greet the British approach, and hundreds of lighter pieces that fired smaller missiles. Guns, rockets, canister, muskets and cliffs, those were Gawilghur's defences, and Dodd reckoned the British stood no chance. No chance at all. The big gun's smoke drifted away in the small breeze. 'They will die here,' Dodd said, 'and we shall chase the survivors south and cut them down like dogs.' He turned and looked at Beny Singh. 'You see the chasm? That is where their demons will die. Their wings will be scorched, they will fall like burning stones to their deaths, and their screams will lull your children to a dreamless sleep.' He knew he spoke true, for Gawilghur was impregnable.

'I take pleasure, no, Dilip, make that I take humble pleasure in reporting the recovery of a quantity of stolen stores.' Captain Torrance paused. Night had just fallen and Torrance uncorked a bottle of arrack and took a sip. 'Am I going too fast for you?'

'Yes, sahib,' Dilip, the middle-aged clerk, answered. 'Humble pleasure,' he said aloud as his pen moved laboriously over the paper, 'in reporting the recovery of a quantity of stolen stores.'

'Add a list of the stores,' Torrance ordered. 'You can do that later. Just leave a space, man.'

'Yes, sahib,' Dilip said.

'I had suspected for some time,' Torrance intoned, then scowled as someone knocked on the door. 'Come,' he shouted, 'if you must.'

Sharpe opened the door and was immediately entangled in the muslin. He fought his way past its folds.

'It's you,' Torrance said unpleasantly.

'Me, sir.'

'You let some moths in,' Torrance complained.

'Sorry, sir.'

'That is why the muslin is there, Sharpe, to keep out moths, ensigns and other insignificant nuisances. Kill the moths, Dilip.'

The clerk dutifully chased the moths about the room, swatting them with a roll of paper. The windows, like the door, were closely screened with muslin on the outside of which moths clustered, attracted by the candles that were set in silver sticks on Torrance's table. Dilip's work was spread on the table, while Captain Torrance lay in a wide hammock slung from the roof beams. He was naked. 'Do I offend you, Sharpe?'

'Offend me, sir?'

'I am naked, or had you not noticed?'

'Doesn't bother me, sir.'

'Nudity keeps clothes clean. You should try it. Is the last of the enemy dead, Dilip?'

'The moths are all deceased, sahib.'

'Then we shall continue. Where were we?'

'"I had suspected for some time,"' Dilip read back the report.

'Surmised is better, I think. I had surmised for some time.' Torrance paused to draw on the mouthpiece of a silver-bellied hookah. 'What are you doing here, Sharpe?'

'Come to get orders, sir.'

'How very assiduous of you. I had surmised for some time that depredations – I can spell it if you cannot, Dilip – were being made upon the stores entrusted to my command. What the devil were you doing, Sharpe, poking about Naig's tents?'

'Just happened to be passing them, sir,' Sharpe said, 'when they caught fire.'

Torrance gazed at Sharpe, plainly not believing a word. He shook his head sadly. 'You look very old to be an ensign, Sharpe?'

'I was a sergeant two months ago, sir.'

Torrance adopted a look of pretended horror. 'Oh, good God,' he said archly, 'good God alive. May all the spavined saints preserve us. You're not telling me you've been made up from the ranks?'

'Yes, sir.'

'Sweet suffering Jesus,' Torrance said. He lay his head back on the hammock's pillow and blew a perfect smoke ring that he watched wobble its way up towards the ceiling. 'Having confidential information as to the identity of the thief, I took steps to apprehend him. You will notice, Sharpe, that I am giving you no credit in this report?'

'No, sir?'

'Indeed I am not. This report will go to Colonel Butters, an appallingly bombastic creature who will, I suspect, attempt to take some of the credit for himself before passing the papers on to Arthur Wellesley who, as you may know, is our commander. A very stern man, our Arthur. He likes things done properly. He plainly had a very stern governess in his nursery.'

'I know the General, sir.'

'You do?' Torrance turned his head to look at Sharpe. 'Socially, perhaps? You and he dine together, do you? Pass the time of day, do you? Hunt together, maybe? Drink port? Talk about old times? Whore together, perhaps?' Torrance was mocking, but there was just an edge of interest in his voice in case Sharpe really did know Sir Arthur.

'I mean I've met him, sir.'

Torrance shook his head as though Sharpe had been wasting his time. 'Do stop calling me "sir". It may be your natural subservience, Sharpe, or more likely it is the natural air of superiority that emanates from my person, but it ill becomes an officer, even one dredged up from the ranks. A search of his tents, Dilip, secured the missing items. I then, in accordance with general orders, hanged the thief as an example. I have the honour to be, et cetera, et cetera.'

'Two thousand muskets are still missing, sir,' Sharpe said. 'Sorry, sir. Didn't mean to call you "sir".'

'If it pleases you to grovel, Sharpe, then do so. Two thousand muskets still missing, eh? I suspect the bugger sold them on, don't you?'

'I'm more interested in how he got them in the first place,' Sharpe said.

'How very tedious of you,' Torrance said lightly.

'I'd suggest talking to Sergeant Hakeswill when he gets back,' Sharpe said.

'I won't hear a word spoken against Obadiah,' Torrance said. 'Obadiah is a most amusing fellow.'

'He's a lying, thieving bastard,' Sharpe said vehemently.

'Sharpe! Please!' Torrance's voice was pained. 'How can you say such wicked things? You don't even know the fellow.'

'Oh, I know him, sir. I served under him in the Havercakes.'

'You did?' Torrance smiled. 'I see we are in for interesting times. Perhaps I should keep the two of you apart. Or perhaps not. Brick!' The last word was shouted towards a door that led to the back of the commandeered house.

The door opened and the black-haired woman slipped past the muslin. 'Captain?' she asked. She blushed when she saw Torrance was naked, and Torrance, Sharpe saw, enjoyed her embarrassment.

'Brick, my dear,' Torrance said, 'my hookah has extinguished itself. Will you attend to it? Dilip is busy, or I would have asked him. Sharpe? May I have the honour of naming you to Brick? Brick? This is Ensign Sharpe. Ensign Sharpe? This is Brick.'

'Pleased to meet you, sir,' the woman said, dropping a brief curtsey before she stooped to the hookah. She had clearly not told Torrance that she had met Sharpe earlier.

'Ma'am,' Sharpe said.

'Ma'am!' Torrance said with a laugh. 'She's called Brick, Sharpe.'

'Brick, sir?' Sharpe asked sourly. The name was utterly unsuited to the delicate-featured woman who now deftly disassembled the hookah.

'Her real name is Mrs Wall,' Torrance explained, 'and she is my laundress, seamstress and conscience. Is that not right, little Brick?'

'If you say so, sir.'

'I cannot abide dirty clothes,' Torrance said. 'They are an abomination unto the Lord. Cleanliness, we are constantly told by tedious folk, is next to godliness, but I suspect it is a superior virtue. Any peasant can be godly, but it is a rare person who is clean. Brick, however, keeps me clean. If you pay her a trifle, Sharpe, she will doubtless wash and mend those rags you are pleased to call a uniform.'

'They're all I've got, sir.'

'So? Walk naked until Brick has serviced you, or does the idea embarrass you?'

'I wash my own clothes, sir.'

'I wish you would,' Torrance said tartly. 'Remind me why you came here, Sharpe?'

'Orders, sir.'

'Very well,' Torrance said. 'At dawn you will go to Colonel Butters's quarters and find an aide who can tell you what is required of us. You then tell Dilip. Dilip then arranges everything. After that you may take your rest. I trust you will not find these duties onerous?'

Sharpe wondered why Torrance had asked for a deputy if the clerk did all the work, then supposed that the Captain was so lazy that he could not be bothered to get up early in the morning to fetch his orders. 'I get tomorrow's orders at dawn, sir,' Sharpe said, 'from an aide of Colonel Butters.'

'There!' Torrance said with mock amazement. 'You have mastered your duties, Ensign. I congratulate you.'

'We already have tomorrow's orders, sahib,' Dilip said from the table where he was copying a list of the recovered stores into Torrance's report. 'We are to move everything to Deogaum. The pioneers' stores are to be moved first, sahib. The Colonel's orders are on the table, sahib, with the chitties. Pioneers' stores first, then everything else.'

'Well, I never!' Torrance said. 'See? Your first day's work is done, Sharpe.' He drew on the hookah which the woman had relit. 'Excellent, my dear,' he said, then held out a hand to stop her from leaving. She crouched beside the hammock, averting her eyes from Torrance's naked body. Sharpe sensed her unhappiness, and Torrance sensed Sharpe's interest in her. 'Brick is a widow, Sharpe,' he said, 'and presumably looking for a husband, though I doubt she's ever dared to dream of marrying as high as an ensign. But why not? The social ladder is there to be climbed and, low a rung as you might be, Sharpe, you still represent a considerable advancement for Brick. Before she joined my service she was a mop-squeezer. From mop-squeezer to an officer's wife! There's progress for you. I think the two of you would suit each other vastly well. I shall play Cupid, or rather Dilip will. Take a letter to the chaplain of the 94th, Dilip. He's rarely sober, but I'm sure he can waddle through the marriage ceremony without falling over.'

'I can't marry, sir!' Sharpe protested.

Torrance, amused at himself, raised an eyebrow. 'You are averse to women? You dislike dear Brick? Or you've taken an oath of celibacy, perhaps?'

Sharpe blushed. 'I'm spoken for, sir.'

'You mean you're engaged? How very touching. Is she an heiress, perhaps?'

Sharpe shrugged. 'She's in Seringapatam,' he said lamely. 'And we're not engaged.'

'But you have an understanding,' Torrance said, 'with this ravishing creature in Seringapatam. Is she black, Sharpe? A black *bibbi*? I'm sure Clare wouldn't mind, would you? A white man in India needs a *bibbi* or two as well as a wife. Don't you agree, Brick?' He turned to the woman, who ignored him. 'The late Mister Wall died of the fever,' Torrance said to Sharpe, 'and in the Christian kindness of my heart I continue to employ his widow. Does that not speak well of my character?'

'If you say so, sir,' Sharpe said.

'I see my attempt to play Cupid is not meeting with success,' Torrance said. 'So, Sharpe, to business. Tomorrow morning I suggest you go to Deogaum, wherever the hell that is.'

'With the bullocks, sir?'

Torrance raised his eyebrows in exasperation. 'You are an officer, Sharpe, not a bullock driver. You don't prod rumps, you leave that to the natives. Go early. Ride there at dawn, and your first duty will be to find me quarters.'

'I don't have a horse,' Sharpe said.

'You don't have a horse? Don't have a horse? Good God alive, man, what bloody use are you? You'll just have to bloody well walk then. I shall find you in Deogaum tomorrow afternoon and God help you if you haven't found me decent quarters. A front room, Sharpe, where Dilip can conduct business. A large room for me, and a hole for Brick. I would also like to have a walled garden with adequate shade trees and a small pool.'

'Where is Deogaum?' Sharpe asked.

'Northwards, sahib,' Dilip answered. 'Close to the hills.'

'Beneath Gawilghur?' Sharpe guessed.

'Yes, sahib.'

Sharpe looked back to Torrance. 'Can I ask a favour of you, sir?'

Torrance sighed. 'If you insist.'

'At Gawilghur, sir, I'd like permission to join the assault party.'

Torrance stared at Sharpe for a long time. 'You want what?' he finally asked.

'I want to be with the attack, sir. There's a fellow inside, see, who killed a friend of mine. I want to see him dead.'

Torrance blinked at Sharpe. 'Don't tell me you're enthusiastic! Good God!' A sudden look of terror came to the Captain's face. 'You're not a Methodist, are you?'

'No, sir.'

Torrance pointed the hookah's mouthpiece towards a corner of the room. 'There is a linen press, Sharpe, d'you see it? Inside it are my clothes. Amidst my clothes you will find a pistol. Take the pistol, remove yourself from my presence, apply the muzzle to your head and pull the trigger. It is a much quicker and less painful way of dying.'

'But you won't mind if I join the attack?'

'Mind? You're not, surely, labouring under the misapprehension that I care about your existence? You think I might mourn you, even after such a short acquaintance? My dear Sharpe, I fear I shall not miss you at all. I doubt I'll even remember your name once you're dead. Of course you can join the assaulting party. Do what you like! Now I suggest you get some sleep. Not here, though, I like my privacy.

Find a tree, perhaps, and slumber beneath its sheltering branches. Good night to you, Sharpe.'

'Good night, sir.'

'And don't let any moths in!'

Sharpe negotiated the muslin and slipped out of the door. Torrance listened to the footsteps go away, then sighed. 'A tedious man, Dilip.'

'Yes, sahib.'

'I wonder why he was made an officer?' Torrance frowned as he sucked on his hookah, then shook his head. 'Poor Naig! Sacrificed to a mere ensign's ambition. How did that wretched Sharpe even know to look in Naig's tent? Did he talk to you?'

'Yes, sahib,' Dilip admitted.

Torrance stared at him. 'Did you let him look at the ledgers?'

'He insisted, sahib.'

'You're a bloody fool, Dilip! A bloody, bloody fool. I should thrash you if I wasn't so tired. Maybe tomorrow.'

'No, sahib, please.'

'Oh, just bugger away off, Dilip,' Torrance snarled. 'And you can go too, Brick.'

The girl fled to the kitchen door. Dilip collected his ink bottle and sand-sprinkler. 'Shall I take the chitties now, sahib, for the morning?'

'Go!' Torrance roared. 'You bore me! Go!' Dilip fled to the front room, and Torrance lay back in the hammock. He was indeed bored. He had nothing to do and nowhere to go. Most nights he would go to Naig's tents and there drink, gamble and whore, but he could hardly visit the green pavilion this night, not after stringing Naig up by the neck. Damn it, he thought. He glanced at the table where a book, a gift from his father, lay unopened. The first volume of *Some Reflections on Paul's Epistle to the Ephesians* by the Reverend Courtney Mallison, and it would be a frigid day in the devil's house before Torrance read that turgid tome. The Reverend Mallison had been Torrance's childhood tutor, and a vicious beast he had been. A whipper, that was Mallison. Loved to whip his pupils. Torrance stared at the ceiling. Money. It was all down to money. Everything in the damned world was down to money. Make money, he thought, and he could go home and make Courtney Mallison's life a misery. Have the bastard on his knees. And Mallison's daughter. Have that prim bitch on her back.

There was a knock on the door. 'I said I didn't want to be disturbed!'

Torrance shouted, but despite his protest the door opened and the muslin billowed inward, letting in a flutter of moths. 'For Christ's sake,' Torrance cursed, then fell abruptly silent.

He fell silent, for the first man through the door was a *jetti*, his bare torso gleaming with oil, and behind him came the tall man with a limp, the same man who had pleaded for Naig's life. His name was Jama, and he was Naig's brother, and his presence made Torrance acutely aware of his nudity. He swung off the hammock and reached for his dressing gown, but Jama twitched the silk garment off the chair back. 'Captain Torrance,' he said with a bow.

'Who let you in?' Torrance demanded.

'I expected to see you in our small establishment tonight, Captain,' Jama said. Where his brother had been plump, noisy and a braggart, Jama was lean, silent and watchful.

Torrance shrugged. 'Maybe tomorrow night?'

'You will be welcome, Captain, as always.' Jama took a small sheaf of papers from his pocket and fanned his face with them. 'Ten thousand welcomes, Captain.'

Ten thousand rupees. That was the value of the papers in Jama's hand, all of them notes signed by Torrance. He had signed far more, but the others he had paid off with supplies filched from the convoys. Jama was here to remind Torrance that his greatest debts remained unpaid. 'About today . . .' Torrance said awkwardly.

'Ah, yes!' Jama said, as though he had momentarily forgotten the reason for his visit. 'About today, Captain. Do tell me about today.' The *jetti* said nothing, just leaned against the wall with folded arms, his oiled muscles shining in the candlelight and his dark eyes fixed immovably on Torrance.

'I've already told you. It wasn't of my doing,' Torrance said with as much dignity as a naked man could muster.

'You were the one who demanded my brother's death,' Jama said.

'What choice did I have? Once the supplies were found?'

'But perhaps you arranged for them to be found?'

'No!' Torrance protested. 'Why the hell would I do that?'

Jama was silent a moment, then indicated the huge man at his side. 'His name is Prithviraj. I once saw him castrate a man with his bare hands.' Jama mimed a pulling action, smiling. 'You'd be astonished at how far a little skin can stretch before it breaks.'

'For God's sake!' Torrance had gone pale. 'It was not my doing!'

'Then whose doing was it?'

'His name is Sharpe. Ensign Sharpe.'

Jama walked to Torrance's table where he turned the pages of *Some Reflections on Paul's Epistle to the Ephesians*. 'This Sharpe,' he asked, 'he was not obeying your orders?'

'Of course not!'

Jama shrugged. 'My brother was careless,' he admitted, 'over confident. He believed that with your friendship he could survive any enquiry.'

'We were doing business,' Torrance said. 'It was not friendship. And I told your brother he should have hidden the supplies.'

'Yes,' Jama said, 'he should. And so I told him also. But even so, Captain, I come from a proud family. You expect me to watch my brother killed and do nothing about it?' He fanned out the notes of Torrance's debts. 'I shall return these to you, Captain, when you deliver Ensign Sharpe to me. Alive! I want Prithviraj to take my revenge. You understand?'

Torrance understood well enough. 'Sharpe's a British officer,' he said. 'If he's murdered there'll be an enquiry. A real enquiry. Heads will be broken.'

'That is your problem, Captain Torrance,' Jama said. 'How you explain his disappearance is your affair. As are your debts.' He smiled and pushed the notes back into the pouch at his belt. 'Give me Sharpe, Captain Torrance, or I shall send Prithviraj to visit you in the night. In the meantime, you will please continue to patronize our establishment.'

'Bastard,' Torrance said, but Jama and his huge companion had already gone. Torrance picked up *Some Reflections on Paul's Epistle to the Ephesians* and slammed the heavy book down on a moth. 'Bastard,' he said again. But on the other hand it was Sharpe who would suffer, not him, so it did not really matter. And what was Sharpe anyway? Nothing but an upstart from the ranks, so who would care if he died? Torrance killed another moth, then opened the kitchen door. 'Come here, Brick.'

'No, sir, please?'

'Shut up. And come here. You can kill these damn moths while I get drunk.'

Filthy drunk, he reckoned, for he had been scared today. He knew he had very nearly got caught when Sharpe had stripped the tent away from the purloined supplies, but by killing Naig quickly Torrance had protected himself, and now the price of his continued survival was Sharpe's death. Arrange that, he thought, and all his troubles would be past. He forced Brick to drink some arrack, knowing how she hated it. Then he drank some himself. Damn Sharpe to hell, he thought, damn the interfering bastard to hell, which was where Sharpe was going anyway so Torrance drank to that happy prospect. Farewell, Mister Sharpe.

CHAPTER 4

Sharpe was not sure how far away Deogaum was, but guessed it was close to twenty miles and that was at least a seven-hour journey on foot, and so it was long before dawn when he stirred Ahmed from his sleep beside the smouldering remains of a bullock-dung fire, then set off under the stars. He tried to teach Ahmed some English. 'Stars,' Sharpe said, pointing.

'Stars,' Ahmed repeated dutifully.

'Moon,' Sharpe said.

'Moon,' Ahmed echoed.

'Sky.'

'Moon?' Ahmed asked, curious that Sharpe was still pointing to the sky.

'Sky, you bugger.'

'Skyoobugger?'

'Never mind,' Sharpe said. He was hungry, and he had forgotten to ask Captain Torrance where he was supposed to draw rations, but their northward route took them through the village of Argaum where the fighting battalions of the army were bivouacked. Unburied bodies still littered the battlefield, and scavenging wild dogs growled from the dark stench as Sharpe and Ahmed walked past. A picquet challenged them at the village, and Sharpe asked the man where he would find the cavalry lines. He could not imagine taking Ahmed to the 74th's mess for breakfast, but Sergeant Eli Lockhart might be more welcoming.

The reveille had sounded by the time Sharpe came to the gully where the horses were picketed and the troopers' campfires were being restored to life. Lockhart scowled at the unexpected visitor through the smoky dawn gloom, then grinned when he recognized Sharpe.

99

'Must be some fighting to do, lads,' he announced, 'the bleeding infantry's here. Good morning, sir. Need our help again?'

'I need some breakfast,' Sharpe admitted.

'Tea, that'll start you off. Smithers! Pork chops! Davies! Some of that bread you're hiding from me. Look lively now!' Lockhart turned back to Sharpe. 'Don't ask me where the chops come from, sir. I might have to lie.' He spat in a tin mug, scoured its interior with the end of his blanket, then filled it with tea. 'There you are, sir. Does your boy want some? Here you are, lad.' Lockhart, a mug of tea in his own hand, then insisted on taking Sharpe to the picketed horses. 'See, sir?' He lifted a horse's leg to show off the new horseshoe. 'My guvnor's beholden to you. I might introduce you after breakfast.'

Sharpe assumed that Lockhart was talking of his troop commander, but once the pork chops and bread had been eaten, the Sergeant led Sharpe across to the lines of the native cavalry, and then to the tent of the 7th Native Cavalry's commanding officer who, it seemed, was in charge of all the army's cavalry. 'He's called Huddlestone,' Lockhart said, 'and he's a decent fellow. He'll probably offer us another breakfast.'

Colonel Huddlestone did indeed insist that both Lockhart and Sharpe join him for a breakfast of rice and eggs. Sharpe was beginning to see that Lockhart was a useful man, someone who was trusted by his officers and liked by his troopers, for Huddlestone greeted the Sergeant warmly and immediately plunged into a conversation about some local horses that had been purchased for remounts and which Huddlestone reckoned would never stand the strain of battle, though Lockhart seemed to feel that a few of them would be adequate. 'So you're the fellow who smoked out Naig?' Huddlestone said to Sharpe after a while.

'Didn't take much doing, sir.'

'No one else did it, man! Don't shy away from credit. I'm damned grateful to you.'

'Couldn't have done it without Sergeant Lockhart, sir.'

'Damned army would come to a stop without Eli, ain't that so?' the Colonel said, and Lockhart, his mouth full of egg, just grinned. Huddlestone turned back to Sharpe. 'So they gave you to Torrance?'

'Yes, sir.'

'He's a lazy bugger,' Huddlestone said vengefully. Sharpe, astonished at the open criticism, said nothing. 'He's one of my own officers,' Huddlestone went on, 'and I confess I wasn't sorry when he asked to be given duty with the bullock train.'

'He asked, sir?' Sharpe found it curious that a man would prefer to be with the baggage when he could be in a fighting unit.

'His uncle is grooming him for a career in the Company,' Huddlestone said. 'An uncle in Leadenhall Street. Know what Leadenhall Street is, Sharpe?'

'Company offices, sir?'

'The very same. The uncle pays him an allowance, and he wants Torrance to get some experience in dealing with *bhinjarries*. Got it all planned out! A few years in the Company's army, another few trading in spices, then home to inherit his uncle's estate and his seat in the Court of Directors. One day we'll all be tugging our forelocks to the lazy bugger. Still, if he wants to run the baggage train it's no skin off our bums, Sharpe. No one likes the job, so Torrance is welcome to it, but my guess is that you'll be doing most of his work.' The Colonel frowned. 'He arrived in India with three English servants! Can you believe it? It ain't as if servants are hard to find here, but Torrance wanted the cachet of white scullions. Two of 'em died of the fever, then Torrance had the nerve to say that one of them hadn't earned the cost of the voyage out and so he's forcing the widow to stay on and pay the debt!' Huddlestone shook his head, then gestured for his servant to pour more tea. 'So what brings you here, Ensign?'

'On my way to Deogaum, sir.'

'He really came to beg his breakfast, Colonel,' Lockhart put in.

'And I've no doubt the Sergeant fed you before you came to steal my victuals?' Huddlestone asked, then grinned. 'You're in luck, Ensign. We're moving up to Deogaum today. You can ride with us.'

Sharpe blushed. 'I've no horse, sir.'

'Eli?' Huddlestone looked at Lockhart.

'I've got a horse he can ride, sir.'

'Good.' Huddlestone blew on his tea. 'Welcome to the cavalry, Sharpe.'

Lockhart found two horses, one for Sharpe and the other for Ahmed. Sharpe, ever uncomfortable on horseback, struggled into the saddle under the cavalry's sardonic gaze, while Ahmed jumped up and kicked back his heels, revelling in being back on a horse.

They went gently northwards, taking care not to tire the horses. Sharpe, as he rode, found himself thinking about Clare Wall, and that made him feel guilty about Simone Joubert, the young French widow who waited for him in Seringapatam. He had sent her there with a southbound convoy and a letter for his friend Major Stokes, and doubtless Simone was waiting for Sharpe to return when the campaign against the Mahrattas was over, but now he needed to warn her that he was being posted back to England. Would she come with him? Did he want her to come? He was not sure about either question, though he felt obscurely responsible for Simone. He could give her a choice, of course, but whenever Simone was faced by a choice she tended to look limp and wait for someone else to make the decision. He had to warn her, though. Would she even want to go to England? But what else could she do? She had no relatives in India, and the nearest French settlements were miles away.

His thoughts were interrupted at mid-morning when Eli Lockhart spurred alongside his horse. 'See it?'

'See what?'

'Up there!' Lockhart pointed ahead and Sharpe, peering through the dust haze thrown up by the leading squadrons, saw a range of high hills. The lower slopes were green with trees, but above the timber line there was nothing but brown and grey cliffs that stretched from horizon to horizon. And at the very top of the topmost bluff he could just see a streak of dark wall broken by a gate-tower. 'Gawilghur!' Lockhart said.

'How the hell do we attack up there?' Sharpe asked.

The Sergeant laughed. 'We don't! It's a job for the infantry. Reckon you're better off attached to that fellow Torrance.'

Sharpe shook his head. 'I have to get in there, Eli.'

'Why?'

Sharpe gazed at the distant wall. 'There's a fellow called Dodd in there, and the bastard killed a friend of mine.'

Lockhart thought for a second. 'Seven hundred guineas Dodd?'

'That's the fellow,' Sharpe said. 'But I'm not after the reward. I just want to see the bugger dead.'

'Me too,' Lockhart said grimly.

'You?'

'Assaye,' Lockhart said brusquely.

'What happened?'

'We charged his troops. They were knocking seven kinds of hell out of the 74th and we caught the buggers in line. Knocked 'em hard back, but we must have had a dozen troopers unhorsed. We didn't stop, though, we just kept after their cavalry and it wasn't till the battle was over that we found our lads. They'd had their throats cut. All of them.'

'That sounds like Dodd,' Sharpe said. The renegade Englishman liked to spread terror. Make a man afraid, Dodd had once told Sharpe, and he won't fight you so hard.

'So maybe I'll go into Gawilghur with you,' Lockhart said.

'Cavalry?' Sharpe asked. 'They won't let cavalry into a real fight.'

Lockhart grinned. 'I couldn't let an ensign go into a fight without help. Poor little bugger might get hurt.'

Sharpe laughed. The cavalry had swerved off the road to pass a long column of marching infantry who had set off before dawn on their march to Deogaum. The leading regiment was Sharpe's own, the 74th, and Sharpe moved even farther away from the road so that he would not have to acknowledge the men who had wanted to be rid of him, but Ensign Venables spotted him, leaped the roadside ditch, and ran to his side. 'Going up in the world, Richard?' Venables asked.

'Borrowed glory,' Sharpe said. 'The horse belongs to the 19th.'

Venables looked slightly relieved that Sharpe had not suddenly been able to afford a horse. 'Are you with the pioneers now?' he asked.

'Nothing so grand,' Sharpe said, reluctant to admit that he had been reduced to being a bullock guard.

Venables did not really care. 'Because that's what we're doing,' he explained, 'escorting the pioneers. It seems they have to make a road.'

'Up there?' Sharpe guessed, nodding towards the fortress that dominated the plain.

'Captain Urquhart says you might be selling your commission,' Venables said.

'Does he?'

'Are you?'

'Are you making an offer?'

'I've got a brother, you see,' Venables explained. 'Three actually. And some sisters. My father might buy.' He took a piece of paper from a pocket and handed it up to Sharpe. 'So if you go home, why not see my pater? That's his address. He reckons one of my brothers should join the army. Ain't any good for anything else, see?'

'I'll think on it,' Sharpe said, taking the paper. The cavalry had stretched ahead and so he clapped his heels back, and the horse jerked forward, throwing Sharpe back in the saddle. For a second he sprawled, almost falling over the beast's rump, then he flailed wildly to catch his balance and just managed to grasp the saddle pommel. He thought he heard laughter as he trotted away from the battalion.

Gawilghur soared above the plain like a threat and Sharpe felt like a poacher with nowhere to hide. From up there, Sharpe reckoned, the approaching British army would look like so many ants in the dust. He wished he had a telescope to stare at the high, distant fortress, but he had been reluctant to spend money. He was not sure why. It was not that he was poor, indeed there were few soldiers richer, yet he feared that the real reason was that he felt fraudulent wearing an officer's sash, and that if he were to buy the usual appurtenances of an officer – a horse and a telescope and an expensive sword – then he would be mocked by those in the army who claimed he should never have been commissioned in the first place. Nor should he, he thought. He had been happier as a sergeant. Much happier. All the same, he wished he had a telescope as he gazed up at the stronghold and saw a great billow of smoke jet from one of the bastions. Seconds later he heard the fading boom of the gun, but he saw no sign of the shot falling. It was as though the cannonball had been swallowed into the warm air.

A mile short of the foothills the road split into three. The sepoy horsemen went westwards, while the 19th Light Dragoons took the right-hand path that angled away from the domineering fortress. The country became more broken as it was cut by small gullies and heaped with low wooded ridges – the first hints of the tumultuous surge of land that ended in the vast cliffs. Trees grew thick in those foothills, and Deogaum was evidently among the low wooded hills. It lay east of Gawilghur, safely out of range of the fortress's guns. A crackle of musketry sounded from a timbered cleft and the 19th Dragoons, riding ahead of Sharpe, spread into a line. Ahmed grinned and made sure his musket was loaded. Sharpe wondered which side the boy was on.

Another spatter of muskets sounded, this time to the west. The Mahrattas must have had men in the foothills. Perhaps they were stripping the villages of the stored grain? The sepoys of the East India Company cavalry had vanished, while the horsemen of the 19th were filing into the wooded cleft. A gun boomed in the fort, and this time Sharpe heard a thump as a cannonball fell to earth like a stone far behind him. A patch of dust drifted from a field where the shot had plummeted, then he and Ahmed followed the dragoons into the gully and the leaves hid them from the invisible watchers high above.

The road twisted left and right, then emerged into a patchwork of small fields and woods. A large village lay beyond the fields – Sharpe guessed it must be Deogaum – then there were shots to his left and he saw a crowd of horsemen burst out of the trees a half-mile away. They were Mahrattas, and at first Sharpe thought they were intent on charging the 19th Light Dragoons, then he realized they were fleeing from the Company cavalry. There were fifty or sixty of the enemy horsemen who, on seeing the blue-and-yellow-coated dragoons, swerved southwards to avoid a fight. The dragoons were turning, drawing sabres and spurring into pursuit. A trumpet sounded and the small fields were suddenly a whirl of horses, dust and gleaming weapons.

Sharpe reined in among a patch of trees, not wanting to be at the centre of a Mahratta cavalry charge. The enemy horse pounded past in a blur of hooves, shining helmets and lance points. The Company cavalry was still a quarter-mile behind when Ahmed suddenly kicked back his heels and shot out of the hiding place to follow the Mahratta cavalry.

Sharpe swore. The little bastard was running back to join the Mahrattas. Not that Sharpe could blame him, but he still felt disappointed. He knew he had no chance of catching Ahmed who had unslung his musket and now rode up behind the rearmost enemy horseman. That man looked round, saw Ahmed was not in British uniform, and so ignored him. Ahmed galloped alongside, then swung his musket by its barrel so that the heavy stock cracked into the Mahratta's forehead.

The man went off the back of his horse as though jerked by a rope. His horse ran on, stirrups flapping. Ahmed reined in, turned and jumped down beside his victim. Sharpe saw the flash of a knife. The sepoy cavalry was closer now, and they might think Ahmed was the enemy, so Sharpe shouted at the boy to come back. Ahmed scrambled back into his saddle and kicked his horse to the trees where Sharpe waited. He had plundered a sabre, a pistol and a leather bag, and had a grin as wide as his face. The bag held two stale loaves of flat bread, some glass beads and a small book in a strange script. Ahmed gave one loaf to Sharpe, threw away the book, draped the cheap beads about his neck and hung the sabre at his waist, then watched as the dragoons cut into the rearward ranks of the fugitives. There was the blacksmith's sound of steel on steel, two horses stumbled in flurries of dust, a man staggered bleeding into a ditch, pistols banged, a lance shivered point downwards in the dry turf, and then the enemy horse was gone and the British and sepoy cavalry reined in.

'Why can't you be a proper servant?' Sharpe asked Ahmed. 'Clean my boots, wash my clothes, make my supper, eh?'

Ahmed, who did not understand a word, just grinned.

'Instead I get some murderous urchin. So come on, you bugger.' Sharpe kicked his horse towards the village. He passed a half-empty tank where some clothes lay to dry on bushes, then he was in the dusty main street which appeared to be deserted, though he was aware of faces watching nervously from dark windows and curtain-hung doorways. Dogs growled from the shade and two chickens scratched in the dust. The only person in sight was a naked holy man who sat cross-legged under a tree, with his long hair cascading to the ground about him. He ignored Sharpe, and Sharpe ignored him. 'We have to find a house,' Sharpe told the uncomprehending Ahmed. 'House, see? House.'

The village headman, the *naique*, ventured into the street. At least Sharpe assumed he was the *naique*, just as the *naique* assumed that the mounted soldier was the leader of the newly arrived cavalrymen. He clasped his hands before his face and bowed to Sharpe, then clicked his fingers to summon a servant carrying a small brass tray on which stood a little cup of arrack. The fierce liquor made Sharpe's head feel suddenly light. The *naique* was talking ten to the dozen, but Sharpe quietened him with a wave. 'No good talking to me,' he said, 'I'm nobody. Talk to him.' He pointed to Colonel Huddlestone who was leading his Indian cavalrymen into the village. The troopers dismounted as Huddlestone talked to the headman. There was a squawk as the two chickens were snatched up. Huddlestone turned at the sound, but his men all looked innocent.

High above Sharpe a gun banged in the fortress. The shot seared out to fall somewhere in the plain where the British infantry marched.

The dragoons came into the village, some with bloodied sabres, and Sharpe surrendered the two horses to Lockhart. Then he searched the street to find a house for Torrance. He saw nothing which had a walled garden, but he did find a small mud-walled home that had a courtyard and he dropped his pack in the main room as a sign of ownership. There was a woman with two small children who shrank away from him. 'It's all right,' Sharpe said, 'you get paid. No one will hurt you.' The woman wailed and crouched as though expecting to be hit. 'Bloody hell,' Sharpe said, 'does no one in this bleeding country speak English?'

He had nothing to do now until Torrance arrived. He could have hunted through the village to discover paper, a pen and ink so he could write to Simone and tell her about going to England, but he decided that chore could wait. He stripped off his belt, sabre and jacket, found a rope bed, and lay down.

Far overhead the fortress guns fired. It sounded like distant thunder. Sharpe slept.

Sergeant Obadiah Hakeswill tugged off his boots, releasing a stench into the room that caused Captain Torrance to close his eyes. 'Good God,' Torrance said weakly. The Captain felt ill enough already. He had drunk the best part of a bottle of arrack, had woken in the night with gripes in the belly, and then slept unevenly until dawn when someone had scratched at his door and Torrance had shouted at the pest to go away, after which he had at last fallen into a deeper sleep. Now he had been woken by Hakeswill who, oblivious of the stench, began to unwrap the cloths that bound his feet. It smelt, Torrance thought, like rotted cheese that had been stored in a corpse's belly. He shifted his chair slightly towards the window and pulled his dressing gown tighter about his chest. 'I'm truly sorry about Naig,' Torrance said. Hakeswill had listened in disbelief to the tale of Naig's death and seemed genuinely saddened by it, just as he had been shocked by the news that Sharpe was now Torrance's assistant.

'The bleeding Scotch didn't want him, sir, did they?' Hakeswill said. 'Never thought the Scotch had much sense, but they had wits enough to get rid of Sharpie.' Hakeswill had uncovered his right foot and Torrance, barely able to endure the stink, suspected there was black fungus growing between the Sergeant's toes. 'Now you've got him, sir,' Hakeswill went on, 'and I pities you, I does. Decent officer like you, sir? Last thing you deserved. Bleeding Sharpie! He ain't got no right to be an officer, sir, not Sharpie. He ain't a gentleman like your good self, sir. He's just a common toad, like the rest of us.'

'So why was he commissioned?' Torrance asked, watching as Hakeswill tugged at the crusted cloth on his left foot.

'On account of saving the General's life, sir. Leastwise, that's what is said.' Hakeswill paused as a spasm made his face twitch. 'Saved Sir Arthur's life at Assaye. Not that I believe it, sir, but Sir Arthur does, and the result of that, sir, is that Sir Arthur thinks bloody Sharpie is a blue-eyed boy. Sharpie farts and Sir Arthur thinks the wind's turned southerly.'

'Does he now?' Torrance asked. That was worth knowing.

'Four years ago, sir,' Hakeswill said, 'I had Sharpie flogged. Would have been a dead 'un too, he would, like he deserved, only Sir Arthur stopped the flogging after two hundred lashes. Stopped it!' The injustice of the act still galled the Sergeant. 'Now he's a bleedin' officer. I tells you, sir, the army ain't what it was. Gone to the dogs, it has.' He pulled the cloth from his left foot, then frowned at his toes. 'I washed them in August,' he said in wonderment, 'but it don't look like it, does it?'

'It is now December, Sergeant,' Torrance said reprovingly.

'A good sluice should last six months, sir.'

'Some of us engage in a more regular toilet,' Torrance hinted.

'You would, sir, being a gentleman. Thing is, sir, I wouldn't normally take the toerags off, only there's a blister.' Hakeswill frowned. 'Haven't had a blister in years! Poor Naig. For a blackamoor he wasn't a bad sort of fellow.'

Naig, Torrance believed, had been as evil a creature as any on the surface of the earth, but he smiled piously at Hakeswill's tribute. 'We shall certainly miss him, Sergeant.'

'Pity you had to hang him, sir, but what choice did you have? Between the devil and a deep blue buggeration, that's where you were, sir. But poor Naig.' Hakeswill shook his head in sad remembrance. 'You should have strung up Sharpie, sir, more's the pity you couldn't. Strung him up proper like what he deserves. A murdering bastard, he is, murdering!' And an indignant Hakeswill told Captain Torrance how Sharpe had tried to kill him, first by throwing him among the Tippoo's tigers, then by trapping him in a courtyard with an elephant trained to kill by crushing men with its forefoot. 'Only the tigers weren't hungry, see, on account of being fed? And as for the elephant, sir, I had me knife, didn't I? I jabbed it in the paw, I did.' He mimed the stabbing action. 'Right in its paw, deep in! It didn't like it. I can't die, sir, I can't die.' The Sergeant spoke hoarsely, believing every word. He had been hanged as a child, but he had survived the gallows and now believed he was protected from death by his own guardian angel.

Mad, Torrance thought, bedlam-mad, but he was nevertheless fascinated by Obadiah Hakeswill. To look at, the Sergeant appeared the perfect soldier; it was the twitch that suggested something more interesting lay behind the bland blue eyes. And what lay behind those childish eyes, Torrance had decided, was a breathtaking malevolence, yet one that was accompanied by an equally astonishing confidence. Hakeswill, Torrance had decided, would murder a baby and find justification for the act. 'So you don't like Mister Sharpe?' Torrance asked.

'I hates him, sir, and I don't mind admitting it. I've watched him, I have, slither his way up the ranks like a bleeding eel up a drain.' Hakeswill had taken out a knife, presumably the one which he had stabbed into the elephant's foot, and now cocked his right heel on his left knee and laid the blade against the blister.

Torrance shut his eyes to spare himself the sight of Hakeswill performing surgery. 'The thing is, Sergeant,' he said, 'that Naig's brother would rather like a private word with Mister Sharpe.'

'Does he now?' Hakeswill asked. He stabbed down. 'Look at that, sir. Proper bit of pus. Soon be healed. Ain't had a blister in years! Reckon it must be the new boots.' He spat on the blade and poked the blister again. 'I'll have to soak the boots in vinegar, sir. So Jama wants Sharpe's goolies, does he?'

'Literally, as it happens. Yes.'

'He can join the bleeding queue.'

'No!' Torrance said sternly. 'It is important to me, Sergeant, that Mister Sharpe is delivered to Jama. Alive. And that his disappearance occasions no curiosity.'

'You mean no one must notice?' Hakeswill's face twitched while he thought, then he shrugged. 'Ain't difficult, sir.'

'It isn't?'

'I'll have a word with Jama, sir. Then you can give Sharpie some orders, and I'll be waiting for him. It'll be easy, sir. Glad to do it for you.'

'You are a comfort to me, Sergeant.'

'That's my job, sir,' Hakeswill said, then leered at the kitchen door where Clare Wall had appeared. 'Sunshine of my life,' he said in what he hoped was a winning tone.

'Your tea, sir,' Clare said, offering Torrance a cup.

'A mug for the Sergeant, Brick! Where are your manners?'

'She don't need manners,' Hakeswill said, still leering at the terrified Clare, 'not with what she's got. Put some sugar in it, darling, if the Captain will spare me some.'

'Give him sugar, Brick,' Torrance ordered.

Hakeswill watched Brick go back to the kitchen. 'A proper little woman, that, sir. A flower, that's what she is, a flower!'

'No doubt you would like to pluck her?'

'It's time I was married,' Hakeswill said. 'A man should leave a son, sir, says so in the scriptures.'

'You want to do some begetting, eh?' Torrance said, then frowned as someone knocked on the outer door. 'Come!' he called.

An infantry captain whom neither man recognized put his head round the door. 'Captain Torrance?'

'That's me,' Torrance said grandly.

'Sir Arthur Wellesley's compliments,' the Captain said, his acid tone suggesting that the compliments would be remarkably thin, 'but is there any reason why the supplies have not moved northwards?'

Torrance stared at the man. For a second he was speechless, then he cursed under his breath. 'My compliments to the General,' he said, 'and my assurances that the bullock train will be on its way immediately.' He waited until the Captain had gone, then swore again.

'What happened, sir?' Hakeswill asked.

'The bloody chitties!' Torrance said. 'Still here. Dilip must have come for them this morning, but I told him to bugger off.' He swore again. 'Bloody Wellesley will pull my guts out backwards for this.'

Hakeswill found the chitties on the table and went to the door, leaving small bloody marks on the floor from his opened blister. 'Dilly! Dilly! You black bastard heathen swine! Here, take these. On your way!'

'Damn!' Torrance said, standing and pacing the small room. 'Damn, damn, damn.'

'Nothing to worry about, sir,' Hakeswill said.

'Easy for you to say, Sergeant.'

Hakeswill grinned as his face was distorted by twitches. 'Just blame someone else, sir,' he said, 'as is usually done in the army.'

'Who? Sharpe? You said yourself he's Wellesley's blue-eyed boy. I'm supposed to blame him? Or you, perhaps?'

Hakeswill tried to calm the Captain down by giving him his cup of tea. 'Blame Dilly, sir, on account of him being a heathen bastard as black as my new boots.'

'He'll simply deny everything when questioned!' Torrance protested.

Hakeswill smiled. 'Won't be in a position to deny anything, sir, will he? On account of being . . .' He paused, stuck his tongue out, opened his eyes wide and made a choking noise.

'Good God, Sergeant,' Torrance said, shuddering at the horrid picture suggested by Hakeswill's contorted face. 'Besides, he's a good clerk! It's damned difficult to replace good men.'

'It's easy, sir. Jama will give us a man. Give us a good man.' Hakeswill grinned. 'It'll make things much easier, sir, if we can trust the clerk as well as each other.'

Torrance flinched at the thought of being in league with Obadiah Hakeswill, yet if he was ever to pay off his debts he needed the Sergeant's cooperation. And Hakeswill was marvellously efficient. He could strip the supplies bare and not leave a trace of his handiwork, always making sure someone else took the blame. And doubtless the Sergeant was right. If Jama could provide a clerk, then the clerk could provide a false set of accounts. And if Dilip was blamed for the late arrival of the pioneers' stores, then Torrance would be off that particularly sharp and nasty hook. As ever, it seemed as though Hakeswill could find his way through the thorniest of problems.

'Just leave it to me, sir,' Hakeswill said. 'I'll look after everything, sir, I will.' He bared his teeth at Clare who had brought his mug of tea. 'You're the flower of womanhood,' he told her, then watched appreciatively as she scuttled back to the kitchen. 'Her and me, sir, are meant for each other. Says so in the scriptures.'

'Not till Sharpe's dead,' Torrance said.

'He'll be dead, sir,' Hakeswill promised, and the Sergeant shivered as he anticipated the riches that would follow that death. Not just Clare Wall, but the jewels. The jewels! Hakeswill had divined that it had been Sharpe who had killed the Tippoo Sultan in Seringapatam, and Sharpe who must have stripped the ruler's body of its diamonds and emeralds and sapphires and rubies, and Sharpe, Hakeswill reckoned, was still hiding those stones. From far away, dulled by the heat of the day, came the sound of artillery firing. Gawilghur, Hakeswill thought, where Sharpe should not reach, on account of Sharpe being Hakeswill's business, and no one else's. I will be rich, the Sergeant promised himself, I will be rich.

Colonel William Dodd stood on the southernmost battlements of Gawilghur with his back against the parapet so that he was staring down into a palace courtyard where Beny Singh had erected a striped pavilion. Small silver bells that tinkled prettily in the small breeze were hung from the pavilion's fringed hem, while under the canopy a group of musicians played the strange, long-necked stringed instruments which made a music that, to Dodd's ears, sounded like the slow strangulation of cats. Beny Singh and a dozen pretty creatures in saris were playing some form of Blind Man's Buff, and their laughter rose to the ramparts, making Dodd scowl, though if truth were told he was inordinately jealous of Beny Singh. The man was plump, short and timid, yet he seemed to work some magical spell on the ladies, while Dodd, who was tall, hard and scarred to prove his bravery, had to make do with a whore.

Damn the Killadar. Dodd turned sharply away and stared over the heat-baked plain. Beneath him, and just far enough to the east to be out of range of Gawilghur's largest guns, the edge of the British encampment showed. From this height the rows of dull white tents looked like speckles. To the south, still a long way off, Dodd could see the enemy baggage train trudging towards its new encampment. It was odd, he thought, that they should make the oxen carry their burdens through the hottest part of the day. Usually the baggage marched just after midnight and camped not long after dawn, but today the great herd was stirring the dust into the broiling afternoon air and it looked, Dodd thought, like a migrating tribe. There were thousands of oxen in the army's train, all loaded with round shot, powder, tools, salt beef, arrack, horseshoes, bandages, flints, muskets, spices, rice, and with them came the merchants' beasts and the merchants' families, and the ox herdsmen had their own families and they all needed more beasts to carry their tents, clothes and food. A dozen elephants plodded in the herd's centre, while a score of dromedaries swayed elegantly behind the elephants. Mysore cavalry guarded the great caravan, while beyond the mounted picquets half-naked grass-cutters spread into the fields to collect fodder that they stuffed into nets and loaded onto yet more oxen.

Dodd glanced at the sentries who guarded the southern stretch of Gawilghur's walls and he saw the awe on their faces as they watched the enormous herd approach. The dust from the hooves rose to smear the southern skyline like a vast sea fog. 'They're only oxen!' Dodd growled to the men. 'Only oxen! Oxen don't fire guns. Oxen don't climb walls.' None of them understood him, but they grinned dutifully.

Dodd walked eastwards. After a while the wall ended, giving way to the bare lip of a precipice. There was no need for walls around much of the perimeters of Gawilghur's twin forts, for nature had provided the great cliffs that were higher than any rampart a man could make, but Dodd, as he walked to the bluff's edge, noted places here and there where an agile man could, with the help of a rope, scramble down the rock face. A few men deserted Gawilghur's garrison every day, and Dodd did not doubt that this was how they escaped, but he did not understand why they should want to go. The fort was impregnable! Why would a man not wish to stay with the victors?

He reached a stretch of wall at the fort's southeastern corner and there, high up on a gun platform, he opened his telescope and stared down into the foothills. He searched for a long time, his glass skittering over trees, shrubs and patches of dry grass, but at last he saw a group of men standing beside a narrow path. Some of the men were in red coats and one was in blue.

'What are you watching, Colonel?' Prince Manu Bappoo had seen Dodd on the rampart and had climbed to join him.

'British,' Dodd said, without taking his eye from the telescope. 'They're surveying a route up to the plateau.'

Bappoo shaded his eyes and stared down, but without a telescope he could not see the group of men. 'It will take them months to build a road up to the hills.'

'It'll take them two weeks,' Dodd said flatly. 'Less. You don't know how their engineers work, sahib, but I do. They'll use powder to break through obstacles and a thousand axemen to widen the tracks. They'll start their work tomorrow and in a fortnight they'll be running guns up to the hills.' Dodd collapsed the telescope. 'Let me go down and break the bastards,' he demanded.

'No,' Bappoo said. He had already had this argument with Dodd who wanted to take his Cobras down into the foothills and there harass the road-makers. Dodd did not want a stand-up fight, a battle of musket line against musket line, but instead wanted to raid, ambush and scare the enemy. He wanted to slow the British work, to dishearten the sappers and, by such delaying tactics, force Wellesley to send forage parties far into the countryside where they would be prey to the Mahratta horsemen who still roamed the Deccan Plain.

Bappoo knew Dodd was right, and that the British road could be slowed by a campaign of harassment, but he feared to let the white-coated Cobras leave the fortress. The garrison was already nervous, awed by the victories of Wellesley's small army, and if they saw the Cobras march out of the fort then many would think they were being abandoned and the trickle of deserters would become a flood.

'We have to slow them!' Dodd snarled.

'We shall,' Bappoo said. 'I shall send *silladars*, Colonel, and reward them for every weapon they bring back to the fort. But you will stay here, and help prepare the defences.' He spoke firmly, showing that the subject was beyond discussion, then offered Dodd a gap-toothed smile and gestured towards the palace at the centre of the Inner Fort. 'Come, Colonel, I want to show you something.'

The two men walked through the small houses that surrounded the palace, past an Arab sentry who protected the palace precincts, then through some flowering trees where monkeys crouched. Dodd could hear the tinkle of the bells where Beny Singh was playing with his women, but that sound faded as the path twisted deeper into the trees. The path ended at a rock face that was pierced by an arched wooden door. Dodd looked up while Bappoo unlocked the door and saw that the great rock slab formed the palace foundations and, when Bappoo thrust back the creaking door, he understood that it led into the palace cellars.

A lantern stood on a shelf just inside the door and there was a pause while Bappoo lit its wick. 'Come,' Bappoo said, and led Dodd into the marvellous coolness of the huge low cellar. 'It is rumoured,' Bappoo said, 'that we store the treasures of Berar in here, and in one sense it is true, but they are not the treasures that men usually dream of.' He stopped by a row of barrels and casually knocked off their lids, revealing that the tubs were filled with copper coins. 'No gold or silver,' Bappoo said, 'but money all the same. Money to hire new mercenaries, to buy new weapons and to make a new army.' Bappoo trickled a stream of the newly minted coins through his fingers. 'We have been lax in paying our men,' he confessed. 'My brother, for all his virtues, is not generous with his treasury.'

Dodd grunted. He was not sure what virtues the Rajah of Berar did possess. Certainly not valour, nor generosity, but the Rajah was fortunate in his brother, for Bappoo was loyal and evidently determined to make up for the Rajah's shortcomings.

'Gold and silver,' Dodd said, 'would buy better arms and more men.'

'My brother will not give me gold or silver, only copper. And we must work with what we have, not with what we dream of.' Bappoo put the lids back onto the barrels, then edged between them to where rack after rack of muskets stood. 'These, Colonel,' he said, 'are the weapons for that new army.'

There were thousands of muskets, all brand new, and all equipped with bayonets and cartridge boxes. Some of the guns were locally made copies of French muskets, but several hundred looked to Dodd to be of British make. He lifted one from the racks and saw the Tower mark on its lock. 'How did you get these?' he asked, surprised.

Bappoo shrugged. 'We have agents in the British camp. They arrange it. We meet some of their supply convoys well to the south and pay for their contents. It seems there are traitors in the British army who would rather make money than seek victory.'

'You buy guns with copper?' Dodd asked scathingly. He could not imagine any man selling a Tower musket for a handful of copper.

'No,' Bappoo confessed. 'To buy the weapons and the cartridges we need gold, so I use my own. My brother, I trust, will repay me one day.'

Dodd frowned at the hawk-faced Bappoo. 'You're using your money to keep your brother on the throne?' he asked and, though he waited for an answer, none came. Dodd shook his head, implying that

Bappoo's nobility was beyond understanding, then he cocked and fired the unloaded musket. The spark of the flint flashed a sparkle of red light against the stone ceiling. 'A musket in its rack kills no one,' he said.

'True. But as yet we don't have the men to carry these muskets. But we will, Colonel. Once we have defeated the British the other kingdoms will join us.' That, Dodd reflected, was true enough. Scindia, Dodd's erstwhile employer, was suing for peace, while Holkar, the most formidable of the Mahratta monarchs, was staying aloof from the contest, but if Bappoo did win his victory, those chieftains would be eager to share future spoils. 'And not just the other kingdoms,' Bappoo went on, 'but warriors from all India will come to our banner. I intend to raise a *compoo* armed with the best weapons and trained to the very highest standard. Many, I suspect, will be sepoys from Wellesley's defeated army and they will need a new master when he is dead. I thought perhaps you would lead them?'

Dodd returned the musket to its rack. 'You'll not pay me with copper, Bappoo.'

Bappoo smiled. 'You will pay me with victory, Colonel, and I shall reward you with gold.'

Dodd saw some unfamiliar weapons farther down the rack. He lifted one and saw it was a hunting rifle. The lock was British, but the filigree decoration on the stock and barrel was Indian. 'You're buying rifles?' he asked.

'No better weapon for skirmishing,' Bappoo said.

'Maybe,' Dodd allowed grudgingly. The rifle was accurate, but slow to load.

'A small group of men with rifles,' Bappoo said, 'backed up by muskets, could be formidable.'

'Maybe,' Dodd said again, then, instead of putting the rifle back onto the rack, he slung it on his shoulder. 'I'd like to try it,' he explained. 'You have ammunition?'

Bappoo gestured across the cellar, and Dodd went and scooped up some cartridges. 'If you've got the cash,' he called back, 'why not raise your new army now. Bring it to Gawilghur.'

'There's no time,' Bappoo said, 'and besides, no one will join us now. They think the British are beating us. So if we are to make our new army, Colonel, then we must first win a victory that will ring through India, and that is what we shall do here at Gawilghur.' He spoke very confidently, for Bappoo, like Dodd, believed Gawilghur to be unassailable. He led the Englishman back to the entrance, blew out the lantern and carefully locked the armoury door.

The two men climbed the slope beside the palace, passing a line of servants who carried drinks and sweetmeats to where Beny Singh whiled away the afternoon. As ever, when Dodd thought of the Killadar, he felt a surge of anger. Beny Singh should have been organizing the fortress's defences, but instead he frittered away his days with women and liquor. Bappoo must have divined Dodd's thoughts, for he grimaced. 'My brother likes Beny Singh. They amuse each other.'

'Do they amuse you?' Dodd asked.

Bappoo paused at the northern side of the palace and there he gazed across the ravine to the Outer Fort which was garrisoned by his Lions of Allah. 'I swore an oath to my brother,' he answered, 'and I am a man who keeps my oaths.'

'There must be those,' Dodd said carefully, 'who would rather see you as Rajah?'

'Of course,' Bappoo answered equably, 'but such men are my brother's enemies, and my oath was to defend my brother against all his enemies.' He shrugged. 'We must be content, Colonel, with what fate grants us. It has granted me the task of fighting my brother's wars, and I shall do that to the best of my ability.' He pointed to the deep ravine that lay between the Outer and the Inner Forts. 'And there, Colonel, I shall win a victory that will make my brother the greatest ruler of all India. The British cannot stop us. Even if they make their road, even if they haul their guns up to the hills, even if they make a breach in our walls and even if they capture the Outer Fort, they must still cross that ravine, and they cannot do it. No one can do it.' Bappoo stared at the steep gorge as if he could already see its rocks soaked in enemy blood. 'Who rules that ravine, Colonel, rules India, and when we have our victory then we shall unlock the cellar and raise an army that will drive the redcoats not just from Berar, but from Hyderabad, from Mysore and from Madras. I shall make my brother Emperor of all southern India, and you and I, Colonel, shall be his warlords.' Bappoo turned to gaze into the dust-smeared immensity of the southern sky. 'It will all belong to my brother,' he said softly, 'but it will begin here. At Gawilghur.'

And here, Dodd suddenly thought, it would end for Bappoo. No man who was willing to endure a feeble wretch like Beny Singh, or protect a cowardly libertine like the Rajah, deserved to be a warlord of all India. No, Dodd thought, he would win his own victory here, and then he would strike against Bappoo and against Beny Singh, and he would raise his own army and use it to strike terror into the rich southern kingdoms. Other Europeans had done it. Benoît de Boigne had made himself richer than the kings of all Christendom, while George Thomas, an illiterate Irish sailor, had risen to rule a princedom for his widowed mistress. Dodd saw himself as a new Prester John. He would make a kingdom from the rotting scraps of India, and he would rule from a new palace in Gawilghur that would be like no other in the world. He would have roofs of gold, walls of white marble and garden paths made from pearls, and men from all India would come to pay him homage. He would be Lord of Gawilghur, Dodd thought, and smiled. Not bad for a miller's son from Suffolk, but Gawilghur was a place to stir dreams for it lifted men's thoughts into the heavens, and Dodd knew that India, above all the lands on God's earth, was a place where dreams could come true. Here a man was either made rich beyond all desire, or else became nothing.

And Dodd would not be nothing. He would be Lord of Gawilghur and the terror of India.

Once the redcoats were defeated.

'Is this the best you could manage, Sharpe?' Torrance enquired, looking about the main room of the commandeered house.

'No, sir,' Sharpe said. 'There was a lovely house just up the road. Big shady courtyard, couple of pools, a fountain and a gaggle of dancing girls, but I thought you might prefer the view from these windows.'

'Sarcasm ill becomes an ensign,' Torrance said, dropping his saddle-bags on the earthen floor. 'Indeed, very little becomes ensigns, Sharpe, except a humble devotion to serving their betters. I suppose the house will have to suffice. Who is that?' He shuddered as he stared at the woman whose house he was occupying.

'She lives here, sir.'

'Not now, she doesn't. Get rid of the black bitch, and her foul children. Brick!'

Clare Wall came in from the sunlight, carrying a sack. 'Sir?'

'I'm hungry, Brick. Find the kitchen. We made a late start, Sharpe,' Torrance explained, 'and missed dinner.'

'I imagine that's why the General wants to see you, sir,' Sharpe said. 'Not because you missed dinner, but because the supplies weren't here on time.'

Torrance stared at Sharpe in horror. 'Wellesley wants to see me?'

'Six o'clock, sir, at his tent.'

'Oh, Christ!' Torrance threw his cocked hat across the room. 'Just because the supplies were a little late?'

'Twelve hours late, sir.'

Torrance glared at Sharpe, then fished a watch from his fob. 'It's half past five already! God help us! Can't you brush that coat, Sharpe?'

'He don't want to see me, sir. Just you.'

'Well, he's bloody well going to see both of us. Clean uniform, Sharpe, hair brushed, paws washed, face scrubbed, Sunday best.' Torrance frowned suddenly. 'Why didn't you tell me you saved Wellesley's life?'

'Is that what I did, sir?'

'I mean, good God, man, he must be grateful to you?' Torrance asked. Sharpe just shrugged. 'You saved his life,' Torrance insisted, 'and that means he's in your debt, and you must use the advantage. Tell him we don't have enough men to run the supply train properly. Put in a good word for me, Sharpe, and I'll repay the favour. Brick! Forget the food! I need a clean stock, boots polished, hat brushed. And give my dress coat a pressing!'

Sergeant Hakeswill edged through the door. 'Your 'ammock, sir,' he said to Torrance, then saw Sharpe and a slow grin spread across his face. 'Look who it isn't. Sharpie!'

Torrance wheeled on the Sergeant. 'Mister Sharpe is an officer, Hakeswill! In this unit we do observe the proprieties!'

'Quite forgot myself, sir,' Hakeswill said, his face twitching, 'on account of being reunited with an old comrade. Mister Sharpe, ever so pleased to see you, sir.'

'Lying bastard,' Sharpe said.

'Ain't officers supposed to observe the properties, sir?' Hakeswill demanded of Torrance, but the Captain had gone in search of his native servant who had charge of the luggage. Hakeswill looked back to Sharpe. 'Fated to be with you, Sharpie.'

'You stay out of my light, Obadiah,' Sharpe said, 'or I'll slit your throat.'

'I can't be killed, Sharpie, can't be killed!' Hakeswill's face wrenched itself in a series of twitches. 'It says so in the scriptures.' He looked Sharpe up and down, then shook his head ruefully. 'I've seen better things dangling off the tails of sheep, I have. You ain't an officer, Sharpie, you're a bleeding disgrace.'

Torrance backed into the house, shouting at his servant to drape the windows with muslin, then turned and hurried to the kitchen to harry Clare. He tripped over Sharpe's pack and swore. 'Whose is this?'

'Mine,' Sharpe said.

'You're not thinking of billeting yourself here, are you, Sharpe?'

'Good as anywhere, sir.'

'I like my privacy, Sharpe. Find somewhere else.' Torrance suddenly remembered he was speaking to a man who might have influence with Wellesley. 'If you'd be so kind, Sharpe. I just can't abide being crowded. An affliction, I know, but there it is. I need solitude, it's my nature. Brick! Did I tell you to brush my hat? And the plume needs a combing.'

Sharpe picked up his pack and walked out to the small garden where Ahmed was sharpening his new *tulwar*. Clare Wall followed him into the sunlight, muttered something under her breath, then sat and started to polish one of Torrance's boots. 'Why the hell do you stay with him?' Sharpe asked.

She paused to look at Sharpe. She had oddly hooded eyes that gave her face an air of delicate mystery. 'What choice do I have?' she asked, resuming her polishing.

Sharpe sat beside her, picked up the other boot and rubbed it with blackball. 'So what's he going to do if you bugger off?'

She shrugged. 'I owe him money.'

'Like hell. How can you owe him money?'

'He brought my husband and me here,' she said, 'paid our passage from England. We agreed to stay three years. Then Charlie died.' She paused again, her eyes suddenly gleaming, then sniffed and began to polish the boot obsessively.

Sharpe looked at her. She had dark eyes, curling black hair and a long upper lip. If she was not so tired and miserable, he thought, she would be a very pretty woman. 'How old are you, love?'

She gave him a sceptical glance. 'Who's your woman in Seringa-patam, then?'

'She's a Frenchie,' Sharpe said. 'A widow, like you.'

'Officer's widow?' Clare asked. Sharpe nodded. 'And you're to marry her?' Clare asked.

'Nothing like that,' Sharpe said.

'Like what, then?' she asked.

'I don't know, really.' Sharpe said. He spat on the boot's flank and rubbed the spittle into the bootblack.

'But you like her?' Clare asked, picking the dirt from the boot's spur. She seemed embarrassed to have posed the question, for she hurried on. 'I'm nineteen,' she said, 'but nearly twenty.'

'Then you're old enough to see a lawyer,' Sharpe said. 'You ain't indentured to the Captain. You have to sign papers, don't you? Or make your mark on a paper. That's how it was done in the foundling home where they dumped me. Wanted to make me into a chimney sweep, they did! Bloody hell! But if you didn't sign indenture papers, you should talk to a lawyer.'

Clare paused, staring at a sad tree in the courtyard's centre that was dying from the drought. 'I wanted to get married a year back,' she said softly, 'and that's what Tom told me. He were called Tom, see? A cavalryman, he was. Only a youngster.'

'What happened?'

'Fever,' she said bleakly. 'But it wouldn't have worked anyway, because Torrance wouldn't ever let me marry.' She began polishing the boot again. 'He said he'd see me dead first.' She shook her head. 'But what's the point in seeing a lawyer? You think a lawyer would talk to me? They like money, lawyers do, and do you know a lawyer in India that ain't in the Company's pocket? Mind you' – she glanced towards the house to make sure she was not being overheard – 'he hasn't got any money either. He gets an allowance from his uncle and his Company pay and he gambles it all away, but he always seems to find more.' She paused. 'And what would I do if I walked away?' She left the question hanging in the warm air, then shook her head. 'I'm miles from bleeding home. I don't know. He was good to me at first. I liked him! I didn't know him then, you see.' She half smiled. 'Funny, isn't it? You think because someone's a gentleman and the son of a clergyman that they have to be kind? But he ain't.' She vigorously brushed the boot's tassel. 'And he's been worse since he met that Hakeswill. I do hate him.' She sighed. 'Just fourteen months to go,' she said wearily, 'and then I'll have paid the debt.'

'Hell, no,' Sharpe said. 'Walk away from the bugger.'

She picked up Torrance's hat and began brushing it. 'I don't have family,' she said, 'so where would I go?'

'You're an orphan?'

She nodded. 'I got work as a house girl in Torrance's uncle's house. That's where I met Charlie. He were a footman. Then Mr Henry, that's his uncle, see, said we should join the Captain's household. Charlie became Captain Torrance's valet. That was a step up. And the money was better, only we weren't paid, not once we were in Madras. He said we had to pay our passage.'

'What the devil are you doing, Sharpe?' Torrance had come into the garden. 'You're not supposed to clean boots! You're an officer!'

Sharpe tossed the boot at Torrance. 'I keep forgetting, sir.'

'If you must clean boots, Sharpe, start with your own. Good God, man! You look like a tinker!'

'The General's seen me looking worse,' Sharpe said. 'Besides, he never did care what men looked like, sir, so long as they do their job properly.'

'I do mine properly!' Torrance bridled at the implication. 'I just need more staff. You tell him that, Sharpe, you tell him! Give me that hat, Brick! We're late!'

In fact Torrance arrived early at the General's tent and had to kick his heels in the evening sunshine. 'What exactly did the General say when he summoned me?' he asked Sharpe.

'He sent an aide, sir. Captain Campbell. Wanted to know where the supplies were.'

'You told him they were coming?'

'Told him the truth, sir.'

'Which was?'

'That I didn't bloody well know where they were.'

'Oh, Christ! Thank you, Sharpe, thank you very much.' Torrance twitched at his sash, making the silk fall more elegantly. 'Do you know what loyalty is?'

Before Sharpe could answer the tent flaps were pushed aside and Captain Campbell ducked out into the sunlight. 'Wasn't expecting you, Sharpe!' he said genially, holding out his hand.

Sharpe shook hands. 'How are you, sir?'

'Busy,' Campbell said. 'You don't have to go in if you don't want.'

'He does,' Torrance said.

Sharpe shrugged. 'Might as well,' he said, then ducked into the tent's yellow light as Campbell pulled back the flap.

The General was in his shirtsleeves, sitting behind a table that was covered with Major Blackiston's sketches of the land bridge to Gawilghur. Blackiston was beside him, travel-stained and tired, while an irascible-looking major of the Royal Engineers stood two paces behind the table. If the General was surprised to see Sharpe he showed no sign of it, but instead looked back to the drawings. 'How wide is the approach?' he asked.

'At its narrowest, sir, about fifty feet.' Blackiston tapped one of the sketches. 'It's wide enough for most of the approach, two or three hundred yards, but just here there's a tank and it squeezes the path cruelly. A ravine to the left, a tank to the right.'

'Fall to your death on one side,' the General said, 'and drown on the other. And doubtless the fifty feet between is covered by their guns?'

'Smothered, sir. Must be twenty heavy cannon looking down the throat of the approach, and God knows how much smaller metal. Plenty.'

Wellesley removed the inkwells that had been serving as weights so that the drawings rolled up with a snap. 'Not much choice, though, is there?' he asked.

'None, sir.'

Wellesley looked up suddenly, his eyes seeming very blue in the tent's half light. 'The supply train is twelve hours late, Captain. Why?' He spoke quietly, but even Sharpe felt a shiver go through him.

Torrance, his cocked hat held beneath his left arm, was sweating. 'I . . . I . . .' he said, too nervous to speak properly, but then he took a deep breath. 'I was ill, sir, and unable to supervise properly, and my clerk failed to issue the chitties. It was a most regrettable occurrence, sir, and I can assure you it will not happen again.'

The General stared at Torrance in silence for a few seconds. 'Colonel Wallace gave you Ensign Sharpe as an assistant? Did Sharpe also fail to obey your orders?'

'I had sent Mister Sharpe ahead, sir,' Torrance said. The sweat was now pouring down his face and dripping from his chin.

'So why did the clerk fail in his duties?'

'Treachery, sir,' Torrance said.

The answer surprised Wellesley, as it was meant to. He tapped his pencil on the table's edge. 'Treachery?' he asked in a low voice.

'It seemed the clerk was in league with a merchant, sir, and had been selling him supplies. And this morning, sir, when he should have been issuing the chitties, he was employed on his own business.'

'And you were too ill to detect his treachery?'

'Yes, sir,' Torrance said almost pleadingly. 'At first, sir, yes, sir.'

Wellesley gazed at Torrance for a few silent seconds, and the Captain had the uncomfortable feeling that the blue eyes saw right into his soul. 'So where is this treacherous clerk now, Captain?' Wellesley asked at last.

'We hanged him, sir,' Torrance said and Sharpe, who had not heard of Dilip's death, stared at him in astonishment.

The General slapped the table, making Torrance jump in alarm. 'You seem very fond of hanging, Captain Torrance?'

'A necessary remedy for theft, sir, as you have made plain.'

'I, sir? I?' The General's voice, when he became angry, did not become louder, but more precise and, therefore, more chilling. 'The general order mandating summary death by hanging for thievery, Captain, applies to men in uniform. King's and Company men only. It does not apply to civilians. Does the dead man have family?'

'No, sir,' Torrance said. He did not really know the answer, but decided it was better to say no than to prevaricate.

'If he does, Captain,' Wellesley said softly, 'and if they complain, then I shall have no choice but to put you on trial, and depend upon it, sir, that trial will be in the civilian courts.'

'I apologize, sir,' Torrance said stiffly, 'for my over-zealousness.'

The General stayed silent for a few seconds. 'Supplies were missing,' he said after a while.

'Yes, sir,' Torrance agreed weakly.

'Yet you never reported the thefts?' Wellesley said.

'I did not believe you wished to be troubled by every mishap, sir,' Torrance said.

'Mishap!' Wellesley snapped. 'Muskets are stolen, and you call that a mishap? Such mishaps, Captain Torrance, lose wars. In future you will inform my staff when such depredations are made.' He stared at

Torrance for a few seconds, then looked at Sharpe. 'Colonel Huddlestone tells me it was you, Sharpe, who discovered the missing supplies?'

'All but the muskets, sir. They're still missing.'

'How did you know where to look?'

'Captain Torrance's clerk told me where to buy supplies, sir.' Sharpe shrugged. 'I guessed they were the missing items, sir.'

Wellesley grunted. Sharpe's answer appeared to confirm Torrance's accusations, and the Captain gave Sharpe a grateful glance. Wellesley saw the glance and rapped the table, demanding Torrance's attention. 'It is a pity, Captain, that we could not have questioned the merchant before you so summarily executed him. May I presume you did interrogate the clerk?'

'My sergeant did, sir, and the wretch confessed to having sold items to Naig.' Torrance blushed as he told the lie, but it was so hot in the tent and he was sweating so heavily that the blush went unnoticed.

'Your sergeant?' Wellesley asked. 'You mean your havildar?'

'Sergeant, sir,' Torrance said. 'I inherited him from Captain Mackay, sir. Sergeant Hakeswill.'

'Hakeswill!' the General said in astonishment. 'What's he still doing here? He should be back with his regiment!'

'He stayed on, sir,' Torrance said, 'with two of his men. His other two died, sir, fever. And he had no alternative orders, sir, and he was too useful to let go, sir.'

'Useful!' Wellesley said. He had been the commanding officer of the 33rd, Hakeswill's regiment, and he knew the Sergeant well. He shook his head. 'If you find him useful, Torrance, then he can stay till Gawilghur's fallen. But then he returns to his regiment. You'll make sure of that, Campbell?'

'Yes, sir,' the aide said. 'But I believe some of the 33rd are on their way here, sir, so the Sergeant can return with them.'

'The 33rd coming here?' Wellesley asked in surprise. 'I ordered no such thing.'

'Just a company, sir,' Campbell explained. 'I believe headquarters detailed them to escort a convoy.'

'Doubtless we can make use of them,' the General said grudgingly. 'Is it awkward for you, Sharpe? Serving with Hakeswill?' Officers who were promoted from the ranks were never expected to serve with their old regiments, and Wellesley was plainly wondering whether Sharpe found his old comrades an embarrassment. 'I daresay you'll get by,' the General said, not waiting for an answer. 'You usually do. Wallace tells me he's recommended you for the Rifles?'

'Yes, sir.'

'That could suit you, Sharpe. Suit you very well. In the meantime, the more you learn about supplies, the better.' The cold eyes looked back to Torrance, though it appeared the General was still talking to Sharpe. 'There is a misapprehension in this army that supplies are of small importance, whereas wars are won by efficient supply, more than they are won by acts of gallantry. Which is why I want no more delays.'

'There will be none, sir,' Torrance said hastily.

'And if there are,' Wellesley said, 'there will be a court martial. You may depend upon that, Captain. Major Elliott?' The General spoke to the engineer who until now had been a spectator of Torrance's discomfiture. 'Tell me what you need to build our road, Major.'

'A hundred bullocks,' Elliott said sourly, 'and none of your spavined beasts, Torrance. I want a hundred prime Mysore oxen to carry timber and road stone. I'll need rice every day for a half-battalion of sepoys and an equivalent number of pioneers.'

'Of course, sir,' Torrance said.

'And I'll take him' – Elliott stabbed a finger at Sharpe – 'because I need someone in charge of the bullocks who knows what he's doing.'

Torrance opened his mouth to protest, then sensibly shut it. Wellesley glanced at Sharpe. 'You'll attach yourself to Major Elliott, Sharpe. Be with him at dawn tomorrow, with the bullocks, and you, Captain Torrance, will ensure the daily supplies go up the road every dawn. And I want no more summary hangings.'

'Of course not, sir.' Torrance, relieved to be let off so lightly, ducked his head in an awkward bow.

'Good day to you both,' the General said sourly, then watched as the two officers left the tent. He rubbed his eyes and stifled a yawn. 'How long to drive the road, Elliott?'

'Two weeks?' the Major suggested.

'You've got one week. One week!' The General forestalled Elliott's protest. 'Good day to you, Elliott.'

The engineer grumbled as he ducked out into the fading light. Wellesley grimaced. 'Is Torrance to be trusted?' he asked.

'Comes from a good family, sir,' Blackiston said.

'So did Nero, as I recall,' Wellesley retorted. 'But at least Torrance has got Sharpe, and even if Sharpe won't make a good officer, he's got the makings of a decent sergeant. He did well to find those supplies.'

'Very well, sir,' Campbell said warmly.

Wellesley leaned back in his chair. A flicker of distaste showed on his face as he recalled the terrible moment when he had been unhorsed at Assaye. He did not remember much of the incident for he had been dazed, but he did recall watching Sharpe kill with a savagery that had astonished him. He disliked being beholden to such a man, but the General knew he would not be alive if Sharpe had not risked his own life. 'I should never have given Sharpe a commission,' he said ruefully. 'A man like that would have been quite content with a fiscal reward. A fungible reward. That's what our men want, Campbell, something that can be turned into rum or arrack.'

'He appears to be a sober man, sir,' Campbell said.

'Probably because he can't afford the drink! Officers' messes are damned expensive places, Campbell, as you well know. I reward Sharpe by plunging him into debt, eh? And God knows if the Rifles are any cheaper. I can't imagine they will be. He needs something fungible, Campbell, something fungible.' Wellesley turned and rummaged in the saddlebags that were piled behind his chair. He brought out the new telescope with the shallow eyepiece that had been a gift from the merchants of Madras. 'Find a goldsmith in the camp followers, Campbell, and see if the fellow can replace that brass plate.'

'With what, sir?'

Nothing too flowery, the General thought, because the glass was only going to be pawned to pay mess bills or buy gin. 'In gratitude, AW,' he said, 'and add the date of Assaye. Then give it to Sharpe with my compliments.'

'It's very generous of you, sir,' Campbell said, taking the glass, 'but perhaps it would be better if you presented it to him?'

'Maybe, maybe. Blackiston! Where do we site guns?' The General unrolled the sketches. 'Candles,' he ordered, for the light was fading fast.

The shadows stretched and joined and turned to night around the British camp. Candles were lit, lanterns hung from ridge-poles and fires fed with bullock dung. The picquets stared at shadows in the darkness, but some, lifting their gaze, saw that high above them the tops of the cliffs were still in daylight and there, like the home of the gods, the walls of a fortress showed deadly black where Gawilghur waited their coming.

CHAPTER 5

The first part of the road was easy enough to build, for the existing track wound up the gentler slopes of the foothills, but even on the first day Major Elliott was filled with gloom. 'Can't do it in a week!' the engineer grumbled. 'Man's mad! Expects miracles. Jacob's ladder, that's what he wants.' He cast a morbid eye over Sharpe's bullocks, all of them prime Mysore beasts with brightly painted horns from which tassels and small bells hung. 'Never did like working with oxen,' Elliott complained. 'Bring any elephants?'

'I can ask for them, sir.'

'Nothing like an elephant. Right, Sharpe, load the beasts with small stones and keep following the track till you catch up with me. Got that?' Elliott hauled himself onto his horse and settled his feet in the stirrups. 'Bloody miracles, that's what he wants,' the Major growled, then spurred onto the track.

'Elliott!' Major Simons, who commanded the half-battalion of sepoys who guarded the pioneers building the road, called in alarm. 'I haven't reconnoitred beyond the small hillock! The one with the two trees.'

'Can't wait for your fellows to wake up, Simons. Got a road to build in a week. Can't be done, of course, but we must look willing. Pinckney! I need a havildar and some stout fellows to carry pegs. Tell 'em to follow me.'

Captain Pinckney, the officer in charge of the East India Company pioneers, spat onto the verge. 'Waste of bloody time.'

'What is?' Sharpe asked.

'Pegging out the route! We follow the footpath, of course. Bloody natives have been scurrying up and down these hills for centuries.' He turned and shouted at a havildar to organize a party to follow Elliott up the hill, then set the rest of his men to loading the oxen's panniers with small stones.

The road made good progress, despite Elliott's misgivings, and three days after they had begun the pioneers cleared a space among the trees to establish a makeshift artillery park where the siege guns could wait while the rest of the road was forged. Sharpe was busy and, because of that, happy. He liked Simons and Pinckney, and even Elliott proved affable. The Major had taken Wellesley's demands that the road be made in a week as a challenge, and he pressed the pioneers hard.

The enemy seemed to be asleep. Elliott would ride far ahead to reconnoitre the route and never once saw a Mahratta. 'Stupid fools,' Elliott said one night beside the fire, 'they could hold us here for months!'

'You still shouldn't ride so far ahead of my picquets,' Simons reproved the Major.

'Stop fussing, man,' Elliott said, and next morning, as usual, he rode out in front to survey the day's work.

Sharpe was again bringing stones up the road that morning. He was walking at the head of his ox train on the wooded stretch above the newly made artillery park. The day's heat was growing and there was little wind in the thick woods of teak and cork trees that covered the low hills. Groups of pioneers felled trees where they might obstruct a gun carriage's progress, and here and there Sharpe saw a white-washed peg showing where Elliott had marked the track. Shots sounded ahead, but Sharpe took no notice. The upland valleys had become a favourite hunting ground for the *shikarees* who used nets, snares and ancient matchlocks to kill hares, wild pigs, deer, quail and partridge that they sold to the officers, and Sharpe assumed a party of the hunters was close to the track, but after a few seconds the firing intensified. The musketry was muffled by the thick leaves, but for a moment the sound was constant, almost at battle pitch, before, as suddenly as it had erupted, it stopped.

His bullock drivers had halted, made nervous by the firing. 'Come on!' Sharpe encouraged them. None of them spoke English, and Sharpe had no idea which language they did speak, but they were good-natured men, eager to please, and they prodded their heavily laden bullocks onwards. Ahmed had unslung his musket and was peering ahead. He suddenly raised the gun to his shoulder, and Sharpe pushed it down before the boy could pull the trigger. 'They're ours,' he told the lad. 'Sepoys.'

A dozen sepoys hurried back through the trees. Major Simons was with them and, as they came closer, Sharpe saw the men were carrying a makeshift stretcher made from tree branches and jackets. 'It's Elliott.' Simons paused by Sharpe as his men hurried ahead. 'Bloody fool got a chest wound. He won't live. Stupid man was too far forward. I told him not to get ahead of the picquets.' Simons took a ragged red handkerchief from his sleeve and wiped the sweat from his face. 'One less engineer.' Sharpe peered at Elliott who was blessedly unconscious. His face had gone pale, and pinkish blood was bubbling at his lips with every laboured breath. 'He won't last the day,' Simons said brutally, 'but I suppose we should get him back to the surgeons.'

'Where are the enemy?' Sharpe asked.

'They ran,' Simons said. 'Half a dozen of the bastards were waiting in ambush. They shot Elliott, took his weapons, but ran off when they saw us.'

Three *shikarees* died that afternoon, ambushed in the high woods, and that night, when the road-builders camped in one of the grassy upland valleys, some shots were fired from a neighbouring wood. The bullets hissed overhead, but none found a target. The picquets blazed back until a havildar shouted at them to hold their fire. Captain Pinckney shook his head. 'I thought it was too good to last,' he said gloomily. 'It'll be slow work now.' He poked the fire around which a half-dozen officers were sitting.

Major Simons grinned. 'If I was the enemy,' he said, 'I'd attack Mister Sharpe's oxen instead of attacking engineers. If they cut our supply line they'd do some real damage.'

'There's no point in shooting engineers,' Pinckney agreed. 'We don't need Royal Engineers anyway. We've been making roads for years. The fellows in the blue coats just get in the way. Mind you, they'll still send us another.'

'If there are any left,' Sharpe said. The campaign had been fatal for the engineers. Two had died blowing up the enemy guns at Assaye, another three were fevered and now Elliott was either dying or already dead.

'They'll find one,' Pinckney grumbled. 'If there's something the

King's army doesn't need then you can be sure they've got a healthy supply of it.'

'The Company army's better?' Sharpe asked.

'It is,' Major Simons said. 'We work for a sterner master than you, Sharpe. It's called book-keeping. You fight for victories, we fight for profits. Leadenhall Street won't pay for fancy engineers in blue coats, not when they can hire plain men like us at half the cost.'

'They could afford me,' Sharpe said. 'Cheap as they come, I am.'

Next morning Simons threw a strong picquet line ahead of the work parties, but no Mahrattas opposed the pioneers who were now widening the track where it twisted up a bare and steep slope that was littered with rocks. The track was ancient, worn into the hills by generations of travellers, but it had never been used by wagons, let alone by heavy guns. Merchants who wanted to carry their goods up the escarpment had used the road leading directly to the fortress's Southern Gate, while this track, which looped miles to the east of Gawilghur, was little more than a series of paths connecting the upland valleys where small farms had been hacked from the jungle. It was supposed to be tiger country, but Sharpe saw none of the beasts. At dawn he had returned to Deogaum to collect rice for the sepoys, and then spent the next four hours climbing back to where the pioneers were working. He was nervous at first, both of tigers and of an enemy ambush, but the worst he suffered was a series of drenching rainstorms that swept up the mountains.

The rain stopped when he reached the working parties who were driving the road through a small ridge. Pinckney was setting a charge of gunpowder that would loosen the rock and let him cut out a mile of looping track. His servant brought a mug of tea that Sharpe drank sitting on a rock. He stared southwards, watching the veils of grey rain sweep across the plain.

'Did Wellesley say anything about sending a new engineer?' Major Simons asked him.

'I just collected the rice, sir,' Sharpe said. 'I didn't see the General.'

'I thought you were supposed to be a friend of his?' Simons observed sourly.

'Everyone thinks that,' Sharpe said, 'except him and me.'

'But you saved his life?'

Sharpe shrugged. 'I reckon so. Either that or stopped him getting captured.'

'And killed a few men doing it, I hear?'

Sharpe looked at the tall Simons with some surprise, for he had not realized that his exploit had become common knowledge. 'Don't remember much about it.'

'I suppose not. Still,' Simons said, 'a feather in your cap?'

'I don't think Wellesley thinks that,' Sharpe said.

'You're a King's officer now, Sharpe,' Simons said enviously. As an East India Company officer he was trapped in the Company's cumbersome system of promotion. 'If Wellesley thrives, he'll remember you.'

Sharpe laughed. 'I doubt it, sir. He ain't the sort.' He turned southwards again because Ahmed had called a warning in Arabic. The boy was pointing downhill and Sharpe stood to see over the crown of the slope. Far beneath him, where the road passed through one of the lush valleys, a small party of horsemen was approaching and one of the riders was in a blue coat. 'Friends, Ahmed!' he called. 'Looks like the new engineer,' Sharpe said to Simons.

'Pinckney will be delighted,' Simons said sarcastically.

Pinckney came back to inspect the approaching party through a telescope, and spat when he saw the blue coat of the Royal Engineers. 'Another interfering bastard to teach me how to suck eggs,' he said. 'So let's blow the charge before he gets here, otherwise he'll tell us we're doing it all wrong.'

A crowd of grinning sepoys waited expectantly about the end of the fuse. Pinckney struck a light, put it to the quickmatch, then watched the sparks smoke their way towards the distant charge. The smoke trail vanished in grass and it seemed to Sharpe that it must have extinguished itself, but then there was a violent coughing sound and the small ridge heaved upwards. Soil and stone flew outwards in a cloud of filthy smoke. The sepoys cheered. The explosion had seemed small to Sharpe, but when the smoke and dust cleared he could see that the ridge now had a deep notch through which the road could climb to the next high valley.

The pioneers went to shovel the loosened earth away and Sharpe sat again. Ahmed squatted beside him. 'What am I going to do with you?' Sharpe asked.

'I go to England,' Ahmed said carefully.

'You won't like it there. Cold as buggery.'

'Cold?'

'Freezing.' Sharpe mimicked a shiver, but plainly it meant nothing to the Arab boy.

'I go to England,' Ahmed insisted.

A half-hour later the new engineer appeared just beneath Sharpe. He wore a wide-brimmed straw hat, rode a grey horse and was trailed by three servants who led pack mules laden with luggage amongst which Sharpe could see a tripod, a surveyor's level and a vast leather tube that he guessed held a telescope. The engineer took off his hat and fanned his face as he rounded the last bend. ''Pon my soul,' he said cheerfully, 'but thank God the horse does the climbing and not me.'

Pinckney had come back to greet the engineer and held out his hand as the blue-coated Major slid from his saddle. 'Captain Pinckney, sir,' he introduced himself.

'Pinckney, eh?' the white-haired engineer said cheerfully. 'I knew a Pinckney in Hertfordshire. He made ploughshares, and damn fine ones too.'

'My uncle Joshua, sir.'

'Then you must be Hugh's boy, yes? An honour!' He shook Pinckney's hand vigorously. 'Major John Stokes, at your service, though I don't suppose you need me, do you? You must have built more roads than I ever did.' Major Stokes looked towards Sharpe who had stood and was now smiling. 'Good God in His blessed heaven,' Stokes said, 'it can't be! But it is! My dear Sharpe! My dear Mister Sharpe. I heard all about your commission! Couldn't be more pleased, my dear Sharpe. An officer, eh?'

Sharpe smiled broadly. 'Only an ensign, sir.'

'Every ladder has a first rung, Sharpe,' Stokes said in gentle reproof of Sharpe's modesty, then held out his hand. 'We shall be mess mates, as they say in the Navy. Well, I never! Mess mates, indeed! And with a Pinckney too! Hugh Pinckney forges mill gears, Sharpe. Never seen a man make better-toothed wheels in all my life.' He clasped Sharpe's hand in both of his. 'They grubbed me out of Seringapatam, Sharpe. Can you believe that? Told me all the other engineers had the pox, and summoned me here just in time to discover that poor Elliott's dead.

I suppose I shouldn't complain. It's awfully good for my promotion prospects.' He let go of Sharpe's hand. 'Oh, and by the way, I travelled north with some of your old comrades! Captain Charles Morris and his company. Not the most charming creature, is he?'

'Not one of my favourites, sir,' Sharpe admitted. Good God! Bloody Morris was here? First Hakeswill, then Morris!

'He didn't want to come,' Stokes said, 'but higher powers deemed that I had to be protected from the ungodly, so they insisted on an infantry escort.' He turned as a rattle of gunfire sounded higher up the escarpment. 'Bless my soul! Is that musketry?'

'Picquet line, sir,' Pinckney explained. 'The enemy harasses us, but they're not thrusting home.'

'They should, they should. A battalion of skirmishers in these hills could keep us at bay for a month! Well, I never, Sharpe! An ensign!' The Major turned back to Pinckney. 'Sharpe and I ran the armoury at Seringapatam for four years.'

'You ran it, sir,' Sharpe said. 'I was just your sergeant.'

'Best sergeant I ever had,' Stokes told Pinckney enthusiastically. 'And it's not "sir"' – he turned to Sharpe – 'but John.' He grinned at Sharpe. 'They were four good years, eh? Best we'll ever have, I daresay. And here you are now, an officer! My dear fellow, I couldn't be more overjoyed.' He sniffed the air. 'Been blowing things up, Pinckney?'

'Cutting through that ridge, sir. I trust you don't mind that we didn't wait for you?'

'Mind? Why should I mind? You go ahead, dear fellow. I'm sure you know your business better than I do. God knows why they need an engineer here at all! Probably to be decorative, eh? Still, I'll make myself useful. I thought I might map the escarpment. Hasn't been done, you see. Of course, Pinckney, if you need advice, just ask away, but I'll probably be at sixes and sevens groping for an answer.' He beamed at the delighted Pinckney, then looked at the rough country through which the road led. 'This is fine landscape, isn't it? Such a relief after the plains. It reminds me of Scotland.'

'There are tigers here, Major,' Sharpe said.

'And there's all kinds of fierce things in Scotland too, Sharpe. I was once posted to Fort William and might as well have been in darkest China! It was worse than Newfoundland. And speaking of America, Sharpe, that young lady you sent me has travelled there. Extraordinary thing to do, I thought, and I advised her to abandon the whole wretched idea. There are bears, I told her, fierce bears, but she wouldn't be persuaded.'

'Simone, sir?' Sharpe asked, at first not believing his ears, then feeling a dreadful premonition.

'A charming creature, I thought. And to be widowed so young!' Stokes tutted and shook his head. 'She went to a fortune teller, one of those naked fellows who make funny faces in the alley by the Hindu temple, and says she was advised to go to a new world. Whatever next, eh?'

'I thought she was waiting for me, sir,' Sharpe said.

'Waiting for you? Good Lord, no. Gone to Louisiana, she says. She stayed in my house for a week – I moved out, of course, to stop any scandal – and then she travelled to Madras with Mrs Pennington. Remember Charlotte Pennington? The clergyman's widow? I can't think the two of them will get along, but your friend said the fortune teller was adamant and so she chose to go.' The Major was eager to give Sharpe the rest of the news from Seringapatam. The armoury was closing down, he said, now that the frontier of the British-held territory was so much farther north, but Stokes had kept himself busy dismantling the town's inner fortifications. 'Very ill made, Sharpe, disgraceful work, quite disgraceful. Walls crumbled to the touch.'

But Sharpe was not listening. He was thinking of Simone. She had gone! By now she was probably in Madras, and maybe already on board a ship. And she had taken his jewels. Only a few of them, true, but enough. He touched the seam of his jacket where a good many of the Tippoo's other jewels were hidden.

'Did Madame Joubert leave any message?' he asked Stokes when the Major paused to draw breath. What did he hope, Sharpe wondered, that Simone would want him to join her in America?

'A message? None, Sharpe. Too busy to write, I daresay. She's a remarkably wealthy woman, did you know? She bought half the raw silk in town, hired a score of bearers and off she went. Every officer in town was leaving a card for her, but she didn't have the time of day for any of them. Off to Louisiana!' Stokes suddenly frowned. 'What is the matter, Sharpe? You look as if you've seen a ghost. You're not sickening, are you?'

'No, no. It's just I thought she might have written.'

'Oh! I see! You were sweet on her!' Stokes shook his head. 'I feel for you, Sharpe, 'pon my soul, I do, but what hope could you have? A woman with her sort of fortune doesn't look at fellows like us! 'Pon my soul, no. She's rich! She'll marry high, Sharpe, or as high as a woman can in French America.'

Her sort of fortune indeed! Simone had no fortune, she had been penniless when Sharpe met her, but he had trusted her. God damn the Frog bitch! Stolen a small fortune. 'It doesn't matter,' he told Stokes, but somehow it did. Simone's betrayal was like a stab to the belly. It was not so much the jewels, for he had kept the greater part of the plunder, but the broken promises. He felt anger and pity and, above all, a fool. A great fool. He turned away from Stokes and stared down the track to where a dozen oxen escorted by two companies of sepoys were trudging towards him. 'I've got work coming,' he said, not wanting to discuss Simone any further.

'I passed those fellows on my way,' Stokes said, 'carrying powder, I think. I do like blowing things up. So just what do you do here, Sharpe?'

'I keep the pioneers supplied with material, sir, and sign in all the convoys.'

'Hope it leaves you time to help me, Sharpe. You and me together again, eh? It'll be like the old days.'

'That'd be good, sir,' Sharpe said with as much enthusiasm as he could muster, then he walked down the track and pointed to where the ox-drivers should drop their barrels of gunpowder. The men crowded about him with their chitties, and he pulled out a pencil and scrawled his initials in the corner of each one, thus confirming that they had completed and were owed for one journey.

The last man also handed Sharpe a sealed paper with his name written in a fine copperplate hand. 'From the clerk, sahib,' the man said, the phrase plainly much practised for he spoke no other English.

Sharpe tore the seal off as he walked back up the hill. The letter was not from the clerk at all, but from Torrance. 'Bloody hell!' he cursed.

'What is it?' Stokes asked.

'A man called Torrance,' Sharpe complained. 'He's in charge of the bullocks. He wants me back at Deogaum because he reckons there are forged chitties in the camp.'

'In the far south of India,' Stokes said, 'they call them *shits*.'

Sharpe blinked at the Major. 'Sorry, sir?'

'You mustn't call me "sir", Sharpe. 'Pon my soul, yes. I had a Tamil servant who was forever asking me to sign his *shits*. Had me all in a dither at first, I can tell you.'

Sharpe crumpled Torrance's note into a ball. 'Why the hell can't Torrance sort out his own *shits*?' he asked angrily. But he knew why. Torrance was scared of another meeting with Wellesley, which meant the Captain would now follow the rules to the letter.

'It won't take long,' Stokes said, 'not if you take my horse. But keep her to a steady walk, Richard, because she's tired. And have her rubbed down and watered while you're sorting out the *shits*.'

Sharpe was touched by Stokes's generosity. 'Are you sure?'

'What are friends for? Go on, Richard! On horseback you'll be home for supper. I'll have my cook brew up one of those *mussallas* you like so much.'

Sharpe left his pack with Stokes's baggage. The big ruby and a score of other stones were in the pack, and Sharpe was half tempted to carry it to Deogaum and back, but if he could not trust Stokes, who could he trust? He tried to persuade Ahmed to stay behind and keep an eye on the baggage, but the boy refused to be parted from Sharpe and insisted on trotting along behind the horse. 'Stokes won't hurt you,' Sharpe told Ahmed.

'I'm your havildar,' Ahmed insisted, hefting his musket and peering about the deserted landscape for enemies. There was none in sight, but Ahmed's gesture reminded Sharpe of Elliott's death and he wondered if he should have waited for the ox convoy to return to Deogaum, for the convoys all had escorts of sepoys or mercenary horsemen. He was tempted to kick the horse into a trot, but he resisted the impulse.

The danger was more acute once he reached the lower hills, for Mahratta horsemen were forever probing the perimeter of the British camp and being chased away by cavalry patrols. Twice he saw horsemen in the distance, but neither group took any notice of Sharpe who was ready to haul Ahmed up onto the horse and then ride for his life if he was threatened. He did not relax until he met a patrol of Madrassi cavalry under the command of a Company lieutenant who escorted him safely to the encampment.

Deogaum was now surrounded by a great spread of tents and makeshift booths, homes to soldiers and camp followers. A dancing bear was performing for a crowd of infantrymen and the animal reminded Sharpe of Major Stokes's words about America. Simone! It was his own damn fault. He should never have trusted the woman. The thought of his own foolishness plunged Sharpe into a black mood that was not helped by the sight of two redcoat privates lounging on a bench outside Torrance's quarters. Neither man moved as Sharpe slid from the horse. He gave the reins to Ahmed and mimed that the boy should rub the grey mare down with straw and then water her.

The two redcoats shifted slightly as if acknowledging Sharpe's presence, but neither man stood. He knew both of them; indeed, not so very long ago he had marched in the same ranks as these two men whose coats had the red facings of the 33rd. Kendrick and Lowry, they were called, and two worse characters it would have been hard to find in any light company. Both were cronies of Hakeswill's, and both had been among the small party Hakeswill had brought north in his failed attempt to arrest Sharpe. 'On your feet,' Sharpe said.

Kendrick glanced at Lowry, who looked back at Kendrick, and the two made faces at each other as though they were surprised by Sharpe's demands. They hesitated just long enough to make their insolence plain, but not quite long enough to make it punishable, then stood to attention. 'Is that your 'orse, Mister Sharpe?' Kendrick asked, stressing the 'mister'.

Sharpe ignored the question and pushed into the house to find a new clerk sitting behind the table. He was a young, good-looking Indian with oiled hair and a very white robe. He wore an apron to protect the robe from ink spots. 'You have business, sahib?' he asked brusquely.

'With Captain Torrance.'

'The Captain is ill.' The Indian, whose English was very good, smiled.

'He's always bloody ill,' Sharpe said and walked past the protesting clerk to push open the inner door.

Torrance was in his hammock, smoking his hookah, and dressed in an Indian gown embroidered with dragons while Sergeant Hakeswill was sitting at a small table counting a pile of coins. 'Sharpe!' Torrance sounded surprised. Hakeswill, looking equally surprised, sullenly stood to attention. 'Wasn't expecting you till this evening,' Torrance said.

'I'm here,' Sharpe said unnecessarily.

'So it is apparent. Unless you're a spectre?'

Sharpe had no time for small talk. 'You've got a problem with chitties?' he asked abruptly.

'Tiresome, isn't it?' Torrance seemed uncomfortable. 'Very tiresome. Sergeant, you have business elsewhere?'

'I've got duties, sir!' Hakeswill snapped.

'Attend to them, dear fellow.'

'Sir!' Hakeswill stiffened, turned to the right, then marched from the room.

'So how are you, Sharpe? Keeping busy?' Torrance had swung himself off the hammock and now scooped the coins into a leather bag. 'I hear poor Elliott died?'

'Shot, sir.'

Torrance shuddered as if the news was personal. 'So very sad,' he sighed, then retied the belt of his elaborate gown. 'I never did thank you, Sharpe, for being so supportive with Sir Arthur.'

Sharpe had not thought he had been supportive at all. 'I just told the truth, sir.'

'My father would be proud of you, and I'm deeply grateful to you. It seems Dilip was in league with Naig.'

'He was?'

Torrance heard the disbelief in Sharpe's voice. 'No other explanation, is there?' he said curtly. 'Someone must have been telling Naig which convoys carried the vital supplies, and it had to be Dilip. I must say I thought Wellesley was damned obtuse! There really is no point in having scruples about hanging natives. There isn't exactly a shortage of them, is there?' He smiled.

'There's something wrong with the chitties?' Sharpe demanded rudely.

'So there is, Sharpe, so there is. Our new clerk discovered the discrepancies. He's a smart young fellow. Sajit!'

The young clerk came into the room, clasped his hands and offered Torrance a slight bow. 'Sahib?'

'This is Ensign Sharpe, Sajit. He's by way of being my deputy and thus as much your sahib as I am.'

Sajit offered Sharpe a bow. 'I am honoured, sahib.'

'Perhaps you could show Mister Sharpe the problematical chitties, Sajit?' Torrance suggested.

Sajit went back to the outer room and returned a moment later with a pile of the grubby paper slips. He placed them on the table, then invited Sharpe to inspect them. All the chitties had Sharpe's initials in the bottom right-hand corner, most of them in pencil, but some had been initialled in ink and Sharpe set those aside. 'I didn't sign any of those,' he said confidently. 'I don't have a pen and ink.'

'You were right, Sajit!' Torrance said.

'You honour me, sahib,' Sajit said.

'And every chitty is a stolen anna,' Torrance said, 'so we have to discover which bullock men gave us the false ones. That's the problem, Sharpe.'

'They've got names on them,' Sharpe said, pointing at the slips of paper. 'You hardly needed to drag me down here to tell you who they were issued to!'

'Please don't be tedious, Sharpe,' Torrance said plaintively. 'Ever since the General put a shot across our bows I am forced to be particular. And the names mean nothing! Nothing! Look' – he scooped up the chitties – 'at least a dozen are assigned to Ram, whoever Ram is. There are probably a dozen Rams out there. What I want you to do, Sharpe, is go round the encampment with Sajit and point out which men have visited the road. Sajit can then identify which bullock men are submitting false claims.'

Sharpe frowned. 'Why doesn't Sajit just identify which men were ordered up the mountain? They must have got their chitties from him?'

'I want to be sure, Sharpe, I want to be sure!' Torrance pleaded.

'My testimony, sahib, would not be believed,' Sajit put in, 'but no one would doubt the word of an English officer.'

'Bloody hell,' Sharpe said. The last thing he felt like doing was wandering about the bullock camp identifying drivers. He was not sure he could do it anyway. 'So why not summon the bullock men here?' he demanded.

'The bad ones would run away, sahib, rather than come,' Sajit said.

'Best to ambush them in their encampment, Sharpe,' Torrance said.

'I'll do my best,' Sharpe grunted.

'I knew you would!' Torrance seemed relieved. 'Do it now, Sharpe, and perhaps you could join me for a late dinner? Say at half past one?'

Sharpe nodded, then went back into the sunlight to wait for Sajit. Kendrick and Lowry had vanished, presumably with Hakeswill. Ahmed had found a bucket of water and Stokes's mare was drinking greedily. 'You can stay here, Ahmed,' Sharpe said, but the boy shook his head. 'You're my bleeding shadow,' Sharpe grumbled.

'Shadow?'

Sharpe pointed to his own shadow. 'Shadow.'

Ahmed grinned, all white teeth in a grubby face. He liked the word. 'Sharpe's shadow!' he said.

Sajit emerged from the house with a pink silk parasol that he offered to Sharpe. Sharpe refused, and the clerk, who had discarded his apron, gratefully shaded himself from the fierce midday sun. 'I am sorry to be troublesome to you, sahib,' he said humbly.

'No trouble,' Sharpe said dourly, following the clerk. Ahmed came behind, leading the Major's mare.

'The boy need not come,' Sajit insisted, glancing behind at the horse which seemed to alarm him.

'You tell him that,' Sharpe said, 'but don't blame me if he shoots you. He's very fond of shooting people.'

Sajit hurried on. 'I think I know, sahib, which is the bad man who is cheating us. He is a fellow from Mysore. He gave me many chitties and swore you signed them in front of him. If you would be so kind as to confirm or deny his story, we shall be finished.'

'Then let's find the bugger and be done with it.'

Sajit led Sharpe through the bullock lines where the wealthier herdsmen had erected vast dark and sagging tents. Women slapped bread dough beside small ox-dung fires, and more piles of the fuel dried in the sun beside each tent entrance. Sharpe looked for Naig's big green tents, but he could not see them and he assumed that whoever had inherited Naig's business had packed up and gone.

'There, sahib, that is the bad man's tent.' Sajit nervously led Sharpe towards a brown tent that stood slightly apart from the others. He stopped a few paces from the entrance and lowered his voice. 'He is called Ranjit, sahib.'

'So fetch the bugger,' Sharpe said, 'and I'll tell you if he's lying or not.'

Sajit seemed nervous of confronting Ranjit for he hesitated, but then plucked up his courage, collapsed the parasol and dropped to the ground to crawl into the tent which sagged so deeply that the doorway was scarce higher than a man's knee. Sharpe heard the murmur of voices, then Sajit backed hurriedly out of the low fringed entrance. He slapped at the dust on his white robes, then looked at Sharpe with a face close to tears. 'He is a bad man, sahib. He will not come out. I told him a sahib was here to see him, but he used rude words!'

'I'll take a look at the bastard,' Sharpe said. 'That's all you need, isn't it? For me to say whether I've seen him or not?'

'Please, sahib,' Sajit said, and gestured at the tent's entrance.

Sharpe took off his hat so it would not tangle with the canvas, hoisted the tent's entrance as high as he could, then ducked low under the heavy brown cloth.

And knew instantly that it was a trap.

And understood, almost in the same instant, that he could do nothing about it.

The first blow struck his forehead, and his vision exploded in streaks of lightning and shuddering stars. He fell backwards, out into the sunlight and someone instantly grabbed one of his ankles and began pulling him into the deep shadow. He tried to kick, tried to push himself against the tent's sides, but another hand seized his second leg, another blow hammered the side of his skull and, mercifully, he knew nothing more.

'He's got a thick skull, our Sharpie,' Hakeswill said with a grin. He prodded Sharpe's prone body and got no reaction. 'Fast asleep, he is.' The Sergeant's face twitched. He had hit Sharpe with the heavy brass-bound butt of a musket and he was amazed that Sharpe's skull was not broken. There was plenty of blood in his black hair, and he would have a bruise the size of a mango by nightfall, but his skull seemed to have taken the two blows without splintering. 'He always was a thick-headed bugger,' Hakeswill said. 'Now strip him.'

'Strip him?' Kendrick asked.

'When his body is found,' Hakeswill explained patiently, 'if it is found, and you can't rely on bleeding blackamoors to do a proper job and hide it, we don't want no one seeing he's a British officer, do we? Not that he is an officer. He's just a jumped-up bit of muck. So strip him, then tie his hands and feet and cover his eyeballs.'

Kendrick and Lowry jerked and tugged Sharpe's coat free, then handed the garment to Hakeswill who ran his fingers along the hems. 'Got it!' he exulted when he felt the lumps in the cloth. He took out

143

a knife, slit the coat and the two privates stared in awe as he eased the glittering jewels out of the tightly sewn seam. It was dark in the shadowed tent, but the stones gleamed bright. 'Get on with it!' Hakeswill said. 'The rest of his clothes off!'

'What are you doing?' Sajit had sidled into the tent and now stared at the jewels.

'None of your bleeding business,' Hakeswill said.

'You have jewels?' Sajit asked.

Hakeswill slid out his bayonet and stabbed it at Sajit, checking the lunge a fraction before the blade would have punctured the clerk's neck. 'The jewels ain't your business, Sajit. The jewels are my business. Your business is Sharpie, got it? I agreed to give him to your bleeding uncle, but I gets what he carries.'

'My uncle will pay well for good stones,' Sajit said.

'Your Uncle Jama's a bleeding monkey who'd cheat me soon as fart at me, so forget the bleeding stones. They're mine.' Hakeswill thrust the first handful into a pocket and started searching the rest of Sharpe's clothes. He slit open all the seams, then cut Sharpe's boots apart to discover a score of rubies hidden in the folded boot-tops. They were small rubies, scarce bigger than peas, and Hakeswill was looking for one large ruby. 'I saw it, I did. The bloody Tippoo had it on his hat. Large as life! Look in his hair.'

Kendrick obediently ran his fingers through Sharpe's blood-encrusted hair. 'Nothing there, Sarge.'

'Turn the bugger over and have a look you know where.'

'Not me!'

'Don't be so bloody squeamish! And tie his hands. Fast now! You don't want the sod waking up, do you?'

The clothes and boots yielded sixty-three stones. There were rubies, emeralds, sapphires and four small diamonds, but no large ruby. Hakeswill frowned. Surely Sharpe would not have sold the ruby? Still, he consoled himself, there was a fortune here, and he could not resist putting all the stones together on a mat and staring at them. 'I do like a bit of glitter,' he breathed as his fingers greedily touched the jewels. He put ten of the smaller stones in one pile, another ten in a second, and pushed the two piles towards Kendrick and Lowry. 'That's your cut, boys. Keep you in whores for the rest of your lives, that will.'

'Perhaps I will tell my uncle about your stones,' Sajit said, staring at the jewels.

'I expect you will,' Hakeswill said, 'and so bleeding what? I ain't as dozy as Sharpie. You won't catch me.'

'Then maybe I shall tell Captain Torrance.' Sajit had positioned himself close to the entrance so that he could flee if Hakeswill attacked him. 'Captain Torrance likes wealth.'

Likes it too much, Hakeswill thought, and if Torrance knew about the stones he would make Hakeswill's life hell until he yielded a share. The Sergeant's face juddered in a series of uncontrollable twitches. 'You're a bright lad, Sajit, ain't you?' he said. 'You might be nothing but a bleeding heathen blackamoor but you've got more than bullock dung for brains, ain't you? Here.' He tossed Sajit three of the stones. 'That keeps your tongue quiet, and if it don't, I'll cut it out and have a feed on it. Partial to a plate of tongue, I am. Nice piece of tongue, knob of butter and some gravy. Proper food, that.' He pushed the rest of the stones into his pocket, then stared broodingly at Sharpe's naked trussed body. 'He had more,' Hakeswill said with a frown, 'I know he had more.' The Sergeant suddenly clicked his fingers. 'What about his pack?'

'What pack?' Lowry asked.

'The bleeding pack he carries, which he shouldn't, being an officer, which he ain't. Where's his pack?'

The privates shrugged. Sajit frowned. 'He had no pack when he came to the Captain's house.'

'You're sure?'

'He came on a horse,' Lowry said helpfully. 'It were a grey horse, and he didn't have no pack.'

'So where's the horse?' Hakeswill demanded angrily. 'We should look in its saddlebags!'

Lowry frowned, trying to remember. 'A bleeding kid had it,' he said at last.

'So where's the kid?'

'He ran off,' Sajit said.

'Ran off?' Hakeswill said threateningly. 'Why?'

'He saw you hit him,' Sajit said. 'I saw it. He fell out of the tent. There was blood on his face.'

'You shouldn't have hit him till he was right inside the tent,' Kendrick said chidingly.

'Shut your bloody face,' Hakeswill said, then frowned. 'So where did the kid run?'

'Away,' Sajit said. 'I chased him, but he climbed onto the horse.'

'Kid don't speak English,' Kendrick said helpfully.

'How the hell do you know that?'

''Cos I talked to him!'

'And who's going to believe a heathen black kid what don't speak English?' Lowry asked.

Hakeswill's face was racked by a quick series of twitches. He suspected he was safe. Lowry was right. Who would believe the kid? Even so the Sergeant wished that Jama's men were coming earlier to fetch Sharpe. Jama himself had gone away from the camp, reckoning that if he was going to murder a British officer then it was best done a long way from the British army. Hakeswill had warned Jama not to expect Sharpe until the evening, and now he had to guard him until dusk. 'I told you to put a bandage on his eyes,' Hakeswill snapped. 'Don't want him to see us!'

'It don't matter if he does,' Kendrick said. 'He ain't going to see the dawn, is he?'

'Got more lives than a basketful of bleeding cats, that one,' Hakeswill said. 'If I had any sense I'd slit his throat now.'

'No!' Sajit said. 'He was promised to my uncle.'

'And your uncle's paying us, yes?'

'That too is agreed,' Sajit said.

Hakeswill stood and walked to Sharpe's unconscious body. 'I put those stripes on his back,' he said proudly. 'Lied through my teeth, I did, and had Sharpie flogged. Now I'll have him killed.' He remembered how Sharpe had flung him among the tigers and his face twitched as he recalled the elephant trying to crush him to death, and in his sudden rage he kicked at Sharpe and went on kicking until Kendrick hauled him away.

'If you kill him, Sarge,' Kendrick said, 'then the blackies won't pay us, will they?'

Hakeswill let himself be pulled away. 'So how will your uncle kill him?' he asked Sajit.

'His *jettis* will do it.'

'I've seen them bastards at work,' Hakeswill said in a tone of admiration. 'Just make it slow. Make it slow and make it bleeding painful.'

'It will be slow,' Sajit promised, 'and very painful. My uncle is not a merciful man.'

'But I am,' Hakeswill said. 'I am. Because I'm letting another man have the pleasure of killing Sharpie.' He spat at Sharpe. 'Dead by dawn, Sharpie. You'll be down with Old Nick, where you ought to be!'

He settled against one of the tent poles and trickled jewels from one palm to the other. Flies crawled among the crusting blood in Sharpe's hair. The Ensign would be dead by dawn, and Hakeswill was a rich man. Revenge, the Sergeant decided, was sweet as honey.

Ahmed saw Sharpe fall back from the tent entrance, saw blood bright on his forehead, then watched as hands seized Sharpe and dragged him into the deep shadows.

Then Sajit, the clerk with the pink umbrella, turned towards him. 'Boy,' he snapped, 'come here!'

Ahmed pretended not to understand, though he understood well enough that he was a witness to something deeply wrong. He backed away, tugging Major Stokes's mare with him. He let the musket slip down from his shoulder and Sajit, seeing the threat, suddenly rushed at him, but Ahmed was even faster. He jumped up to sprawl across the saddle and, without bothering to seat himself properly, kicked the horse into motion. The startled mare leaped away as Ahmed hauled himself onto her back. The stirrups were too long for him, but Ahmed had been raised with horses and could have ridden the mare bareback, blindfolded and back to front. He swerved southwards, galloping between tents, fires and grazing bullocks, and leaving Sajit far behind. A woman shouted a protest as he nearly galloped over her children. He slowed the mare as he reached the edge of the encampment and looked back to see that he had left Sajit far behind.

What the hell should he do? He knew no one in the British camp. He looked up at the high summit where Gawilghur just showed. He supposed his old comrades in Manu Bappoo's Lions of Allah were up there, but his uncle, with whom he had travelled from Arabia, was dead and buried in Argaum's black earth. He knew other soldiers in the regiment, but he also feared them. Those other soldiers wanted Ahmed to be their servant, and not just to cook for them and clean their weapons. Sharpe alone had shown him friendliness, and Sharpe now needed help, but Ahmed did not know how to provide it. He thought about the problem as he knotted the stirrup leathers.

The plump, red-faced and white-haired man in the hills had been friendly, but how was Ahmed to talk to him? He decided he ought to try and so he turned the horse, planning to ride her all about the camp perimeter and then back up the road into the hills, but an officer of the camp picquets saw him. The man was riding a horse and he spurred it close to Ahmed and noted the British saddle cloth. 'What are you doing, boy?' he asked. The officer presumed Ahmed was exercising the horse, but Ahmed took fright at the challenge and kicked back.

'Thief!' the officer shouted and gave chase. 'Stop! Thief!'

A sepoy turned with his musket and Ahmed nudged the horse so that she ran the man down. There was a group of houses close by and Ahmed turned towards them, jumped a garden wall, thumped through some beds of vegetables, jumped another wall, ducked under some fruit trees, jumped a hedge and splashed through a muddy pond before kicking the horse up a bank and into some trees. The officer had not dared follow him through the gardens, but Ahmed could hear the hue and cry beyond the houses. He patted the mare's neck as she threaded through the trees, then curbed her at the wood's edge. There was about a half-mile of open country, then more thick woods that promised safety if only the tired mare could make the distance without faltering. 'If Allah wills it,' Ahmed said, then kicked the horse into a gallop.

His pursuers were well behind, but they saw him break cover and now a dozen horsemen were chasing him. Someone fired at him. He heard the musket shot, but the ball went nowhere near him. He leaned over the mane and just let the horse run. He looked back once and saw the pursuers bunching in his path, and then he was in the trees and he twisted northwards, cut back west, then went north again, going ever deeper into the woods until at last he slowed the blowing horse so that the sound of her thumping hooves would not betray him.

He listened. He could hear other horses blundering through the leaves, but they were not coming any closer, and then he began to wonder if it would not be better to let himself be caught after all, for surely someone among the British would speak his language? Maybe if he went all the way to where the men were making the road in the hills he would be too late to help Sharpe. He felt miserable, utterly unsure what he should do, and then he decided he must go back and find help within the encampment and so he turned the horse back towards his pursuers.

And saw a musket pointing straight at his throat.

The man holding the musket was an Indian and had one of the spiralling brass helmets that the Mahrattas wore. He was a cavalryman, but he had picketed his horse a few yards away and had crept up on Ahmed on foot. The man grinned.

Ahmed wondered if he should just kick the tired mare and risk his luck, but then another Mahratta stepped from the leaves, and this one held a curved *tulwar*. A third man appeared, and then more men came, all mounted, to surround him.

And Ahmed, who knew he had panicked and failed, wept.

It seemed to Dodd that Prince Manu Bappoo's policy of rewarding freebooters with cash for weapons captured from the British was failing miserably. So far they had fetched in three ancient matchlocks that must have belonged to *shikarees*, a broken musket of local manufacture, and a fine pistol and sword that had been taken from an engineer officer. No scabbard for the sword, of course, but the two trophies, so far as Dodd was concerned, were the only evidence that the Mahrattas had tried to stop the British approach. He pestered Manu Bappoo, pleading to be allowed to take his Cobras down to where the pioneers were driving the road, but the Rajah's brother adamantly refused to let Dodd's men leave the fortress.

Dodd himself was allowed to leave, but only to exercise his horse, which he did each day by riding west along the brink of the plateau. He did not go far. There was a tempting price on his head, and though no enemy cavalry had been seen on the plateau since the engineer had made his reconnaissance, Dodd still feared that he might be captured, and so he only rode until he could see the British works far beneath him. Then, protected by a handful of Bappoo's horsemen, he would stare through a telescope at the ant-like figures labouring so far below. He watched the road widen, and lengthen, and one morning he saw that two battalions of infantry had camped in one of the high valleys, and next day he saw the beginnings of an artillery park: three guns, a forage cart, a spare wheel wagon and four ammunition limbers.

He cursed Bappoo, knowing that his Cobras could destroy that small park and hurl the British into dazed confusion, yet the Prince was content to let the enemy climb the escarpment unopposed. The road was being remade, yet even so it was still steep enough in places to need a hundred men to haul one gun. Yet day by day Dodd saw the number of guns increase in the artillery park, then inch up the hill and he knew it would not be long before the British reached the plateau and their besieging forces would seal off the narrow isthmus of rock that led from the cliffs to the great fortress.

And still Manu Bappoo made no proper effort to harry the redcoats. 'We shall stop them here,' the Prince told Dodd, 'here,' and he would gesture at Gawilghur's walls, but William Dodd was not so sure that the redcoats would be stopped so easily. Bappoo might be convinced of the fortress's strength, but Bappoo knew nothing of modern siege craft.

Each morning, as he returned from his excursion along the cliff top, Dodd would dismount as he reached the isthmus and give his horse to one of his escort so that he could walk the attackers' route. He tried to see the fortress as the redcoats would see it, tried to anticipate where their attack would come and how it would be made.

It was, he had to admit, a brutal place to attack. Two great walls protected the Outer Fort, and though the British could undoubtedly breach those walls with cannon fire, the two ramparts stood on a steep slope so that the attackers would need to fight their way uphill to where the defenders would be waiting among the ruins of the breaches. And those breaches would be flanked by the massive round bastions that were too big to be collapsed by the twelve- or eighteen-pounder guns Dodd expected the British to deploy. The bastions would spit round shot, musket balls and rockets down into the British who would be struggling towards the nearer breach, their approach route getting ever narrower until it was finally constricted by the vast tank of water that blocked most of the approach. Dodd walked the route obsessively and could almost feel sorry for the men who would have to do it under fire.

A hundred paces from the fort, where the defenders' fire would be most lethal, the attackers would be squeezed between the reservoir and the cliff edge, compressed into a space just twenty paces wide. Dodd stood in that space each day and stared up at the double walls and counted the artillery pieces. Twenty-two cannon were pointing at him and when the redcoats came those barrels would be loaded with canister, and besides those heavy guns there was a mass of smaller weapons, the murderers and spitfires that could be held by one man and which could blast out a fistful of stone scraps or pistol balls. True, the British would have destroyed some of the larger guns, but the barrels could be mounted on new carriages and resited behind the vast bastions so that the attackers, if they even succeeded in climbing up to the breach, would be enfiladed by cannon fire. And to reach that far they would need to fight uphill against Bappoo's Arabs, and against the massed musketry of the garrison.

It was a prospect so daunting that Prince Manu Bappoo expected most of the attackers would sheer away from the breaches and run to the Delhi Gate, the Outer Fort's northern entrance. That gate would undoubtedly have been shattered by British cannon fire, but once inside its arch the attackers would find themselves in a trap. The road inside the gate curled up beside the wall, with another great wall outside it, so that anyone on the cobbles was dwarfed by the stone ramparts on either side, and those would be lined with men firing down or else throwing the great rocks that Bappoo had ordered piled onto the firesteps. Inch by bloody inch the redcoats would fight their way up the narrow road between the walls, only to turn the corner to see an even greater gate standing in front of them, and one, moreover, that could not be reached by the besiegers' cannon fire. Thus, Bappoo reckoned, the British assault would be thwarted.

Dodd was not so sure. The Prince was right in thinking that there was no way in through the Delhi Gate, but Dodd suspected the breaches would be less formidable. He had begun to see weaknesses in the ancient walls, old cracks that were half hidden by weeds and lichen, and he knew the skill of the British gunners. The wall would break easily, and that meant the breaches would be big and wide, and Dodd reckoned the British would fight their way through. It might be a hard fight, but they would win it. And that meant the British would capture the Outer Fort.

But Dodd did not express that opinion to Bappoo, nor did he urge the Prince to build an earthen glacis outside the wall to soak up the fire of the breaching batteries. Such a glacis would delay the British for days, even weeks, but Dodd encouraged the Prince to believe that the Outer Fort was impregnable, for in that misapprehension lay Dodd's opportunity.

Manu Bappoo had once told Dodd that the Outer Fort was a trap. An enemy, if they captured the Outer Fort, would think their battle won, but then they would come to Gawilghur's central ravine and find a second, even greater fort, waiting on its far side. But for Dodd the Outer Fort was Manu Bappoo's trap. If Manu Bappoo lost the Outer Fort then he, like the enemy, would have to cross the ravine and climb to the Inner Fort, and it was there that Dodd commanded and, try as Dodd might, he could see no weaknesses in the Inner Fort's defences. Neither Manu Bappoo nor the British could ever cross the ravine, not if Dodd opposed them.

The Inner Fort was quite separate from the Outer. No wall joined them, only a track that dropped steeply to the bed of the ravine and then climbed, even more steeply, to the intricate gateway of the Inner Fort. Dodd used that track each day, and he tried to imagine himself as an attacker. Twenty more guns faced him from the Inner Fort's single wall as he descended the ravine, and none of those guns would have been dismounted by cannon fire. Muskets would be pouring their shot down into the rocky ravine and rockets would be slashing bloodily through the British ranks. The redcoats would die here like rats being pounded in a bucket, and even if some did survive to climb the track towards the gate, they would only reach Gawilghur's last horror.

That horror was the entrance, where four vast gates barred the Inner Fort, four gates set one after another in a steep passage that was flanked by towering walls. There was no other way in. Even if the British breached the Inner Fort's wall it would not help, for the wall was built on top of the precipice which formed the southern side of the ravine, and no man could climb that slope and hope to survive. The only way in was through the gate, and Wellesley, Dodd had learned, did not like lengthy sieges. He had escaladed Ahmednuggur, surprising its defenders by sending men with ladders against the unbreached walls, and Dodd was certain that Wellesley would similarly try to rush the Inner Fort. He could not approach the wall, perched on its cliff, so he would be forced to send his men into the ghastly entrance that twisted as it climbed, and for every steep step of the way, between each of the four great gates, they would be pounded by muskets, crushed by stones, blasted by cannon and savaged by rockets dropped from the parapets. It could not be done. Dodd's Cobras would be on the firesteps and the redcoats would be beneath them, and the redcoats would die like cattle.

Dodd had no great opinion of Indian rockets, but he had stockpiled more than a thousand above the Inner Fort's murderous entrance, for within the close confines of the walled road the weapons would prove lethal. The rockets were made of hammered tin, each one about sixteen inches long and four or five inches in diameter, with a bamboo stick the height of a man attached to each tin cylinder that was crammed with powder. Dodd had experimented with the weapon and found that a lit rocket tossed down into the gate passage would sear and bounce from wall to wall, and even when it finally stopped careering madly about the roadway, it went on belching out a torch of flame that would scorch trapped men terribly. A dozen rockets dropped between two of the gates might kill a score of men and burn another score half to death. Just let them come, Dodd prayed as he climbed each morning towards the Inner Fort. Let them come! Let them come and let them take the Outer Fort, for then Manu Bappoo must die and the British would then come to Dodd and die like the Prince.

And afterwards the fugitives of their beaten army would be pursued south across the Deccan Plain. Their bodies would rot in the heat and their bones whiten in the sun, and the British power in India would be broken and Dodd would be Lord of Gawilghur.

Just let the bastards come.

That evening Sergeant Hakeswill pushed aside the folds of muslin to enter Captain Torrance's quarters. The Captain was lying naked in his hammock where he was being fanned by a bamboo punkah that had been rigged to a ceiling beam. His native servant kept the punkah moving by tugging on a string, while Clare Wall trimmed the Captain's fingernails. 'Not too close, Brick,' Torrance said. 'Leave me enough to scratch with, there's a good girl.' He raised his eyes to Hakeswill. 'Did you knock, Sergeant?'

'Twice, sir,' Hakeswill lied, 'loud and clear, sir.'

'Brick will have to ream out my ears. Say good evening to the Sergeant, Brick. Where are our manners tonight?'

Clare lifted her eyes briefly to acknowledge Hakeswill's presence and mumbled something barely audible. Hakeswill snatched off his hat. 'Pleasure to see you, Mrs Wall,' he said eagerly, 'a proper pleasure, my jewel.' He bobbed his head to her and winked at Torrance, who flinched.

'Brick,' Torrance said, 'the Sergeant and I have military matters to discuss. So take yourself to the garden.' He patted her hand and watched her leave. 'And no listening at the window!' he added archly. He waited until Clare had sidled past the muslin that hung over the kitchen entrance, then leaned precariously from the hammock to pick up a green silk robe that he draped over his crotch. 'I would hate to shock you, Sergeant.'

'Beyond shock, sir, me, sir. Ain't nothing living I ain't seen naked, sir, all of 'em naked as needles, and never once was I shocked, sir. Ever since they strung me up by the neck I've been beyond shock, sir.'

And beyond sense, too, Torrance thought, but he suppressed the comment. 'Has Brick left the kitchen?'

Hakeswill peered past the muslin. 'She's gone, sir.'

'She's not at the window?'

Hakeswill checked the window. 'On the far side of the yard, sir, like a good girl.'

'I trust you've brought me news?'

'Better than news, sir, better than news.' The Sergeant crossed to the table and emptied his pocket. 'Your notes to Jama, sir, all of them. Ten thousand rupees, and all paid off. You're out of debt, sir, out of debt.'

Relief seared through Torrance. Debt was a terrible thing, a dreadful thing, yet seemingly inescapable if a man was to live to the full. Twelve hundred guineas! How could he ever have gambled that much away? It had been madness! Yet now it was paid, and paid in full. 'Burn the notes,' he ordered Hakeswill.

Hakeswill held the notes into a candle flame one by one, then let them shrivel and burn on the table. The draught from the punkah disturbed the smoke and scattered the little scraps of black ash that rose from the small fires. 'And Jama, sir, being a gentleman, despite being an heathen bastard blackamoor, added a thankee,' Hakeswill said, putting some gold coins on the table.

'How much?'

'Seven hundred rupees there, sir.'

'He gave us more, I know that. You're cheating me, Sergeant.'

'Sir!' Hakeswill straightened indignantly. 'On my life, sir, and I speak as a Christian, I ain't ever cheated a soul in my life, sir, not unless they deserved it, in which case they gets it right and proper, sir, like it says in the scriptures.'

Torrance stared at Hakeswill. 'Jama will be back in the camp in a day or two. I can ask him.'

'And you will find, sir, that I have treated you foursquare and straight, sir, on the nail, sir, on the drumhead, as one soldier to another.' Hakeswill sniffed. 'I'm hurt, sir.'

Torrance yawned. 'You have my sincerest, deepest and most fervent apologies, Sergeant. So tell me about Sharpe.'

Hakeswill glanced at the punkah boy. 'Does that heathen speak English, sir?'

'Of course not.'

'Sharpie's no more, sir.' Hakeswill's face twitched as he remembered the pleasure of kicking his enemy. 'Stripped the bastard naked, sir, gave him a headache he won't ever forget, not that he's got long to remember anything now on account of him being on his way to meet his executioner, and I kept him trussed up till Jama's men came to fetch him. Which they did, sir, so now he's gone, sir. Gone for bleeding ever, just as he deserves.'

'You stripped him?' Torrance asked, puzzled.

'Didn't want the bastards dropping off a body all dressed up in an officer's coat, sir, even though the little bleeder should never have worn one, him being nothing more than a jumped-up dribble of dried toad-spittle, sir. So we stripped him and burned the uniform, sir.'

'And nothing went wrong?'

Hakeswill's face twitched as he shrugged. 'His boy got away, but he didn't make no trouble. Just vanished. Probably went back to his mummy.'

Torrance smiled. All was done, all was solved. Even better, he could resume his trade with Jama, though perhaps with a little more circumspection than in the past. 'Did Sajit go with Sharpe?' he asked, knowing he would need an efficient clerk if he was to hide the treacherous transactions in the ledger.

'No, sir. He's with me, sir, outside, sir.' Hakeswill jerked his head towards the front room. 'He wanted to go, sir, but I gave him a thumping on account of us needing him here, sir, and after that he was as good as gold, sir, even if he is an heathen bit of scum.'

Torrance smiled. 'I am vastly in your debt, Sergeant Hakeswill,' he said.

'Just doing my duty, sir.' Hakeswill's face twitched as he grinned and gestured towards the garden window. 'And hoping for a soldier's reward, sir.'

'Brick, you mean?' Torrance asked.

'Me heart's desire, sir,' Hakeswill said hoarsely. 'Her and me, sir, made for each other. Says so in the scriptures.'

'Then the fruition of the prophecy must wait a while,' Torrance said, 'because I need Brick to look after me, and your duty, Sergeant, is to assume Mister Sharpe's responsibilities. We shall wait till someone notices that he's missing, then claim that he must have been ambushed by Mahrattas while on his way here. Then you'll go up the mountain to help the engineers.'

'Me, sir?' Hakeswill sounded alarmed at the prospect of having to do some real work. 'Up the mountain?'

'Someone has to be there. You can't expect me to do it!' Torrance said indignantly. 'Someone must stay here and shoulder the heavier responsibilities. It won't be for long, Sergeant, not for long. And once the campaign is over I can assure you that your heart's desires will be fully met.' But not, he decided, before Hakeswill paid him the money Clare owed for her passage out from England. That money could come from the cash that Jama had given Hakeswill this night which, Torrance was sure, was a great deal more than the Sergeant had admitted. 'Make yourself ready, Sergeant,' Torrance ordered. 'Doubtless you will be needed up the road tomorrow.'

'Yes, sir,' Hakeswill said sullenly.

'Well done, good and faithful Hakeswill,' Torrance said grandly. 'Don't let any moths in as you leave.'

Hakeswill went. He had three thousand three hundred rupees in his pocket and a fortune in precious stones hidden in his cartridge box. He would have liked to have celebrated with Clare Wall, but he did not doubt that his chance would come and so, for the moment, he was a satisfied man. He looked at the first stars pricking the sky above

Gawilghur's plateau and reflected that he had rarely been more content. He had taken his revenge, he had become wealthy, and thus all was well in Obadiah Hakeswill's world.

CHAPTER 6

Sharpe knew he was in an ox cart. He could tell that from the jolting motion and from the terrible squeal of the ungreased axles. The ox carts that followed the army made a noise like the shrieking of souls in perdition.

He was naked, bruised and in pain. It hurt even to breathe. His mouth was gagged and his hands and feet were tied, but even if they had been free he doubted he could have moved for he was wrapped in a thick dusty carpet. Hakeswill! The bastard had ambushed him, stripped him and robbed him. He knew it was Hakeswill, for Sharpe had heard the Sergeant's hoarse voice as he was rolled into the rug. Then he had been carried out of the tent and slung into the cart, and he was not sure how long ago that had been because he was in too much pain and he kept slipping in and out of a dreamlike daze. A nightmare daze. There was blood in his mouth, a tooth was loose, a rib was probably cracked and the rest of him simply ached or hurt. His head throbbed. He wanted to be sick, but knew he would choke on his vomit because of the gag and so he willed his belly to be calm.

Calm! The only blessing was that he was alive, and he suspected that was no blessing at all. Why had Hakeswill not killed him? Not out of mercy, that was for sure. So presumably he was to be killed somewhere else, though why Hakeswill had run the terrible risk of having a British officer tied hand and foot and smuggled past the picquet line Sharpe could not tell. It made no sense. All he did know was that by now Obadiah Hakeswill would have teased Sharpe's gems from their hiding places. God damn it all to hell. First Simone, now Hakeswill, and Hakeswill, Sharpe realized, could never have trapped Sharpe if Torrance had not helped.

But knowing his enemies would not help Sharpe now. He knew he

158

had as much hope of living as those dogs who were hurled onto the mud flats beside the Thames in London with stones tied to their necks. The children used to laugh as they watched the dogs struggle. Some of the dogs had come from wealthy homes. They used to be snatched and if their owners did not produce the ransom money within a couple of days, the dogs were thrown to the river. Usually the ransom was paid, brought by a nervous footman to a sordid public house near the docks, but no one would ransom Sharpe. Who would care? Dust from the rug was thick in his nose. Just let the end be quick, he prayed.

He could hear almost nothing through the rug. The axle squealing was the loudest noise, and once he heard a thump on the cart's side and thought he heard a man laugh. It was night-time. He was not sure how he knew that, except that it would make sense, for no one would try to smuggle a British officer out in daylight, and he knew he had lain in the tent for a long time after Hakeswill had hit him. He remembered ducking under the tent's canvas, remembered a glimpse of the brass-bound musket butt, and then it was nothing but a jumble of pain and oblivion. A weight pressed on his waist, and he guessed after a while that a man was resting his feet on the rug. Sharpe tested the assumption by trying to move and the man kicked him. He lay still again. One dog had escaped, he remembered. It had somehow slipped the rope over its neck and had paddled away downstream with the children shrieking along the bank and hurling stones at the frightened head. Did the dog die? Sharpe could not remember. God, he thought, but he had been a wild child, wild as a hawk. They had tried to beat the wildness out of him, beat him till the blood ran, then told him he would come to a bad end. They had prophesied that he would be strung up by the neck at Tyburn Hill. Dick Sharpe dangling, pissing down his legs while the rope burned into his gullet. But it had not happened. He was an officer, a gentleman, and he was still alive, and he pulled at the tether about his wrists, but it would not shift.

Was Hakeswill riding in the cart? That seemed possible, and suggested the Sergeant wanted somewhere safe and private to kill Sharpe. But how? Quick with a knife? That was a forlorn wish, for Hakeswill was not merciful. Perhaps he planned to repay Sharpe by putting him beneath an elephant's foot and he would scream and writhe until the great weight would not let him scream ever again and his bones would crack and splinter like eggshells. Be sure your sin will find you out. How many times had he heard those words from the Bible? Usually thumped into him at the foundling home with a blow across the skull for every syllable, and the blows would keep coming as they chanted the reference. The Book of Numbers, chapter thirty-two, verse twenty-three, syllable by syllable, blow by blow, and now his sin was finding him out and he was to be punished for all the unpunished offences. So die well, he told himself. Don't cry out. Whatever was about to happen could not be worse than the flogging he had taken because of Hakeswill's lies. That had hurt. Hurt like buggery, but he had not cried out. So take the pain and go like a man. What had Sergeant Major Bywaters said as he had thrust the leather gag into Sharpe's mouth? 'Be brave, boy. Don't let the regiment down.' So he would be brave and die well, and then what? Hell, he supposed, and an eternity of torment at the hands of a legion of Hakeswills. Just like the army, really.

The cart stopped. He heard feet thump on the wagon boards, the murmur of voices, then hands seized the rug and dragged him off. He banged hard down onto the ground, then the rug was picked up and carried. Die well, he told himself, die well, but that was easier said than done. Not all men died well. Sharpe had seen strong men reduced to shuddering despair as they waited for the cart to be run out from under the gallows, just as he had seen others go into eternity with a defiance so brittle and hard that it had silenced the watching crowd. Yet all men, the brave and the cowardly, danced the gallows dance in the end, jerking from a length of Bridport hemp, and the crowd would laugh at their twitching antics. Best puppet show in London, they said. There was no good way to die, except in bed, asleep, unknowing. Or maybe in battle, at the cannon's mouth, blown to kingdom come in an instant of oblivion.

He heard the footsteps of the men who carried him slap on stone, then heard a loud murmur of voices. There were a lot of voices, all apparently talking at once and all excited, and he felt the rug being jostled by a crowd and then he seemed to be carried down some steps and the crowd was gone and he was thrown onto a hard floor. The voices seemed louder now, as if he was indoors, and he was suddenly possessed by the absurd notion that he had been brought into a cockfighting arena like the one off Vinegar Street where, as a child, he had earned farthings by carrying pots of porter to spectators who were alternatively morose or maniacally excited.

He lay for a long time. He could hear the voices, even sometimes a burst of laughter. He remembered the fat man in Vinegar Street, whose trade, rat-catching, took him to the great houses in west London that he reconnoitred for his thieving friends. 'You'd make a good snaffler, Dicky,' he'd say to Sharpe, then he would clutch Sharpe's arm and point to the cockerels waiting to fight. 'Which one'll win, lad, which one?' And Sharpe would make a haphazard choice and, as often as not, the bird did win. 'He's a lucky boy,' the rat-catcher would boast to his friends as he tossed Sharpe a farthing. 'Nipper's got the luck of the devil!'

But not tonight, Sharpe thought, and suddenly the rug was seized, unwound, and Sharpe was spilt naked onto hard stones. A cheer greeted his appearance. Light flared in Sharpe's eyes, dazzling him, but after a while he saw he was in a great stone courtyard lit by the flames of torches mounted on pillars that surrounded the yard. Two white-robed men seized him, dragged him upright and pushed him onto a stone bench where, to his surprise, his hands and feet were loosed and the gag taken from his mouth. He sat flexing his fingers and gasping deep breaths of humid air. He could see no sign of Hakeswill.

He could see now that he was in a temple. A kind of cloister ran around the courtyard and, because the cloister was raised three or four feet, it made the stone-paved floor into a natural arena. He had not been so wrong about the cock-fighting pit, though Vinegar Street had never aspired to ornately carved stone arches smothered with writhing gods and snarling beasts. The raised cloister was packed with men who were in obvious good humour. There were hundreds of them, all anticipating a night's rare entertainment. Sharpe touched his swollen lip and winced at the pain. He was thirsty, and with every deep breath his bruised or broken ribs hurt. There was a swelling on his forehead that was thick with dried blood. He looked about the crowd, seeking one friendly face and finding none. He just saw Indian peasants with dark eyes that reflected the flame light. They must have come from every village within ten miles to witness whatever was about to happen.

In the centre of the courtyard was a small stone building, fantastically carved with elephants and dancing girls, and crowned by a stepped tower that had been sculpted with yet more gods and animals painted red, yellow, green and black. The crowd's noise subsided as a man showed at the doorway of the small shrine and raised his arms as a signal for silence. Sharpe recognized the man. He was the tall, thin, limping man in the green and black striped robe who had pleaded with Torrance for Naig's life, and behind him came a pair of *jettis*. So that was the sum of it. Revenge for Naig, and Sharpe realized that Hakeswill had never intended to kill him, only deliver him to these men.

A murmur ran through the spectators as they admired the *jettis*. Vast brutes, they were, who dedicated their extraordinary strength to some strange Indian god. Although Sharpe had met *jettis* before and had killed some in Seringapatam, he did not fancy his chances against these two bearded brutes. He was too weak, too thirsty, too bruised, too hurt, while these two fanatics were tall and hugely muscled. Their bronze skin had been oiled so that it gleamed in the flame light. Their long hair was coiled about their skulls, and one had red lines painted on his face, while the other, who was slightly shorter, carried a long spear. Each man wore a loincloth and nothing else. They glanced at Sharpe, then the taller man prostrated himself before a small shrine. A dozen guards came from the courtyard's rear and lined its edge. They carried muskets tipped with bayonets.

The tall man in the striped robe clapped his hands to silence the crowd's last murmurs. It took a while, for still more spectators were pushing into the temple and there was scarce room in the cloister. Somewhere outside a horse neighed. Men shouted protests as the newcomers shoved their way inside, but at last the commotion ended and the tall man stepped to the edge of the stone platform on which the small shrine stood. He spoke for a long time, and every few moments his words would provoke a growl of agreement, and then the crowd would look at Sharpe and some would spit at him. Sharpe stared sullenly back at them. They were getting a rare night's amusement, he reckoned. A captured Englishman was to be killed in front of them, and Sharpe could not blame them for relishing the prospect. But he was damned if he would die easy. He could do some damage, he reckoned, maybe not much, but enough so that the *jettis* remembered the night they were given a redcoat to kill.

The tall man finished his speech, then limped down the short flight of steps and approached Sharpe. He carried himself with dignity, like a man who knows his own worth to be high. He stopped a few paces from Sharpe and his face showed derision as he stared at the Englishman's sorry state. 'My name,' he said in English, 'is Jama.'

Sharpe said nothing.

'You killed my brother,' Jama said.

'I've killed a lot of men,' Sharpe said, his voice hoarse so that it scarcely carried the few paces that separated the two men. He spat to clear his throat. 'I've killed a lot of men,' he said again.

'And Naig was one,' Jama said.

'He deserved to die,' Sharpe said.

Jama sneered at that answer. 'If my brother deserved to die then so did the British who traded with him.'

That was probably true, Sharpe thought, but he said nothing. He could see some pointed helmets at the back of the crowd and he guessed that some of the Mahratta horsemen who still roamed the Deccan Plain had come to see his death. Maybe the same Mahrattas who had bought the two thousand missing muskets, muskets that Hakeswill had supplied and Torrance had lied about to conceal the theft.

'So now you will die,' Jama said simply.

Sharpe shrugged. Run to the right, he was thinking, and grab the nearest musket, but he knew he would be slowed by the pain. Besides, the men on the cloister would jump down to overpower him. But he had to do something. Anything! A man could not just be killed like a dog.

'You will die slowly,' Jama said, 'to satisfy the debt of blood that is owed to my family.'

'You want a death,' Sharpe asked, 'to balance your brother's death?'

'Exactly so,' Jama said gravely.

'Then kill a rat,' Sharpe said, 'or strangle a toad. Your brother deserved to die. He was a thief.'

'And you English have come to steal all India,' Jama said equably. He looked again at Sharpe's wounds, and seemed to get satisfaction from them. 'You will soon be pleading for my mercy,' he said. 'Do you know what *jettis* are?'

'I know,' Sharpe said.

'Prithviraj,' Jama said, gesturing towards the taller *jetti* who was bowing before the small altar, 'has castrated a man with his bare hands. He will do that to you and more, for tonight I have promised these

163

people they will see the death of a hundred parts. You will be torn to pieces, Englishman, but you will live as your body is divided, for that is a *jetti*'s skill. To kill a man slowly, without weapons, tearing him piece by piece, and only when your screams have assuaged the pain of my brother's death will I show you mercy.' Jama gave Sharpe one last look of disdain, then turned and walked back to the shrine's steps.

Prithviraj leaned forward and rang a tiny handbell to draw the god's attention, then put his hands together and bowed his head a last time. The second *jetti*, the one with the spear, watched Sharpe with an expressionless face.

Sharpe forced himself to stand. His back ached and his legs were weak so that he tottered, making the crowd laugh at him. He took a step to his right, but the closest guard just edged away. A carved stool had been fetched from the shrine and Jama was now sitting at the top of the steps. A huge bat flickered in and out of the torchlight. Sharpe walked forward, testing his legs, and was amazed he could stand at all. The crowd jeered his faltering gait, and the sound made Prithviraj turn from his devotions. He saw that Sharpe posed no danger and so turned back to the god.

Sharpe staggered. He did it deliberately, making himself look weaker than he really was. He swayed, pretending that he was about to fall, then took some slurred sideways steps to get close to one of the guards. Seize a musket, he told himself, then ram its muzzle into Jama's face. He swayed sideways again, and the closest guard just stepped back and levelled the bayonet at Sharpe. The dozen sentries plainly had orders to keep Sharpe inside the *jetti*'s killing ground. Sharpe measured the distance, wondering if he could get past the bayonet to seize the musket, but a second guard came to reinforce the first.

Then Prithviraj stood.

He was a bloody giant, Sharpe thought, a giant with an oiled skin and upper arms as thick as most men's thighs. The crowd murmured in admiration again, and then Prithviraj undid his loincloth and let it fall so that he was naked like Sharpe. The gesture seemed to imply that he sought no advantage over his opponent, though as the huge man came down from the shrine the second *jetti* took care to stay close beside him. Two against one, and the second had a spear, and Sharpe had nothing. He glanced at the burning torches, wondering if he could seize one and brandish it as a weapon, but they were mounted too high. Christ, he thought, but do something! Anything! Panic began to close in on him, fluttering like the bat which swooped into the flame light again.

He backed away from the *jettis* and the crowd jeered him. He did not care. He was watching Prithviraj. A slow-moving man, too musclebound to be quick, and Sharpe guessed that was why the second *jetti* was present. His job would be to herd Sharpe with the glittering spear, and afterwards to hold him still as Prithviraj tore off fingers, toes and ears. So take the spearman first, Sharpe told himself, put the bastard down and take his weapon. He edged to his left, circling the courtyard to try and position himself closer to the spear-carrying *jetti*. The crowd sighed as he moved, enjoying the thought that the English-man would put up a fight.

The spear followed Sharpe's movements. He would have to be quick, Sharpe thought, desperately quick, and he doubted he could do it. Hakeswill's kicking had slowed him, but he had to try and so he kept on circling, then abruptly charged in to attack the spearman, but the weapon was jabbed towards him and Prithviraj was much faster than Sharpe had expected and leaped to catch him, and Sharpe had to twist awkwardly away. The crowd laughed at his clumsiness.

'Accept your death,' Jama called. A servant was fanning the mer-chant's face.

Sweat poured down Sharpe's cheeks. He had been forced towards that part of the courtyard nearest the temple's entrance where there were two stone flights of stairs leading up to the cloister. The steps, jutting into the yard, formed a bay in which Sharpe suddenly realized he was trapped. He moved sideways, but the spear-carrying *jetti* covered him. The two men knew he was cornered now and came slowly towards him and Sharpe could only back away until his spine touched the cloister's edge. One of the spectators kicked him, but with more malice than force. The *jettis* came on slowly, wary in case he suddenly broke to right or left. Prithviraj was flexing his huge fingers, making them supple for the night's work. Scraps of smouldering ash whirled away from the torches, one settling on Sharpe's shoulder. He brushed it off.

'Sahib?' a voice hissed from behind Sharpe. 'Sahib?'

Prithviraj looked calm and confident. No bloody wonder, Sharpe thought. So kick the naked bugger in the crotch. He reckoned that was his last chance. One good kick, and hope that Prithviraj doubled over. Either that or run onto the spear and hope the blade killed him quickly.

'Sahib!' the voice hissed again. Prithviraj was turning sideways so that he would not expose his groin to Sharpe, then he beckoned for the other *jetti* to close in on the Englishman and drive him out from the wall with his spear. 'You bugger!' the voice said impatiently.

Sharpe turned to see that Ahmed was on hands and knees among the legs of the spectators, and what was more the child was pushing forward the hilt of the *tulwar* he had captured at Deogaum. Sharpe leaned on the cloister edge and the crowd, seeing him rest against the stone, believed he had given up. Some groaned for they had been anticipating more of a fight, but most of the watching men just jeered at him for being a weakling.

Sharpe winked at Ahmed, then reached for the *tulwar*. He seized the handle, pushed away from the stone and turned, dragging the blade from the scabbard that was still in Ahmed's grasp. He turned fast as a striking snake, the curved steel silver-red in the courtyard's flame light, and the *jettis*, thinking he was a beaten man, were not prepared. The man with the spear was closest, and the curved blade slashed across his face, springing blood, and he instinctively clutched his eyes and let the spear drop. Sharpe moved to the right, scooped up the fallen spear, and Prithviraj at last looked worried.

The guards raised their muskets. Sharpe heard the clicks as the dogheads were hauled back. So let them shoot him, he thought, for that was a quicker death than being dismembered and gelded by a naked giant. Jama was standing, one hand in the air, reluctant to let his guards shoot Sharpe before he had suffered pain. The wounded *jetti* was on his knees, his hands clutched to his face which was streaming blood.

Then a musket fired, its sound unnaturally loud in the confines of the courtyard's carved walls. One of the guards flinched as the musket ball whipped past his head to chip a flake of stone from one of the decorated arches. Then a voice shouted from the cloister by the temple entrance. The man spoke in an Indian language, and he spoke to Jama who was staring appalled as a group of armed men pushed their way to the very front of the crowd.

It was Syud Sevajee who had fired, and who had spoken to Jama, and who now grinned down at Sharpe. 'I've told him it must be a fair fight, Ensign.'

'Me against him?' Sharpe jerked his chin at Prithviraj.

'We came for entertainment,' Syud Sevajee said, 'the least you can do is provide us with some.'

'Why don't you just shoot the bugger and have done with it?'

Sevajee smiled. 'This crowd will accept the result of a fair fight, Ensign. They might not like it if I simply rescue you. Besides, you don't want to be in my debt, do you?'

'I'm in your debt already,' Sharpe said, 'up to my bloody eyeballs.' He turned and looked at Prithviraj who was waiting for a sign from Jama. 'Hey! Goliath!' Sharpe shouted. 'Here!' He threw the *tulwar* at the man, keeping the spear. 'You want a fair fight? So you've got a weapon now.'

The pain seemed to have vanished and even the thirst had gone away. It was like that moment at Assaye when he had been surrounded by enemies, and suddenly the world had seemed a calm, clear-cut place full of delicious opportunity. He had a chance now. He had more than a chance, he was going to put the big bastard down. It was a fair fight, and Sharpe had grown up fighting. He had been bred to it from the gutter, driven to it by poverty and inured to it by desperation. He was nothing if he was not a fighter, and now the crowd would get the bloody sport they wanted. He hefted the spear. 'So come on, you bastard!'

Prithviraj stooped and picked up the *tulwar*. He swung it in a clumsy arc, then looked again at Jama.

'Don't look at him, you great ox! Look at me!' Sharpe went forward, the spear low, then he raised the blade and lunged towards the big man's belly and Prithviraj made a clumsy parry that rang against the spear blade. 'You'll have to put more strength into it than that,' Sharpe said, pulling back the spear and standing still to tempt the *jetti* forward. Prithviraj stepped towards him, swung the blade and Sharpe stepped back so that the *tulwar*'s tip slashed inches from his chest.

'You have to be quick,' Sharpe said, and he feinted right, spun away and walked back to the left leaving Prithviraj off balance. Sharpe turned and lunged with the spear, pricking the big man's back and leaving a trickle of blood. 'Ain't the same, is it, when the other fellow's got a weapon?' He smiled at the *jetti*. 'So come on, you daft pudding. Come on!'

The crowd was silent now. Prithviraj seemed puzzled. He had not expected to fight, not with a weapon, and it was plain he was not accustomed to a *tulwar*. 'You can give up,' Sharpe said. 'You can kneel down and give up. I won't kill you if you do that, but if you stay on your feet I'll pick you apart like a joint of bloody meat.'

Prithviraj did not understand a word, but he knew Sharpe was dangerous and he was trying to work out how best to kill him. He glanced at the spear, wishing he had that weapon instead of the *tulwar*, but Sharpe knew the point should always beat the edge, which was why he had kept the spear. 'You want it quick or slow, Sevajee?' Sharpe called.

'Whichever you prefer, Ensign,' Sevajee said, smiling. 'It is not for the audience to tell the actors how the play should go.'

'Then I'll make it quick,' Sharpe said, and he pointed at Prithviraj with his free hand and motioned that the *jetti* could kneel down. 'Just kneel,' he said, 'and I'll spare you. Tell him that, Sevajee!'

Sevajee called out in an Indian language and Prithviraj must have decided the offer was an insult, for he suddenly ran forward, *tulwar* swinging, and Sharpe had to step quickly aside and parry one of the cuts with the spear's staff. The blade cut a sliver of wood from the shaft, but went nowhere near Sharpe.

'No good doing that,' Sharpe said. 'You're not making hay, you great pudding, you're trying to stay alive.'

Prithviraj attacked again, but all he could think to do was make great swings with the blade, any one of which might have slit Sharpe into two, but the attacks were clumsy and Sharpe backed away, always circling around to the middle of the courtyard so that he was not trapped against its edges. The crowd, sensing that Prithviraj might win, began to urge him on, but some noticed that the Englishman was not even trying to fight yet. He was taunting the *jetti*, he was evading him and he was keeping his spear low.

'I thought you said it would be quick,' Sevajee said.

'You want it over?' Sharpe asked. He crouched, raising the spear blade, and the motion checked Prithviraj who stared at him warily. 'What I'm going to do,' Sharpe said, 'is cut your belly open, then slit your throat. Are you ready?' He went forward, jabbing the spear, still low, and Prithviraj backed away, trying to parry the small lunges, but Sharpe dragged the spear back each time before the parry could connect, and Prithviraj frowned. He seemed hypnotized by the shining blade that flickered like a snake's tongue, and behind it Sharpe was grinning at him and taunting him, and Prithviraj tried to counter-attack once, but the spear slashed up to within an inch of his face and he went on stepping backwards. Then he backed into the blinded *jetti* who still crouched on the flagstones and Prithviraj staggered as he lost his balance.

Sharpe came up from the crouch, the spear lancing forward and the wild parry came far too late and suddenly the blade was punching and tearing through the skin and muscle of the *jetti*'s stomach. Sharpe twisted the leaf-shaped steel so that it did not get trapped in the flesh and then he ripped it out, and blood washed across the temple floor and Prithviraj was bending forward as if he could seal the pain in his belly by folding over, and then the spear sliced from the side to slash across his throat.

The crowd sighed.

Prithviraj was on the stones now, curled up with blood bubbling from his sliced belly and pulsing from his neck.

Sharpe kicked the *tulwar* from the *jetti*'s unresisting hand, then turned and looked at Jama. 'You and your brother did business with Captain Torrance?'

Jama said nothing.

Sharpe walked towards the shrine. The guards moved to stop him, but Sevajee's men raised their muskets and some, grinning, jumped down into the courtyard. Ahmed also jumped down and snatched the *tulwar* from the flagstones. Prithviraj was on his side now, dying.

Jama stood as Sharpe reached the steps, but he could not move fast with his limp and suddenly the spear was at his belly. 'I asked you a question,' Sharpe said.

Jama still said nothing.

'You want to live?' Sharpe asked. Jama looked down at the spear blade that was thick with blood. 'Was it Torrance who gave me to you?' Sharpe asked.

'Yes,' Jama said.

'If I see you again,' Sharpe said, 'I'll kill you. If you go back to the British camp I'll hang you like your brother, and if you so much as send a message to Torrance, I'll follow you to the last corner on God's earth and I'll castrate you with my bare hands.' He jabbed the spear just enough to prick Jama's belly, then turned away. The crowd was silent, cowed by Sevajee's men and by the ferocity they had witnessed in the temple courtyard. Sharpe tossed away the spear, pulled Ahmed towards him and patted the boy's head. 'You're a good lad, Ahmed. A bloody good lad. And I need a drink. By Christ, I'm thirsty.'

But he was also alive.

Which meant some other men would soon be dead.

Because Sharpe was more than alive. He was angry. Angry as hell. And wanting revenge.

Sharpe borrowed a cloak from one of Sevajee's men, then pulled himself up behind Ahmed onto Major Stokes's horse. They rode slowly away from the village where the torches guttered in the temple towards the smear of red light that betrayed where the British encampment lay some miles to the west. Sevajee talked as they rode, telling Sharpe how Ahmed had fled straight into the arms of his men. 'Luckily for you, Ensign,' the Indian said, 'I recognized him.'

'Which is why you sent for help, isn't it?' Sharpe asked sarcastically. 'It's why you fetched some redcoats to get me out of that bloody tent.'

'Your gratitude touches me deeply,' Sevajee said with a smile. 'It took us a long time to make sense of what your boy was saying, and I confess we didn't wholly believe him even then, and by the time we thought to take him seriously, you were already being carried away. So we followed. I thought we might fetch some entertainment from the evening, and so we did.'

'Glad to be of service, sahib,' Sharpe said.

'I knew you could beat a *jetti* in a fair fight.'

'I beat three at once in Seringapatam,' Sharpe said, 'but I don't know as it was a fair fight. I'm not much in favour of fair fights. I like them to be unfair. Fair fights are for gentlemen who don't know any better.'

'Which is why you gave the sword to the *jetti*,' Sevajee observed drily.

'I knew he'd make a bollocks of it,' Sharpe said. He was tired suddenly, and all the aches and throbs and agony had come back. Above him the sky was brilliant with stars, while a thin sickle moon hung just above the faraway fortress. Dodd was up there, Sharpe thought, another life to take. Dodd and Torrance, Hakeswill and his two men. A debt to be paid by sending all the bastards to hell.

'Where shall I take you?' Sevajee asked.

'Take me?'

'You want to go to the General?'

'Christ, no.' Sharpe could not imagine complaining to Wellesley. The cold bugger would probably blame Sharpe for getting into trouble. Stokes, maybe? Or the cavalry? Sergeant Lockhart would doubtless welcome him, but then he had a better idea. 'Take me to wherever you're camped,' he told Sevajee.

'And in the morning?'

'You've got a new recruit,' Sharpe said. 'I'm one of your men for now.'

Sevajee looked amused. 'Why?'

'Why do you think? I want to hide.'

'But why?'

Sharpe sighed. 'D'you think Wellesley will believe me? If I go to Wellesley he'll think I've got sunstroke, or he'll reckon I'm drunk. And Torrance will stand there with a plum in his bloody mouth and deny everything, or else he'll blame Hakeswill.'

'Hakeswill?' Sevajee asked.

'A bastard I'm going to kill,' Sharpe said. 'And it'll be easier if he doesn't know I'm still alive.' And this time, Sharpe vowed, he would make sure of the bastard. 'My only worry,' he told Sevajee, 'is Major Stokes's horse. He's a good man, Stokes.'

'That horse?' Sevajee asked, nodding at the grey mare.

'You reckon a couple of your fellows could return it to him in the morning?'

'Of course.'

'Tell him I got thrown from the saddle and snatched up by the enemy,' Sharpe said. 'Let him think I'm a prisoner in Gawilghur.'

'And meanwhile you'll be one of us?' Sevajee asked.

'I've just become a Mahratta,' Sharpe said.

'Welcome,' said Sevajee. 'And what you need now, Sharpe, is some rest.'

'I've had plenty of rest,' Sharpe said. 'What I need now are some clothes, and some darkness.'

'You need food too,' Sevajee insisted. He glanced up at the sliver of moon above the fort. It was waning. 'Tomorrow night will be darker,' he promised, and Sharpe nodded. He wanted a deep darkness, a shadowed blackness, in which a living ghost could hunt.

Major Stokes was grateful for the return of his horse, but saddened over Sharpe's fate. 'Captured!' he told Sir Arthur Wellesley. 'And my own fault too.'

'Can't see how that can be, Stokes.'

'I should never have let him ride off on his own. Should have made him wait till a group went back.'

'Won't be the first prison cell he's seen,' Wellesley said, 'and I daresay it won't be the last.'

'I shall miss him,' Stokes said, 'miss him deeply. A good man.'

Wellesley grunted. He had ridden up the improved road to judge its progress for himself and he was impressed, though he took care not to show his approval. The road now snaked up into the hills and one more day's work would see it reach the edge of the escarpment. Half the necessary siege guns were already high on the road, parked in an upland meadow, while bullocks were trudging up the lower slopes with their heavy burdens of round shot that would be needed to break open Gawilghur's walls. The Mahrattas had virtually ceased their raids on the road-makers ever since Wellesley had sent two battalions of sepoys up into the hills to hunt the enemy down. Every once in a while a musket shot would be fired from a long distance, but the balls were usually spent before they reached a target. 'Your work won't end with the road,' Wellesley told Stokes, as the General and his staff followed the engineer on foot towards some higher ground from where they could inspect the fortress.

'I doubted it would, sir.'

'You know Stevenson?'

'I've dined with the Colonel.'

'I'm sending him up here. His troops will make the assault. My men will stay below and climb the two roads.' Wellesley spoke curtly, almost offhandedly. He was proposing to divide his army into two again, just as it had been split for most of the war against the Mahrattas. Stevenson's part of the army would climb to the plateau and make the main assault on the fortress. That attack would swarm across the narrow neck of land to climb the breaches, but to stop the enemy from throwing all their strength into the defence of the broken wall Wellesley proposed sending two columns of his own men up the steep tracks that led directly to the fortress. Those men would have to approach unbroken walls up slopes too steep to permit artillery to be deployed, and Wellesley knew those columns could never hope to break into Gawilghur. Their job was to spread the defenders thin, and to block off the garrison's escape routes while Colonel Stevenson's men did the bloody work. 'You'll have to establish Stevenson's batteries,' Wellesley told Stokes. 'Major Blackiston's seen the ground' – he indicated his aide – 'and he reckons two eighteens and three iron twelves should suffice. Major Blackiston, of course, will give you whatever advice he can.'

'No glacis?' Stokes directed the question to Blackiston.

'Not when I was there,' Blackiston said, 'though of course they could have made one since. I just saw curtain walls with a few bastions. Ancient work, by the look of it.'

'Fifteenth-century work,' Wellesley put in and, when he saw that the two engineers were impressed by his knowledge, he shrugged. 'Syud Sevajee claims as much, anyway.'

'Old walls break fastest,' Stokes said cheerfully. The two big guns, with the three smaller cannon, would batter the wall head on to crumble the ancient stone that was probably unprotected by a glacis of embanked earth to soak up the force of the bombardment, and the Major had yet to find a fortress wall in India that could resist the strike of an eighteen-pounder shot travelling half a mile every two seconds. 'But you'll want some enfilading fire,' he warned Wellesley.

'I'll send you some more twelves,' Wellesley promised.

'A battery of twelves and an howitzer,' Stokes suggested. 'I'd like to drop some nasties over the wall. There's nothing like an howitzer for spreading gloom.'

'I'll send an howitzer,' Wellesley promised. The enfilading batteries would fire at an angle through the growing breaches to keep the enemy from making repairs, and the howitzer, which fired high in the air so that its shells dropped steeply down, could bombard the repair parties behind the fortress ramparts. 'And I want the batteries established quickly,' Wellesley said. 'No dallying, Major.'

'I'm not a man to dally, Sir Arthur,' Stokes said cheerfully. The Major was leading the General and his staff up a particularly steep patch of road where an elephant, supplemented by over sixty sweating sepoys, forced an eighteen-pounder gun up the twisting road. The officers dodged the sepoys, then climbed a knoll from where they could stare across at Gawilghur.

By now they were nearly as high as the stronghold itself and the profile of the twin forts stood clear against the bright sky beyond. It formed a double hump. The narrow neck of land led from the plateau to the first, lower hump on which the Outer Fortress stood. It was that fortress which would receive Stokes's breaching fire, and that fortress which would be assailed by Stevenson's men, but beyond it the ground dropped into a deep ravine, then climbed steeply to the much larger second hump on which the Inner Fortress with its palace and its lakes and its houses stood. Sir Arthur spent a long time staring through his glass, but said nothing.

'I'll warrant I can get you into the smaller fortress,' Stokes said, 'but how do you cross the central ravine into the main stronghold?'

It was that question that Wellesley had yet to answer in his own mind, and he suspected there was no simple solution. He hoped that the attackers would simply surge across the ravine and flood up the second slope like an irresistible wave that had broken through one barrier and would now overcome everything in its path, but he dared not admit to such impractical optimism. He dared not confess that he was condemning his men to an attack on an Inner Fortress that would have unbreached walls and well-prepared defenders. 'If we can't take it by escalade,' he said curtly, collapsing his glass, 'we'll have to dig breaching batteries in the Outer Fortress and do it the hard way.'

In other words, Stokes thought, Sir Arthur had no idea how it was to be done. Only that it must be done. By escalade or by breach, and by God's mercy, if they were lucky, for once they were into the central ravine the attackers would be in the devil's hands.

It was a hot December day, but Stokes shivered, for he feared for the men who must go up against Gawilghur.

Captain Torrance had enjoyed a remarkably lucky evening. Jama had still not returned to the camp, and his big green tents with their varied delights stood empty, but there were plenty of other diversions in the British camp. A group of Scottish officers, augmented by a sergeant who played the flute, gave a concert, and though Torrance had no great taste for chamber music he found the melodies were in tune with his jaunty mood. Sharpe was gone, Torrance's debts were paid, he had survived, and he had strolled on from the concert to the cavalry lines where he knew he would find a game of whist. Torrance had succeeded in taking fifty-three guineas from an irascible major and another twelve from a whey-cheeked ensign who kept scratching his groin. 'If you've got the pox,' the Major had finally said, 'then get the hell to a surgeon.'

'It's lice, sir.'

'Then for Christ's sake stop wriggling. You're distracting me.'

'Scratch on,' Torrance had said, laying down a winning hand. He had yawned, scooped up the coins, and bid his partners a good night.

'It's devilish early,' the Major had grumbled, wanting a chance to win his money back.

'Duty,' Torrance had said vaguely, then he had strolled to the merchant encampment and inspected the women who fanned themselves in the torrid night heat. An hour later, well pleased with himself, he had returned to his quarters. His servant squatted on the porch, but he waved the man away.

Sajit was still at his candle-lit desk, unclogging his pen of the soggy paper scraps that collected on the nib. He stood, touched his inky hands together and bowed as Torrance entered. 'Sahib.'

'All well?'

'All is well, sahib. Tomorrow's chitties.' He pushed a pile of papers across the desk.

'I'm sure they're in order,' Torrance said, quite confident that he spoke true. Sajit was proving to be an excellent clerk. He went to the door of his quarters, then turned with a frown. 'Your uncle hasn't come back?'

'Tomorrow, sahib, I'm sure.'

'Tell him I'd like a word. But not if he comes tonight. I don't want to be disturbed tonight.'

'Of course not, sahib.' Sajit offered another bow as Torrance negotiated the door and the muslin screen.

The Captain shot the iron bolt, then chased down the few moths that had managed to get past the muslin. He lit a second lamp, piled the night's winnings on the table, then called for Clare. She came sleepy-eyed from the kitchen.

'Arrack, Brick,' Torrance ordered, then peeled off his coat while Clare unstoppered a fresh jar of the fierce spirit. She kept her eyes averted as Torrance stripped himself naked and lay back in his hammock. 'You could light me a hookah, Brick,' he suggested, 'then sponge me down. Is there a clean shirt for the morning?'

'Of course, sir.'

'Not the darned one?'

'No, sir.'

He turned his head to stare at the coins which glittered so prettily in the smoky lamplight. In funds again! Winning! Perhaps his luck had turned. It seemed so. He had lost so much money at cards in the last month that he had thought nothing but ruin awaited him, but now the goddess of fortune had turned her other cheek. Rule of halves, he told himself as he sucked on the hookah. Save half, gamble the other half. Halve the winnings and save half again. Simple really. And now that Sharpe was gone he could begin some careful trading once more, though how the market would hold up once the Mahrattas were defeated he could not tell. Still, with a slice of luck he might make sufficient money to set himself up in a comfortable civilian life in Madras. A carriage, a dozen horses and as many women servants. He would have an harem. He smiled at the thought, imagining his father's disgust. An harem, a courtyard with a fountain, a wine cellar deep beneath his house that should be built close to the sea so that cooling breezes could waft through its windows. He would need to spend an hour or two at the office each week, but certainly not more for there were always Indians to do the real work. The buggers would cheat him, of course, but there seemed plenty of money to go around so long as a man did not gamble it away. Rule of halves, he told himself again. The golden rule of life.

The sound of singing came from the camp beyond the village. Torrance did not recognize the tune, which was probably some Scottish song. The sound drifted him back to his childhood when he had sung in the cathedral choir. He grimaced, remembering the frosty mornings when he had run in the dark across the close and pushed open the cathedral's great side door to be greeted by a clout over the ear because he was late. The choristers' cloudy breath had mingled with the smoke of the guttering candles. Lice under the robes, he remembered. He had caught his first lice off a counter-tenor who had held him against a wall behind a bishop's tomb and hoisted his robe. I hope the bastard's dead, he thought.

Sajit yelped. 'Quiet!' Torrance shouted, resenting being jarred from his reverie. There was silence again, and Torrance sucked on the hookah. He could hear Clare pouring water in the yard and he smiled as he anticipated the soothing touch of the sponge.

Someone, it had to be Sajit, tried to open the door from the front room. 'Go away,' Torrance called, but then something hit the door a massive blow. The bolt held, though dust sifted from crevices in the plaster wall either side of the frame. Torrance stared in shock, then twitched with alarm as another huge bang shook the door, and this time a chunk of plaster the size of a dinner plate fell from the wall. Torrance swung his bare legs out of the hammock. Where the devil were his pistols?

A third blow reverberated round the room, and this time the bracket holding the bolt was wrenched out of the wall and the door swung in onto the muslin screen. Torrance saw a robed figure sweep the screen aside, then he threw himself over the room and pawed through his discarded clothes to find his guns.

A hand gripped his wrist. 'You won't need that, sir,' a familiar voice said, and Torrance turned, wincing at the strength of the man's grip. He saw a figure dressed in blood-spattered Indian robes, with a *tulwar* scabbarded at his waist and a face shrouded by a head cloth. But Torrance recognized his visitor and blanched. 'Reporting for duty, sir,' Sharpe said, taking the pistol from Torrance's unresisting grip.

Torrance gaped. He could have sworn that the blood on the robe was fresh for it gleamed wetly. There was more blood on a short-bladed knife in Sharpe's hand. It dripped onto the floor and Torrance gave a small pitiful mew.

'It's Sajit's blood,' Sharpe said. 'His penknife too.' He tossed the wet blade onto the table beside the gold coins. 'Lost your tongue, sir?'

'Sharpe?'

'He's dead, sir, Sharpe is,' Sharpe said. 'He was sold to Jama, remember, sir? Is that the blood money?' Sharpe glanced at the rupees on the table.

'Sharpe,' Torrance said again, somehow incapable of saying any-thing else.

'I'm his ghost, sir,' Sharpe said, and Torrance did indeed look as though a spectre had just broken through his door. Sharpe tutted and shook his head in self-reproof. 'I'm not supposed to call you "sir", am I, sir? On account of me being a fellow officer and a gentleman. Where's Sergeant Hakeswill?'

'Sharpe!' Torrance said once more, collapsing onto a chair. 'We heard you'd been captured!'

'So I was, sir, but not by the enemy. Leastwise, not by any proper enemy.' Sharpe examined the pistol. 'This ain't loaded. What were you hoping to do, sir? Beat me to death with the barrel?'

'My robe, Sharpe, please,' Torrance said, gesturing to where the silk robe hung on a wooden peg.

'So where is Hakeswill, sir?' Sharpe asked. He had pushed back his head cloth and now opened the pistol's frizzen and blew dust off the pan before scraping at the layer of caked powder with a fingernail.

'He's on the road,' Torrance said.

'Ah! Took over from me, did he? You should keep this pistol clean, sir. There's rust on the spring, see? Shame to keep an expensive gun so shabbily. Are you sitting on your cartridge box?'

Torrance meekly raised his bottom to take out his leather pouch which held the powder and bullets for his pistols. He gave the bag to Sharpe, thought about fetching the robe himself, then decided that any untoward move might upset his visitor. 'I'm delighted to see you're alive, Sharpe,' he said.

'Are you, sir?' Sharpe asked.

'Of course.'

'Then why did you sell me to Jama?'

'Sell you? Don't be ridiculous, Sharpe. No!' The cry came as the pistol barrel whipped towards him, and it turned into a moan as the barrel slashed across his cheek. Torrance touched his face and winced at the blood on his fingers. 'Sharpe –' he began.

'Shut it, sir,' Sharpe said nastily. He perched on the table and poured some powder into the pistol barrel. 'I talked to Jama last night. He tried to have me killed by a couple of *jettis*. You know what *jettis* are, sir? Religious strongmen, sir, but they must have been praying to the wrong God, for I cut one's throat and left the other bugger blinded.' He paused to select a bullet from the pouch. 'And I had a chat with

178

Jama when I'd killed his thugs and he told me lots of interesting things. Like that you traded with him and his brother. You're a traitor, Torrance.'

'Sharpe –'

'I said shut it!' Sharpe snapped. He pushed the bullet into the pistol's muzzle, then drew out the short ramrod and shoved it down the barrel. 'The thing is, Torrance,' he went on in a calmer tone, 'I know the truth. All of it. About you and Hakeswill and about you and Jama and about you and Naig.' He smiled at Torrance, then slotted the short ramrod back into its hoops. 'I used to think officers were above that sort of crime. I knew the men were crooked, because I was crooked, but you don't have much choice, do you, when you've got nothing? But you, sir, you had everything you wanted. Rich parents, proper schooling.' Sharpe shook his head.

'You don't understand, Sharpe.'

'But I do, sir. Now look at me. My ma was a whore, and not a very good one by all accounts, and she went and died and left me with nothing. Bloody nothing! And the thing is, sir, that when I go to General Wellesley and I tells him about you selling muskets to the enemy, who's he going to believe? You, with your proper education, or me with a dead frow as a mother?' Sharpe looked at Torrance as though he expected an answer, but none came. 'He's going to believe you, sir, isn't he? He'd never believe me, on account of me not being a proper gentleman who knows his Latin. And you know what that means, sir?'

'Sharpe?'

'It means justice won't be done, sir. But, on the other hand, you're a gentleman, so you knows your duty, don't you?' Sharpe edged off the table and gave the pistol, butt first, to Torrance. 'Hold it just in front of your ear,' he advised Torrance, 'or else put it in your mouth. Makes more mess that way, but it's surer.'

'Sharpe!' Torrance said, and found he had nothing to say. The pistol felt heavy in his hand.

'It won't hurt, sir,' Sharpe said comfortingly. 'You'll be dead in the blink of an eyelid.' He began scooping the coins off the table into Torrance's pouch. He heard the heavy click as the pistol was cocked, then glanced round to see that the muzzle was pointing at his face. He frowned and shook his head in disappointment. 'And I thought you were a gentleman, sir.'

'I'm not a fool, Sharpe,' Torrance said vengefully. He stood and took a pace closer to the Ensign. 'And I'm worth ten of you. Up from the ranks? You know what that makes you, Sharpe? It makes you a brute, a lucky brute, but it don't make you a real officer. You're not going to be welcome anywhere, Sharpe. You'll be endured, Sharpe, because officers have manners, but they won't welcome you because you ain't a proper officer. You weren't born to it, Sharpe.' Torrance laughed at the look of horrified outrage on Sharpe's face. 'Christ, I despise you!' he said savagely. 'You're like a dressed-up monkey, Sharpe, only you can't even wear clothes properly! I could give you lace and braid, and you'd still look like a peasant, because that's what you are, Sharpe. Officers should have style! They should have wit! And all you can do is grunt. You know what you are, Sharpe? You're an embarrassment, you're . . .' He paused, trying to find the right insult, and shook his head in frustration as the words would not come. 'You're a lump, Sharpe! That's what you are, a lump! And the kindest thing is to finish you off.' Torrance smiled. 'Goodbye, Mister Sharpe.' He pulled the trigger.

The flint smashed down on the steel and the spark flashed into the empty pan.

Sharpe reached out in the silence and took the pistol from Torrance's hand. 'I loaded it, sir, but I didn't prime it. On account of the fact that I might be a lump, but I ain't any kind of fool.' He pushed Torrance back into the chair, and Torrance could only watch as Sharpe dropped a pinch of powder into the pan. He flinched as Sharpe closed the frizzen, then shuddered as Sharpe walked towards him.

'No, Sharpe, no!'

Sharpe stood behind Torrance. 'You tried to have me killed, sir, and I don't like that.' He pressed the pistol into the side of the Captain's head.

'Sharpe!' Torrance pleaded. He was shaking, but he seemed power-less to offer any resistance, then the muslin curtain from the kitchen was swept aside and Clare Wall came into the room. She stopped and stared with huge eyes at Sharpe.

'Clare!' Torrance pleaded. 'Fetch help! Quickly now!' Clare did not move. 'Fetch help, my dear!' Torrance said. 'She'll be a witness against you, Sharpe.' Torrance had turned to look at Sharpe and was babbling now. 'So the best thing you can do is to put the gun down. I'll say nothing about this, nothing! Just a touch of fever in you, I expect. It's all a misunderstanding and we shall forget it ever happened. Maybe we could share a bottle of arrack? Clare, my dear, maybe you could find a bottle?'

Clare stepped towards Sharpe and held out her hand.

'Fetch help, my dear,' Torrance said, 'he's not going to give you the gun.'

'He is,' Sharpe said, and he gave Clare the pistol.

Torrance breathed a great sigh of relief, then Clare clumsily turned the gun and pointed it at Torrance's head. The Captain just stared at her.

'Eyes front, Captain,' Sharpe said, and turned Torrance's head so that the bullet would enter from the side, just as it might if Torrance had committed suicide. 'Are you sure?' he asked Clare.

'God help me,' she said, 'but I've dreamed of doing this.' She straightened her arm so that the pistol's muzzle touched Torrance's temple.

'No!' he called. 'No, please! No!'

But she could not pull the trigger. Sharpe could see she wanted to, but her finger would not tighten and so Sharpe took the gun from her, edged her gently aside, then pushed the barrel into Torrance's oiled hair. 'No, please!' the Captain appealed. He was weeping. 'I beg you, Sharpe. Please!'

Sharpe pulled the trigger, stepping back as a gush of blood spouted from the shattered skull. The sound of the pistol had been hugely loud in the small room that was now hazed with smoke.

Sharpe knelt and pushed the pistol into Torrance's dead hand, then picked up the pouch with its gold and thrust it into Clare's hands. 'We're going,' he told her, 'right now.'

She understood the haste and, without bothering to fetch any of her belongings, followed him back into the outer room where Sajit's body lay slumped over the table. His blood had soaked the chitties. Clare whimpered when she saw the blood. 'I didn't really mean to kill him,' Sharpe explained, 'then realized he'd be a witness if I didn't.' He saw the fear on Clare's face. 'I trust you, love. You and me? We're the same, aren't we? So come on, let's get the hell out of here.'

Sharpe had already taken the three jewels from Sajit and he added those to the pouch of gold, then went to the porch where Ahmed stood guard. No one seemed to have been alarmed by the shot, but it was not wise to linger. 'I've got you some gold, Ahmed,' Sharpe said.

'Gold!'

'You know that word, you little bugger, don't you?' Sharpe grinned, then took Clare's hand and led her into the shadows. A dog barked briefly, a horse whinnied from the cavalry lines, and afterwards there was silence.

CHAPTER 7

Dodd needed to practise with the rifle and so, on the day that the British reached the top of the high escarpment, he settled himself in some rocks at the top of the cliff and gauged the range to the party of sepoys who were levelling the last few yards of the road. Unlike a musket, the rifle had proper sights, and he set the range at two hundred yards, then propped the barrel in a stone cleft and aimed at a blue-coated engineer who was standing just beneath the sweating sepoys. A gust of wind swept up the cliffs, driving some circling buzzards high up into the air. Dodd waited until the wind settled, then squeezed the trigger.

The rifle slammed into his shoulder with surprising force. The smoke blotted his view instantly, but another billow of wind carried it away and he was rewarded by the sight of the engineer bent double. He thought he must have hit the man, but then saw the engineer had been picking up his straw hat that must have fallen as he reacted to the close passage of the spinning bullet. The engineer beat dust from the hat against his thigh and stared up at the drifting patch of smoke.

Dodd wriggled back out of view and reloaded the rifle. It was hard work. The barrel of a rifle, unlike a musket, had spiralling grooves cast into the barrel to spin the bullet. The spin made the weapon extraordinarily accurate, but the grooves resisted the rammer, and the resistance was made worse because the bullet, if it was to be spun by the grooves, had to fit the barrel tightly. Dodd wrapped a bullet in one of the small greased leather patches that gave the barrel purchase, then grunted as he shoved the ramrod hard down. One of the Mahratta cavalrymen who escorted Dodd on his daily rides shouted a warning, and Dodd peered over the rock to see that a company of sepoy infantry was scrambling to the top of the slope. The first of them were already on the plateau and coming towards him. He primed the rifle, settled it on the makeshift firestep again and reckoned that he had not allowed for the effect of the wind on the last bullet. He aimed at the sepoys' officer, a man whose small round spectacles reflected the sun, and, letting the barrel edge slightly windwards, he fired again.

The rifle hammered back onto his shoulder. Smoke billowed as Dodd ran to his horse and clambered into the saddle. He slung the rifle, turned the horse and saw that the red-coated officer was on the ground with two of his men kneeling beside him. He grinned. Two hundred paces!

A wild volley of musketry followed the Mahratta horsemen as they rode westwards towards Gawilghur. The balls rattled on rocks or whistled overhead, but none of the cavalrymen was touched. After half a mile Dodd stopped, dismounted and reloaded the rifle. A troop of sepoy cavalry was climbing the last few yards of the road, the men walking as they led their horses around the final steep bend. Dodd found another place to rest the rifle, then waited for the cavalry to approach along the cliff's edge.

He kept the sights at two hundred yards. He knew that was very long range, even for a rifle, but if he could hit at two hundred yards then he was confident of killing at a hundred or at fifty.

'Sahib!' The commander of his escort was worried by the more numerous sepoy cavalry who had now mounted and were trotting towards them.

'In a minute,' Dodd called back. He picked his target, another officer, and waited for the man to ride into the rifle's sights. The wind was fitful. It gusted, blowing dust into Dodd's right eye and making him blink. Sweat trickled down his face. The approaching cavalry had sabres drawn and the blades glittered in the sun. One man carried a dusty pennant on a short staff. They came raggedly, twisting between the rocks and low bushes. Their horses kept their heads low, tired after the effort of climbing the steep hill.

The officer curbed his horse to let his men catch up. The wind died to nothing and Dodd squeezed the trigger and flinched as the heavy stock slammed into his bruised shoulder.

'Sahib!'

'We're going,' Dodd said, and he put his left foot into the stirrup and heaved himself into the saddle. A glance behind showed a riderless horse and a score of men spurring forward to take revenge. Dodd laughed, slung the rifle, and kicked his horse into a canter. He heard a shout behind as the sepoy cavalry were urged into the pursuit, but Dodd and his escort were mounted on fresh horses and easily outstripped the sepoys.

Dodd curbed his horse on the neck of rocky land that led to Gawilghur's Outer Fort. The walls were thick with men who watched the enemy's approach, and the sight of those spectators gave Dodd an idea. He threw the rifle to the commander of his escort. 'Hold it for me!' he ordered, then turned his horse to face the pursuing horsemen. He waved his escort on towards the fortress and drew his sword. It was a beautiful weapon, European made, then sent to India where craftsmen had given it a hilt of gold shaped like an elephant's head. The escort commander, charged with protecting Dodd's life, wanted to stay, but Dodd insisted he ride on. 'I'll join you in five minutes,' he promised.

Dodd barred the road. He glanced behind him once, just to check that the Outer Fort's ramparts were crowded with men, then he looked back to the approaching cavalry. They slowed as they reached the rock isthmus. They could have kept galloping, and Dodd would then have turned his horse and outrun them, but instead they curbed their sweating horses and just stood watching him from a hundred paces away. They knew what he wanted, but Dodd saluted them with his sword just to make certain they understood his challenge. A havildar urged his horse forward, but then an English voice summoned him back and the man reluctantly turned.

The English officer drew his sabre. He had lost his hat in the gallop along the edge of the cliff and had long fair hair that was matted with sweat and dirt. He wore a black and scarlet jacket and was mounted on a tall bay gelding that was white with sweat. He saluted Dodd by holding his sabre up, hilt before his face, then he touched the gelding's flanks with the tips of his spurs and the horse walked forward. Dodd spurred his own horse and the two slowly closed. The Englishman went into a trot, then clapped his heels to drive his horse into a canter and Dodd saw the puffs of dust spurting from the gelding's hooves. He kept his horse at a walk, only touching it into a trot at the very last second as the Englishman stood in his stirrups to deliver a scything cut with the sabre.

Dodd tweaked the rein and his horse swerved to the left, then he was turning it back right, turning it all the way, and the sabre had missed his head by a scant two inches and he had not even bothered to parry with his sword. Now he spurred the horse on, following the officer who was trying to turn back, and the Englishman was still half turned, still tugging on the reins, as Dodd attacked. The sabre made an awkward parry that just managed to deflect the sword's thrust. Dodd hacked back as he passed, felt the blade thump home, then he hauled on the reins and was turning again, and the Englishman was also turning so that the two horses seemed to curl around each other, nose to tail, and the sabre and sword rang together. Dodd was taller than his opponent, but the young Englishman, who was a lieutenant and scarce looked a day over eighteen, was strong, and Dodd's blow had hardly broken the weave of his coat. He gritted his teeth as he hacked at Dodd, and Dodd parried, parried again and the two blades locked, hilt against hilt, and Dodd heaved to try and throw the young man off balance.

'You're Dodd, aren't you?' the Lieutenant said.

'Seven hundred guineas to you, boy.'

'Traitor,' the young Englishman spat.

Dodd heaved, then kicked the Lieutenant's horse so that it moved forward and he tried to slash back with his disengaged sword, but the Lieutenant turned the horse in again. The men were too close to fight properly, close enough to smell each other's breath. The Lieutenant's stank of tobacco. They could hit their opponent with their sword hilts, but not use the blades' lengths. If either horse had been properly schooled they could have been walked sideways away from the impasse, but the horses would only go forward and Dodd was the first to take the risk by using his spurs. He used them savagely, startling his horse so that it leaped ahead, and even so he flinched from the expected slash as the sabre whipped towards his spine, but the Lieutenant was slow and the blow missed.

Dodd rode twenty paces up the track towards the watching sepoys, then turned again. The Lieutenant was gaining confidence and he grinned as the tall man charged at him. He lowered the sabre, using its point like a spearhead, and urged his weary gelding into a trot. Dodd also had his sword at the lunge, elbow locked, and the two horses closed at frightening speed and then, at the very last second,

Dodd hauled on his rein and his horse went right, to the Lieutenant's unguarded side, and he brought the sword back across his body and then cut it forward in one fluid motion so that the blade raked across the Lieutenant's throat. The sabre was still coming across to the parry when the blood spurted. The Lieutenant faltered and his horse stopped. The young man's sword arm fell, and Dodd was turning. He came alongside his opponent whose jacket was now dark with blood, and he rammed the sword into the Lieutenant's neck a second time, this time point first, and the young man seemed to shake like a rat in a terrier's jaws.

Dodd hauled his sword free, then scabbarded it. He leaned over and took the sabre from the dying man's unresisting hand, then pushed the Lieutenant so that he toppled from the horse. One of his feet was trapped in a stirrup, but as Dodd seized the gelding's rein and hauled it round towards the fortress, the boot fell free and the young man was left sprawling amidst his blood on the dusty road as Dodd led his trophy homewards.

The Indians on the ramparts cheered. The sepoys spurred forward and Dodd hurried ahead of them, but the Madrassi cavalrymen only rode as far as their officer's body where they dismounted. Dodd rode on, waving the captured sabre aloft.

A gun fired from the fort and the ball screamed over the rocky isthmus to crash home among the cavalrymen gathered about their officer. A second gun fired, and suddenly the British cavalry and their riderless horses were running away and the cheers on the wall redoubled. Manu Bappoo was on the big buttress close to the gatehouse and he first pointed an admonitory finger at Dodd, chiding him for taking such a risk, then he touched his hands together, in thanks for Dodd's victory, and finally raised his arms above his head to salute the hero. Dodd laughed and bowed his head in acknowledgement and saw, to his surprise, that his white coat was red with the Lieutenant's blood. 'Who would have thought the young man had so much blood in him?' he asked the leader of his escort at the fortress gate.

'Sahib?' the man answered, puzzled.

'Never mind.' Dodd took the rifle back, then spurred his horse into Gawilghur's Delhi Gate. The men on the ramparts that edged the paved entranceway cheered him home.

He did not pause to speak to Manu Bappoo, but instead rode through the Outer Fortress and out of its southern gate, then led his captured horse down the steep path which slanted across the face of the ravine. At the bottom the path turned sharply to the left before climbing to the Inner Fort's massive gateway. The four heavy gates that barred the entranceway were all opened for him, and the hooves of his two horses echoed from the high walls as he clattered up the winding passage. One by one the gates crashed shut behind and the thick locking bars were dropped into their brackets.

His groom waited beyond the last gate. Dodd swung down from his horse and gave both reins to the man, ordering him to water the captured horse before he rubbed it down. He handed his sword to his servant and told him to clean the blood from the blade and only then did he turn to face Beny Singh who had come waddling from the palace garden. The Killadar was dressed in a green silk robe and was attended by two servants, one to hold a parasol above Beny Singh's perfumed head and the other clasping the Killadar's small white lap dog. 'The cheering,' Beny Singh asked anxiously, 'what was it? The guns were firing?' He stared in horror at the blood soaked into Dodd's coat. 'You're wounded, Colonel?'

'There was a fight,' Dodd said, and waited while one of the servants translated for the Killadar. Dodd spoke a crude Marathi, but it was easier to use interpreters.

'The *djinns* are here!' Beny Singh wailed. The dog whimpered and the two servants looked nervous.

'I killed a *djinn*,' Dodd snarled. He reached out and took hold of Beny Singh's plump hand and forced it against his wet coat. 'It isn't my blood. But it is fresh.' He rubbed the Killadar's hand into the gory patch, then raised the plump fingers to his mouth. Keeping his eyes on Beny Singh's eyes, he licked the blood from the Killadar's hand. 'I am a *djinn*, Killadar,' Dodd said, letting go of the hand, 'and I lap the blood of my enemies.'

Beny Singh recoiled from the clammy touch of the blood. He shuddered, then wiped his hand on his silk robe. 'When will they assault?'

'A week?' Dodd guessed. 'And then they will be defeated.'

'But what if they get in?' Beny Singh asked anxiously.

'Then they will kill you,' Dodd said, 'and afterwards rape your wife, your concubines and your daughters. They'll line up for the pleasure, Killadar. They'll rut like hogs,' and Dodd grunted like a pig and jerked his groin forward, driving Beny Singh back.

'They won't!' the Killadar declared.

'Because they won't get in,' Dodd said, 'because some of us are men, and we will fight.'

'I have poison!' Beny Singh said, not comprehending Dodd's last words. 'If they look like winning, Colonel, you'll send me word?'

Dodd smiled. 'You have my promise, sahib,' he said with a pretended humility.

'Better my women should die,' Beny Singh insisted.

'Better that you should die,' Dodd said, 'unless you want to be forced to watch the white *djinns* take their pleasure on your dying women.'

'They wouldn't!'

'What else do they want in here?' Dodd asked. 'Have they not heard of the beauty of your women? Each night they talk of them around their fires, and every day they dream of their thighs and their breasts. They can't wait, Killadar. The pleasures of your women pull the redcoats towards us.'

Beny Singh fled from the horrid words and Dodd smiled. He had come to realize that only one man could command here. Beny Singh was the fortress commander and though he was a despicable coward he was also a friend of the Rajah's, and that friendship ensured the loyalty of much of Gawilghur's standing garrison. The rest of the fortress defenders were divided into two camps. There were Manu Bappoo's soldiers, led by the remnants of the Lions of Allah and loyal to the Prince, and Dodd's Cobras. But if only one of the three leaders was left, then that man would rule Gawilghur, and whoever ruled Gawilghur could rule all India.

Dodd touched the stock of the rifle. That would help, and Beny Singh's abject terror would render the Killadar harmless. Dodd smiled and climbed to the ramparts from where, with a telescope, he watched the British heave the first gun up to the edge of the plateau. A week, he thought, maybe a day more, and then the British would come to his slaughter. And make his wildly ambitious dreams come true.

'The fellow was using a rifle!' Major Stokes said in wonderment. 'I do declare, a rifle! Can't have been anything else at that range. Two hundred paces if it was an inch, and he fanned my head! A much underestimated weapon, the rifle, don't you think?'

'A toy,' Captain Morris said. 'Nothing will replace muskets.'

'But the accuracy!' Stokes declared.

'Soldiers can't use rifles,' Morris said. 'It would be like giving knives and forks to hogs.' He twisted in the camp chair and gestured at his men, the 33rd's Light Company. 'Look at them! Half of them can't work out which end of a musket is which. Useless buggers. Might as well arm the bastards with pikes.'

'If you say so,' Stokes said disapprovingly. His road had reached the plateau and now he had to begin the construction of the breaching batteries, and the 33rd's Light Company, which had escorted Stokes north from Mysore, had been charged with the job of protecting the sappers who would build the batteries. Captain Morris had been unhappy with the orders, for he would have much preferred to have been sent back south rather than be camped by the rock isthmus that promised to be such a lively place in these next few days. There was a chance that Gawilghur's garrison might sally out to destroy the batteries, and even if that danger did not materialize, it was a certainty that the Mahratta gunners on the Outer Fort's walls would try to break down the new works with cannon fire.

Sergeant Hakeswill approached Stokes's tent. He looked distracted, so much so that his salute was perfunctory. 'You heard the news, sir?' He spoke to Morris.

Morris squinted up at the Sergeant. 'News,' he said heavily, 'news? Can't say I have, Sergeant. The enemy has surrendered, perhaps?'

'Nothing so good, sir, nothing so good.'

'You look pale, man!' Stokes said. 'Are you sickening?'

'Heart-sick, sir, that's what I am in my own self, sir, heart-sick.' Sergeant Hakeswill sniffed heavily, and even cuffed at a non-existent tear on his twitching cheek. 'Captain Torrance,' he announced, 'is dead, sir.' The Sergeant took off his shako and held it against his breast. 'Dead, sir.'

'Dead?' Stokes said lightly. He had not met Torrance.

'Took his own life, sir, that's what they do say. He killed his clerk with a knife, then turned his pistol on himself.' The Sergeant demonstrated the action by pretending to point a pistol at his own head and pulling the trigger. He sniffed again. 'And he was as good an officer as ever I did meet, and I've known many in my time. Officers and gentlemen, like your own good self, sir,' he said to Morris.

Morris, as unmoved by Torrance's death as Stokes, smirked. 'Killed his clerk, eh? That'll teach the bugger to keep a tidy ledger.'

'They do say, sir,' Hakeswill lowered his voice, 'that he must have been unnatural.'

'Unnatural?' Stokes asked.

'With his clerk, sir, pardon me for breathing such a filthy thing. Him and the clerk, sir. 'Cos he was naked, see, the Captain was, and the clerk was a handsome boy, even if he was a blackamoor. He washed a lot, and the Captain liked that.'

'Are you suggesting it was a lovers' tiff?' Morris asked, then laughed.

'No, sir,' Hakeswill said, turning to stare across the plateau's edge into the immense sky above the Deccan Plain, 'because it weren't. The Captain weren't ever unnatural, not like that. It weren't a lovers' tiff, sir, not even if he was naked as a needle. The Captain, sir, he liked to go naked. Kept him cool, he said, and kept his clothes clean, but there weren't nothing strange in it. Not in him. And he weren't a man to be filthy and unnatural. He liked the *bibbis*, he did. He was a Christian. A Christian gentleman, that's what he was, and he didn't kill himself. I knows who killed him, I do.'

Morris gave Stokes a shrug, as if Hakeswill's maunderings were beyond understanding.

'But the nub of the thing is, sir' – Hakeswill turned back to face Morris and stood to attention – 'that I ain't with the bullocks no more, sir. I've got orders, sir, to be back with you where I belongs, sir, seeing as some other officer has got Captain Torrance's duties and he didn't want me no more on account of having his own sergeant.' He replaced his shako, then saluted Morris. 'Under orders, sir! With Privates Kendrick and Lowry, sir. Others have taken over our bullocking duties, sir, and we is back with you like we always wanted to be. Sir!'

'Welcome back, Sergeant,' Morris said laconically. 'I'm sure the company will be overjoyed at your return.'

'I knows they will, sir,' Hakeswill said. 'I'm like a father to them, sir, I am,' Hakeswill added to Stokes.

Stokes frowned. 'Who do you think killed Captain Torrance, Sergeant?' he asked, and when Hakeswill said nothing, but just stood with his face twitching, the Major became insistent. 'If you know, man, you must speak! This is a crime! You have a duty to speak.'

Hakeswill's face wrenched itself. 'It were him, sir.' The Sergeant's eyes widened. 'It were Sharpie, sir!'

Stokes laughed. 'Don't be so absurd, man. Poor Sharpe is a prisoner! He's locked away in the fortress, I've no doubt.'

'That's what we all hear, sir,' Hakeswill said, 'but I knows better.'

'A touch of the sun,' Morris explained to Stokes, then waved the Sergeant away. 'Put your kit with the company, Sergeant. And I'm glad you're back.'

'Touched by your words, sir,' Hakeswill said fervently, 'and I'm glad to be home, sir, back in me own kind where I belong.' He saluted again, then swivelled on his heel and marched away.

'Salt of the earth,' Morris said.

Major Stokes, from his brief acquaintance with Hakeswill, was not sure of that verdict, but he said nothing. Instead he wandered a few paces northwards to watch the sappers who were busy scraping at the plateau's thin soil to fill gabions that had been newly woven from green bamboo. The gabions, great wicker baskets stuffed with earth, would be stacked as a screen to soak up the enemy gunfire while the battery sites were being levelled. Stokes had already decided to do the initial work at night, for the vulnerable time for making batteries close to a fortress was the first few hours, and at night the enemy gunfire was likely to be inaccurate.

The Major was making four batteries. Two, the breaching ones, would be constructed far down the isthmus among an outcrop of great black boulders that lay less than a quarter-mile from the fortress. The rocks, with the gabions, would provide the gunners some protection from the fortress's counter-fire. Sappers, hidden from the fort by the lie of the land, were already driving a road to the proposed site of the breaching guns. Two other batteries would be constructed to the east of the isthmus, on the edge of the plateau, and those guns would enfilade the growing breaches.

There would be three breaches. That decision had been made when Stokes, early in the dawn, had crept as close to the fortress as he had dared and, hidden among the tumbled rocks above the half-filled tank, had examined the Outer Fort's wall through his telescope. He had stared a long time, counting the gun embrasures and trying to estimate how many men were stationed on the bastions and firesteps. Those were details that did not really concern him for Stokes's business was confined to breaking the walls, but what he saw encouraged him.

There were two walls, both built on the steep slope which faced the plateau. The slope was so steep that the base of the inner wall showed high above the parapet of the outer wall, and that was excellent news, for making a breach depended on being able to batter the base of a wall. These walls, built so long ago, had never been designed to stop artillery, but to deter men. Stokes knew he could lay his guns so that they would hammer both walls at once, and that when the ancient stonework crumbled, the rubble would spill forward down the slope to make natural ramps up which the attackers could climb.

The masonry seemed to have stayed largely unrepaired since it had been built. Stokes could tell that, for the dark stones were covered with grey lichen and thick with weeds growing from the gaps between the blocks. The walls looked formidable, for they were high and well provided with massive bastions that would let the defenders provide flanking fire, but Stokes knew that the dressed stone of the two walls' outer faces merely disguised a thick heart of piled rubble, and once the facing masonry was shattered the rubble would spill out. A few shots would then suffice to break the inner faces. Two days' work, he reckoned. Two days of hard gunnery should bring the walls tumbling down.

Stokes had not made his reconnaissance alone, but had been accompanied by Lieutenant Colonel William Kenny of the East India Company who would lead the assault on the breaches. Kenny, a lantern-jawed and taciturn man, had lain beside Stokes. 'Well?' he had finally asked after Stokes had spent a silent five minutes examining the walls.

'Two days' work, sir,' Stokes said. If the Mahrattas had taken the trouble to build a glacis it would have been two weeks' work, but such was their confidence that they had not bothered to protect the base of the outer wall.

Kenny grunted. 'If it's that easy, then give me two holes in the inner wall.'

'Not the outer?' Stokes asked.

'One will serve me there,' Kenny said, putting an eye to his own telescope. 'A good wide gap in the nearer wall, Stokes, but not too near the main gate.'

'We shall avoid that,' the Major said. The main gate lay to the left so that the approach to the fortress was faced by high walls and bastions rather than by a gate vulnerable to artillery fire. However, this gate was massively defended by bastions and towers, which suggested it would be thick with defenders.

'Straight up the middle,' Kenny said, wriggling back from his viewpoint. 'Give me a breach to the right of that main bastion, and two on either side of it through the inner wall, and we'll do the rest.'

It would be easy enough to break down the walls, but Stokes still feared for Kenny's men. Their approach was limited by the existence of the great reservoir that lay on the right of the isthmus. The water level was low, and scummed green, but the tank still constricted the assault route so that Kenny's men would be squeezed between the water and the sheer drop to the left. That slender space, scarce more than fifty feet at its narrowest, would be furious with gunfire, much of it coming from the firesteps above and around the main gate that flanked the approach. Stokes had already determined that his enfilading batteries should spare some shot for that gate in an attempt to unseat its cannon and unsettle its defenders.

Now, under the midday sun, the Major wandered among the sappers filling the gabions. He tested each one, making certain that the sepoys were ramming the earth hard into the wicker baskets, for a loosely filled gabion was no use. The finished gabions were being stacked on ox carts, while other carts piled with powder and shot waited nearby. All was being done properly, and the Major stared out across the plateau where the newly arrived troops were making their camp. The closest tents, ragged and makeshift, belonged to a troop of Mahratta horsemen who had allied themselves with the British. Stokes, watching the robed guards who sat close to the tents, decided it would be best if he locked his valuables away and made sure his servant kept an eye on the trunk. The rest of the Mahratta horsemen had trotted north-wards, going to seek springs or wells, for it was dry up here on the plateau. Dry and cooler than on the plain, though it was still damned hot. Dust devils whirled between the farther tent rows where muskets were stacked in neat tripods. Some shirt-sleeved officers, presumably from the East India Company battalions, were playing cricket on a smoother stretch of turf, watched by bemused sepoys and men from the Scotch Brigade.

'Not their game, sir, is it, sir?' Hakeswill's voice disturbed Stokes.

The Major turned. 'Eh?'

'Cricket, sir. Too complicated for blackamoors and Scotchmen, sir, on account of it being a game that needs brains, sir.'

'Do you play, Sergeant?'

'Me, sir? No, sir. No time for frittering, sir, being as I'm a soldier back to front, sir.'

'It does a man good to have a pastime,' Stokes said. 'Your Colonel, now, he plays the violin.'

'Sir Arthur does, sir?' Hakeswill said, plainly not believing Stokes. 'He's never done it near me, sir.'

'I assure you he does,' Stokes said. He was irritated by Hakeswill's presence. He disliked the man intensely, even though Hakeswill had spent only a short time as Sharpe's substitute. 'So what is it, Sergeant?'

Hakeswill's face twitched. 'Come to be of use to you, sir.'

The reply puzzled Stokes. 'I thought you'd been returned to company duties?'

'That I am, sir, and not before time. But I was thinking of poor Sharpie, sir, as you tell me he languishes in the heathens' jail, sir, which I did not know, sir, until you told me.'

Stokes shrugged. 'He's probably being fairly treated. The Mahrattas aren't renowned for being unduly cruel to prisoners.'

'I was wondering if he left his pack with you, sir?'

'Why would he do that?' Stokes asked.

'I was just wondering, sir. Officers don't like carrying their baggage everywhere, sir, not if they want to keep their dignity, and if he did leave his pack with you, sir, then I thought as how we might relieve you of the responsibility, sir, seeing as how Mister Sharpe was a comrade of ours for so long. That's what I was thinking, sir.'

Stokes bridled, but was not certain why. 'It isn't a heavy responsibility, Sergeant.'

'Never thought it was, sir, but it might be a nuisance to you, sir, seeing as how you're charged with other duties, and I would relieve you of the responsibility, sir.'

Stokes shook his head. 'As it happens, Sergeant, Mister Sharpe did leave his pack with me, and I promised him I would keep it safe, and I'm not a man to break promises, Sergeant. I shall keep it.'

'As you chooses, sir!' Hakeswill said sourly. 'Just thought it was a Christian act, sir.' He turned and marched away. Stokes watched him, then shook his head and turned back to gaze at the growing encampment.

Tonight, he thought, tonight we shall make the batteries, and tomorrow the big guns will be hauled forward. Another day to fill the magazines with powder and shot and then the stone-breaking could begin. Two days of battering, of dust and rubble and smoke, and then the cricketers could lead the charge across the isthmus. Poor men, Stokes thought, poor men.

'I hate night actions,' Captain Morris complained to Hakeswill.

'Because of Serry-apatam, sir? A right dog's mess, that was.' The battalion had attacked a wood outside Seringapatam by night and the companies had become separated, some became lost, and the enemy had punished them.

Morris attached his scabbard to its slings and pulled his hat on. It was dark outside, and soon the oxen would drag the gabions forward to the position Stokes had chosen for the breaching batteries. It would be a prime moment for the enemy to sally out of the fortress, so Morris and his company must form a picquet line ahead of the proposed batteries. They must watch the fortress and, if an attack was made, they must resist it, then slowly fall back, protecting the sappers until the reserve troops, a battalion of sepoys, could be brought forward from the plateau. With any luck, Morris fervently hoped, the enemy would stay in bed.

'Evening, Morris!' Major Stokes was indecently cheerful. 'Your lads are ready?'

'They are, sir.'

Stokes led Morris a few yards from his tent and stared towards the fortress that was nothing but a dark shape in the night beyond the closer blackness of the rocks. 'The thing is,' Stokes said, 'that they're bound to see our lanterns and must hear the carts, so they're liable to unleash a pretty furious artillery barrage. Maybe rockets as well. But take no heed of it. Your only job is to watch for infantry coming from the gate.'

'I know, sir.'

'So don't use your muskets! I hear musket fire, Captain, and I think infantry. Then I send for the Madrassi lads, and the next moment the whole place is swarming with redcoats who can't tell who's who in the dark. So no firing, you understand? Unless you see enemy infantry. Then send a message to me, fight the good fight and wait for support.'

Morris grunted. He had been told this twice already, and did not need the instructions a third time, but he still turned to the company which was paraded and ready. 'No one's to fire without my express permission, you understand?'

'They understands, sir,' Hakeswill answered for the company. 'One musket shot without permission and the culprit's earned himself a skinned back, sir.'

Morris took the company forward, following the old road that led directly to the gateway of the Outer Fort. The night was horribly dark, and within a few paces of leaving the engineers' encampment, Morris could hardly see the road at all. His men's boots scuffed loud on the hard-packed stones. They went slowly, feeling their way and using what small light came from the merest sliver of moon that hung like a silver blade above Gawilghur.

'Permission to speak, sir?' Hakeswill's hoarse voice sounded close to Morris.

'Not too loud, Sergeant.'

'Like a mouse, sir, quiet I will be, but, sir, if we're here, does that mean we'll be joining the assault on the fort, sir?'

'God, no,' Morris said fervently.

Hakeswill chuckled. 'I thought I should ask, sir, on account of making a will.'

'A will?' Morris asked. 'You need a will?'

'I have some wealth,' Hakeswill said defensively. And soon, he reckoned, he would have even more, for he had cleverly confirmed his surmise that Sharpe's missing pack was in Major Stokes's keeping.

'You have some wealth, do you?' Morris asked sarcastically. 'And who the hell will you leave it to?'

'Your own self, sir, if you'll forgive me, sir. No family, apart from the army, sir, which is mother's milk to me.'

'By all means make your will,' Morris said. 'Connors can draw one up for you.' Connors was the company clerk. 'I trust, of course, that the document proves redundant.'

'Whatever that means, sir, I hopes the same.'

The two men fell silent. The dark loom of the fortress was much closer now, and Morris was nervous. What was the point of this futile exercise anyway? He would be damned if he would be able to see any enemy infantrymen, not in this pitch black, unless the fools decided to carry a lantern. Some lights showed in Gawilghur. There was a glow above the Outer Fort that must have been cast by the fires and lights in the Inner Fort, while closer Morris could see a couple of flickering patches where fires or torches burned inside the nearer defences. But those scattered lights would not help him see an enemy force debouching from the gate.

'Far enough,' he called. He was not really sure if he had gone close enough to the fort, but he had no fancy to go further, and so he stopped and hissed at Hakeswill to spread the men westwards across the isthmus. 'Five paces between each pair of men, Sergeant.'

'Five paces it is, sir.'

'If anyone sees or hears anything, they're to pass the message back here to me.'

'They'll do so, sir.'

'And no fool's to light a pipe, you hear me? Don't want the enemy spraying us with canister because some blockhead needs tobacco.'

'Your orders is noted, sir. And where would you want me, sir?'

'Far end of the line, Sergeant.' Morris was the sole officer with the company, for both his lieutenant and ensign had the fever and so had stayed in Mysore. But Hakeswill, he reckoned, was as good as any lieutenant. 'You can order men to fire if you're certain you see the enemy, but God help you if you're wrong.'

'Very good, sir,' Hakeswill said, then hissed at the men to spread out. They vanished into the blackness. For a moment there was the sound of boots, the thump of musket stocks hitting rocks and the grunts as the redcoats settled, but then there was silence. Or near silence. The wind sighed at the cliff's edge while, from the fort, there drifted a plangent and discordant music that rose and fell with the wind's vagaries. Worse than bagpipes, Morris thought sourly.

The first axle squeals sounded as the oxen dragged the gabions forward. The noise would be continuous now and, sooner or later, the enemy must react by opening fire. And what chance would he have of seeing anything then, Morris wondered. The gun flashes would blind him. The first he would see of an enemy would be the glint of starlight on a blade. He spat. Waste of time.

'Morris!' a voice hissed from the dark. 'Captain Morris!'

'Here!' He turned towards the voice, which had come from behind him on the road back to the plateau. 'Here!'

'Colonel Kenny,' the voice said, still in a sibilant whisper. 'Don't mind me prowling around.'

'Of course not, sir.' Morris did not like the idea of a senior officer coming to the picquet line, but he could hardly send the man away. 'Honoured to have you, sir,' he said, then hissed a warning to his men. 'Senior officer present, don't be startled. Pass the word on.'

Morris heard Kenny's footsteps fade to his right. There was the low murmur of a brief conversation, then silence again, except for the demonic squeal of the ox-cart axles. A moment later a lantern light showed from behind the rocks where Stokes was making one of his main batteries. Morris braced himself for the enemy reaction, but the fortress stayed silent.

The noise grew louder as the sappers heaved the gabions from the carts and manhandled them up onto the rocks to form the thick bastion. A man swore, others grunted and the great baskets thumped on stone. Another lantern was unmasked, and this time the man carrying it stepped up onto the rocks to see where the gabions were being laid. A voice ordered him to get down.

The fort at last woke up. Morris could hear footsteps hurrying along the nearer firestep, and he saw a brief glow as a linstock was plucked from a barrel and blown into red life. 'Jesus,' he said under his breath, and a moment later the first gun fired. The flame stabbed bright as a lance from the walls, its glare momentarily lighting all the rocky isthmus and the green-scummed surface of the tank, before it was blotted out by the rolling smoke. The round shot screamed overhead, struck a rock and ricocheted wildly up into the sky. A second gun fired, its flame lighting the first smoke cloud from within so that it seemed as if the wall of the fort was edged with a brief vaporous luminance. The ball struck a gabion, breaking it apart in a spray of earth. A man groaned. Dogs were barking in the British camp and inside the fortress.

Morris stared towards the dark gateway. He could see nothing, because the guns' flames had robbed him of his night vision. Or rather he could see wraithlike shapes which he knew were more likely to be his imagination than the approach of some savage enemy. The guns were firing steadily now, aiming at the small patch of lantern light, but then more lights, brighter ones, appeared to the west of the isthmus, and some of the gunners switched their aim, not knowing that Stokes had unveiled the second lights as a feint.

Then the first rockets were fired, and they were even more dazzling than the guns. The fiery trails seemed to limp up from the fort's bastions, seething smoke and sparks, then they leaped up into the air, wobbling in their flight, to sear over Morris's head and slash north towards the camp. None went near their targets, but their sound and the flaming exhausts were nerve-racking. The first shells were fired, and they added to the night's din as they cracked apart among the rocks to whistle shards of shattered casing over the struggling sappers. The firing was deliberate as the gun captains took care to lay their pieces before firing, but still there were six or seven shots every minute, while the rockets were more constant. Morris tried to use the brightness of the rocket trails to see the ground between his hiding place and the fort, but there was too much smoke, the shadows flickered wildly, and his imagination made movement where there was none. He held his fire, reckoning he would hear the gate open or the sound of enemy footsteps. He could hear the defenders shouting on the wall, either calling insults to the enemy hidden in the dark or else encouraging each other.

Hakeswill, at the very right-hand end of the line, cowered among the rocks. He had been sheltering with Kendrick and Lowry, but the enemy cannonade had driven him still further right to where there was a deep cleft. He knew he was safe there, but even so every screaming rocket made him flinch, while the sound of the shells exploding and the round shots cracking against stone made him draw his knees up into his chest. He knew there was a senior officer visiting the picquet line because the message telling of the Colonel's presence had been passed down the line. Kenny's visit struck Hakeswill as a daft thing for any man with gold braid on his coat to do, but when the Colonel hissed his name aloud he kept silent. At least he assumed it was the visiting officer, for the summons was insistent and authoritative, but Hakeswill ignored it. He did not want to draw attention to himself in case the heathen blackamoor gunners aimed their cannon at him. Let the officer hiss away, he decided, and a moment later the man went away.

'Who are you?' a low voice asked Private Kendrick just a few yards from Hakeswill's hiding place.

'Kendrick, sir.'

'To me, Private. I need your help.'

Kendrick slipped back towards the voice. Bastard interfering officer, he thought, but he had to obey. 'Where are you, sir?' he asked.

'Here, man! Hurry, now, hurry!'

Kendrick slipped on a slanting stone and sat down with a bump. A rocket slashed overhead, spewing fire and sparks, and in its brief light he saw a shadow above him, then felt a blade at his throat. 'One noise,' the voice hissed, 'and you're dead.'

Kendrick went very still. He did not make any noise at all, but he still died.

A lucky shell struck a pair of oxen, disembowelling the beasts that lowed pitifully as they collapsed onto the road. 'Get them out of the way!' a voice roared, and sepoys struggled with the massive animals, cutting their harnesses and pulling the dying beasts into the rocks. Other men ran the empty cart back to the encampment, making way for the next wagon to drag more gabions forward. 'Kill them!' the officer ordered. 'Use your bayonets! No musket fire!' The sepoys finished off the oxen, stabbing again and again into their thick necks while the bloody hooves thrashed violently. Another shell landed nearby, slicing its fragments among the rocks. The road was slippery with spilled guts over which the next cart rolled impassively, its axle screeching like a demon.

'All well, soldier?' a voice asked Private Lowry.

'Yes, sir.'

'I'm Colonel Kenny,' the man said, dropping down beside Lowry.

'Yes, sir,' Lowry acknowledged nervously.

'See anything?'

'Nothing, sir,' Lowry said, then gasped as he felt a blade at his throat.

'Where's Hakeswill?' the voice hissed in his ear, and Lowry suddenly knew this was not Colonel Kenny who had him in a tight grip.

'Dunno, sir,' Lowry said, then began to cry out, but the cry was cut off as the blade sawed deep into his gullet.

A ball, fired low, struck plumb on the great boulder that sheltered Hakeswill and the Sergeant whimpered as he tried to wriggle deeper into the cleft. A rocket landed thirty paces behind him and began to chase its tail, whirling about on the turf, scattering sparks, until it finally lodged against a rock and burned itself out in a display of small blue flames. Another round shot hammered into the gabions, but now they were well stacked and the ball's impact was soaked up by the tight-packed soil.

A whistle blew from the battery site, then blew twice more. Morris, relieved by the sound, called to the men to his right. 'Back to the road! Pass it on! Back to the road!' Thank God the worst of the ordeal was over! Now he was supposed to withdraw to the battery, ready to protect it through the remaining hours of the dark night, but Morris knew he would feel a good deal safer once he was behind the gabions, just as he knew that the cessation of the work would probably persuade the Mahrattas to cease fire. 'Close on me!' he called to his company. 'Hurry!'

The message was passed along the picquet line and the men ran at a crouch back to where Morris waited. They bumped into each other as they gathered, then squatted as Morris called for Hakeswill.

'Not here, sir,' Sergeant Green finally decided.

'Count the men, Sergeant,' Morris ordered.

Sergeant Green numbered the men off. 'Three missing, sir,' he reported. 'Hakeswill, Lowry and Kendrick.'

'Damn them,' Morris said. A rocket hissed up from the gatehouse, twisted in the night to leave a crazy trail of flame-edged smoke, then dived down to the left, far down, plunging into the ravine that edged the isthmus. The light of the exhaust flashed down the steep cliffs, finally vanishing a thousand feet below Morris. Two guns fired together, their balls hammering towards the fake lanterns. The battery lanterns had vanished, evidence that the sappers had finished their work.

'Take the men to the battery,' Morris ordered Green. 'Garrard? You stay with me.'

Morris did not want to do anything heroic, but he knew he could not report that he had simply lost three men, so he took Private Tom Garrard west across the tumbled ground where the picquet line had been stretched. They called out the names of the missing men, but no reply came.

It was Garrard who stumbled over the first body. 'Don't know who it is, sir, but he's dead. Bloody mess, he is.'

Morris swore and crouched beside the body. A rocket's bright passage showed him a slit throat and a spill of blood. It also revealed that the man had been stripped of his coat which lay discarded beside the corpse. The sight of the gaping throat made Morris gag.

'There's another here, sir,' Garrard called from a few paces away.

'Jesus!' Morris twisted aside, willing himself not to throw up, but the bile was sour in his throat. He shuddered, then managed to take a deep breath. 'We're going.'

'You want me to look for the other fellow, sir?' Garrard asked.

'Come on!' Morris fled, not wanting to stay in this dark charnel house.

Garrard followed.

The gunfire died. A last rocket stitched sparks across the stars, then Gawilghur was silent again.

Hakeswill cowered in his hiding place, shuddering as the occasional flare of an exploding shell or passing rocket cast lurid shadows into the narrow cleft. He thought he heard Lowry call aloud, but the sound was so unexpected, and so quickly over, he decided it was his nerves. Then, blessedly, he heard the whistle that signalled that the sappers were done with their work, and a moment later he heard the message being called along the line. 'Back to the road! Back to the road!'

The rockets and guns were still battering the night, so Hakeswill stayed where he was until he sensed that the fury of the fire was diminishing, then he crept out of his cleft and, still keeping low, scuttled eastwards.

'Hakeswill!' a voice called nearby.

He froze.

'Hakeswill?' The voice was insistent.

Some instinct told the Sergeant that there was mischief in the dark, and so Hakeswill crouched lower still. He heard something moving in the night, the scrape of leather on stone, the sound of breathing, but the man did not come close to Hakeswill who, petrified, edged on another pace. His hand, feeling the ground ahead of him, suddenly found something wet and sticky. He flinched, brought his fingers to his nose and smelt blood.

'Jesus,' he swore under his breath. He groped again, and this time found a corpse. His hands explored the face, the open mouth, then found the gaping wound in the neck. He jerked his hand back.

It had to be Lowry or Kendrick, for this was about where he had left the two privates, and if they were dead, or even if only one of them was dead, then it meant that Captain Torrance's death had been no lovers' tiff. Not that Hakeswill had ever believed it was. He knew who it was. Bloody Sharpe was alive. Bloody Sharpe was hunting his enemies, and three, maybe four, were already dead. And Hakeswill knew he would be next.

'Hakeswill!' the voice hissed, but farther away now.

A gun fired from the fort and in its flash Hakeswill saw a cloaked shape to his north. The man was crossing the skyline, not far from Hakeswill, but at least he was going away. Sharpe! It had to be Sharpe! And a terror grew in Hakeswill so that his face twitched and his hands shook.

'Think, you bugger,' he told himself, 'think!'

And the answer came, a sweet answer, so obvious that he wondered why he had taken so long to find it.

Sharpe was alive, he was not a prisoner in Gawilghur, but haunting the British camp, which meant that there was one place that would be utterly safe for Hakeswill to go. He could go to the fortress, and Sharpe would never reach him there for the rumour in the camp was that the assault on Gawilghur was likely to be a desperate and bloody business. Likely to fail, some men said, and even if it did not, Hakeswill could always pretend he had been taken prisoner. All he wanted at this moment was to be away from Sharpe and so he sidled southwards, down the hill, and once he reached the flatter ground, he ran towards the now dark walls of the fort through the drifting skeins of foul-smelling powder smoke.

He ran past the tank, along the approach road, and round to the left where the great gatehouse loomed above him in the dark. And once there he pounded on the massive, iron-studded doors.

No one responded.

He pounded again, using the butt of his musket, scared witless that the sound would bring an avenging horror from the dark behind, and suddenly a small wicket gate in the larger door was pulled open to flood flame light into the night.

'I'm a deserter!' Hakeswill hissed. 'I'm on your side!'

Hands seized him and pulled him through the small doorway. A smoking torch burned high on the wall to show Hakeswill the long, narrow entranceway, the dark ramparts, and the dark faces of the men who had him prisoner. 'I'm on your side!' he shouted as the gate was closed behind him and his musket was snatched away. 'I'm on your side!'

A tall, hawk-faced man strode down the stone road. 'Who are you?' he asked in English.

'I'm someone willing to fight for you, sir. Willing and able, sir. Old soldier, sir.'

'My name is Manu Bappoo,' the man said in a sibilant voice, 'and I command here.'

'Very good, sir. Sahib, I mean, very good.' Hakeswill bobbed his head. 'Hakeswill, sir, is my name. Sergeant Obadiah Hakeswill.'

Manu Bappoo stared at the redcoat. He disliked deserters. A man who deserted his flag could not be trusted under any other flag, but the news that a white soldier had run from the enemy ranks could only hearten his garrison. Better, he decided, to leave this man alive as a witness to the enemy's crumbling morale than shoot him out of hand. 'Take him to Colonel Dodd,' he ordered one of his men. 'Give him back his firelock. He's on our side.'

So Hakeswill was inside Gawilghur and among the enemy. But he was safe from the terror that had turned his life to sudden nightmare. He was safe from Sharpe.

CHAPTER 8

The sappers who had emplaced the gabions were too excited to go to sleep and instead were milling about a pair of smoky fires. Their laughter rose and fell on the night wind. Major Stokes, pleased with their work, had produced three jars of arrack as a reward, and the jugs were being passed from hand to hand.

Sharpe watched the small celebration and then, keeping to the shadows among Syud Sevajee's encampment, he went to a small tent where he stripped off his borrowed Indian robes before crawling under the flap. In the dark he blundered into Clare who, kept awake by the sound of the bombardment and then by the voices of the sappers, put up a hand and felt bare flesh. 'You're undressed!' She sounded alarmed.

'Not quite,' Sharpe said, then understood her fear. 'My clothes were soaking,' he explained, 'so I took them off. Didn't want to wet the bed, eh? And I've still got my shirt on.'

'Is it raining? I didn't hear it.'

'It was blood,' he said, then rummaged under the blanket he had borrowed from Syud Sevajee and found Torrance's pouch.

Clare heard the rattle of stones. 'What is it?'

'Just stones,' he said, 'pebbles.' He put the twenty jewels he had retrieved from Kendrick and Lowry into the pouch, stowed it safe under the blanket, then lay down. He doubted he had found every stone, but he reckoned he had retrieved most of them. They had been loose in the two privates' pockets, not even hidden away in their coat seams. God, he felt tired and his body had still not recovered from Hakeswill's kicking. It hurt to breathe, the bruises were tender and a tooth was still loose.

'What happened out there?' Clare asked.

'The engineers put the gabions in place. When it's light they'll scrape the gun platform and make the magazines, and tomorrow night they'll bring up the guns.'

'What happened to you?' Clare amended her question.

Sharpe was silent for a while. 'I looked up some old friends,' he said. But he had missed Hakeswill, damn it, and Hakeswill would be doubly alert now. Still, a chance would come. He grinned as he remembered Morris's scared voice. The Captain was a bully to his men and a toadie to his superiors.

'Did you kill someone?' Clare asked.

'Two men,' he admitted, 'but it should have been three.'

'Why?'

He sighed. 'Because they were bad men,' he said simply, then reflected it was a true answer. 'And because they tried to kill me,' he added, 'and they robbed me. You knew them,' he went on. 'Kendrick and Lowry.'

'They were horrid,' Clare said softly. 'They used to stare at me.'

'Can't blame them for that, love.'

She was silent for a while. The laughter of the sappers was subsiding as men drifted towards their tents. The wind gusted at the tent's entrance and brought the smell of burnt powder from the rocky isthmus where patches of grass still flamed around the exhausted rocket tubes. 'Everything's gone wrong, hasn't it?' Clare said.

'It's being put right,' Sharpe replied.

'For you,' she said.

Again she was silent, and Sharpe suspected she was crying. 'I'll get you home to Madras,' he said.

'And what'll happen to me there?'

'You'll be all right, lass. I'll give you a pair of my magic pebbles.'

'What I want,' she said softly, 'is to go home. But I can't afford it.'

'Marry a soldier,' Sharpe said, 'and be carried home with him.' He thought of Eli Lockhart who had been admiring Clare from a distance. They would suit each other, Sharpe thought.

She was crying very softly. 'Torrance said he'd pay my way home when I'd paid off the debt,' she said.

'Why would he make you work for one passage, then give you another?' Sharpe asked. 'He was a lying bastard.'

'He seemed so kind at first.'

'We're all like that,' Sharpe said. 'Soft as lights when you first meet a woman, then you get what you want and it changes. I don't know. Maybe not every time.'

'Charlie wasn't like that,' Clare said.

'Charlie? Your husband?'

'He was always good to me.'

Sharpe lay back. The light of the dying fires flickered in the tent's loose weave. If it rained, he thought, the cloth would leak like a pepper pot. 'There are good men and bad,' he said.

'What are you?' Clare asked.

'I think I'm good,' he said, 'but I don't know. All the time I get into trouble, and I only know one way out. I can fight. I can do that all right.'

'Is that what you want? To fight?'

'God knows what I want.' He laughed softly. 'I wanted to be an officer more than I'd wanted anything in my life! I dreamed of it, I did. I wanted it so bad that it hurt, and then the dream came true and it woke me up and I wondered why I'd wanted it so much.' He paused. Syud Sevajee's horses stamped their feet softly behind the tent. 'Some buggers are trying to persuade me to leave the army. Sell the commission, see? They don't want me.'

'Why not?'

'Because I piss in their soup, lass.'

'So will you leave?'

He shrugged. 'Don't want to.' He thought about it. 'It's like a club, a society. They don't really want me, so they chuck me out, and then I have to fight my way back in. But why do I do it if they don't want me? I don't know. Maybe it'll be different in the Rifles. I'll try 'em, anyway, and see if they're different.'

'You want to go on fighting?' Clare asked.

'It's what I'm good at,' Sharpe said. 'And I do enjoy it. I mean I know you shouldn't, but there ain't any other excitement like it.'

'None?'

'Well, one.' He grinned in the dark.

There was a long silence, and he thought Clare had fallen asleep, but then she spoke again. 'How about your French widow?'

'She's gone,' Sharpe said flatly.

'Gone?'

'She buggered off, love. Took some money of mine and went. Gone to America, I'm told.'

Clare lay in silence again. 'Don't you worry about being alone?' she asked after a while.

'No.'

'I do.'

He turned towards her, propped himself on an elbow and stroked her hair. She stiffened as he touched her, then relaxed to the gentle pressure of his hand. 'You ain't alone, lass,' Sharpe said. 'Or only if you want to be. You got trapped, that's all. It happens to everyone. But you're out now. You're free.' He stroked her hair down to her neck and felt warm bare skin under his hand. She did not move and he softly stroked farther down. 'You're undressed,' he said.

'I was warm,' she said in a small voice.

'What's worse?' Sharpe asked. 'Being warm or being lonely?'

He thought she smiled. He could not tell in the dark, but he thought she smiled. 'Being lonely,' she said very softly.

'We can look after that,' he said, lifting the thin blanket and moving to her side.

She had stopped crying. Somewhere outside a cock crowed and the eastern cliffs were touched with the first gold of the day. The fires on the rocky neck of land flickered and died, their smoke drifting like patches of thin mist. Bugles called from the main encampment, summoning the redcoats to the morning parade. The night picquets were relieved as the sun rose to flood the world with light.

Where Sharpe and Clare slept.

'You abandoned the dead men?' Wellesley growled.

Captain Morris blinked as a gust of wind blew dust into one of his eyes. 'I tried to bring the bodies in,' he lied, 'but it was dark, sir. Very dark. Colonel Kenny can vouch for that, sir. He visited us.'

'I visited you?' Kenny, lean, tall and irascible, was standing beside the General. 'I visited you?' he asked again, his inflection rising to outrage.

'Last night, sir,' Morris answered in plaintive indignation. 'On the picquet line.'

'I did no such thing. Sun's gone to your head.' Kenny glowered at Morris, then took a snuff box from a pocket and placed a pinch on his hand. 'Who the devil are you, anyway?' he added.

'Morris, sir. 33rd.'

'I thought we had nothing but Scots and sepoys here,' Kenny said to Wellesley.

'Captain Morris's company escorted a convoy here,' Wellesley answered.

'A light company, eh?' Kenny said, glancing at Morris's epaulettes. 'You might even be useful. I could do with another company in the assault party.' He snorted the snuff, stopping one nostril at a time. 'It cheers my boys up,' he added, 'seeing white men killed.' Kenny commanded the first battalion of the 11th Madrassi Regiment.

'What's in your assault unit now?' Wellesley asked.

'Nine companies,' Kenny said. 'The grenadiers and two others from the Scotch Brigade, the flankers from my regiment and four others. Good boys, all of them, but I daresay they won't mind sharing the honours with an English light company.'

'And I've no doubt you'll welcome a chance to assault a breach, Morris?' Wellesley asked drily.

'Of course, sir,' Morris said, cursing Kenny inwardly.

'But in the meantime,' Wellesley went on coldly, 'bring your men's bodies in.'

'Yes, sir.'

'Do it now.'

Sergeant Green took a half-dozen men down the neck of land, but they only found two bodies. They were expecting three, but Sergeant Hakeswill was missing. The enemy, seeing the redcoats among the rocks above the reservoir, opened fire and the musket balls smacked into stones and ricocheted up into the air. Green took a bullet in the heel of his boot. It did not break the skin of his foot, but the blow hurt and he hopped on the short, dry grass. 'Just grab the buggers and drag them away,' he said. He wondered why the enemy did not fire their cannon, and just then a gun discharged a barrel of canister at his squad. The balls hissed all about the men, but miraculously none was hit as the soldiers seized Kendrick and Lowry by their feet and ran back towards the half-completed battery where Captain Morris waited. Both the dead men had slit throats.

Once safe behind the gabions the corpses were treated more decorously by being placed on makeshift stretchers. Colonel Kenny intercepted the stretcher-bearers to examine the corpses which were already smelling foul. 'They must have sent a dozen cut-throats out of the fort,' he reckoned. 'You say there's a sergeant missing?'

'Yes, sir,' Morris answered.

'Poor fellow must be a prisoner. Be careful tonight, Captain! They'll probably try again. And I assure you, Captain, if I decide to take a stroll this evening, it won't be to your picquet line.'

That night the 33rd's Light Company again formed a screen in front of the new batteries, this time to protect the men dragging up the guns. It was a nervous night, for the company was expecting throat-slitting Mahrattas to come silently through the darkness, but nothing stirred. The fortress stayed silent and dark. Not a gun fired and not a rocket flew as the British cannon were hauled to their new emplacements and as powder charges and round shot were stacked in the newly made ready magazines.

Then the gunners waited.

The first sign of dawn was a grey lightening of the east, followed by the flare of reflected sun as the first rays lanced over the world's rim to touch the summit of the eastern cliffs. The fortress walls showed grey-black. Still the gunners waited. A solitary cloud glowed livid pink on the horizon. Smoke rose from the cooking fires inside the fortress where the flags hung limp in the windless air. Bugles roused the British camp which lay a half-mile behind the batteries where officers trained telescopes on Gawilghur's northern wall.

Major Stokes's job was almost finished. He had made the batteries, and now the gunners must unmake the walls, but first Stokes wanted to be certain that the outermost breach would be made in the right place. He had fixed a telescope to a tripod and now he edged it from side to side, searching the lichen-covered stones just to the right of a bastion in the centre of the wall. The wall sloped back slightly, but he was sure he could see a place where the old stones bulged out of alignment, and he watched that spot as the sun rose and cast a hint of shadow where the stones were not quite true. Finally he screwed the telescope's mount tight shut, so that the tube could not move, then summoned the gun captain of the battery's eighteen-pounder. A major actually commanded this battery, but he insisted that his sergeant go to the spyglass. 'That's your target,' Stokes told the Sergeant.

The Sergeant stooped to the telescope, then straightened to see over the glass, then stooped again. He was chewing a wad of tobacco and had no lower front teeth so that the yellow spittle ran down his chin in a continuous dribble. He straightened, then stooped a third time. The telescope was powerful, and all he could see in the glass circle was a vertical joint between two great stones. The joint was some four feet above the wall's base, and when it gave way the wall would spill forward down the slope to make the ramp up which the attackers could swarm. 'Smack on the joint, sir?' the Sergeant asked in a Northumbrian accent so pronounced that Stokes did not at first understand him.

'Low on the joint,' Stokes said.

'Low it is, sir,' the Sergeant said, and stooped to squint through the glass once more. 'The joint gapes a bit, don't it?'

'It does,' Stokes said.

The Sergeant grunted. For a while, he reckoned, the battering would drive the stones in, sealing the gap, but there was pressure there and the wall must eventually give way as the battered stones weakened. 'That bugger'll burst like an abscess,' the Sergeant said happily, straightening from the telescope. He returned to his gun and barked at his men to make some minute adjustments to its trail. He himself heaved on the elevating screw, though as yet the gun was still masked by some half-filled gabions that blocked the embrasure. Every few seconds the Sergeant climbed onto the trail to see over the gabions, then he would demand that the gun was shifted a half-inch left or a finger's breadth to the right as he made another finicky adjustment to the screw. He tossed grass in the air to gauge the wind, then twisted the elevation again to raise the barrel a tiny amount. 'Stone cold shot,' he explained to Stokes, 'so I'm pointing her a bit high. Maybe a half turn more.' He hammered the screw with the heel of his hand. 'Perfect,' he said.

The *puckalees* were bringing water which they poured into great wooden tubs. The water was not just to slake the gunners' thirst and soak the sponges that cleaned out the barrels between shots, but was also intended to cool the great weapons. The sun was climbing, it promised to be a searing hot day, and if the huge guns were not drenched intermittently with water they could overheat and explode the powder charges prematurely. The Sergeant was choosing his shot now, rolling two eighteen-pounder balls up and down a stretch of bare earth to judge which was the more perfect sphere. 'That one,' he said, spitting tobacco juice onto his chosen missile.

Morris's Light Company trailed back up the road, going to the camp where they would sleep. Stokes watched them pass and thought of Sharpe. Poor Sharpe, but at least, from wherever he was imprisoned inside the fortress, he would hear the siege guns and know that the redcoats were coming. If they got through the breach, Stokes thought gloomily, or if they ever managed to cross the fortress's central ravine. He tried to suppress his pessimism, telling himself that his job was simply to make the breach, not win the whole victory.

The chosen shot was rolled into the gun's muzzle, then rammed down onto the canvas bags of powder. The Sergeant took a length of wire that hung looped on his belt and rammed it through the cannon's touch-hole, piercing the canvas bag beneath, then selected a priming tube, a reed filled with finely milled powder, and slid it down into the powder charge, but leaving a half-inch of the reed protruding above the touch-hole. 'Ready when you are, sir,' he told the Major command-ing the battery who, in turn, looked at Stokes.

Stokes shrugged. 'I imagine we wait for Colonel Stevenson's per-mission.'

The gunners in the second breaching battery which lay fifty yards west of the first had trained their telescopes over the gabions to watch where the first shot fell. The scar it left in the wall would be their aiming mark. The two enfilading batteries also watched. Their work would begin properly when the first of the three breaches was made, but till then their twelve-pounders would be aimed at the cannon mounted on Gawilghur's ramparts, trying to dismount them or tumble their embrasures into rubble.

'That wall won't last long,' the battery Major, whose name was Plummer, opined. He was staring at the wall through Stokes's telescope.

'We'll have it opened up today,' Stokes agreed.

'Thank God there ain't a glacis,' Plummer said.

'Thank God, indeed,' Stokes echoed piously, but he had been think-ing about that lack and was not so sure now that it was a blessing. Perhaps the Mahrattas understood that their real defence was the great central ravine, and so were offering nothing but a token defence of the Outer Fort. And how was that ravine to be crossed? Stokes feared that he would be asked for an engineering solution, but what could he do? Fill the thing with soil? That would take months.

Stokes's gloomy presentiments were interrupted by an aide who had been sent by Colonel Stevenson to enquire why the batteries were silent. 'I suspect those are your orders to open fire, Plummer,' Stokes said.

'Unmask!' Plummer shouted.

Four gunners clambered up onto the bastion and manhandled the half-filled gabions out of the cannon's way. The Sergeant squinted down the barrel a last time, nodded to himself, then stepped aside. The other gunners had their hands over their ears. 'You can fire, Ned!' Plummer called to the Sergeant, who took a glowing linstock from a protective barrel, reached across the gun's high wheel and touched the fire to the reed.

The cannon hammered back a full five yards as the battery filled with acrid smoke. The ball screamed low across the stony neck of land to crack against the fort's wall. There was a pause. Defenders were running along the ramparts. Stokes was peering through the glass, waiting for the smoke to thin. It took a full minute, but then he saw that a slab of stone about the size of a soup plate had been chipped from the wall. 'Two inches to the right, Sergeant,' he called chidingly.

'Must have been a puff of wind, sir,' the Sergeant said, 'puff of bloody wind, 'cos there weren't a thing wrong with gun's laying, begging your pardon, sir.'

'You did well,' Stokes said with a smile, 'very well.' He cupped his hands and shouted at the second breaching battery. 'You have your mark! Fire on!' A billow of smoke erupted from the fortress wall, followed by the bang of a gun and a howl as a round shot whipped overhead. Stokes jumped down into the battery, clutching his hat. 'It seems we've woken them up,' he remarked as a dozen more Mahratta guns fired. The enemy's shots smacked into the gabions or ricocheted wildly along the rocky ground. The second British battery fired, the noise of its guns echoing off the cliff face to tell the camp far beneath that the siege of Gawilghur had properly begun.

Private Tom Garrard of the 33rd's Light Company had wandered to the edge of the cliff to watch the bombardment of the fortress. Not that there was much to see other than the constantly replenished cloud of smoke that shrouded the rocky neck of land between the batteries and the fortress, but every now and then a large piece of stone would fall from Gawilghur's wall. The fire from the defences was furious, but it seemed to Garrard that it was ill aimed. Many of the shots bounced over the batteries, or else buried themselves in the great piles of protective gabions. The British fire, on the other hand, was slow and sure. The eighteen-pound round shots gnawed at the wall and not one was wasted. The sky was cloudless, the sun rising ever higher and the guns were heating so that after every second shot the gunners poured buckets of water on the long barrels. The metal hissed and steamed, and sweating *puckalees* hurried up the battery road with yet more skins of water to replenish the great vats.

Garrard was sitting by himself, but he had noticed a ragged Indian was watching him. He ignored the man, hoping he would go away, but the Indian edged closer. Garrard picked up a fist-sized stone and tossed it up and down in his right hand as a hint that the man should go away, but the threat of the stone only made the Indian edge closer. 'Sahib!' the Indian hissed.

'Bugger off,' Garrard growled.

'Sahib! Please!'

'I've got nothing worth stealing, I don't want to buy anything, and I don't want to roger your sister.'

'I'll roger your sister instead, sahib,' the Indian said, and Garrard twisted round, the stone drawn back ready to throw, then he saw that the dirty robed man had pushed back his grubby white head cloth and was grinning at him. 'You ain't supposed to chuck rocks at officers, Tom,' Sharpe said. 'Mind you, I always wanted to, so I can't blame you.'

'Bloody hell!' Garrard dropped the stone and held out his right hand. 'Dick Sharpe!' He suddenly checked his outstretched hand. 'Do I have to call you "sir"?'

'Of course you don't,' Sharpe said, taking Garrard's hand. 'You and me? Friends from way back, eh? Red sash won't change that, Tom. How are you?'

'Been worse. Yourself?'

'Been better.'

Garrard frowned. 'Didn't I hear that you'd been captured?'

'Got away, I did. Ain't a bugger born who can hold me, Tom. Nor you.' Sharpe sat next to his friend, a man with whom he had marched in the ranks for six years. 'Here.' He gave Garrard a strip of dried meat.

'What is it?'

'Goat. Tastes all right, though.'

The two sat and watched the gunners at work. The closest guns were in the two enfilading batteries, and the gunners were using their twelve-pounders to systematically bring down the parapets of the ramparts above Gawilghur's gate. They had already unseated a pair of enemy guns and were now working on the next two embrasures. An ox-drawn limber had just delivered more ammunition, but, on leaving the battery, the limber's wheel had loosened and five men were now standing about the canted wheel arguing how best to mend it. Garrard pulled a piece of stringy meat from between his teeth. 'Pull the broken wheel off and put on a new one,' he said scornfully. 'It don't take a major and two lieutenants to work that out.'

'They're officers, Tom,' Sharpe said chidingly, 'only half brained.'

'You should know.' Garrard grinned. 'Buggers make an inviting target, though.' He pointed across the plunging chasm which separated the plateau from the Inner Fort. 'There's a bloody great gun over there. Size of a bloody hay wain, it is. Buggers have been fussing about it for a half-hour now.'

Sharpe stared past the beleaguered Outer Fort to the distant cliffs. He thought he could see a wall where a gun might be mounted, but he was not sure. 'I need a bloody telescope.'

'You need a bloody uniform.'

'I'm doing something about that,' Sharpe said mysteriously.

Garrard slapped at a fly. 'What's it like then?'

'What's what like?'

'Being a Jack-pudding?'

Sharpe shrugged, thought for a while, then shrugged again. 'Don't seem real. Well, it does. I dunno.' He sighed. 'I mean I wanted it, Tom, I wanted it real bad, but I should have known the bastards wouldn't want me. Some are all right. Major Stokes, he's a fine fellow, and there are others. But most of them? God knows. They don't like me, anyway.'

'You got 'em worried, that's why,' Garrard said. 'If you can become an officer, so can others.' He saw the unhappiness on Sharpe's face. 'Wishing you'd stayed a sergeant, are you?'

'No,' Sharpe said, and surprised himself by saying it so firmly. 'I can do the job, Tom.'

'What job's that, for Christ's sake? Sitting around while we do all the bloody work? Having a servant to clean your boots and scrub your arse?'

'No,' Sharpe said, and he pointed across the shadowed chasm to the Inner Fort. 'When we go in there, Tom, we're going to need fellows who know what the hell they're doing. That's the job. It's beating hell out of the other side and keeping your own men alive, and I can do that.'

Garrard looked sceptical. 'If they let you.'

'Aye, if they let me,' Sharpe agreed. He sat in silence for a while, watching the far gun emplacement. He could see men there, but was not sure what they were doing. 'Where's Hakeswill?' he asked. 'I looked for him yesterday, and the bugger wasn't on parade with the rest of you.'

'Captured,' Garrard said.

'Captured?'

'That's what Morris says. Me, I think the bugger ran. Either ways, he's in the fort now.'

'You think he ran?'

'We had two fellows murdered the other night. Morris says it were the enemy, but I didn't see any of the buggers, but there was some fellow creeping round saying he was a Company colonel, only he weren't.' Garrard stared at Sharpe and a slow grin came to his face. 'It were you, Dick.'

'Me?' Sharpe asked straight-faced. 'I was captured, Tom. Only escaped yesterday.'

'And I'm the king of bloody Persia. Lowry and Kendrick were meant to arrest you, weren't they?'

'It was them who died?' Sharpe asked innocently.

Garrard laughed. 'Serve them bloody right. Bastards, both of them.' An enormous blossom of smoke showed at the distant wall on the top of the cliffs. Two seconds later the sound of the great gun bellowed all around Sharpe and Garrard, while the massive round shot struck the stalled limber just behind the enfilading battery. The wooden vehicle shattered into splinters and all five men were hurled to the ground where they jerked bloodily for a few seconds and then were still. Fragments of stone and wood hissed past Sharpe. 'Bloody hell,' Garrard said admiringly, 'five men with one shot!'

'That'll teach 'em to keep their heads down,' Sharpe said. The sound of the enormous gun had drawn men from their tents towards the plateau's edge. Sharpe looked round and saw that Captain Morris was among them. The Captain was in his shirtsleeves, staring at the great cloud of smoke through a telescope. 'I'm going to stand up in a minute,' Sharpe said, 'and you're going to hit me.'

'I'm going to do what?' Garrard asked.

'You're going to thump me. Then I'm going to run, and you're going to chase me. But you're not to catch me.'

Garrard offered his friend a puzzled look. 'What are you up to, Dick?'

Sharpe grinned. 'Don't ask, Tom, just do it.'

'You are a bloody officer, aren't you?' Garrard said, grinning back. 'Don't ask, just do it.'

'Are you ready?' Sharpe asked.

'I've always wanted to clobber an officer.'

'On your feet then.' They stood. 'So hit me,' Sharpe said. 'I've tried to pinch some cartridges off you, right? So give me a thump in the belly.'

'Bloody hell,' Garrard said.

'Go on, do it!'

Garrard gave Sharpe a half-hearted punch, and Sharpe shoved him back, making him fall, then he turned and ran along the cliff's edge. Garrard shouted, scrambled to his feet and began to pursue. Some of the men who had gone to fetch the five bodies moved to intercept Sharpe, but he dodged to his left and disappeared among some bushes. The rest of the 33rd's Light Company was whooping and shouting in pursuit, but Sharpe had a long lead on them and he twisted in and out of the shrubs to where he had picketed one of Syud Sevajee's horses. He pulled the peg loose, hauled himself into the saddle and kicked back his heels. Someone yelled an insult at him, but he was clear of the camp now and there were no mounted picquets to pursue him.

A half-hour later Sharpe returned, trotting with a group of native horsemen coming back from a reconnaissance. He peeled away from them and dismounted by his tent where Ahmed waited for him. While Sharpe and Garrard had made the diversion the boy had been thieving and he grinned broadly as Sharpe ducked into the hot tent. 'I have every things,' Ahmed said proudly.

He had taken Captain Morris's red coat, his sash and his sword-belt with its sabre. 'You're a good lad,' Sharpe said. He needed a red coat, for Colonel Stevenson had given orders that every man who went into Gawilghur with the attackers must be in uniform so that they were not mistaken for the enemy. Syud Sevajee's men, who planned to hunt down Beny Singh, had been issued with some threadbare old sepoys' jackets, some of them still stained with the blood of their previous owners, but none of the jackets had fitted Sharpe. Even Morris's coat would be a tight fit, but at least he had a uniform now. 'No trouble?' Sharpe asked Ahmed.

'No bugger saw me,' the boy said proudly. His English was improving every day, though Sharpe worried that it was not quite the King's English. Ahmed grinned again as Sharpe gave him a coin that he stuffed into his robes.

Sharpe folded the jacket over his arm and stooped out of the tent. He was looking for Clare and saw her a hundred paces away, walking with a tall soldier who was dressed in a shirt, black trousers and spurred boots. She was deep in conversation, and Sharpe felt a curious pang of jealousy as he approached, but then the soldier turned round, frowned at Sharpe's ragged appearance, then recognized the man under the head cloth. He grinned. 'Mister Sharpe,' he said.

'Eli Lockhart,' Sharpe said. 'What the hell are the cavalry doing here?' He jerked his thumb towards the fort that was edged with white smoke as the defenders tried to hammer the British batteries. 'This is a job for real soldiers.'

'Our Colonel persuaded the General that Mister Dodd might make a run for it. He reckoned a dozen cavalrymen could head him off.'

'Dodd won't run,' Sharpe said. 'He won't have space to get a horse out.'

'So we'll go in with you,' Lockhart said. 'We've got a quarrel with Mister Dodd, remember?'

Clare was looking shy and alarmed, and Sharpe reckoned she did not want Sergeant Lockhart to know that she had spent time with Ensign Sharpe. 'I was looking for Mrs Wall,' he explained to Lockhart. 'If you can spare me a few minutes, Ma'am?'

Clare shot Sharpe a look of gratitude. 'Of course, Mister Sharpe.'

'It's this jacket, see?' He held out Morris's coat. 'It's got red facings and turnbacks, and I need white ones.' He took off his head cloth. 'I wondered if you could use this. I know it's a bit filthy, and I hate to trouble you, Ma'am, but I don't reckon my sewing's up to making turnbacks, cuffs and collars.'

'You could take that captain's badge off while you're about it, love,' Lockhart suggested to Clare, 'and the skirmisher's wings. Don't reckon Mister Sharpe wants that coat's real owner to recognize it.'

'I'd rather he didn't,' Sharpe admitted.

Clare took the coat, gave Sharpe another grateful look, then hurried towards Sevajee's tents. Lockhart watched her go. 'Been wanting a chance to talk to her for three years,' he said wonderingly.

'So you found it, eh?'

Lockhart still watched her. 'A rare-looking woman, that.'

'Is she? I hadn't really noticed,' Sharpe lied.

'She said you'd been kind to her,' Lockhart said.

'Well, I tried to help, you know how it is,' Sharpe said awkwardly.

'That bloody man Torrance killed himself and she had nowhere to go. And you found her, eh? Most officers would try to take advantage of a woman like that,' Lockhart said.

'I'm not a proper officer, am I?' Sharpe replied. He had seen the way that Clare looked at the tall cavalryman, and how Lockhart had stared at her, and Sharpe reckoned that it was best to stand aside.

'I had a wife,' Lockhart said, 'only she died on the voyage out. Good little woman, she was.'

'I'm sorry,' Sharpe said.

'And Mrs Wall,' Lockhart went on, 'lost her husband.' Widow meets widower. Any minute now, Sharpe thought, and the word fate would be used. 'It's destiny,' Lockhart said in a tone of wonderment.

'So what are you going to do about her?' Sharpe asked.

'She says she ain't got a proper home now,' Lockhart said, 'except the tent you lent her, and my Colonel won't mind me taking a wife.'

'Have you asked her?'

'More or less,' Lockhart said, blushing.

'And she said yes?'

'More or less,' Lockhart said again, blushing more deeply.

'Bloody hell,' Sharpe said admiringly, 'that's quick!'

'Real soldiers don't wait,' Lockhart said, then frowned. 'I heard a rumour you'd been snaffled by the enemy?'

'Got away,' Sharpe said vaguely. 'Buggers were careless.' He turned and watched as an errant rocket from the fort soared up into the cloudless sky to leave a thickening pile of smoke through which, eventually, it tumbled harmlessly to earth. 'Are you really joining the attack?' he asked Lockhart.

'Not in the front rank,' Lockhart said. 'I ain't a fool. But Colonel Huddlestone says we can go in and look for Dodd. So we'll wait for you boys to do the hard work, then follow.'

'I'll look out for you.'

'And we'll keep an eye on you,' Lockhart promised. 'But in the meantime I'll go and see if someone needs a needle threaded.'

'You do that,' Sharpe said. He watched the cavalryman walk away, and saw, at the same time, that Ahmed had been evicted from Clare's tent with Sharpe's few belongings. The boy looked indignant, but Sharpe guessed their exile from the tent would not last long, for Clare would surely move to the cavalryman's quarters before nightfall. Ding dong, he thought, wedding bells. He took the pouch with its jewels from Ahmed, then, while his uniform was being tailored, he went to watch the guns gnaw and batter at the fort.

The young horseman who presented himself at the gate of Gawilghur's Inner Fort was tall, arrogant and self-assured. He was dressed in a white silk robe that was tied at the waist with a red leather belt from which a golden-hilted *tulwar* hung in a gem-encrusted scabbard, and he did not request that the gates be opened, but rather demanded it. There was, in truth, no good reason to deny his orders, for men were constantly traversing the ravine between the two forts and Dodd's Cobras were accustomed to opening and closing the gates a score of times each day, but there was something in the young man's demeanour that annoyed Gopal. So he sent for Colonel Dodd.

Dodd arrived a few moments later with the twitching English Sergeant at his side. The horseman rounded on Dodd, shouting at him to punish Gopal, but Dodd just spat, then turned to Hakeswill. 'Why would a man be riding a horse out of this gate?'

'Wouldn't know, sir,' Hakeswill said. The Sergeant was now dressed in a white coat that was crossed with a black sash as a sign of rank, though quite what rank the sash denoted was uncertain.

'There's nowhere to exercise a horse,' Dodd said, 'not unless he plans to ride through the Outer Fort into the English camp. Ask him his business, Gopal.'

The young man refused to answer. Dodd shrugged, drew his pistol and aimed it at the horseman's head. He cocked the gun and the sound of the hammer engaging echoed loudly from the ramparts. The young man blanched and shouted at Gopal.

'He says, sahib, that he is on an errand for the Killadar,' Gopal explained to Dodd.

'What errand?' Dodd demanded. The young man plainly did not want to answer, but Dodd's grim face and the levelled pistol persuaded him to take a sealed packet from the pouch that hung from his belt. He showed Dodd the Killadar's seal, but Dodd was not impressed by the red wax with its impression of a snake curled about a knife blade. 'Who is it addressed to?' he demanded, gesturing that the young man turn the package over.

The horseman obeyed and Dodd saw that the packet was addressed to the commanding officer of the British camp. It must have been written by a clerk who was unfamiliar with the English language, for it was atrociously spelt, but the words were unmistakable and Dodd stepped forward and seized the horse's bridle. 'Haul him out of the saddle, Gopal,' Dodd ordered, 'hold him in the guardroom and send a man to fetch Manu Bappoo.'

The young man attempted a momentary resistance, even half drawing his *tulwar* from its precious scabbard, but a dozen of Dodd's men easily overpowered him. Dodd himself turned away and climbed the steps to the rampart, motioning Hakeswill to follow him. 'It's obvious what the Killadar is doing,' Dodd growled. 'He's trying to make peace.'

'I thought we couldn't be defeated here, sir,' Hakeswill said in some alarm.

'We can't,' Dodd said, 'but Beny Singh is a coward. He thinks life should be nothing but women, music and games.'

Which sounded just splendid to Obadiah Hakeswill, but he said nothing. He had presented himself to Dodd as an aggrieved British soldier who believed the war against the Mahrattas was unfair. 'We ain't got no business here, sir,' he had said, 'not in heathen land. It belongs to the blackamoors, don't it? And there ain't nothing here for a redcoat.'

Dodd had not believed a word of it. He suspected Hakeswill had

222

fled the British army to avoid trouble, but he could hardly blame the Sergeant for that. Dodd himself had done the same, and Dodd did not care about Hakeswill's motives, only that the Sergeant was willing to fight. And Dodd believed his men fought better when white men gave them orders. 'There's a steadiness about the English, Sergeant,' he had told Hakeswill, 'and it gives the natives bottom.'

'It gives them what, sir?' Hakeswill had asked.

Dodd had frowned at the Sergeant's obtuseness. 'You ain't Scotch, are you?'

'Christ no, sir! I ain't a bleeding Scotchman, nor a Welshman. English, sir, I am, through and through, sir.' His face twitched. 'English, sir, and proud of it.'

So Dodd had given Hakeswill a white jacket and a black sash, then put him in charge of a company of his Cobras. 'Fight well for me here, Sergeant,' he told Hakeswill when the two men reached the top of the rampart, 'and I'll make you an officer.'

'I shall fight, sir, never you mind, sir. Fight like a demon, I will.'

And Dodd believed him, for if Hakeswill did not fight then he risked being captured by the British, and God alone knew what trouble he would then face. Though in truth Dodd did not see how the British could penetrate the Inner Fort. He expected them to take the Outer Fort, for there they had a flat approach and their guns were already blasting down the breaches, but they would have a far greater problem in capturing the Inner Fort. He showed that problem now to Hakeswill. 'There's only one way in, Sergeant, and that's through this gate. They can't assault the walls, because the slope of the ravine is too steep. See?'

Hakeswill looked to his left and saw that the wall of the Inner Fort was built on an almost sheer slope. No man could climb that and hope to assail a wall, even a breached wall, which meant that Dodd was right and the attackers would have to try and batter down the four gates that barred the entranceway, and those gates were defended by Dodd's Cobras. 'And my men have never known defeat, Sergeant,' Dodd said. 'They've watched other men beaten, but they've not been outfought themselves. And here the enemy will have to beat us. Have to! But they can't. They can't.' He fell silent, his clenched fists resting on the firestep. The sound of the guns was constant, but the only sign of the bombardment was the misting smoke that hung over the far side of the Outer Fort. Manu Bappoo, who commanded there, was now hurrying back towards the Inner Fort and Dodd watched the Prince climb the steep path to the gates. The hinges squealed as, one after the other, the gates were opened to let Bappoo and his aides in. Dodd smiled as the last gate was unbarred. 'Let's go and make some mischief,' he said, turning back to the steps.

Manu Bappoo had already opened the letter that Gopal had given to him. He looked up as Dodd approached. 'Read it,' he said simply, thrusting the folded paper towards the Colonel.

'He wants to surrender?' Dodd asked, taking the letter.

'Just read it,' Bappoo said grimly.

The letter was clumsily written, but intelligible. Beny Singh, as Killadar of the Rajah of Berar's fortress of Gawilghur, was offering to yield the fort to the British on the sole condition that the lives of all the garrison and their dependants were spared. None was to be hurt, none was to be imprisoned. The British were welcome to confiscate all the weaponry in the fort, but they were to allow Gawilghur's inhabitants to leave with such personal property as could be carried away on foot or horseback.

'Of course the British will accept!' Manu Bappoo said. 'They don't want to die in the breaches!'

'Has Beny Singh the authority to send this?' Dodd asked.

Bappoo shrugged. 'He's Killadar.'

'You're the general of the army. And the Rajah's brother.'

Bappoo stared up at the sky between the high walls of the entrance-way. 'One can never tell with my brother,' he said. 'Maybe he wants to surrender? But he hasn't told me. Maybe, if we lose, he can blame me, saying he always wanted to yield.'

'But you won't yield?'

'We can win here!' Bappoo said fiercely, then turned towards the palace as Gopal announced that the Killadar himself was approaching.

Beny Singh must have been watching his messenger's progress from the palace, for now he hurried down the path and behind him came his wives, concubines and daughters. Bappoo walked towards him, followed by Dodd and a score of his white-coated soldiers. The Killadar must have reckoned that the sight of the women would soften Bappoo's heart, but the Prince's face just became harder. 'If you want to surrender,' he shouted at Beny Singh, 'then talk to me first!'

'I have authority here,' Beny Singh squeaked. His little lap dog was in his arms, its small tongue hanging out as it panted in the heat.

'You have nothing!' Bappoo retorted. The women, pretty in their silk and cotton, huddled together as the two men met beside the snake pit.

'The British are making their breaches,' Beny Singh protested, 'and tomorrow or the day after they'll come through! We shall all be killed!' He wailed the prophecy. 'My daughters will be their playthings and my wives their servants.' The women shuddered.

'The British will die in the breaches,' Bappoo retorted.

'They cannot be stopped!' Beny Singh insisted. 'They are *djinns*.'

Bappoo suddenly shoved Beny Singh back towards the rock pit where the snakes were kept. The Killadar cried aloud as he tripped and fell backwards, but Bappoo had kept hold of Beny Singh's yellow silk robe and now he held on tight so that the Killadar did not fall. Hakeswill sidled to the pit's edge and saw the monkey bones. Then he saw a curving, flickering shape slither across the pit's shadowed floor and he quickly stepped back.

Beny Singh whimpered. 'I am the Killadar! I am trying to save lives!'

'You're supposed to be a soldier,' Bappoo said in his hissing voice, 'and your job is to kill my brother's enemies.' The women screamed, expecting to see their man fall to the pit's floor, but Manu Bappoo kept a firm grip on the silk. 'And when the British die in the breaches,' he said to Beny Singh, 'and when their survivors are harried south across the plain, who do you think will get the credit for the victory? The Killadar of the fort, that is who! And you would throw that glory away?'

'They are *djinns*,' Beny Singh said, and he looked sideways at Obadiah Hakeswill whose face was twitching, and he screamed. 'They are *djinns*!'

'They are men, as feeble as other men,' Bappoo said. He reached out with his free hand and took hold of the white dog by the scruff of its neck. Beny Singh whimpered, but did not resist. The dog struggled in Manu Bappoo's grip. 'If you try to surrender the fortress again,' Manu Bappoo said, 'then this will be your fate.' He let the dog drop. It yelped as it fell into the pit, then howled piteously as it struck the rock floor. There was a hiss, a scrabble of paws, a last howl, then

225

silence. Beny Singh uttered a shriek of pity for his dog before babbling that he would rather give his women poison to drink than risk that they should become prey to the terrible besiegers.

Manu Bappoo shook the hapless Killadar. 'Do you understand me?' he demanded.

'I understand!' Beny Singh said desperately.

Manu Bappoo hauled the Killadar safely back from the pit's edge. 'You will go to the palace, Beny Singh,' he ordered, 'and you will stay there, and you will send no more messages to the enemy.' He pushed the Killadar away, then turned his back on him. 'Colonel Dodd?'

'Sahib?'

'A dozen of your men will make certain that the Killadar sends no messages from the palace. If he does, you may kill the messenger.'

Dodd smiled. 'Of course, sahib.'

Bappoo went back to the beleaguered Outer Fort while the Killadar slunk back to the hilltop palace above its green-scummed lake. Dodd detailed a dozen men to guard the palace's entrance, then went back to the rampart to brood over the ravine. Hakeswill followed him there. 'Why's the Killadar so scared, sir? Does he know something we don't?'

'He's a coward, Sergeant.'

But Beny Singh's fear had infected Hakeswill who imagined a vengeful Sharpe come back from the dead to pursue him through the nightmare of a fortress fallen. 'The bastards can't get in, sir, can they?' he asked anxiously.

Dodd recognized Hakeswill's fear, the same fear he felt himself, the fear of the ignominy and shame of being recaptured by the British and then condemned by a merciless court. He smiled. 'They will probably take the Outer Fort, Sergeant, because they're very good, and because our old comrades do indeed fight like *djinns*, but they cannot cross the ravine. Not if all the powers of darkness help them, not if they besiege us for a year, not if they batter down all these walls and destroy the gates and flatten the palace by gunfire, because they will still have to cross the ravine, and it cannot be done. It cannot be done.'

And who rules Gawilghur, Dodd thought, reigns in India.

And within a week he would be Rajah here.

* * *

Gawilghur's walls, as Stokes had guessed, were rotten. The first breach, in the outer wall, took less than a day to make. In mid-afternoon the wall had still been standing, though a cave had been excavated into the dusty rubble where Stokes had pointed the guns, but quite suddenly the whole rampart collapsed. It slid down the brief slope in a cloud of dust which slowly settled to reveal a steep ramp of jumbled stone leading into the space between the two walls. A low stub of the wall's rear face still survived, but an hour's work served to throw that remnant down.

The gunners changed their aim, starting the two breaches in the higher inner wall, while the enfilading batteries, which had been gnawing at the embrasures to dismount the enemy's guns, began firing slantwise into the first breach to dissuade the defenders from building obstacles at the head of the ramp. The enemy guns, those which survived, redoubled their efforts to disable the British batteries, but their shots were wasted in the gabions or overhead. The big gun which had inflicted such slaughter fired three times more, but its balls cracked uselessly into the cliff face, after which the Mahratta gunners mysteriously gave up.

Next day the two inner breaches were made, and now the big guns concentrated on widening all three gaps in the walls. The eighteen-pounder shots slammed into rotten stone, gouging out the wall's fill to add to the ramps. By evening the breaches were clearly big enough and now the gunners aimed their pieces at the enemy's remaining cannon. One by one they were unseated or their embrasures shattered. A constant shroud of smoke hung over the rocky neck of land. It hung thick and pungent, twitching every time a shot whipped through. The enfilading twelve-pounders fired shells into the breaches, while the howitzer lobbed more shells over the walls.

The British guns fired deep into dusk, and minute by minute the enemy response grew feebler as their guns were wrecked or thrown off the firesteps. Only as black night dropped did the besiegers' hot guns cease fire, but even now there would be no respite for the enemy. It was at night that the defenders could turn the breaches into deathtraps. They could bury mines in the stony ramps, or dig wide trenches across the breach summits or make new walls behind the raw new openings, but the British kept one heavy gun firing throughout the darkness. They loaded the eighteen-pounder with canister and, three times an hour, sprayed the area of the breaches with a cloud of musket balls to deter any Mahratta from risking his life on the rubbled slopes.

Few slept well that night. The cough of the gun seemed unnaturally loud, and even in the British camp men could hear the rattle as the musket balls whipped against Gawilghur's wounded walls. And in the morning, the soldiers knew, they would be asked to go to those walls and climb the tumbled ramps and fight their way through the shattered stones. And what would wait for them? At the very least, they suspected, the enemy would have mounted guns athwart the breaches to fire across the attack route. They expected blood and pain and death.

'I've never been into a breach,' Garrard told Sharpe. The two men met at Syud Sevajee's tents, and Sharpe had given his old friend a bottle of arrack.

'Nor me,' Sharpe said.

'They say it's bad.'

'They do,' Sharpe agreed bleakly. It was supposedly the worst ordeal that any soldier could face.

Garrard drank from the stone bottle, wiped its lip, then handed it to Sharpe. He admired Sharpe's coat in the light of the small campfire. 'Smart bit of cloth, Mister Sharpe.'

The coat had been given new white turnbacks and cuffs by Clare Wall, and Sharpe had done his best to make the jacket wrinkled and dusty, but it still looked expensive. 'Just an old coat, Tom,' he said dismissively.

'Funny, isn't it? Mister Morris lost a coat.'

'Did he?' Sharpe asked. 'He should be more careful.' He gave Garrard the bottle, then climbed to his feet. 'I've got an errand, Tom.' He held out his hand. 'I'll look for you tomorrow.'

'I'll look out for you, Dick.'

Sharpe led Ahmed through the camp. Some men sang around their fires, others obsessively honed bayonets that were already razor sharp. A cavalryman had set up a grinding stone and a succession of officers' servants brought swords and sabres to be given a wicked edge. Sparks whipped off the stone. The sappers were doing their last job, making ladders from bamboo that had been carried up from the plain. Major Stokes supervised the job, and his eyes widened in joy as he saw Sharpe approaching through the firelight. 'Richard! Is it you? Dear me, it is!

Well, I never! And I thought you were locked up in the enemy's dungeons! You escaped?'

Sharpe shook Stokes's hand. 'I never got taken to Gawilghur. I was held by some horsemen,' he lied, 'but they didn't seem to know what to do with me, so the buggers just let me go.'

'I'm delighted, delighted!'

Sharpe turned and looked at the ladders. 'I didn't think we were making an escalade tomorrow?'

'We're not,' Stokes said, 'but you never know what obstacles have to be overcome inside a fortress. Sensible to carry ladders.' He peered at Ahmed who was now dressed in one of the sepoy's coats that had been given to Syud Sevajee. The boy wore the red jacket proudly, even though it was a poor, threadbare and bloodstained thing. 'I say,' Stokes admired the boy, 'but you do look like a proper soldier. Don't he just?' Ahmed stood to attention, shouldered his musket and made a smart about-turn. Major Stokes applauded. 'Well done, lad. I'm afraid you've missed all the excitement, Sharpe.'

'Excitement?'

'Your Captain Torrance died. Shot himself, by the look of things. Terrible way to go. I feel sorry for his father. He's a cleric, did you know? Poor man, poor man. Would you like some tea, Sharpe? Or do you need to sleep?'

'I'd like some tea, sir.'

'We'll go to my tent,' Stokes said, leading the way. 'I've still got your pack, by the way. You can take it with you.'

'I'd rather you kept it another day,' Sharpe said, 'I'll be busy tomorrow.'

'Busy?' Stokes asked.

'I'm going in with Kenny's troops, sir.'

'Dear God,' Stokes said. He stopped and frowned. 'I've no doubt we'll get through the breaches, Richard, for they're good breaches. A bit steep, perhaps, but we should get through, but God only knows what waits beyond. And I fear that the Inner Fort may be a much bigger obstacle than any of us have anticipated.' He shook his head. 'I ain't sanguine, Sharpe, I truly ain't.'

Sharpe had no idea what sanguine meant, though he did not doubt that Stokes's lack of it did not augur well for the attack. 'I have to go into the fort, sir. I have to. But I wondered if you'd keep an eye on

Ahmed here.' He took hold of the boy's shoulder and pulled him forward. 'The little bugger will insist on coming with me,' Sharpe said, 'but if you keep him out of trouble then he might survive another day.'

'He can be my assistant,' Stokes said happily. 'But, Richard, can't I persuade you to the same employment? Are you ordered to accompany Kenny?'

'I'm not ordered, sir, but I have to go. It's personal business.'

'It will be bloody in there,' Stokes warned. He walked on to his tent and shouted for his servant.

Sharpe pushed Ahmed towards Stokes's tent. 'You stay here, Ahmed, you hear me? You stay here!'

'I come with you,' Ahmed insisted.

'You bloody well stay,' Sharpe said. He twitched Ahmed's red coat. 'You're a soldier now. That means you take orders, understand? You obey. And I'm ordering you to stay here.'

The boy scowled, but he seemed to accept the orders, and Stokes showed him a place where he could sleep. Afterwards the two men talked, or rather Sharpe listened as Stokes enthused about some fine quartz he had discovered in rocks broken open by the enemy's counter-battery fire. Eventually the Major began yawning. Sharpe finished his tea, said his good night and then, making certain that Ahmed did not see him go, he slipped away into the dark.

He still could not sleep. He wished Clare had not gone to Eli Lockhart, although he was glad for the cavalryman that she had, but her absence made Sharpe feel lonely. He walked to the cliff's edge and he stood staring across the great gulf towards the fortress. A few lights showed in Gawilghur, and every twenty minutes or so the rocky isthmus would be lit by the monstrous flame of the eighteen-pounder gun. The balls would rattle against stone, then there would be silence except for the distant sound of singing, the crackle of insects and the soft sigh of the wind against the cliffs. Once, when the great gun fired, Sharpe distinctly saw the three ragged holes in the two walls. And why, he wondered, was he so intent on going into those deathtraps? Was it revenge? Just to find Hakeswill and Dodd? He could wait for the attackers to do their work, then stroll into the fort unopposed, but he knew he would not choose that easy path. He would go with Kenny's men and he would fight his way into Gawilghur for no other reason than pride. He was failing as an officer. The 74th had rejected him, the Rifles did not yet know him, so Sharpe must take a reputation back to England if he was to stand any chance of success.

So tomorrow he must fight. Or else he must sell his commission and leave the army. He had thought about that, but he wanted to stay in uniform. He enjoyed the army, he even suspected he was good at the army's business of fighting the King's enemies. So tomorrow he would do it again, and thus demonstrate that he deserved the red sash and the sword.

So in the morning, when the drums beat and the enemy guns beat even harder, Sharpe would go into Gawilghur.

CHAPTER 9

At dawn there was a mist in Deogaum, a mist that sifted through the rain trees and pooled in the valleys and beaded on the tents. 'A touch of winter, don't you think?' Sir Arthur Wellesley commented to his aide, Campbell.

'The thermometer's showing seventy-eight degrees, sir,' the young Scotsman answered drily.

'Only a touch of winter, Campbell, only a touch,' the General said. He was standing outside his tent, a cup and saucer in one hand, staring up through the wisps of mist to where the rising sun threw a brilliant light on Gawilghur's soaring cliffs. A servant stood behind with Wellesley's coat, hat and sword, a second servant held his horse, while a third waited to take the cup and saucer. 'How's Harness?' the General asked Campbell.

'I believe he now sleeps most of the time, sir,' Campbell replied. Colonel Harness had been relieved of the command of his brigade. He had been found ranting in the camp, demanding that his Highlanders form fours and follow him southwards to fight against dragons, papists and Whigs.

'Sleeps?' the General asked. 'What are the doctors doing? Pouring rum down his gullet?'

'I believe it is tincture of opium, sir, but most likely flavoured with rum.'

'Poor Harness,' Wellesley grunted, then sipped his tea. From high above him there came the sound of a pair of twelve-pounder guns that had been hauled to the summit of the conical hill that reared just south of the fortress. Wellesley knew those guns were doing no good, but he had stubbornly insisted that they fire at the fortress gate that looked out across the vast plain. The gunners had warned the General that

232

the weapons would be ineffective, that they would be firing too far and too high above them, but Wellesley had wanted the fortress to know that an assault might come from the south as well as across the rocky isthmus to the north, and so he had ordered the sappers to drag the two weapons up through the entangling jungle and to make a battery on the hill top. The guns, firing at their maximum elevation, were just able to throw their missiles to Gawilghur's southern entrance, but by the time the round shot reached the gate it was spent of all force and simply bounced back down the steep slope. But that was not the point. The point was to keep some of the garrison looking southwards, so that not every man could be thrown against the assault on the breaches.

That assault would not start for five hours yet, for before Lieutenant Colonel Kenny led his men against the breaches, Wellesley wanted his other attackers to be in place. Those were two columns of redcoats that were even now climbing the two steep roads that twisted up the great cliffs. Colonel Wallace, with his own 74th and a battalion of sepoys, would approach the Southern Gate, while the 78th and another native battalion would climb the road which led to the ravine between the forts. Both columns could expect to come under heavy artillery fire, and neither could hope to break into the fortress, but their job was only to distract the defenders while Kenny's men made for the breaches.

Wellesley drained the tea, made a wry face at its bitter taste and held out the cup and saucer for the servant. 'Time to go, Campbell.'

'Yes, sir.'

Wellesley had thought about riding to the plateau and entering the fortress behind Kenny, but he guessed his presence would merely distract men who had enough problems to face without worrying about their commander's approval. Instead he would ride the steep southern road and join Wallace and the 74th. All those men could hope for was that the other attackers got inside the Inner Fort and opened the Southern Gate, or else they would have to march ignominiously back down the hill to their encampment. It was all or nothing, Wellesley thought. Victory or disgrace.

He mounted, waited for his aides to assemble, then touched his horse's flank with his spurs. God help us now, he prayed, God help us now.

* * *

Lieutenant Colonel Kenny examined the breaches through a telescope that he had propped on a rock close to one of the breaching batteries. The guns were firing, but he ignored the vast noise as he gazed at the stone ramps which his men must climb. 'They're steep, man,' he grumbled, 'damned steep.'

'The walls are built on a slope,' Major Stokes pointed out, 'so the breaches are steep of necessity.'

'Damned hard to climb though,' Kenny said.

'They're practical,' Stokes declared. He knew the breaches were steep, and that was why the guns were still firing. There was no hope of making the breaches less steep, the slope of the hill saw to that, but at least the continued bombardment gave the attacking infantry the impression that the gunners were attempting to alleviate the difficulties.

'You've made holes in the walls,' Kenny said, 'I'll grant you that. You've made holes, but that don't make them practical holes, Stokes. They're damned steep.'

'Of necessity,' Stokes repeated patiently.

'We ain't monkeys, you know,' Kenny complained.

'I think you'll find them practical, sir,' Stokes said emolliently. He knew, and Kenny knew, that the breaches could not be improved and must therefore be attempted. Kenny's grumbling, Stokes suspected, was a disguise for nerves, and Stokes could not blame the man. He would not have wanted to carry a sword or musket up those rugged stone slopes to whatever horrors the enemy had prepared on the other side.

Kenny grunted. 'I suppose they'll have to suffice,' he said grudgingly, snapping his telescope shut. He flinched as one of the eighteen-pounders roared and billowed smoke all about the battery, then he strode into the acrid cloud, shouting for Major Plummer, the gunner officer.

Plummer, powder-stained and sweating, loomed out of the smoke. 'Sir?'

'You'll keep your pieces firing till we're well on the breaches?'

'I will, sir.'

'That should keep their damned heads down,' Kenny said, then fished a watch from his fob. 'I make it ten minutes after nine.'

'Eight minutes after,' Plummer said.

'Exactly nine o'clock,' Stokes said, tapping his watch to see if the hands were stuck.

'We'll use my timepiece,' Kenny decreed, 'and we'll move forward on the strike of ten o'clock. And remember, Plummer, keep firing till we're there! Don't be chary, man, don't stop just because we're close to the summit. Batter the bastards! Batter the bastards!' He frowned at Ahmed who was staying close to Stokes. The boy was wearing his red coat which was far too big for him, and Kenny seemed on the point of demanding an explanation for the boy's odd garb, then abruptly shrugged and walked away.

He went to where his men crouched on the track that led to the fortress gate. They were sheltered from the defenders by the lie of the land, but the moment they advanced over a small rocky rise they would become targets. They then had three hundred yards of open ground to cross, and as they neared the broken walls they would be squeezed into the narrow space between the tank and the precipice where they could expect the fire of the defenders to be at its fiercest. After that it was a climb to the breaches and to whatever horrors waited out of sight.

The men sat, trying to find what small shade was offered by bushes or rocks. Many were half drunk, for their officers had issued extra rations of arrack and rum. None carried a pack, they had only their muskets, their ammunition and bayonets. A few, not many, prayed. An officer of the Scotch Brigade knelt bare-headed amongst a group of his men, and Kenny, intrigued by the sight, swerved towards the kneeling soldiers to hear them softly repeating the twenty-third psalm. Most men just sat, heads low, consumed by their thoughts. The officers forced conversation.

Behind Kenny's thousand men was a second assault force, also composed of sepoys and Scotsmen, which would follow Kenny into the breach. If Kenny failed then the second storming party would try to go farther, but if Kenny succeeded they would secure the Outer Fort while Kenny's troops went on to assault the Inner. Small groups of gunners were included in both assault groups. Their orders were to find whatever serviceable cannon still existed in the Outer Fort and turn them against the defenders beyond the ravine.

An officer wearing the white facings of the 74th picked his way up the track between the waiting troops. The man had a cheap Indian sabre at his waist and, unusually for an officer, was carrying a musket and cartridge box. Kenny hailed him. 'Who the devil are you?'

'Sharpe, sir.'

The name rang a bell in Kenny's mind. 'Wellesley's man?'

'Don't know about that, sir.'

Kenny scowled at the evasion. 'You were at Assaye, yes?'

'Yes, sir,' Sharpe admitted.

Kenny's expression softened. He knew of Sharpe and he admired a brave man. 'So what the devil are you doing here, Sharpe? Your regiment is miles away! They're climbing the road from Deogaum.'

'I was stranded here, sir,' Sharpe said, deciding there was no point in trying to deliver a longer explanation, 'and there wasn't time to join the 74th, sir, so I was hoping to go with my old company. That's Captain Morris's men, sir.' He nodded up the track to where the 33rd's Light Company was gathered among some boulders. 'With your permission of course, sir.'

'No doubt Morris will be glad of your help, Sharpe,' Kenny said, 'as will I.' He was impressed by Sharpe's appearance, for the Ensign was tall, evidently strong and had a roguish fierceness about his face. In the breach, the Colonel knew, victory or defeat as often as not came down to a man's skill and strength, and Sharpe looked as if he knew how to use his weapons. 'Good luck to you, Sharpe.'

'And the best to you, sir,' Sharpe said warmly.

He walked on, his borrowed musket heavy on his shoulder. Eli Lockhart and Syud Sevajee were waiting with their men among the third group, the soldiers who would occupy the fort after the assault troops had done their work, if, indeed, the leading two thousand men managed to get through the walls. A rumour was spreading that the breaches were too steep and that no one could carry a weapon and climb the ramps at the same time. The men believed they would need to use their hands to scramble up the stony piles, and so they would be easy targets for any defenders at the top of the breaches. The gunners, they grumbled, should have brought down more of the wall, if not all of it, and the proof of that assertion was the guns' continual firing. Why would the guns go on gnawing at the wall if the breaches were already practical? They could hear the strike of round shot on stone, hear the occasional tumble of rubble, but what they could not

236

hear was any fire from the fortress. The bastards were saving their fire for the assault.

Sharpe edged among sepoys who were carrying one of Major Stokes's bamboo ladders. The dark faces grinned at him, and one man offered Sharpe a canteen which proved to contain a strongly spiced arrack. Sharpe took a small sip, then amused the sepoys by pretending to be astonished by the liquor's fierceness. 'That's rare stuff, lads,' Sharpe said, then walked on towards his old comrades. They watched his approach with a mixture of surprise, welcome and apprehension. When the 33rd's Light Company had last seen Sharpe he had been a sergeant, and not long before that he had been a private strapped to the punishment triangle; now he wore a sword and sash. Although officers promoted from the ranks were not supposed to serve with their old units, Sharpe had friends among these men and if he was to climb the steep rubble of Gawilghur's breaches then he would rather do it among friends.

Captain Morris was no friend, and he watched Sharpe's approach with foreboding. Sharpe headed straight for his old company commander. 'Good to see you, Charles,' he said, knowing that his use of the Christian name would irritate Morris. 'Nice morning, eh?'

Morris looked left and right as though seeking someone who could help him confront this upstart from his past. Morris had never liked Sharpe, indeed he had conspired with Obadiah Hakeswill to have Sharpe flogged in the hope that the punishment would end in death, but Sharpe had survived and had been commissioned. Now the bastard was being familiar, and there was nothing Morris could do about it. 'Sharpe,' he managed to say.

'Thought I'd join you, Charles,' Sharpe said airily. 'I've been stranded up here, and Kenny reckoned I might be useful to you.'

'Of course,' Morris said, conscious of his men's gaze. Morris would have liked to tell Sharpe to bugger a long way off, but he could not commit such impoliteness to a fellow officer in front of his men. 'I never congratulated you,' he forced himself to say.

'No time like the present,' Sharpe said.

Morris blushed. 'Congratulations.'

'Thank you, Charles,' Sharpe said, then turned and looked at the company. Most grinned at him, but a few men avoided his gaze. 'No Sergeant Hakeswill?' Sharpe asked guilelessly.

'He was captured by the enemy,' Morris said. The Captain was staring at Sharpe's coat which was not quite big enough and looked, somehow, familiar.

Sharpe saw Morris frowning at the jacket. 'You like the coat?' he asked.

'What?' Morris asked, confused by his suspicions and by Sharpe's easy manner. Morris himself was wearing an old coat that was disfigured by brown cloth patches.

'I bought the coat after Assaye,' Sharpe said. 'You weren't there, were you?'

'No.'

'Nor at Argaum?'

'No,' Morris said, stiffening slightly. He resented the fact that Sharpe had survived those battles and was now suggesting, however delicately, that the experience gave him an advantage. The truth was that it did, but Morris could not admit that any more than he could admit his jealousy of Sharpe's reputation.

'So what are our orders today?' Sharpe asked.

Morris could not accustom himself to this confident Sharpe who treated him as an equal and he was tempted not to answer, but the question was reasonable and Sharpe was undoubtedly an officer, if merely an ensign. 'Once we're through the first wall,' Morris answered unhappily, 'Kenny's going to attack the left-hand upper breach and he wants us to seal off the right upper breach.'

'Sounds like a decent morning's work,' Sharpe said happily, then raised a hand to Garrard. 'How are you, Tom?'

'Pleased you're here, sir.'

'Couldn't let you babies go into a breach without some help,' Sharpe said, then held out his hand to Sergeant Green. 'Good to see you, Sergeant.'

'Grand to see you too, sir,' Green said, shaking Sharpe's hand. 'I heard you'd been commissioned and I hardly dared believe it!'

'You know what they say about scum, Sergeant,' Sharpe said. 'Always floats to the top, eh?' Some of the men laughed, especially when Sharpe glanced at Morris who had, indeed, expressed that very opinion not long before. Others scowled, for there were plenty in the company who resented Sharpe's good fortune.

One of them, a dark-faced man called Crowley, spat. 'You always were a lucky bastard, Sharpie.'

Sharpe seemed to ignore the remark as he stepped through the seated company and greeted more of his old friends, but when he was behind Crowley he turned abruptly and pushed out the butt of his slung musket so that the heavy stock thumped into the private's head. Crowley let out a yelp and turned to see Sharpe standing above him. 'The word, Crowley,' Sharpe said menacingly, 'is "sir".'

Crowley met Sharpe's gaze, but could not hold it. 'Yes, sir,' he said meekly.

'I'm sorry I was careless with the musket, Crowley,' Sharpe said.

There was another burst of laughter, making Morris scowl, but he was quite uncertain of how to deal with Sharpe and so he said nothing. Watson, a Welsh private who had joined the regiment rather than face an assize court, jerked a thumb towards the fort. 'They say the breaches are too steep, Mister Sharpe.'

'Nothing to what you Welsh boys climb every day in the mountains,' Sharpe said. He had borrowed Major Stokes's telescope shortly after dawn and stared at the breaches, and he had not much liked what he had seen, but this was no time to tell the truth. 'We're going to give the buggers a right bloody thrashing, lads,' he said instead. 'I've fought these Mahrattas twice now and they don't stand. They look good, but press home on the bastards and they turn and run like jack rabbits. Just keep going, boys, keep fighting, and the buggers'll give up.'

It was the speech Morris should have made to them, and Sharpe had not even known he was going to make any kind of speech when he opened his mouth, but somehow the words had come. And he was glad, for the men looked relieved at his confidence, then some of them looked nervous again as they watched a sepoy coming up the track with a British flag in his hands. Colonel Kenny and his aides walked behind the man, all with drawn swords. Captain Morris drank deep from his canteen, and the smell of rum wafted to Sharpe.

The guns fired on, crumbling the breaches' shoulders and filling the air with smoke and dust as they tried to make the rough way smooth. Soldiers, sensing that the order to advance was about to be given, stood and hefted their weapons. Some touched rabbits' feet hidden in pockets, or whatever other small token gave them a fingerhold on life.

One man vomited, another trembled. Sweat poured down their faces.

'Four ranks,' Morris said.

'Into ranks! Quick now!' Sergeant Green snapped. An howitzer shell arced overhead then plummeted towards the fort trailing its wisp of fuse smoke. Sharpe heard the shell explode, then watched another shell follow. A man dashed out of the ranks into the rocks, lowered his trousers and emptied his bowels. Everyone pretended not to notice until the smell struck them, then they jeered as the embarrassed man went back to his place. 'That's enough!' Green said.

A sepoy drummer with an old-fashioned mitred shako on his head gave his drum a couple of taps, while a piper from the Scotch Brigade filled his bag then settled the instrument under his elbow. Colonel Kenny was looking at his watch. The guns fired on, their smoke drifting down to the waiting men. The sepoy with the flag was at the front of the forming column, and Sharpe guessed the enemy must be able to see the bright tip of the colour above the rocky crest.

Sharpe took the bayonet from his belt and slotted it onto the musket. He was not wearing the sabre that Ahmed had stolen from Morris, for he knew the weapon would be identifiable, and so he had a *tulwar* that he had borrowed from Syud Sevajee. He did not trust the weapon. He had seen too many Indian blades break in combat. Besides he was used to a musket and bayonet.

'Fix bayonets!' Morris ordered, prompted by the sight of Sharpe's blade.

'And save your fire till you're hard in the breach,' Sharpe added. 'You've got one shot, lads, so don't waste it. You won't have time to reload till you're through both walls.'

Morris scowled at this unasked-for advice, but the men seemed grateful for it, just as they were grateful that they were not in the front ranks of Kenny's force. That honour had gone to the Grenadier Company of the 94th who thus formed the Forlorn Hope. Usually the Hope, that group of men who went first into a breach to spring the enemy traps and fight down the immediate defenders, was composed of volunteers, but Kenny had decided to do without a proper Forlorn Hope. He wanted to fill the breaches quickly and so overwhelm the defences by numbers, and thus hard behind the Scotch Brigade's grenadiers were two more companies of Scots, then came the sepoys and Morris's men. Hard and fast, Kenny had told them, hard and fast.

Leave the wounded behind you, he had ordered, and just get up the damned breaches and start killing.

The Colonel looked at his watch a last time, then snapped its lid shut and put it into a pocket. He took a breath, hefted his sword, then shouted one word. 'Now!'

And the flag went forward across the crest and behind it came a wave of men who hurried towards the walls.

For a few seconds the fortress was silent, then the first rocket was fired. It seared towards the advancing troops, trailing its plume of thick smoke, then abruptly twisted and climbed into the clear sky.

Then the guns began.

Colonel William Dodd saw the errant rocket twist into the sky, falter amidst a growing tumult of its own smoke, then fall. Manu Bappoo's guns began to fire and Dodd knew, though he could not see over the loom of the Outer Fort, that the British attack was coming. 'Gopal!' he called to his second in command.

'Sahib?'

'Close the gates.'

'Sahib?' Gopal frowned at the Colonel. It had been agreed with Manu Bappoo that the four gates that barred the entranceway to the Inner Fort would be left open so that the defenders of the Outer Fort could retreat swiftly if it was necessary. Dodd had even posted a company to guard the outermost gate to make sure that no British pursuers could get in behind Manu Bappoo's men, yet now he was suggesting that the gates should be shut? 'You want me to close them, sahib?' Gopal asked, wondering if he had misheard.

'Close them, bar them and forget them,' Dodd said happily, 'and pull the platoon back inside the fort. I have another job for them.'

'But, sahib, if –'

'You heard me, Jemadar! Move!'

Gopal ran to do Dodd's bidding, while the Colonel himself walked along the firestep that edged the entranceway to make certain that his orders were being obeyed. He watched, satisfied, as the troops guarding the outer gate were brought back into the fortress and then as, one by one, the four vast gates were pushed shut. The great locking bars, each as thick as a man's thigh, were dropped into their metal brackets. The Outer Fort was now isolated. If Manu Bappoo repelled the British then it would be a simple matter to open the gates again, but if he lost, and if he fled, then he would find himself trapped between Dodd's Cobras and the advancing British.

Dodd walked to the centre of the firestep and there climbed onto an embrasure so that he could talk to as many of his men as possible. 'You will see that I have shut the gates,' he shouted, 'and they will stay shut! They will not be opened except by my express permission. Not if all the maharajahs of India stand out there and demand entrance! The gates stay shut. Do you understand?'

The white-coated soldiers, or at least those few who spoke some English, nodded while the rest had Dodd's orders translated. None showed much interest in the decision. They trusted their Colonel, and if he wanted the gates kept closed, then so be it.

Dodd watched the smoke thicken on the far side of the Outer Fort. A grim struggle was being waged there, but it was nothing to do with him. He would only begin to fight when the British attacked across the ravine, but their attacks would achieve nothing. The only way into the Inner Fort was through the gates, and that was impossible. The British might batter down the first gate with cannon fire, but once through the arch they would discover that the entranceway turned sharply to the left, so their gun could not fire through the passage to batter down the three other doors. They would have to fight their way up the narrow passage, try to destroy the successive gates with axes, and all the while his men would be pouring slaughter on them from the flanking walls.

'Sahib?' Gopal called, and Dodd turned to see that the Jemadar was pointing up the path that led to the palace. Beny Singh had appeared on the path, flanked by a servant carrying a parasol to protect the Killadar from the hot sun.

'Send him up here, Jemadar!' Dodd shouted back.

Dodd felt a quiet exaltation at the neatness of his tactics. Manu Bappoo was already cut off from safety, and only Beny Singh was now left as a rival to Dodd's supremacy. Dodd was tempted to cut the Killadar down here and now, but the murder would have been witnessed by members of the garrison who were still loyal to Beny Singh, and so instead Dodd greeted the Killadar with a respectful bow. 'What's happening?' Beny Singh demanded. He was breathing hard from the effort of climbing to the firestep, then he cried out in dismay because the guns on the southern wall of the Outer Fort, those guns that overlooked the ravine, had suddenly opened fire to pump gouts of grey-white smoke.

'I fear, sahib,' Dodd said, 'that the enemy are overwhelming the fort.'

'They're doing what?' The Killadar, who was dressed for battle in a clean white robe girdled by a red cummerbund and hung with a jewelled scabbard, looked horrified. He watched the smoke spread across the ravine. He was puzzled because it was not at all clear what the nearer guns were firing at. 'But the enemy can't get in here!'

'There are other British soldiers approaching, sahib,' Dodd said, and he pointed to the smoke cloud above the ravine. The guns on the near side of the Outer Fort, most of them small three- and five-pounder cannon, were aiming their pieces westwards, which meant that British troops must be approaching up the steep road which led from the plain. Those troops were still out of Dodd's sight, but the gunnery from the Outer Fort was eloquent proof of their presence. 'There must be redcoats coming towards the ravine,' Dodd explained, 'and we never foresaw that the British might assault in more than one place.' Dodd told the lie smoothly. 'I have no doubt they have men coming up the southern road too.'

'They do,' the Killadar confirmed.

Dodd shuddered, as though the news overwhelmed him with despair. 'We shall do our best,' he promised, 'but I cannot defend everything at once. I fear the British will gain the victory this day.' He bowed to the Killadar again. 'I am so very sorry, sahib. But you can gain an immortal reputation by joining the fight. We might lose today's battle, but in years to come men will sing songs about the defiance of Beny Singh. And how better for a soldier to die, sahib, than with a sword in his hand and his enemies dead about his feet?'

Beny Singh blanched at the thought. 'My daughters!' he croaked.

'Alas,' Dodd said gravely, 'they will become soldiers' toys. But you should not worry, sahib. In my experience the prettiest girls usually find a soldier to defend them. He is usually a big man, crude and forceful, but he stops the other men from raping his woman, except his friends, of course, who will be allowed some liberties. I am sure your wives and daughters will find men eager to protect them.'

Beny Singh fled from Dodd's reassurances. Dodd smiled as the

Killadar ran, then turned and walked towards Hakeswill who was posted in the bastion above the innermost gate. The Sergeant had been issued with a sword to accompany his black sash. He slammed to attention as Dodd approached him. 'Stand easy, Mister Hakeswill,' Dodd said. Hakeswill relaxed slightly. He liked being called 'Mister', it somehow seemed appropriate. If that little bastard Sharpe could be a mister and wear a sword, then so could he. 'I shall have a job for you in a few minutes, Mister Hakeswill,' Dodd said.

'I shall be honoured, sir,' Hakeswill replied.

Dodd watched the Killadar hurry up the path towards the palace. 'Our honoured commander,' he said sarcastically, 'is taking some bad news to the palace. We must give the news time to take root there.'

'Bad news, sir?'

'He thinks we're going to lose,' Dodd explained.

'I pray not, sir.'

'As do I, Mister Hakeswill, as do I. Fervently!' Dodd turned to watch the gunners in the Outer Fort and he saw how puny their small cannon were and he reckoned that such fire would not hold up the redcoats for long. The British would be in the ravine in half an hour, maybe less. 'In ten minutes, Mister Hakeswill, you will lead your company to the palace and you will order the Arab guards to come and defend the walls.'

Hakeswill's face twitched. 'Don't speak their heathen language, sir, begging your pardon, sir.'

'You don't need their language. You've got a musket, use it. And if anyone questions your authority, Mister Hakeswill, you have my permission to shoot them.'

'Shoot them, sir? Yes, sir. With pleasure, sir.'

'Anyone at all, Mister Hakeswill.'

Hakeswill's face twitched again. 'That fat little bugger, sir, him what was just here with the curly moustache . . .'

'The Killadar? If he questions you . . .'

'I shoot the bugger, sir.'

'Exactly.' Dodd smiled. He had seen into Hakeswill's soul and discovered it was black as filth, and perfect for his purposes. 'Do it for me, Mister Hakeswill, and I shall gazette you as a captain in the Cobras. Your havildar speaks some English, doesn't he?'

'A kind of English, sir,' Hakeswill said.

'Make sure he understands you. The palace guards are to be despatched to the walls.'

'They will, sir, or else they'll be dead 'uns.'

'Very good,' Dodd said. 'But wait ten minutes.'

'I shall, sir. And good day to you, sir.' Hakeswill saluted, about-turned and marched down the ramparts.

Dodd turned back to the Outer Fort. Rockets seared out of the smoke cloud above which Manu Bappoo's flag still hung. Faintly, very faintly, Dodd could hear men shouting, but the sound was being drowned by the roar of the guns which unsettled the silver-grey monkeys in the ravine. The beasts turned puzzled black faces up towards the men on the Inner Fort's walls as though they could find an answer to the noise and stink that was consuming the day.

A day which, to Dodd's way of thinking, was going perfectly.

The 33rd's Light Company had been waiting a little to the side of the track and Captain Morris deliberately stayed there, allowing almost all of Kenny's assault troops to go past before he led his men out of the rocks. He thus ensured that he was at the rear of the assault, a place which offered the greatest measure of safety.

Once Morris moved his men onto the fort's approach road he deliberately fell in behind a sepoy ladder party so that his progress was impeded. He walked at the head of his men, but turned repeatedly. 'Keep in files, Sergeant!' he snapped at Green more than once.

Sharpe walked alongside the company, curbing his long stride to the slow pace set by Morris. It took a moment to reach the small crest in the road, but then they were in sight of the fortress and Sharpe could only stare in awe at the weight of fire that seemed to pour from the battered walls.

The Mahrattas' bigger guns had been unseated, but they possessed a myriad of smaller cannon, some little larger than blunderbusses, and those weapons now roared and coughed and spat their flames towards the advancing troops so that the black walls were half obscured behind the patchwork of smoke that vented from every embrasure. Rockets added to the confusion. Some hissed up into the sky, but others seared into the advancing men to slice fiery passages through the ranks.

The leading company had not yet reached the outer breach, but was hurrying into the narrow space between the precipice to the east and the tank to the west. They jostled as their files were compressed, and then the gunfire seemed to concentrate on those men and Sharpe had an impression of blood misting the air as the round shot slammed home at a range of a mere hundred paces. There were big round bastions on either flank of the breach, and their summits were edged with perpetual flame as the defenders took turns to blast muskets down into the mass of attackers. The British guns were still firing, their shots exploding bursts of dust and stone from the breach, or else hammering into the embrasures in an effort to dull the enemy's fire.

An aide came running back down the path. 'Hurry!' he called. 'Hurry!'

Morris made no effort to hasten his pace. The leading Scots were past the tank now and climbing the gentle slope towards the walls, but that slope became ever steeper as it neared the breach. The man with the flag was in front, then he was engulfed by Highlanders racing to reach the stones. Kenny led them, sword in hand. Muskets suddenly flamed from the breach summit, obscuring it with smoke, and then an eighteen-pounder shot churned up the smoke and threw up a barrowload of broken stone amidst which an enemy musket wheeled. Sharpe quickened his pace. He could feel a kind of rage inside, and he wondered if that was fear, but there was an excitement too, and an anxiety that he would miss the fight.

He could see the fight clearly enough, for the breach was high above the approach road and the Scots, scrambling up using their hands, were clearly visible. The British gunners were still firing, hammering round shot just inches over the Scotsmen's heads to keep the summit of the breach clear of the enemy, and then, abruptly, the guns stopped and the redcoats climbed into the dust that hung thick above the shattered stones. A mass of Arabs climbed the breach's inner slope, coming to oppose the Scots, and scimitars rang against bayonets. The red coats of the attackers were turned pink by the stone dust. Colonel Kenny was in the front rank, straddling a chunk of masonry as he parried a scimitar. He lunged, piercing an enemy's throat, then stepped forward, downwards, knowing he was across the summit and oblivious of the muskets that flamed above him from the upper wall. The British gunners, their weapons relaid, started to fire at the upper wall, driving the defenders away from the firestep. The Scots rammed their bayonets forward, kicked the dead off the blades, stepped over the corpses and followed Kenny down to the space inside the walls. 'This way!' Kenny shouted. 'This way!' He led the rush of men to the left, to where the inner breach waited, its slope twitching as the round shot slammed home. Some Arabs, fleeing the Scotsmen's snarling rage, died as they tried to climb the inner breach and were struck by the cannonballs. Blood spattered across the inner wall, smeared the ramp, then was whitened by the dust.

Kenny glanced behind to make sure that the column was close behind him. 'Keep them coming,' he shouted to an aide who stood on the summit of the first breach. 'Keep them coming!' Kenny spat a mouthful of dust, then shouted at the Scots to start the ascent of the second breach.

'Hurry! Hurry!' Kenny's aides who were still outside the walls urged on the column. The rearmost ranks of the Colonel's assault party were stringing out, and the second storming group was not far behind. 'Close up!' the aides urged the laggards. 'Close up!'

Morris reluctantly quickened. The sepoys carrying the ladders were running down the slight slope which led to the narrow space beside the tank where the enemy's guns were aimed. All along Gawilghur's walls the smoke jetted, the flames spat and the rockets blasted out in gouts of smoke and streams of sparks. Even arrows were being fired. One clattered on a rock near Sharpe, then spun into the grass.

The Scots were climbing the inner breach now, and a stream of men was vanishing over the rocky summit of the outer breach. No mines had awaited the attackers, and no cannon had been placed athwart the breach to blast them as they flooded through the wall. Sepoys scrambled up the stones.

'Hurry!' the aides shouted. 'Hurry!'

Sharpe ran down the slope towards the tank. His canteen and haversack thumped on his waist, and sweat poured down his face. 'Slow down!' Morris shouted at him, but Sharpe ignored the call. The company was breaking apart as the more eager of the men hurried to catch up with Sharpe and the others dallied with Morris. 'Slow down, damn you!' Morris called to Sharpe again.

'Keep going!' Kenny's aides shouted. Two of them had been posted beside the tank and they gestured the men on. The round shot of the breaching batteries hammered above their heads making a noise like great barrels rolling across floorboards, then cracked into the smoke-rimmed upper wall. A green and red flag waved there. Sharpe saw an Arab aim a musket, then smoke obscured the sight. A small cannonball struck a sepoy, throwing him back and smearing the stony road with blood and guts. Sharpe leaped the sprawling body and saw he had reached the reservoir. The water was low and scummed green. Two Scots and a sepoy lay on the sun-baked mud, their blood seeping into the cracks that crazed the bank. A musket ball hammered into the mud, then a small round shot lashed into the rear of Morris's company and bowled over two men. 'Leave them!' an aide shouted. 'Just leave them!' A rocket smashed close by Sharpe's head, enveloping him in smoke and sparks. A wounded man crawled back beside the road, trailing a shattered leg. Another, blood oozing from his belly, collapsed on the mud and lapped at the filthy water.

Sharpe half choked on the thick smoke as he stumbled up the rising ground. Big black round shot lay here, left from the cannonade that had made the first breach. Two redcoat bodies had been heaved aside, three others twitched and called for help, but Kenny had posted another aide here to keep the troops moving. Dust spurted where musket balls lashed into the ground, then Sharpe was on the breach itself, half lost his balance as he climbed the ramp, and then was pushed from behind. Men jostled up the stones, clambered up, hauled themselves up with one hand while the other gripped their musket. Sharpe put his hand on a smear of blood. The dusty rubble was almost too hot to touch, and the ramp was much longer than Sharpe had anticipated. Men shouted hoarsely as they climbed, and still the bullets thudded down. An arrow struck and quivered in a musket stock. A rocket crashed into the flood of men, parting it momentarily as the carcass flamed madly where it had lodged between a boulder and a cannonball. Someone unceremoniously dumped a dead Scotsman on top of the hissing rocket and the press of men clambered on up over the corpse.

Once at the summit the attackers turned to their left and ran down the inside of the breach to the dry grass that separated the two walls. A fight was going on in the left-hand breach, and men were bunching behind it, but Sharpe could see the Scots were gradually inching up the slope. By God, he thought, but they were almost in! The British guns had ceased firing for fear of hitting their own men.

Sharpe turned right, going to the second inner breach that Morris's company was supposed to seal off. High above him, from the firestep of the inner wall, defenders leaned over to fire down into the space between the ramparts. Sharpe seemed to be running through a hail of bullets that magically did not touch him. Smoke wreathed about him, then he saw the broken stones of the breach in front and he leaped onto them and clambered upwards. 'I'm with you, Dick!' Tom Garrard shouted just behind, then a man appeared in the smoke above Sharpe and heaved down a baulk of wood.

The timber struck Sharpe on the chest, throwing him back onto Garrard who clutched at him as the two men fell on the stones. Sharpe swore as a fusillade of musket fire came down from the breach summit. A handful of men was with him, maybe six or seven, but none seemed to be hit. They crouched behind him, waiting for orders. 'No farther!' Morris shouted. 'No farther!'

'Bugger him,' Sharpe said, and he picked up his musket. Just then the British guns, seeing that the right-hand breach was still occupied by the Mahrattas, opened fire again and the balls hammered into the stones just a few feet over Sharpe's head. One defender was caught smack in the belly by an eighteen-pounder shot and it seemed to Sharpe that the man simply disintegrated in a red shower. Sharpe ducked as the blood poured down the stones, trickling past him and Garrard in small torrents. 'Jesus,' Sharpe said. Another round shot slammed into the breach, the sound of the ball's strike as loud as thunder. Shards of stone whipped past Sharpe, and he seemed to be breathing nothing but hot dust.

'No farther!' Morris said. 'Here! To me! Rally! Rally!' He was crouched under the inner wall, safe from the defenders on the breach, though high above him, on the undamaged firestep, Arab soldiers still leaned out to fire straight down. 'Sharpe! Come here!' Morris ordered.

'Come on!' Sharpe shouted. Bugger Morris, and bugger all the other officers who said you could put a racing saddle on a carthorse, but the beast would not go quick. 'Come on!' he shouted again as he clambered up the stones, and suddenly there were more men to his right, but they were Scots, and he saw that the leading men of the second assault group had reached the fortress. A red-haired lieutenant led them, a claymore in his hand.

The Lieutenant was climbing the centre of the breach, while Sharpe was trying to clamber up the steeper flank. The Highlanders went past

Sharpe, screaming at the enemy, and the sight of their red coats made the British gunners cease fire, and immediately the breach summit filled with robed men who carried curved swords with blades as thick as cleavers. Swords clashed, muskets crashed, and the red-haired Lieutenant shook like a gaffed eel as a scimitar sliced into his belly. He turned and fell towards Sharpe, dropping his claymore. A line of defenders was now firing down the breach, while a huge Arab, who looked seven feet tall to Sharpe, stood in the centre with a reddened scimitar and dared any man to challenge him. Two did, and both he threw back in a shower of blood. 'Light Company!' Sharpe shouted. 'Give those bastards fire! Fire!'

Some muskets banged behind him and the row of defenders seemed to stagger back, but they closed up again, rallied by the huge man with the bloodstained scimitar. Sharpe had his left hand on the broken shoulder of the wall and he used it to haul himself up, then twisted aside as the closest Arabs turned and fired at him. The balls whiplashed past as a flaming lump of wadding struck Sharpe on the cheek. He let go of the wall and fell backwards as a grinning man tried to stab him with a bayonet. Dear God, but the breach was steep! His cheek was burnt and his new coat scorched. The Scots tried again, surging up the centre of the breach to be met by a line of Arab blades. More Arabs came from inside the fortress and poured a volley of musket fire down the face of the ramp. Sharpe aimed his musket at the tall Arab and pulled the trigger. The gun hammered into his shoulder, but when the smoke cleared the big man was still standing and still fighting. The Arabs were winning here, they were pressing down the face of the breach and chanting a blood-curdling war cry as they killed. A man rammed a bayonet at Sharpe, he parried it with his own, but then an enemy grasped Sharpe's musket by the muzzle and tugged it upwards. Sharpe cursed, but held on, then saw a scimitar slashing towards him and so he let go of the musket and fell back again. 'Bastards,' he swore, then saw the dead Scottish Lieutenant's claymore lying on the stones. He picked it up and swept it at the ankles of the Arabs above him, and the blade bit home and threw one man down, and the Scots were charging up the breach again, climbing over their own dead and screaming a raw shout of hate that was matched by the Arabs' cries of victory.

Sharpe climbed again. He balanced on the steep stones and hacked with the claymore, driving the enemy back. He scrambled up two more feet, wreathed in bitter smoke, and reached the spot where he could grip the wall at the edge of the breach. All he could do now was hold onto the stone with his left hand and thrust and swing with the sword. He drove men back, but then the big Arab saw him and came across the breach, bellowing at his comrades to leave the redcoat's death to his scimitar. He raised the sword high over his head, like an executioner taking aim, and Sharpe was off balance. 'Push me, Tom!' he shouted, and Garrard put a hand on Sharpe's arse and shoved him hard upwards just as the scimitar started downwards, but Sharpe had let go of the wall and reached out to hook his left hand behind the tall man's ankle. He tugged hard and the man shouted in alarm as his feet slid out from under him and as he bumped down the breach's flank. 'Now kill him!' Sharpe bellowed and a half-dozen redcoats attacked the fallen man with bayonets as Sharpe hacked at the Arabs coming to the big man's rescue. His claymore clashed with scimitars, the blades ringing like blacksmith's hammers on anvils. The big man was twisting and twitching as the bayonets stabbed again and again through his robes. The Scots were back, thrusting and snarling up the centre, and Sharpe forced himself up another step. Garrard was beside him now, and the two were only a step from the summit of the breach. 'Bastards! Bastards!' Sharpe was panting as he hacked and lunged, but the Arabs' robes seemed to soak up the blows, then suddenly, almost miraculously, they backed away from him. A musket fired from inside the fortress and one of the Arabs crumpled down onto the breach's inner ramp, and Sharpe realized that the men who had fought their way through the left-hand breach must have turned and come to attack this breach from the inside. 'Come on!' he roared, and he was on the summit at last and there were Scots and Light Company men all about him as they spilt down into the Outer Fortress where a company of the Scotch Brigade waited to welcome them. The defenders were fleeing to the southern gate which would lead them to the refuge of the Inner Fort.

'Jesus,' Tom Garrard said, leaning over to catch his breath.

'Are you hurt?' Sharpe asked.

Garrard shook his head. 'Jesus,' he said again. Some enemy gunners, who had stayed with their weapons till the last minute, jumped down from the firestep, dodged past the tired redcoats scattered inside the wall and fled southwards. Most of the Scots and sepoys were too breathless to pursue them and contented themselves with some musket shots. A dog barked madly until a sepoy kicked the beast into silence.

Sharpe stopped. It seemed suddenly quiet, for the big guns were silent at last and the only muskets firing were from the Mahrattas defending the gatehouse. A few small cannon were firing to the south, but Sharpe could not see them, nor guess what their target was. The highest part of the fort lay to his right, and there was nothing on the low summit but dry grassland and a few thorny trees. No defenders gathered there. To his left he could see Kenny's men assaulting the gatehouse. They were storming the steps to the parapet where a handful of Arabs were making a stand, though they stood no chance, for over a hundred redcoats now gathered under the wall and were firing up at the firestep. The defenders' robes turned red. They were trapped now between the musket balls and the bayonets of the men climbing the steps, and though some tried to surrender, they were all killed. The other Mahrattas had fled, gone over the high ground in the centre of the Outer Fort to the ravine and to the larger fort beyond.

A vat stood in an embrasure of the wall and Sharpe heaved himself up and found, as he had hoped, that the barrel contained water for the abandoned guns. They were very small cannon, mostly mounted on iron tripods, but they had inflicted a hard punishment on the men crammed along the fort's approach. The dead and wounded had been pushed aside to make way for the stream of men approaching the breaches. Major Stokes was among them, Ahmed at his side, and Sharpe waved to them, though they did not see him. He dipped his hands in the water, slung it over his face and hair, then stooped and drank. It was filthy stuff, stagnant and bitter with powder debris, but he was desperately thirsty.

A cheer sounded as Colonel Kenny's men hoisted the British flag above the captured Delhi Gate. Manu Bappoo's flag was being folded by an aide, to be carried back to Britain. A squad of Scotsmen unbarred the big inner gate, then the outer one, to let even more redcoats into the fort that had fallen so quickly. Exhausted men slumped in the wall's shade, but Kenny's officers were shouting at them to find their units, to load their muskets and move on south.

'I think our orders are to guard the breach,' Morris suggested as Sharpe jumped down from the firestep.

'We go on,' Sharpe said savagely.

'We –'

'We go on, sir,' Sharpe said, investing the 'sir' with a savage scorn.

'Move, move, move!' a major shouted at Morris. 'The job ain't done yet! Move on!' He waved southwards.

'Sergeant Green,' Morris said reluctantly, 'gather the men.'

Sharpe walked up the hill, going to the high spot in the fort, and once there he stared southwards. Beneath him the ground fell away, gently at first, then steeply until it disappeared in a rocky ravine that was deep in shadow. But the far slope was sunlit, and that slope was a precipitous climb to an unbreached wall, and at the wall's eastern end was a massive gatehouse, far bigger than the one that had just been captured, and that far gatehouse was thick with soldiers. Some had white coats, and Sharpe knew those men. He had fought them before. 'Bloody hell,' he said softly.

'What is it?'

Sharpe turned and saw Garrard had followed him. 'Looks bloody nasty to me, Tom.'

Garrard stared at the Inner Fort. From here he could see the palace, the gardens and the defences, and suddenly those defences were blotted out by smoke as the guns across the ravine opened fire on the redcoats who now spread across the Outer Fort. The round shot screamed past Sharpe and Garrard. 'Bloody hell,' Sharpe said again. He had just fought his way through a breach to help capture a fort, only to find that the day's real work had scarcely begun.

Manu Bappoo had hoped to defend the breaches by concentrating his best fighters, the Lions of Allah, at their summits, but that hope had been defeated by the British guns that had continued to fire at the breaches until the redcoats were almost at the top of the ramps. No defender could stand in the breach and hope to live, not until the guns ceased fire, and by then the leading attackers were almost at the summit and so the Lions of Allah had been denied the advantage of higher ground.

The attackers and defenders had clashed amidst the dust and smoke at the top of the breach and there the greater height and strength of the Scotsmen had prevailed. Manu Bappoo had raged at his men, he had fought in their front rank and taken a wound in his shoulder, but his Arabs had retreated. They had gone back to the upper breaches, and there the redcoats, helped by their remorseless cannon, had prevailed again, and Bappoo knew the Outer Fort was lost. In itself that was no great loss. Nothing precious was stored in the Outer Fort, it was merely an elaborate defence to slow an attacker as he approached the ravine, but Bappoo was galled by the swiftness of the British victory. For a while he swore at the redcoats and tried to rally his men to defend the gatehouse, but the British were now swarming over the breaches, the gunners on the walls were abandoning their weapons, and Bappoo knew it was time to pull back into the stronghold of the Inner Fort. 'Go back!' he shouted. 'Go back!' His white tunic was soaked in his own blood, but the wound was to his left shoulder and he could still wield the gold-hilted *tulwar* that had been a gift from his brother. 'Go back!'

The defenders retreated swiftly and the attackers seemed too spent to pursue. Bappoo waited until the last, and then he walked backwards, facing the enemy and daring them to come and kill him, but they simply watched him go. In a moment, he knew, they would reorganize themselves and advance to the ravine, but by then he and his troops would be safely locked within the greater fortress.

The last sight Bappoo had of the Delhi Gate was of an enemy flag being hauled to the top of the pole that had held his own flag, then he dropped down the steep slope and was hustled through the south gate by his bodyguard. The path now ran obliquely down the steep side of the ravine before turning a hairpin bend to climb to the Inner Fort. The first of his men were already scrambling up that farther path. The gunners on the southern wall, who had been trying to stop the redcoats approaching on the road from the plain, now abandoned their small cannon and joined the retreat. Bappoo could only follow them with tears in his eyes. It did not matter that the battle was not lost, that the Inner Fort still stood and was likely to stand through all eternity, he had been humiliated by the swiftness of the defeat. 'Hurry, sahib,' one of his aides said.

'The British aren't following,' Bappoo said tiredly, 'not yet.'

'Those British,' the aide said, and pointed west to where the road from the plain climbed to the ravine. And there, at the bend where the road disappeared about the flank of the steep slope, was a company of redcoats. They wore kilts, and Bappoo remembered them from

Argaum. If those men hurried, they might cut off Bappoo's retreat and so he quickened his pace.

It was not till he reached the bottom of the ravine that he realized something was wrong. The leading groups of his men had reached the Inner Fort, but instead of streaming into the gate they were milling about on the slope beneath. 'What's happening?' he asked.

'The gates are shut, sahib,' his aide said in wonderment.

'They'll open any minute,' Bappoo said, and turned as a musket bullet whistled down from the slope behind him. The British who had captured the Outer Fort had at last advanced to the edge of the ravine and beneath them they saw the mass of retreating enemy, so they began to fire down. 'Hurry!' Bappoo shouted, and his men pushed on up the hill, but still the gates did not open.

The British fire became heavier. Redcoats were lining the hilltop now and pouring musket fire into the ravine. Bullets ricocheted from the stone sides and flicked down into the press of men. Panic began to infect them, and Bappoo shouted at them to be calm and return the fire, while he pushed through the throng to discover why the Inner Fort's gates were closed. 'Dodd!' he shouted as he came close. 'Dodd!'

Colonel Dodd's face appeared above the rampart. He looked quite calm, though he said nothing.

'Open the gate!' Bappoo shouted angrily.

Dodd's response was to raise the rifle to his shoulder.

Bappoo stared up into the muzzle. He knew he should run or twist away, but the horror of fate kept him rooted to the path. 'Dodd?' he said in puzzlement, and then the rifle was blotted out by the smoke of its discharge.

The bullet struck Bappoo on the breastbone, shattering it and driving scraps of bone deep into his heart. The Prince took two shuddering breaths and then was dead.

His men gave a great wail as the news of their Prince's death spread, and then, unable to endure the plunging fire from the Outer Fort, and denied entrance to the Inner, they fled west towards the road which dropped to the plain.

But the road was blocked. The Highlanders of the 78th were nearing its summit and they now saw a great panicked mass surging towards them. The Scotsmen had endured the artillery fire of the Outer Fort during their long climb, but now those guns had been abandoned. To their right the cliffs soared up to the Inner Fort, while to their left was a precipice above a dizzying gorge.

There was only room for twelve men to stand abreast on the road, but Colonel Chalmers, who led the 78th, knew that was space enough. He formed his leading half-company into three ranks with the front row kneeling. 'You'll fire by ranks,' he said quietly.

The panicked defenders ran towards the kilted Highlanders, who waited until every shot could kill. 'Front rank, fire!' Chalmers said.

The muskets started, and one by one the three ranks fired, and the steady fusillade tore into the approaching fugitives. Some tried to turn and retreat, but the press behind was too great, and still the relentless fire ripped into them, while behind them redcoats came down from the Outer Fort to attack their rear.

The first men jumped off the cliff, and their terrible screams faded as they plunged down to the rocks far beneath. The road was thick with bodies and running with blood.

'Advance twenty paces!' Chalmers ordered.

The Highlanders marched, halted, knelt and began firing again. Bappoo's survivors, betrayed by Dodd, were trapped between two forces. They were stranded in a hell above emptiness, a slaughter in the high hills. There were screams as men tumbled to their deaths far beneath and still the fire kept coming. It kept coming until there was nothing left but quivering men crouching in terror on a road that was rank with the stench of blood, and then the redcoats moved forward with bayonets.

The Outer Fort had fallen and its garrison had been massacred.

And William Dodd, renegade, was Lord of Gawilghur.

CHAPTER 10

Mister Hakeswill was not sure whether he was a lieutenant in William Dodd's eyes, but he knew he was a Mister and he dimly apprehended that he could be much more. William Dodd was going to win, and his victory would make him ruler of Gawilghur and tyrant of all the wide land that could be seen from its soaring battlements. Mister Hakeswill was therefore well placed, as Dodd's only white officer, to profit from the victory and, as he approached the palace on Gawilghur's summit, Hakeswill was already imagining a future that was limited only by the bounds of his fancy. He could be a rajah, he decided. 'I shall have an harem,' he said aloud, earning a worried look from his Havildar. 'An harem I'll have, all of me own. *Bibbis* in silk, but only when it's cold, eh? Rest of the time they'll have to be naked as needles.' He laughed, scratched at the lice in his crotch, then lunged with his sword at one of the peacocks that decorated the palace gardens. 'Bad luck, them birds,' Hakeswill told the Havildar as the bird fled in a flurry of bright severed feathers. 'Bad luck, they are. Got the evil eye, they do. Know what you should do with a peacock? Roast the bugger. Roast it and serve it with 'taters. Very nice, that.'

'Yes, sahib,' the Havildar said nervously. He was not certain he liked this new white officer whose face twitched so compulsively, but Colonel Dodd had appointed him and the Colonel could do no wrong as far as the Havildar was concerned.

'Haven't tasted a 'tater in months,' Hakeswill said wistfully. 'Christian food, that, see? Makes us white.'

'Yes, sahib.'

'And I won't be sahib, will I? Your highness, that's what I'll be. Your bleeding highness with a bedful of bare *bibbis*.' His face twitched as a bright idea occurred to him. 'I could have Sharpie as a servant.

Cut off his goolies first, though. Snip snip.' He bounded enthusiastically up a stone staircase, oblivious of the sound of gunfire that had erupted in the ravine just north of the Inner Fort. Two Arab guards moved to bar the way, but Hakeswill shouted at them. 'Off to the walls, you scum! No more shirking! You ain't guarding the royal pisspot any longer, but has to be soldiers. So piss off!'

The Havildar ordered the two men away and, though they were reluctant to abandon their post, they were overawed by the number of bayonets that faced them. So, just like the guards who had stood at the garden gate, they fled. 'So now we look for the little fat man,' Hakeswill said, 'and give him a bloodletting.'

'We must hurry, sahib,' the Havildar said, glancing back at the wall above the ravine where the gunners were suddenly at work.

'God's work can't be hurried,' Hakeswill answered, pulling at one of the latticed doors that led into the palace, 'and Colonel Dodd will die of old age on that wall, sonny. Ain't a man alive who can get through that gate, and certainly not a pack of bleeding Scotchmen. Bugger this door.' He raised his right foot and battered down the locked lattice with his boot.

Hakeswill had expected a palace dripping with gold, festooned with silk and paved with polished marble, but Gawilghur had only ever been a summer refuge, and Berar had never been as wealthy as other Indian states, and so the floors were common stone, the walls were painted in limewash and the curtains were of cotton. Some fine furniture of ebony inlaid with ivory stood in the hallway, but Hakeswill had no eye for such chairs, only for jewels, and he saw none. Two bronze jars and an iron cuspidor stood by the walls where lizards waited motionless, while a brass poker, tongs and fire shovel, cast in Birmingham, mounted on a stand and long bereft of any hearth, had pride of place in a niche. The hallway had no guards, indeed no one was in sight and the palace seemed silent except for a faint sound of choking and moaning that came from a curtained doorway at the far end of the hall. The noise of the guns was muffled. Hakeswill hefted his sword and edged towards the curtain. His men followed slowly, bayonets ready, eyes peering into every shadow.

Hakeswill swept the curtain aside with the blade, and gasped.

The Killadar, with a *tulwar* slung at his side and a small round shield strapped to his left arm, stared at Hakeswill above the bodies of his wives, concubines and daughters. Eighteen women were on the floor. Most were motionless, but some still writhed as the slow pain of the poison worked its horrors. The Killadar was in tears. 'I could not leave them for the English,' he said.

'What did he say?' Hakeswill demanded.

'He preferred they should die than be dishonoured,' the Havildar translated.

'Bleeding hell,' Hakeswill commented. He stepped down into the sunken floor where the women lay. The dead had greenish dribbles coming from their mouths and their glassy eyes stared up at the lotuses painted on the ceiling, while the living jerked spasmodically. The cups from which they had drunk the poison lay on the tiled floor. 'Some nice *bibbis* here,' Hakeswill said ruefully. 'A waste!' He stared at a child, no more than six or seven. There was a jewel about her neck and Hakeswill stooped, grasped the pendant and snapped the chain. 'Bleeding waste,' he said in disgust, then used his sword blade to lift the sari of a dying woman. He raised the silk to her waist, then shook his head. 'Look at that!' he said. 'Just look at that! What a bleeding waste!'

The Killadar roared in anger, drew his *tulwar* and ran down the steps to drive Hakeswill from his women. Hakeswill, alarmed, backed away, then remembered he was to be a rajah and could not show timidity in front of the Havildar and his men, so he stepped forward again and thrust the sword forward in a clumsy lunge. It might have been clumsy, but it was also lucky, for the Killadar had stumbled on a body and was lurching forward, his *tulwar* flailing as he sought his balance, and the tip of Hakeswill's blade ripped into his throat so that a spray of blood pulsed onto the dead and the dying. The Killadar gasped as he fell. His legs twitched as he tried to bring the *tulwar* round to strike at Hakeswill, but his strength was going and the Englishman was above him now. 'You're a *djinn*!' the Killadar said hoarsely.

The sword stabbed into Beny Singh's neck. 'I ain't drunk, you bastard,' Hakeswill said indignantly. 'Ain't seen a drop of mother's milk in three years!' He twisted the sword blade, fascinated by the way the blood pulsed past the steel. He watched until the blood finally died to a trickle, then jerked the blade free. 'That's him gone,' Hakeswill said. 'Another bloody heathen gone down to hell, eh?'

The Havildar stared in horror at Beny Singh and at the corpses drenched with his blood.

'Don't just stand there, you great pudding!' Hakeswill snapped. 'Get back to the walls!'

'The walls, sahib?'

'Hurry! There's a battle being fought, or ain't you noticed? Go on! Off with you! Take the company and report to Colonel Dodd as how the fat little bugger's dead. Tell him I'll be back in a minute or two. Now off with you! Quick!'

The Havildar obeyed, taking his men back through the hallway and out into the sunlight that was being hazed by the smoke rising from the ravine. Hakeswill, left alone in the palace, stooped to his work. All the dead wore jewellery. They were not great jewels, not like the massive ruby that the Tippoo Sultan had worn on his hat, but there were pearls and emeralds, sapphires and small diamonds, all mounted in gold, and Hakeswill busied himself delving through the bloodied silks to retrieve the scraps of wealth. He crammed the stones into his pockets where they joined the gems he had taken from Sharpe, and then, when the corpses were stripped and searched, he roamed the palace, snarling at servants and threatening scullions, as he ransacked the smaller rooms. The rest of the defenders could fight; Mister Hakeswill was getting rich.

The fight in the ravine was now a merciless massacre. The garrison of the Outer Fort was trapped between the soldiers who had captured their stronghold and the kilted Highlanders advancing up the narrow road, and there was no escape except over the precipice, and those who jumped, or were pushed by the panicking mass, fell onto the shadowed rocks far below. Colonel Chalmers's men advanced with bayonets, herding the fugitives towards Kenny's men who greeted them with more bayonets. A thousand men had garrisoned the Outer Fort, and those men were now dead or doomed, but seven thousand more defenders waited within the Inner Fort and Colonel Kenny was eager to attack them. He tried to order men into ranks, tugging them away from the slaughter and shouting for gunners to find an enemy cannon that could be fetched from the captured ramparts and dragged to face the massive gate of the Inner Fort, but the redcoats had an easier target in the huddled fugitives and they enthusiastically killed the helpless enemy, and all the while the guns of the Inner Fort fired down at the redcoats while rockets slammed into the ravine to add to the choking fog of powder smoke.

The slaughter could not endure. The beaten defenders threw down their guns and fell to their knees, and gradually the British officers called off the massacre. Chalmers's Highlanders advanced up the road that was now slippery with blood, driving the few prisoners in front of them. Wounded Arabs crawled or limped. The survivors were stripped of their remaining weapons and sent under sepoy guard back up to the Outer Fort, and for every step of their way they suffered from the fire that flamed and crackled from the Inner Fort. Finally, exhausted, they were taken out through the Delhi Gate and told to wait beside the tank. The parched prisoners threw themselves at the green-scummed water and some, seeing that the sepoy guards were few in number, slipped away northwards. They went without weapons, masterless fugitives who posed no threat to the British camp, which was guarded by a half-battalion of Madrassi sepoys.

The northern face of the ravine, which looked towards the uncon-quered Inner Fort, was now crowded with some three thousand red-coats, most of whom did nothing but sit in whatever small shade they could find and grumble that the *puckalees* had not fetched water. Once in a while a man would fire a musket across the ravine, but the balls were wild at that long range, and the enemy fire, which had been heavy during the massacre on the western road, gradually eased off as both sides waited for the real struggle to begin.

Sharpe was halfway down the ravine, seated beneath a stunted tree on which the remnants of some red blossom hung dry and faded. A tribe of black-faced, silver-furred monkeys had fled the irruption of men into the rocky gorge, and those beasts now gathered behind Sharpe where they gibbered and screamed. Tom Garrard and a dozen men of the 33rd's Light Company had gathered around Sharpe, while the rest of the company was lower down the ravine among some rocks. 'What happens now?' Garrard asked.

'Some poor bastards have to get through that gate,' Sharpe said.

'Not you?'

'Kenny will call us when he needs us,' Sharpe said, nodding towards the lean Colonel who had at last organized an assault party at the bottom of the track which slanted up towards the gate. 'And he bloody will, Tom. It ain't going to be easy getting through that gate.' He touched the scorch mark on his cheek. 'That bloody hurts!'

'Put some butter on it,' Garrard said.

'And where do I get bleeding butter here?' Sharpe asked. He shaded his eyes and peered at the complex ramparts above the big gate, trying to spot either Dodd or Hakeswill, but although he could see the white jackets of the Cobras, he could not see a white man on the ramparts. 'It's going to be a long fight, Tom,' he said.

The British gunners had succeeded in bringing an enemy five-pounder cannon to the edge of the ravine. The sight of the gun pro-voked a flurry of fire from the Inner Fort, wreathing its gatehouse in smoke as the round shot screamed across the ravine to plunge all around the threatening gun. Somehow it survived. The gunners rammed it, aimed it, then fired a shot that bounced just beneath the gate, ricocheted up into the woodwork, but fell back.

The defenders kept firing, but their smoke obscured their aim and the small captured cannon had been positioned behind a large low rock that served as a makeshift breastwork. The gunners elevated the barrel a trifle and their next shot struck plumb on the gates, breaking a timber. Each successive shot splintered more wood and was greeted by an ironic cheer from the redcoats who watched from across the ravine. The gate was being demolished board by board, and at last a round shot cracked into its locking bar and the half-shattered timbers sagged on their hinges.

Colonel Kenny was gathering his assault troops at the foot of the ravine. They were the same men who had gone first into the breaches of the Outer Fort, and their faces were stained with powder burns, with dust and sweat. They watched the destruction of the outer gate of the Inner Fort and they knew they must climb the path into the enemy's fire as soon as the gun had done its work. Kenny summoned an aide. 'You know Plummer?' he asked the man.

'Gunner Major, sir?'

'Find him,' Kenny said, 'or any gunner officer. Tell them we might need a light piece up in the gateway.' He pointed with a reddened sword at the Inner Fort's gatehouse. 'The passage ain't straight,' he explained to the aide. 'Get through the gate and we turn hard left. If our axemen can't deal with the other gates we'll need a gun to blow them in.'

The aide climbed back up to the Outer Fort, looking for a gunner. Kenny talked to his men, explaining that once they were through the shattered gate they would find themselves faced by another and that the infantry were to fire up at the flanking firesteps to protect the axemen who would try to hack their way through the successive obstacles. 'If we put up enough fire,' Kenny said, 'the enemy'll take shelter. It won't take long.' He looked at his axemen, all of them huge sappers, all carrying vast-bladed axes that had been sharpened to wicked edges.

Kenny turned and watched the effect of the five-pounder shots. The gate's locking bar had been struck plumb, but the gate still held. A badly aimed shot cracked into the stone beside the gate, starting up dust, then a correction to the gun sent a ball hammering into the bar again and the thick timber broke and the remnants of the gates fell inwards. 'Forward!' Kenny shouted. 'Forward!'

Four hundred redcoats followed the Colonel up the narrow track that led to the Inner Fort. They could not run to the assault, for the hill was too steep; they could only trudge into the fury of Dodd's fusillade. Cannon, rockets and muskets blasted down the hill to tear gaps in Kenny's ranks.

'Give them fire!' an officer on the ravine's northern side shouted at the watching redcoats, and the men loaded their muskets and fired at the smoke-masked gatehouse. If nothing else, the wild fire might keep the defenders' heads down. Another cannon had been fetched from the Outer Fort, and now added its small round shots to the fury that beat audibly on the gatehouse ramparts. Those ramparts were thick with the powder smoke gouted by the defenders' cannon and muskets and it was that smoke which protected Kenny's men as they hurried up the last few yards to the broken gate. 'Protect the sappers!' Kenny shouted and then, his sword in his hand, he clambered over the broken timbers and led his attackers into the entrance passage.

Facing Kenny was a stone wall. He had expected it, but even so he was astonished by the narrowness of the passage that turned sharply to his left and then climbed steeply to the second unbroken gate. 'There it is!' he shouted, and led a surge of men up the cobbled road towards the iron-studded timbers.

And hell was loosed.

The firesteps above the gateway passage were protected by the outer wall's high rampart, and Dodd's men, though they could hear the musket balls beating against the stones, were safe from the wild fire that lashed across the deep ravine. But the redcoats beneath them, the men following Colonel Kenny into the passage, had no protection. Musket fire, stones and rockets slashed into a narrow space just twenty-five paces long and eight wide. The leading axemen were among the first to die, beaten down by bullets. Their blood splashed high on the walls. Colonel Kenny somehow survived the opening salvo, then he was struck on the shoulder by a lump of stone and driven to the ground. A rocket slashed past his face, scorching his cheek, but he picked himself up and, sword in numbed hand, shouted at his men to keep going. No one could hear him. The narrow space was filled with noise, choking with smoke in which men died and rockets flared. A musket ball struck Kenny in the hip and he twisted, half fell, but forced himself to stand and, with blood pouring down his white breeches, limped on. Then another musket ball scored down his back and threw him forward. He crawled on blood-slicked stones, sword still in his hand, and shuddered as a third ball hit him in the back. He still managed to reach the second gate and reared up to strike it with his sword, and then a last musket ball split his skull and left him dead at the head of his men. More bullets plucked at his corpse.

Kenny's surviving men tried to brave the fire. They tried to climb the slope to the second gate, but the murderous fire did not cease, and the dead made a barrier to the living. Some men attempted to fire up at their tormentors on the firestep, but the sun was high now and they aimed into a blinding glare, and soon the redcoats began to back down the passage. The weltering fire from above did not let up. It flayed the Scotsmen, ricocheted between the walls, struck dead and dying and living, while the rockets, lit and tossed down, seared like great comets between the stone walls and filled the space with a sickening smoke. The dead were burned by rocket flames which exploded their cartridge boxes to pulse gouts of blood against the black walls, but the smoke hid the survivors who, under its cover, stumbled back to the hill outside the fortress. They left a stone-walled passage filled with the dying and the dead, trickling with blood, foul with smoke and echoing with the moans of the wounded.

'Cease fire!' Colonel Dodd shouted. 'Cease fire!'

The smoke cleared slowly and Dodd stared down at a pit of carnage in which a few bodies twitched. 'They'll come again soon,' Dodd warned his Cobras. 'Fetch more stones, make sure your muskets are loaded. More rockets!' He patted his men on the shoulders, congratulating them. They grinned at him, pleased with their work. It was like killing rats in a barrel. Not one Cobra had been hit, the first enemy assault had failed and the others, Dodd was certain, would end in just the same way. The Lord of Gawilghur was winning his first victory.

Major Stokes had found Sharpe shortly before Kenny made his assault, and the two men had been joined first by Syud Sevajee and his followers, then by the dozen cavalrymen who accompanied Eli Lockhart. All of them, Stokes, Sevajee and Lockhart, had entered the Outer Fort after the fight for the breaches was finished, and now they stood watching the failure of Kenny's assault. The survivors of the attack were crouching just yards from the broken entrance that boiled with smoke, and Sharpe knew they were summoning the courage to charge again. 'Poor bastards,' he said.

'No choice in the matter,' Stokes said bleakly. 'No other way in.'

'That ain't a way in, sir,' Sharpe said dourly, 'that's a fast road to a shallow grave.'

'Overwhelm them,' Stokes said, 'that's the way to do it. Overwhelm them.'

'Send more men to be killed?' Sharpe asked angrily.

'Get a gun over that side,' Stokes suggested, 'and blast the gates down one after the other. Only way to prise the place open, Sharpe.'

The covering fire that had blazed across the ravine died when it was obvious the first attack had failed, and the lull encouraged the defenders to come to the outer embrasures and fire down at the stalled attackers.

'Give them fire!' an officer shouted from the bed of the ravine, and again the muskets flared across the gorge and the balls spattered against the walls.

Major Stokes had levelled his telescope at the gate where the thick smoke had at last dissipated. 'It ain't good,' he admitted. 'It opens onto a blank wall.'

'It does what, sir?' Eli Lockhart asked. The cavalry Sergeant was looking aghast at the horror across the ravine, grateful perhaps that the cavalry was never asked to break into such deathtraps.

'The passage turns,' Stokes said. 'We can't fire straight up the entranceway. They'll have to drag a gun right into the archway.'

'They'll never make it,' Sharpe said. Any gun positioned in the outer arch would get the full fury of the defensive fire, and those defenders were protected by the big outer wall. The only way Sharpe could see of getting into the fortress was by battering the whole gatehouse flat, and that would take days of heavy cannon fire.

'The gates of hell,' Stokes said softly, staring through his glass at the bodies left inside the arch.

'Can I borrow the telescope, sir?' Sharpe asked.

'Of course.' Stokes cleaned the eyepiece on the hem of his jacket. 'It ain't a pretty sight though.'

Sharpe took the glass and aimed it across the ravine. He gave the gatehouse a cursory glance, then edged the lens along the wall which led westwards from the besieged gate. The wall was not very high, perhaps only twelve or fifteen feet, much lower than the great ramparts about the gatehouse, and its embrasures did not appear to be heavily manned. But that was hardly a surprise, for the wall stood atop a precipice. The defences straight ahead were not the wall and its handful of defenders, but the stony cliff which fell down into the ravine.

Stokes saw where Sharpe was aiming the glass. 'No way in there, Richard.'

Sharpe said nothing. He was staring at a place where weeds and small shrubs twisted up the cliff. He tracked the telescope from the bed of the ravine to the base of the wall, searching every inch, and he reckoned it could be climbed. It would be hard, for it was perilously steep, but if there was space for bushes to find lodgement, then a man could follow, and at the top of the cliff there was a brief area of grass between the precipice and the wall. He took the telescope from his eye. 'Has anyone seen a ladder?'

'Back up there.' It was Ahmed who answered.

'Where, lad?'

'Up there.' The Arab boy pointed to the Outer Fort. 'On the ground,' he said.

Sharpe twisted and looked at Lockhart. 'Can you boys fetch me a ladder?'

'What are you thinking of?' Lockhart asked.

'A way in,' Sharpe said, 'a bloody way in.' He gave the telescope to Stokes. 'Get me a ladder, Sergeant,' he said, 'and I'll fix those buggers properly. Ahmed? Show Sergeant Lockhart where you saw the ladder.'

'I stay with you,' the boy said stubbornly.

'You bloody don't.' Sharpe patted the boy on the head, wondering what Ahmed made of the slaughter that had been inflicted on his countrymen in the ravine, but the boy seemed blessedly unaffected. 'Go and help the Sergeant,' he told Ahmed.

Ahmed led the cavalrymen uphill. 'What are you doing, Richard?' Stokes asked.

'We can climb up to the wall,' Sharpe said, pointing to where the trail of weeds and bushes snaked up the other side of the ravine. 'Not you, sir, but a light company can do it. Go up the ravine, send a ladder up and cross the wall.'

Stokes trained the telescope and stared at the opposing cliff for a long while. 'You might get up,' he said dubiously, 'but then what?'

Sharpe grinned. 'We attack the gatehouse from the back, sir.'

'One company?'

'Where one company can go, sir, another can follow. Once they see we're up there, other men will come.' He still held the great claymore which was too big to fit into the scabbard of his borrowed sword, but now he discarded that scabbard and shoved the claymore into his belt. He liked the sword. It was heavy, straight-bladed and brutal, not a weapon for delicate work, but a killer. Something to give a man confidence. 'You stay here, sir,' he told Stokes, 'and look after Ahmed for me. The little bugger would love to get in a fight, but he ain't got the sense of a louse when it comes to a scrap and he's bound to get killed. Tom!' he called to Garrard, then beckoned that he and the rest of the 33rd's Light Company should follow him down to where Morris sheltered among the rocks. 'When Eli gets here with the ladder, sir,' he added to Stokes, 'send him down.'

Sharpe ran down the ravine's steep side into the smoke-reeking shadows where Morris was seated under a tree making a meal out of bread, salt beef and whatever liquor was left in his canteen. 'Don't have enough food for you, Sharpe,' he said.

'Not hungry,' Sharpe lied.

'You're sweating, man,' Morris complained. 'Why don't you find yourself some shade? There's nothing we can do until the gunners knock that bloody gatehouse flat.'

'There is,' Sharpe said.

Morris cocked a sceptical eye up at Sharpe. 'I've had no orders, Ensign,' he said.

'I want you and the Light Company, sir,' Sharpe said respectfully. 'There's a way up the side of the ravine, sir, and if we can get a ladder to the top then we can cross the wall and go at the bastards from the back.'

Morris tipped the canteen to his mouth, drank, then wiped his lips. 'If you, twenty like you and the Archangel Gabriel and all the bloody saints asked me to climb the ravine, Sharpe, I would still say no. Now for Christ's sake, man, stop trying to be a bloody hero. Leave it to the poor bastards who are under orders, and go away.' He waved a hand.

'Sir,' Sharpe pleaded, 'we can do it! I've sent for a ladder.'

'No!' Morris interrupted loudly, attracting the attention of the rest of the company. 'I am not giving you my company, Sharpe. For God's sake, you're not even a proper officer! You're just a bumped-up sergeant! A bloody ensign too big for your boots and, allow me to remind you, Mister Sharpe, forbidden by army regulations to serve in this regiment. Now go away and leave me in peace.'

'I thought you'd say that, Charles,' Sharpe said ruefully.

'And stop calling me Charles!' Morris exploded. 'We are not friends, you and I. And kindly obey my order to leave me in peace, or had you not noticed that I outrank you?'

'I had noticed. Sorry, sir,' Sharpe said humbly and he started to turn away, but suddenly whipped back and seized Morris's coat. He dragged the Captain back into the rocks, going so fast that Morris was momentarily incapable of resistance. Once among the rocks, Sharpe let go of the patched coat and thumped Morris in the belly. 'That's for the flogging you gave me, you bastard,' he said.

'What the hell do you think you're doing, Sharpe?' Morris asked, scrambling away on his bottom.

Sharpe kicked him in the chest, leaned down, hauled him up and thumped him on the jaw. Morris squealed with pain, then gasped as Sharpe backhanded him across the cheek, then struck him again. A group of men had followed and were watching wide-eyed. Morris turned to appeal to them, but Sharpe hit him yet again and the Captain's eyes turned glassy as he swayed and collapsed. Sharpe bent over him. 'You might outrank me,' he said, 'but you're a piece of shit, Charlie, and you always were. Now can I take the company?'

'No,' Morris said through the blood on his lips.

'Thank you, sir,' Sharpe said, and stamped his boot hard down on Morris's head, driving it onto a rock. Morris gasped, choked, then lay immobile as the breath scraped in his throat.

Sharpe kicked Morris's head again, just for the hell of it, then turned, smiling. 'Where's Sergeant Green?'

'Here, sir.' Green, looking anxious, pushed through the watching men. 'I'm here, sir,' he said, staring with astonishment at the immobile Morris.

'Captain Morris has eaten something that disagreed with him,' Sharpe said, 'but before he was taken ill he expressed the wish that I should temporarily take command of the company.'

Sergeant Green looked at the battered, bleeding Captain, then back to Sharpe. 'Something he ate, sir?'

'Are you a doctor, Sergeant? Wear a black plume on your hat, do you?'

'No, sir.'

'Then stop questioning my statements. Have the company paraded, muskets loaded, no bayonets fixed.' Green hesitated. 'Do it, Sergeant!' Sharpe roared, startling the watching men.

'Yes, sir!' Green said hurriedly, backing away.

Sharpe waited until the company was in its four ranks. Many of them looked at him suspiciously, but they were powerless to challenge his authority, not while Sergeant Green had accepted it. 'You're a light company,' Sharpe said, 'and that means you can go where other soldiers can't. It makes you an elite. You know what that means? It means you're the best in the bloody army, and right now the army needs its best men. It needs you. So in a minute we'll be climbing up there' – he pointed to the ravine – 'crossing the wall and carrying the fight to the enemy. It'll be hard work for a bit, but not beyond a decent light company.' He looked to his left and saw Eli Lockhart leading his men down the side of the ravine with one of the discarded bamboo ladders. 'I'll go first,' he told the company, 'and Sergeant Green will go last. If any man refuses to climb, Sergeant, you're to shoot the bugger.'

'I am, sir?' Green asked nervously.

'In the head,' Sharpe said.

Major Stokes had followed Lockhart and now came up to Sharpe. 'I'll arrange for some covering fire, Sharpe,' he said.

'That'll be a help, sir. Not that these men need much help. They're the 33rd's Light Company. Best in the army.'

'I'm sure they are,' Stokes said, smiling at the seventy men who, seeing a major with Sharpe, supposed that the Ensign really did have the authority to do what he was proposing.

Lockhart, in his blue and yellow coat, waited with the ladder. 'Where do you want it, Mister Sharpe?'

'Over here,' Sharpe said. 'Just pass it up when we've reached the top. Sergeant Green! Send the men in ranks! Front rank first!' He walked to the side of the ravine and stared up his chosen route. It looked steeper from here, and much higher than it had seemed when he was staring through the telescope, but he still reckoned it was climbable. He could not see the Inner Fort's wall, but that was good, for neither could the defenders see him. All the same, it was bloody steep. Steep enough to give a mountain goat pause, yet if he failed now then he would be on a charge for striking a superior officer, so he really had no choice but to play the hero.

So he spat on his bruised hands, looked up one last time, then started to climb.

The second assault on the Inner Fort's gatehouse fared no better than the first. A howling mass of men charged through the wreckage of the shattered gate, stumbled on the dead and dying as they turned up the passage, but then the killing began again as a shower of missiles, rockets and musket fire turned the narrow, steep passage into a charnel house. An axeman succeeded in reaching the second gate and he stood above Colonel Kenny's scorched body to sink his blade deep into the timber, but he was immediately struck by three musket balls and dropped back, leaving the axe embedded in the dark, iron-studded wood. No one else went close to the gate, and a major, appalled at the slaughter, called the men back. 'Next time,' he shouted at them, 'we designate firing parties to give cover. Sergeant! I want two dozen men.'

'We need a cannon, sir,' the Sergeant answered with brutal honesty.

'They say one's coming.' The aide whom Kenny had sent to fetch a cannon had returned to the assault party. 'They say it'll take time, though,' he added, without explaining that the gunner officer had declared it would take at least two hours to manhandle a gun and ammunition across the ravine.

The Major shook his head. 'We'll try without the gun,' he said.

'God help us,' the Sergeant said under his breath.

Colonel Dodd had watched the attackers limp away. He could not help smiling. This was so very simple, just as he had foreseen. Manu Bappoo was dead and the Havildar had returned from the palace with the welcome news of Beny Singh's murder, which meant that Gawilghur had a new commander. He looked down at the dead and dying redcoats who lay among the small flickering blue flames of the spent rockets. 'They've learned their lesson, Gopal,' he told his Jemadar, 'so next time they'll try to keep us quiet by firing bigger volleys up at the firesteps. Toss down rockets, that'll spoil their aim.'

'Rockets, sahib.'

'Lots of rockets,' Dodd said. He patted his men on their backs. Their faces were singed by the explosions of the powder in their muskets' pans, they were thirsty and hot, but they were winning, and they knew it. They were his Cobras, as well trained as any troops in India, and they would be at the heart of the army that Dodd would unleash from this fortress to dominate the lands the British must relinquish when their southern army was broken.

'Why don't they give up?' Gopal asked Dodd. A sentry on the wall had reported that the bloodied attackers were forming to charge again.

'Because they're brave men, Jemadar,' Dodd said, 'but also stupid.'

The furious musket fire had started again from across the ravine, a sign that a new attack would soon come into the blood-slick gateway. Dodd drew his pistol, checked it was loaded, and walked back to watch the next failure. Let them come, he thought, for the more who died here, the fewer would remain to trouble him as he pursued the beaten remnant south across the Deccan Plain. 'Get ready!' he called. Slow matches burned on the firestep and his men crouched beside them with rockets, waiting to light the fuses and toss the terrible weapons down into the killing place.

A defiant cheer sounded, and the redcoats came again to the slaughter.

*   *   *

The cliff face was far steeper than Sharpe had anticipated, though it was not sheer rock, but rather a series of cracks in which plants had taken root, and he found that he could pull himself up by using stony outcrops and the thick stalks of the bigger shrubs. He needed both hands. Tom Garrard came behind, and more than once Sharpe trod on his friend's hands. 'Sorry, Tom.'

'Just keep going,' Garrard panted.

It became easier after the first ten feet, for the face now sloped away, and there was even room for two or three men to stand together on a weed-covered ledge. Sharpe called for the ladder and it was pushed up to him by the cavalrymen. The bamboo was light and he hooked the top rung over his right shoulder and climbed on upwards, following a jagged line of rocks and bushes that gave easy footing. A line of redcoats trailed him, muskets slung. There were more bushes to Sharpe's left, shielding him from the ramparts, but after he had climbed twenty feet those bushes ended and he prayed that the defenders would all be staring at the beleaguered gatehouse rather than at the precipice below. He pulled himself up the last few feet, cursing the ladder that seemed to get caught on every protrusion. The sun beat off the stone and the sweat poured down him. He was panting when he reached the top, and now there was nothing but steep, open ground between him and the wall's base. Fifty feet of rough grass to cross and then he would be at the wall.

He crouched at the edge of the cliff, waiting for the men to catch up. Still no one had seen him from the walls. Tom Garrard dropped beside him. 'When we go, Tom,' Sharpe said, 'we run like bloody hell. Straight to the wall. Ladder up, climb like rats and jump over the bloody top. Tell the lads to get over fast. Bastards on the other side are going to try and kill us before we can get reinforced, so we're going to need plenty of muskets to fend the buggers off.'

Garrard peered up at the embrasures. 'There's no one there.'

'There's a few there,' Sharpe said, 'but they ain't taking much notice. Dozy, they are,' he added, and thank God for that, he thought, for a handful of defenders with loaded muskets could stop him dead. And dead is what he had better be after striking Morris, unless he could cross the ramparts and open the gates. He peered up at the battlements as more men hauled themselves over the edge of the cliff. He guessed the wall was lightly manned by little more than a picquet line, for no one would have anticipated that the cliff could be climbed, but he also guessed that once the redcoats appeared the defenders would quickly reinforce the threatened spot.

Garrard grinned at Sharpe. 'Did you thump Morris?'

'What else could I do?'

'He'll have you court-martialled.'

'Not if we win here,' Sharpe said. 'If we get those gates open, Tom, we'll be bloody heroes.'

'And if we don't?'

'We'll be dead,' Sharpe said curtly, then turned to see Eli Lockhart scrambling onto the grass. 'What the hell are you doing here?' Sharpe demanded.

'I got lost,' Lockhart said, and hefted a musket he had taken from a soldier below. 'Some of your boys ain't too keen on being heroes, so me and my boys are making up the numbers.'

And it was not just Lockhart's cavalrymen who were climbing, but some kilted Highlanders and sepoys who had seen the Light Company scrambling up the cliff and decided to join in too. The more the merrier, Sharpe decided. He counted heads and saw he had thirty men, and more were coming. It was time to go, for the enemy would not stay asleep for long. 'We have to get over the wall fast,' he told them all, 'and once we're over, we form two ranks.'

He stood and hefted the ladder high over his head, holding it with both hands, then ran up the steep grass. His boots, which were Syud Sevajee's cast-offs, had smooth soles and slipped on the grass, but he stumbled on, and went even faster when he heard an aggrieved shout from high above him. He knew what was coming next and he was still thirty feet from the walls, a sitting target, and then he heard the bang of the musket and saw the grass flatten ahead of him as the gases from the barrel lashed downwards. Smoke eddied around him, but the ball had thumped into one of the ladder's thick uprights, and then another musket fired and he saw a fleck of turf dance up.

'Give them fire!' Major Stokes roared from the bottom of the ravine. 'Give them fire!'

A hundred redcoats and sepoys blasted up at the walls. Sharpe heard the musket shots clatter on the stone, and then he was hard under the rampart and he dropped the leading end of the ladder and rammed it into the turf and swung the other end up and over. A bloody escalade, he thought. A breach and an escalade, all in one day, and he pulled the claymore out from his belt and pushed Garrard away from the foot of the ladder. 'Me first,' he growled, and began to climb. The rungs were springy and he had the terrible thought that maybe they would break after the first few men had used the ladder, and then a handful of soldiers would be trapped inside the fortress where they would be cut down by the Mahrattas, but there was no time to dwell on that fear, just to keep climbing. The musket balls rattled the stones to left and right in a torrent of fire that had driven the defenders back from the parapet, but at any second Sharpe would be alone up there. He roared a shout of defiance, reached the top of the ladder and extended his free hand to grip the stone. He hauled himself through the embrasure. He paused, trying to get a sense of what lay beyond, but Garrard shoved him and he had no option but to spring through the embrasure.

There was no firestep! Jesus, he thought, and jumped. It was not a long jump down, maybe eight or ten feet, for the ground was higher on the inner side of the wall. He sprawled on the turf and a musket bullet whipped over his back. He rolled, got to his feet, and saw that the defenders had low wooden platforms that they had been using to peer over the top of the wall. Those defenders were running towards him now, but they were few, very few, and already Sharpe had five redcoats on his side of the wall, and more were coming. But so was the enemy, some from the west and more from the east. 'Tom! Look after those men.' Sharpe pointed westwards, then he turned the other way and dragged three men into a crude rank. 'Present!' he called. The muskets went up into their shoulders. 'Aim low, boys,' he said. 'Fire!'

The muskets coughed out smoke. A Mahratta slid on the grass. The others turned and ran, appalled at the stream of men now crossing the wall. It was a curious mix of English skirmishers, Highland infantry, sepoys, cavalrymen and even some of Syud Sevajee's followers in their borrowed red jackets. 'Two ranks!' Sharpe shouted. 'Quick now! Two ranks! Tom! What's happening behind me?'

'Buggers have gone, sir.'

'Two ranks!' Sharpe shouted again. He could not see the gatehouse from here because the hill inside the wall bulged outwards and hid the great ramparts from him, but the enemy was forming two hundred paces eastwards. The wall's defenders, in brown jackets, were joining a company of white-coated Cobras who must have been in reserve and those men would have to be defeated before Sharpe could hope to advance on the gatehouse. He glanced up the hill and saw nothing there except a building half hidden by trees in which monkeys gibbered. No defenders there, thank God, so he could ignore his right flank.

A Scottish sergeant had shoved and tugged the men into two ranks. 'Load!' Sharpe said, though most of the men were already loaded. 'Sergeant?'

'Sir?'

'Advance along the wall. No one's to fire till I give the word. Sergeant Green?' Sharpe called, waited. 'Sergeant Green!' Green had evidently not crossed the wall yet, or maybe he had not even climbed the cliff. 'Sergeant Green!' Sharpe bellowed again.

'Why do you need him?' a voice called.

It was a Scottish captain. Christ, Sharpe thought, but he was out-ranked. 'To bring the next group on!'

'I'll do it,' the Scotsman said, 'you go!'

'Advance!' Sharpe shouted.

'By the centre!' the Sergeant shouted. 'March!'

It was a ragged advance. The men had no file-closers and they spread out, but Sharpe did not much care. The thing was to close on the enemy. That had always been McCandless's advice. Get close and start killing, because there's bugger all you can do at long range, though the Scottish Colonel would never have used that word. This is for you, McCandless, Sharpe thought, this one's for you, and it struck him that this was the first time he had ever taken troops into formal battle, line against line, muskets against muskets. He was nervous, and made even more nervous by the fact that he was leading a makeshift company in full view of the thousands of redcoats on the ravine's northern slope. It was like being trapped on stage in a full theatre; lose here, he thought, and all the army would know. He watched the enemy officer, a tall man with a dark face and a large moustache. He looked calm and his men marched in three tight ranks. Well trained, Sharpe thought, but then no one had ever said William Dodd could not whip troops into shape.

The Cobras stopped when the two units were a hundred paces apart.

They levelled their muskets and Sharpe saw his men falter. 'Keep going!' he ordered. 'Keep going!'

'You heard the man!' the Scottish Sergeant bellowed. 'Keep going!'

Sharpe was at the right-hand flank of his line. He glanced behind to see more men running to catch up, their equipment flapping as they stumbled over the uneven ground. Christ, Sharpe thought, but I'm inside! We're in! And then the Cobras fired.

And Sharpe, ensign and bullock driver, had a battle on his hands.

The redcoats stormed the gatehouse a third time, this attempt led by two squads who hugged the walls either side of the passage and then turned their muskets up to blast the defenders on the opposite firestep. The tactic seemed to work, for they ripped off their first volley and under its cover a third squad comprised of axemen charged over the dead and dying and scrambled up the steep stone path towards the second gate.

Then the lit rockets began to drop from on high. They struck the bodies and then flamed into life and ricocheted madly about the confined space. They tore into the two musket squads, flamed among the axemen, choked men with their smoke, burned them with flame and exploded to strew the carnage with more blood and guts. The axemen never even reached the gate. They died under the musket fire that followed the rockets, or else, wounded, they tried to crawl back through the thick smoke. Rocks hurtled down from the flanking firesteps, pulping the dead and the living into horror. The survivors fled, defeated again.

'Enough!' Colonel Dodd shouted at his men. 'Enough!' He peered down into the stone chamber. It looked like something from hell, a place where broken things twitched in blood beneath a reeking pall of smoke. The rocket carcasses still burned. The wounded cried for help that was not coming, and Dodd felt an elation sear through him. It was even easier than he had dared to hope.

'Sahib!' Gopal said urgently. 'Sahib?'

'What?'

'Sahib, look!' Gopal was pointing westwards. There was smoke and the crackling sound of a musket fight. The noise and smoke were coming from just beyond the curve of the hill so Dodd could not see what was happening, but the sound was enough to convince him that a considerable fight had broken out a quarter-mile away, and that might not have mattered, except that the smoke and the noise came from inside the wall.

'Jesus!' Dodd swore. 'Find out what's happening, Gopal. Quick!' He could not lose. He must not lose. 'Where's Mister Hakeswill?' he shouted, wanting the deserter to take over Gopal's responsibilities on the firestep, but the twitching Sergeant had vanished. The musketry went on, but beneath Dodd there were only moans and the smell of burning flesh. He stared westwards. If the damned redcoats had crossed the wall then he would need more infantry to drive them out and seal whatever place they had found to penetrate the Inner Fort. 'Havildar!' He summoned the man who had accompanied Hakeswill to the palace. 'Go to the Southern Gate and tell them to send a battalion here. Quick!'

'Sahib,' the man said, and ran.

Dodd found that he was shaking slightly. It was just a small tremor in his right hand which he stilled by gripping the gold elephant-shaped hilt of his sword. There was no need to panic, he told himself, everything was under control, but he could not rid himself of the thought that there would be no escape from this place. In every other fight since he had defected from British service he had made certain of a route along which he could retreat, but from this high fortress on its soaring bluff there was no way out. He must win, or else he must die. He watched the smoke to the west. The firing was constant now, suggesting that the enemy was inside the fort in force. His hand twitched, but this time he did not notice as, for the first time in weeks, the Lord of Gawilghur began to fear defeat.

The volley from the company of white-coated Cobras hammered towards Sharpe's men, but because they were spread more widely than usual many of the balls wasted themselves in the gaps between the files. Some men went down, and the rest instinctively checked, but Sharpe shouted at them to keep marching. The enemy was hidden in smoke, but Sharpe knew they would be reloading. 'Close the files, Sergeant,' he shouted.

'Close up! Close up!' the Scots Sergeant called. He glanced at Sharpe, suspecting that he was taking the small company too close to the enemy. The range was already down to sixty yards.

Sharpe could just see one of the Indians through the smoke. The man was the left flanker of the front rank, a small man, and he had bitten off his cartridge and was pouring the powder down the muzzle of his musket. Sharpe watched the bullet go in and the ramrod come up ready to plunge down into the barrel. 'Halt!' he called.

'Halt!' the Sergeant echoed.

'Present!'

The muskets came up into the men's shoulders. Sharpe reckoned he had about sixty men in the two ranks, fewer than the enemy's three ranks, but enough. More men were running up from the ladder all the time. 'Aim low,' he said. 'Fire!'

The volley slammed into the Cobras who were still loading. Sharpe's men began to reload themselves, working fast, nervous of the enemy's next volley.

Sharpe watched the enemy bring their muskets up. His men were half hidden by their own musket smoke. 'Drop!' he shouted. He had not known he was going to give the order until he heard himself shout it, but it suddenly seemed the sensible thing to do. 'Flat on the ground!' he shouted. 'Quick!' He dropped himself, though only to one knee, and a heartbeat later the enemy fired and their volley whistled over the prostrate company. Sharpe had slowed his men's loading process, but he had kept them alive and now it was time to go for the kill. 'Load!' he shouted, and his men climbed to their feet. This time Sharpe did not watch the enemy, for he did not want to be affected by their timing. He hefted the claymore, comforted by the blade's heaviness.

'Prepare to charge!' he shouted. His men were pushing their ramrods back into their musket hoops, and now they pulled out their bayonets and twisted them onto blackened muzzles. Eli Lockhart's cavalrymen, some of whom only had pistols, drew their sabres.

'Present!' Sharpe called, and the muskets went up into the shoulders again. Now he did look at the enemy and saw that most of them were still ramming.

'Fire!' The muskets flamed and the scraps of wadding spat out after the bullets to flicker their small flames in the grass. 'Charge!' Sharpe shouted, and he led the way from the right flank, the claymore in his hand. 'Charge!' he shouted again and his small company, sensing that they had only seconds before the enemy's muskets were loaded, ran with him.

Then a blast of musketry sounded to Sharpe's right and he saw that the Scottish Captain had formed a score of men on the flank and had poured in a volley that struck the Cobras just before Sharpe's charge closed the gap.

'Kill them!' Sharpe raged. Fear was whipping inside him, the fear that he had mistimed this charge and that the enemy would have a volley ready just yards before the redcoats struck home, but he was committed now, and he ran as hard as he could to break into the white-coated ranks before the volley came.

The Havildar commanding the Cobra company had been appalled to see the redcoats charging. He should have fired, but instead he ordered his men to fix their own bayonets and so the enemy was still twisting the blades onto their muskets when the leading redcoats burst through the smoke. Sharpe hacked his heavy sword at the front rank, felt it bite and slide against bone, twisted it free, lunged, kicked at a man, and suddenly Eli Lockhart was beside him, his sabre slashing down, and two Highlanders were stabbing with bayonets. Sharpe hacked with the sword two-handed, fighting in a red rage that had come from the nervousness that had assailed him during the charge. A sepoy trapped the Cobras' Havildar, feinted with the bayonet, parried the *tulwar*'s counter-lunge, then stabbed the enemy in the belly. The white coats were running now, fleeing back towards the smoke that boiled up from the gatehouse which lay beyond the bulge of the hill. Tom Garrard, his bayonet bloodied to the hilt, kicked at a wounded man who was trying to aim his musket. Other men stooped to search the dead and dying.

The Scottish Captain came in from the flank. He had the winged epaulettes of a light company. 'I didn't know the 74th were up here,' he greeted Sharpe, 'or is it the 33rd?' He peered at Sharpe's coat, and Sharpe saw that Clare's newly sewn facings had been torn in the climb, revealing the old red material beneath.

'I'm a lost sheep, sir,' Sharpe said.

'A very welcome lost sheep,' the Captain said, holding out his hand. 'Archibald Campbell, Scotch Brigade. Brought my company up here, just in case they got bored.'

'Richard Sharpe, 74th,' Sharpe said, shaking Campbell's hand, 'and bloody glad to see you, sir.' Sharpe suddenly wanted to laugh. His force, which had pierced the Inner Fort's defences, was a ragged mix of Indians and British, cavalrymen and infantry. There were kilted Highlanders from the 78th, some of Campbell's men from the 94th, maybe half of the 33rd's Light Company, and a good number of sepoys.

Campbell had climbed one of the low timber platforms that had let the defenders peer over the firestep, and from its vantage point he stared at the gatehouse which lay a quarter-mile eastwards.

'Are you thinking what I'm thinking, Mister Sharpe?' he asked.

'I'm thinking we should take the gatehouse,' Sharpe said, 'and open the gates.'

'Me too.' He shifted to make room for Sharpe on the small platform. 'They'll no doubt be trying to evict us soon, eh? We'd best make haste.'

Sharpe stared at the gatehouse where a great smear of smoke showed above the ramparts that were thick with white-coated Cobras. A shallow flight of stone stairs led from inside the fortress to the firestep, and the gates could not be opened until that firestep was cleared of the enemy. 'If I take the firestep,' he suggested to Campbell, 'you can open the gates?'

'That seems a fair division of labour,' Campbell said, jumping down from the platform. He had lost his hat and a shock of curly black hair hung over his narrow face. He grinned at Sharpe. 'I'll take my company and you can have the rest, eh?' Campbell strode up the hill, shouting for his own Light Company to form in a column of three ranks.

Sharpe followed Campbell off the platform and summoned the remaining men into line. 'Captain Campbell's going to open the gates from the inside,' he told them, 'and we're going to make it possible by clearing the parapets of the bastards. It's a fair distance to the gate, but we've got to get there fast. And when we get there, the first thing we do is fire a volley up at the firestep. Clean some of the buggers off before we go up there. Load your muskets now. Sergeant Green!'

Green, red-faced from the effort of climbing up the ravine and running to join Sharpe, stepped forward. 'I'm here, sir, and sir –'

'Number off twenty men, Green,' Sharpe ordered the panting Sergeant. 'You'll stay down below and provide covering fire while we climb the steps, understand?'

'Twenty men, sir? Yes, sir, I will, sir, only it's Mister Morris, sir.' Green sounded embarrassed.

'What about him?' Sharpe asked.

'He's recovered, sir. His tummy, sir, it got better' – Green managed to keep a straight face as he delivered that news – 'and he said no one else was to climb the cliff, sir, and he sent me to fetch the men what had climbed it back down again. That's why I'm here, sir.'

'No, you're not,' Sharpe said. 'You're here to number off twenty men who'll give the rest of us covering fire.'

Green hesitated, looked at Sharpe's face, then nodded. 'Right you are, sir! Twenty men, covering fire.'

'Thank you, Sergeant,' Sharpe said. So Morris was conscious again, and probably already making trouble, but Sharpe could not worry about that. He looked at his men. They numbered seventy or eighty now, and still more Scotsmen and sepoys were coming up the cliff and crossing the wall. He waited until they all had loaded muskets and their ramrods were back in their hoops. 'Just follow me, lads, and when we get there kill the bastards. Now!' He turned and faced east. 'Come on!'

'At the double!' Campbell called to his company. 'Forward!'

The fox was in the henhouse. Feathers would fly.

CHAPTER 11

The 74th, climbing the road that led from the plain to Gawilghur's Southern Gate, could hear the distant musketry sounding like a burning thorn grove. It crackled, flared up to a crescendo, then faded again. At times it seemed as though it would die altogether and then, just as sweating men decided the battle must be over, it rattled loud and furious once more. There was nothing the 74th could do to help. They were still three hundred feet beneath the fortress and from now on they would be within killing range of the guns mounted on Gawilghur's south-facing ramparts. Those guns had been firing at the 74th for over an hour now, but the range had been long and the downward angle steep, so that not a ball had struck home. If the 74th had had their own artillery, they could have fired back, but the slope was too steep for any gun to fire effectively. The gunners would have had to site their cannon on a steep upwards ramp, and every shot would have threatened to turn the guns over. The 74th could go no farther, not without taking needless casualties, and so Wellesley halted them. If the defenders on the southern wall looked few he might contemplate an escalade, but the sepoys carrying the ladders had fallen far behind the leading troops so no such attack could be contemplated yet. Nor did the General truly expect to try such an assault, for the 74th's task had always been to keep some of the fort's defenders pinned to their southern walls while the real attack came from the north. That purpose, at least, was being accomplished, for the walls facing the steep southern slope looked thick with defenders.

Sir Arthur Wellesley dismounted from his horse and climbed to a vantage point from which he could stare at the fortress. Colonel Wallace and a handful of aides followed, and the officers settled by some rocks from where they tried to work out what the noise of the battle meant. 'No guns,' Wellesley said after cocking his head to the distant sound.

'No guns, sir?' an aide asked.

'There's no sound of cannon fire,' Colonel Wallace explained, 'which surely means the Outer Fort is taken.'

'But not the Inner?' the aide asked.

Sir Arthur did not even bother to reply. Of course the Inner Fort was not taken, otherwise the sound of fighting would have died away altogether and fugitives would be streaming from the Southern Gate towards the muskets of the 74th. And somehow, despite his misgivings, Wellesley had dared to hope that Kenny's assault would wash over both sets of ramparts, and that by the time the 74th reached the road's summit the great Southern Gate would already have been opened by triumphant redcoats. Instead a green and gold flag hung from the gate-tower which bristled with the muskets of its defenders.

Wellesley now wished that he had ridden to the plateau and followed Kenny's men through the breaches. What the hell was happening? He had no way of reaching the plateau except to ride all the way down to the plain and then back up the newly cut road, a distance of over twenty miles. He could only wait and hope. 'You'll advance your skirmishers, Colonel?' he suggested to Wallace. The 74th's skirmishers could not hope to achieve much, but at least their presence would confirm the threat to the southern walls and so pin those defenders down. 'But spread them out,' Wellesley advised, 'spread them well out.' By scattering the Light Company across the hot hillside he would protect them from cannon fire.

Beyond the southern ramparts, far beyond, a pillar of smoke smeared the sky grey. The sound of firing rose and fell, muted by the hot air that shimmered over the fort's black walls. Wellesley fidgeted and hoped to God his gamble would pay off and that his redcoats, God alone knew how, had found a way into the fort that had never before fallen.

'Give them fire!' Major Stokes roared at the men on the ravine's northern side. 'Give them fire!' Other officers took up the call, and the men who had been watching the fight across the ravine loaded their firelocks and began peppering the gatehouse with musket balls.

Stokes had climbed back up the northern side of the ravine so that he could see across the farther wall, and he now watched as the two small groups of redcoats advanced raggedly over the hillside. A column was farthest away, while the nearer men were in a line, and both advanced on the strongly garrisoned gatehouse which had just repelled yet another British attack through the broken gate. Those defenders would now turn their muskets on the new attackers and so Stokes roared at men to fire across the ravine. The range was terribly long, but any distraction would help. The gunners who had smashed down the gate fired at the parapets, their shots chipping at stone. 'Go, man, go!' Stokes urged Sharpe. 'Go!'

Captain Morris, his mouth swollen and bleeding, and with a bruise blackening one eye and another disfiguring his forehead, staggered up the hillside. 'Major Stokes!' he called petulantly. 'Major Stokes.'

Stokes turned to him. His first reaction was that Morris must have been wounded trying to cross the wall, and he decided he must have misjudged the man who was not, after all, such a coward. 'You need a surgeon, Captain?'

'That bloody man, Sharpe! He hit me! Hit me! Stole my company. I want charges levelled.'

'Hit you?' Stokes asked, bemused.

'Stole my company!' Morris said in outrage. 'I ordered him to go away, and he hit me! I'm telling you, sir, because you're a senior officer. You can talk to some of my men, sir, and hear their story. Some of them witnessed the assault, and I shall look for your support, sir, in the proceedings.'

Stokes wanted to laugh. So that was how Sharpe had found the men! 'I think you'd better forget bringing charges against Mister Sharpe,' the engineer said.

'Forget bringing charges?' Morris exclaimed. 'I will not! I'll break the bastard!'

'I doubt it,' Stokes said.

'He hit me!' Morris protested. 'He assaulted me!'

'Nonsense,' Stokes said brusquely. 'You fell over. I saw you do it. Tripped and tumbled. And that's precisely what I'll allege at any court martial. Not that there'll be a court martial. You simply fell over, man, and now you're suffering from delusions! Maybe it's a touch of the sun, Captain? You should be careful, otherwise you'll end up like poor

Harness. We shall ship you home and you'll end your days in bedlam with chains round your ankles.'

'Sir! I protest!' Morris said.

'You protest too much, Captain,' Stokes said. 'You tripped, and that's what I shall testify if you're foolish enough to bring charges. Even my boy saw you trip. Ain't that so, Ahmed?' Stokes turned to get Ahmed's agreement, but he had vanished. 'Oh, God,' Stokes said, and started down the hill to find the boy.

But sensed he was already too late.

The first hundred paces of Sharpe's advance were easy enough, for the sun-baked ground was open and his men were still out of sight of the gatehouse. The few defenders who had manned the wall above the ravine had fled, but as soon as the redcoats breasted the slope of the hill to see the gatehouse ahead, the enemy musketry began. 'Keep running!' Sharpe shouted, though it was hardly a run. They staggered and stumbled, their scabbards and haversacks banging and flapping, and the sun burned down relentlessly and the dry ground spurted puffs of dust as enemy musket balls flicked home. Sharpe was dimly aware of a cacophony of musketry from his left, the fire of the thousands of redcoats on the other side of the ravine, but the gatehouse defenders were sheltered by the outer parapet. A group of those defenders was manhandling a cannon round to face the new attack. 'Just keep going!' Sharpe called, the breath rasping in his throat. Christ, but he was thirsty. Thirsty, hungry and excited. The gatehouse was fogged by smoke as its defenders fired their muskets at the unexpected attack that was coming out of the west.

Off to his right Sharpe could see more defenders, but they were not firing, indeed they were not even formed in ranks. Instead they bunched beside a low wall that seemed to edge some gardens and supinely watched the confrontation. A building reared up beyond that, half obscured by trees. The place was huge! Hilltop after hilltop lay within the vast ring of Gawilghur's Inner Fort, and there had to be a thousand places for the enemy to assemble a force to attack Sharpe's open right flank, but he dared not worry about that possibility. All that mattered now was to reach the gatehouse and kill its defenders and so let a torrent of redcoats through the entrance.

The cannon fired from the gatehouse. The ball struck the dry ground fifty yards ahead of Sharpe and bounced clean over his head. The smoke of the gun spread in front of the parapet, spoiling the aim of the defenders, and Sharpe blessed the gunners and prayed that the smoke would linger. He had a stitch in his side, and his ribs still hurt like hell from the kicking that Hakeswill had given him, but he knew they had surprised this enemy, and an enemy surprised was already half beaten.

The smoke thinned and the muskets flamed from the wall again, making more smoke. Sharpe turned to shout at his men. 'Come on! Hurry!' He was crossing a stretch of ground where some of the garrison had made pathetic little lodges of thin branches propped against half dead trees and covered with sacking. Ash showed where fires had burned. It was a dumping ground. There was a rusting iron cannon carriage, a stone trough that had split in two and the remains of an ancient windlass made of wood that had been sun-whitened to the colour of bone. A small brown snake twisted away from him. A woman, thin as the snake and clutching a baby, fled from one of the shelters. A cat hissed at him from another. Sharpe dodged between the small trees, kicking up dust, breathing dust. A musket ball flicked up a puff of fire ash, another clanged off the rusting gun carriage.

He blinked through the sweat that stung his eyes to see that the gate passage's inner wall was lined with white-coated soldiers. The wall was a good hundred paces long, and its firestep was reached by climbing the flight of stone steps that led up beside the innermost gate. Campbell and his men were running towards that gate and Sharpe was now alongside them. He would have to fight his way up the stairs, and he knew that it would be impossible, that there were too many defenders, and he flinched as the cannon fired again, only this time it belched a barrelful of canister that threw up a storm of dust devils all about Sharpe's leading men.

'Stop!' he shouted. 'Stop! Form line!' He was close to the wall, damned close, not more than forty paces. 'Present!' he shouted, and his men raised their muskets to aim at the top of the wall. Smoke still hid half the rampart, though the other half was clear and the defenders were firing fast. A Scotsman staggered backwards and a sepoy folded over silently and clutched his bleeding belly. A small dog yapped at the soldiers. The smoke was clearing from the mouth of the cannon. 'You've got one volley,' Sharpe called, 'then we charge. Sergeant

Green? I don't want your men to fire now. Wait till we reach the top of the steps, then give us covering fire.' Sharpe wanted to lash out with his boot at the damned dog, but he forced himself to show calm as he paced down the front of the line. 'Aim well, boys, aim well! I want that wall cleared.' He stepped into a space between two files. 'Fire!'

The single volley flamed towards the top of the wall and Sharpe immediately ran at the steps without waiting to see the effect of the fire. Campbell was already at the innermost gate, lifting its heavy bar. He had a dozen men ready to enter the passageway, while the rest of his company faced back into the fort's interior to fight off any of the garrison who might come down from the buildings on the hill.

Sharpe took the steps two at a time. This is bloody madness, he thought. Suicide in a hot place. Should have stayed in the ravine. The sun beat off the stones so that it was like being in an oven. There were men with him, though he could not see who they were, for he was only aware of the top of the stairs, and of the men in white who were turning to face him with bayonets, and then Green's first volley slammed into them, and one of the men spun sideways, spurting a spray of blood from his scalp, and the others instinctively twitched away from the volley and Sharpe was there, the claymore slashing in a haymaker's sweep that bounced off the wounded man's skull to drive a second man over the wall's unprotected edge and into the passageway.

Where the innermost gate was opening, scraping on the stone and squealing on its huge hinges as Campbell's men heaved on the vast doors.

A bayonet lunged at Sharpe, catching his coat, and he hammered the hilt of the claymore down onto the man's head, then brought up his knee. Lockhart was beside him, fighting with a cold-blooded ferocity, his sabre spattering drops of blood with every cut or lunge. 'Over there!' Lockhart shouted to his men, and a half-dozen of the cavalrymen ran across the top of the archway to challenge the defenders on the outer walkway. Tom Garrard came up on Sharpe's right and plunged his bayonet forward in short, disciplined strokes. More men ran up the stairs and pushed at those in front so that Sharpe, Lockhart and Garrard were shoved forward against the enemy who had no space to use their bayonets. The press of men also protected Sharpe from the enemy's muskets. He beat down with the heavy sword, using his height to dominate the Indians who were keening a high-pitched war cry. A bayonet hit Sharpe plumb on his hip bone and he felt the steel grind on bone and he slammed the claymore's hilt down onto the man's head to crumple his shako, then down again to beat the man to the ground. The bayonet fell away and Sharpe climbed over the stunned man to slash at another defender. A musket banged close by him and he felt the scorch of the barrel flame on his burnt cheek. The press of men was thick, too thick to make progress, even though he beat at them with the sword which he cut downwards with both hands. 'Throw them over the bloody side!' Lockhart shouted, and the tall cavalryman slashed his sabre, just missing Sharpe, but the hissing blade drove the enemy frantically back and two of them, caught on the edge of the firestep, screamed and fell to where they were beaten to death by the musket butts of Campbell's Highlanders. Campbell himself was running to the next gate. Two more gates to unbar and the way would be open, but the Cobras were thick on the walls and Dodd was screaming at them to shoot into the press of men, attackers and defenders alike, and so throw back the impudent handful of redcoats who had turned his rear.

Then the attackers outside the fort, who had despaired of making another charge into the smoke- and blood-stinking alley where so many had died, heard the fight on the ramparts and so they came back, flooding into the shadow of the arch and there aiming up at the firesteps. The muskets hammered, more men came, and the Cobras were assailed from in front and from below. 'Rockets!' Dodd shouted, and some of his men lit the missiles and tossed them down into the passageway, but they were nervous of the attackers coming along the top of the rampart. Those attackers were big men, crazed with battle, slashing with swords and bayonets as they snarled their way along the wall. Sergeant Green's men fired from below, picking off defenders and forcing others to duck.

'Fire across! Fire across!' Captain Campbell, down in the passageway, had seen the defenders thickening in front of the men attacking along the tops of the walls and now he cupped his hands and shouted at the men behind the front ranks of the attackers. 'Fire across!' He pointed, showing them that they should angle their fire over the passageway to strike the defenders on the opposite wall and the men, understanding him, loaded their muskets. It took a few seconds, but at last the crossfire began and the pressure in front of Sharpe gave way. He swung the huge sword backhanded, half severing a man's head, twisted the blade, thrust it into a belly, twisted it again, and suddenly the Cobras were backing away, terrified of the bloody blades.

The second gate was opened. Campbell was the first man through and now there was only one gate left. His sergeant had brought a score of men into the passageway and those Scotsmen began to fire up at the walls, and the Cobras were crumbling now because there were redcoats below them on both sides, and more were hacking their way along the rampart, and the defenders were pinned in a small place with nowhere to go. The only steps to the gateway's firestep were in redcoat hands, and Dodd's men could either jump or surrender. A piper had started playing, and the mad skirl of the music drove the attackers to a new fury as they closed on the remnants of Dodd's Cobras. The redcoats were screaming a terrible war cry that was a compound of rage, madness and sheer terror. Sharpe's tattered white facings were now so soaked in blood that it looked as if he wore the red-trimmed coat of the 33rd again. His arm was tired, his hip was a great aching sore, and the wall was still not clear. A musket ball snatched at his sleeve, another fanned his bare head, and then he snarled at an enemy, cut again, and Campbell had the last bar out of its brackets and his men were heaving on the gate, and the attackers who had come from outside the fort were pulling on it, while beyond the outermost arch, on the slope above the ravine, an officer beckoned to all the troops waiting to the north.

A cheer sounded, and a flood of redcoats ran down into the ravine and up the track towards the Inner Fort. They smelt loot and women. The gates were open. The fortress in the sky had fallen.

Dodd was the last man on Sharpe's wall. He knew he was beaten, but he was no coward, and he came forward, sword in hand, then recognized the bloody man opposing him. 'Sergeant Sharpe,' he said, and raised his gold-hilted sword in an ironic salute. He had once tried to persuade Sharpe to join him in the Cobras, and Sharpe had been tempted, but fate had kept him in his red coat and brought him to this last meeting on Gawilghur's ramparts.

'I'm Mister Sharpe now, you bastard,' Sharpe said, and he waved Lockhart and Garrard back, then jumped forward, cutting with the claymore, but Dodd parried it easily and lunged at Sharpe, piercing his coat and glancing the sword point off a rib. Dodd stepped back, flicked the claymore aside, and lunged again, and this time the blade cut into Sharpe's right cheek, opening it clean up to the bone beside his eye.

'Marked for life,' Dodd said, 'though I fear it won't be a long life, Mister Sharpe.' Dodd thrust again and Sharpe parried desperately, deflecting the blade more by luck than skill, and he knew he was a dead man because Dodd was too good a swordsman. McCandless had warned him of this. Dodd might be a traitor, but he was a soldier, and a good one.

Dodd saw Sharpe's sudden caution, and smiled. 'They made an officer out of you, did they? I never knew the British army had that much sense.' He advanced again, sword low, inviting an attack from Sharpe, but then a redcoat ran past Sharpe, sabre swinging, and Dodd stepped fast back, surprised by the sudden charge, although he parried it with an instinctive skill. The force of the parry knocked the redcoat off balance and Dodd, still with a smile, lunged effortlessly to skewer the redcoat's throat. It was Ahmed, and Sharpe, recognizing the boy, roared with rage and ran at Dodd who flicked the sword back, blood streaming from its tip, and deflected the claymore's savage cut, turned his blade beneath it and was about to thrust the slim blade into Sharpe's belly when a pistol banged and Dodd was thrown hard back, blood showing on his right shoulder. His sword arm, numbed by the pistol bullet, hung low.

Sharpe walked up to him and saw the fear in Dodd's eyes. 'This is for McCandless,' he said, and kicked the renegade in the crotch. Dodd gasped and bent double. 'And this is for Ahmed,' Sharpe said, and swept the claymore up so that its heavy blade ripped into Dodd's throat, and Sharpe, still holding the sword double-handed, pulled it hard back and the steel sawed through sinew and muscle and gullet so that the firestep was suddenly awash with blood as the tall Dodd collapsed. Eli Lockhart, the long horse pistol still smoking in his hand, edged Sharpe aside to make certain Dodd was dead. Sharpe was stooped by Ahmed, but the boy was dying. Blood bubbled at his throat as he tried to breathe. His eyes looked up into Sharpe's face, but there was no recognition there. His small body heaved frantically, then was still. He had gone to his paradise. 'You stupid bastard,' Sharpe said, tears trickling to dilute the blood pouring from his cheek. 'You stupid little bastard.'

Lockhart used his sabre to cut the ropes holding the flag above the gatehouse and a roar of triumph sounded from the ravine as the flag came down. Then Lockhart helped Sharpe strip Ahmed of his red jacket and, lacking a British flag to hoist, they pulled the faded, blood-reddened coat up to the top of the pole. Gawilghur had yielded.

Sharpe cuffed tears and blood from his face. Lockhart was grinning at him, and Sharpe forced a smile in return. 'We did it, Eli.'

'We bloody did.' Lockhart held out a hand and Sharpe gripped it.

'Thank you,' Sharpe said fervently, then he let go of the cavalryman's hand and kicked Dodd's corpse. 'Look after that body, Eli. It's worth a fortune.'

'That's Dodd?'

'That's the bastard. That corpse is worth seven hundred guineas to you and Clare.'

'You and me, sir,' Lockhart said. The Sergeant looked as ragged and bloody as Sharpe. His blue jacket was torn and bloodstained. 'We'll share the reward,' he said, 'you and me, sir.'

'No,' Sharpe said, 'he's all yours. I just wanted to see the bastard dead. That's reward enough for me.' Blood was pouring from his cheek to add to the gore on his coat. He turned to Garrard who was leaning against the parapet, gasping for air. 'Look after the boy for me, Tom.'

Garrard, seeing that Ahmed was dead, frowned in puzzlement.

'I'm going to give him a proper burial,' Sharpe explained, then he turned and walked down the wall where exhausted redcoats rested among the dead and dying Cobras, while beneath them, in the passage that Campbell had opened, a stream of soldiers poured unopposed into the fort.

'Where are you going?' Garrard shouted after Sharpe.

Sharpe did not answer. He just walked on. He had another enemy to hunt, and an even richer reward to win.

The defenders were hunted down and killed. Even when they tried to surrender, they were killed, for their fortress had resisted and that was the fate of garrisons that showed defiance. Blood-maddened redcoats, fed on arrack and rum, roamed the vast stronghold with bayonets and greed both sharpened. There was little enough loot, but plenty of women, and so the screaming began.

Some defenders, knowing Gawilghur's geography, slipped to those parts of the perimeter where no wall faced outwards and dangerously narrow paths led down the cliffs. They streamed like ants down the rock, going to oblivion. Some hid, knowing that the rage of the attackers would soon enough be exhausted. Those who could not escape or find a hiding place died.

Flies buzzed in the palace where the dead were already stinking in the heat. Officers wandered the rooms, marvelling at their poverty. They had expected to find another mansion like the Tippoo Sultan's palace, a glittering trove of gems, gold, ivory and silk, but the Rajah of Berar had never been rich. Some discovered the cellars and they noted the great armoury, but were more interested in the barrels of cash, though when they saw the coins were all of copper they spat in disgust. A company of sepoys found some silver plate that they cut apart with their bayonets. Syud Sevajee had found his enemy, his father's murderer, but Beny Singh was already dead and Sevajee could do little more than spit on his corpse.

Beneath the palace, redcoats splashed in the lake, slaking their thirst. Some had discarded their red jackets, hanging them from the trees, and a ragged man, who had slipped unseen from the palace, stole one of the coats and pulled it on before limping towards the captured gatehouse. He was a white man, and wore a pair of dirty trousers and a ragged shirt, while a white coat and a black sash were bundled under one arm. His hair was lank, his skin filthy, and his face twitched as he shuffled along the path. No one took any notice of him, for he looked like any other redcoat who had found his small scrap of loot, and so Obadiah Hakeswill slunk northwards with a fortune in jewels concealed in his shabby clothes. He reckoned he had only to get through the gate, and across the Outer Fort, and then he would run. Where? He did not know. Just run. He was rich now, but he would still need to steal a horse. There would be plenty of officers' horses in the camp, and maybe he would be lucky and find a dead man's horse so that the loss would not be noticed for days. Then he would ride southwards. South to Madras, and in Madras he could sell the jewels, buy proper clothes and become a gentleman. Obadiah Hakeswill, Gent. Then he would go home. Home to England. Be a rich gentleman there.

He ignored the redcoats. The buggers had won, and it was not fair. He could have been a rajah, but at least he was as rich as any rajah, and so he sidled down the dusty path and the gatehouse was not very far away now. An officer was ahead, standing with a drawn claymore beside the snake pit and staring down into its horror, and then he turned and walked towards Hakeswill. The officer was hatless, bloody-faced, and Obadiah limped off the track, praying that he would not be noticed. The officer went safely past and Hakeswill breathed a silent prayer of thanks and swerved back to the track. Only a trickle of men came through the gate now, and most of them were too intent on joining the plundering to care about a single man limping the other way. Hakeswill grinned, knowing he would get away. He would be a gentleman.

Then a sword point pricked his spine and Hakeswill froze.

'I've been looking for you for days, Obadiah,' a hated voice said, and Hakeswill turned to look up into Sharpe's face, but the face was half hidden by blood, which was why he had not recognized the officer standing beside the snake pit.

'I was a prisoner,' Hakeswill whined, 'a prisoner.'

'You're a bloody liar.'

'For the love of God, help me.' Obadiah pretended not to recognize Sharpe, pretended to be mad. He twitched and moaned, let spittle dribble from his mouth and twisted his hands in submission. 'Locked me up,' he said, 'the heathen bastards locked me up. Ain't seen daylight in days.'

Sharpe leaned forward and snatched the coat that was bundled under Hakeswill's arm. Hakeswill stiffened, and Sharpe smiled as he saw the flash of anger in the Sergeant's eyes. 'Want the coat back, Obadiah? So fight me for it.'

'I was a prisoner,' Hakeswill insisted, no longer moaning like a mad thing.

Sharpe shook the coat open. 'So why's the jacket white, Obadiah? You're a bleeding liar.' He felt the coat's pockets, felt the hard lumps and knew his jewels were safe again. Hakeswill's eyes glinted with a terrible and frustrated rage. 'Go on, Obadiah,' Sharpe said, 'fight me.'

'I was a prisoner,' Hakeswill said, and he glanced to his right, hoping he could make a run for it, for though he might have lost the jewels in the coat, he had others in his trousers. And Sharpe, he now saw, had a wound in the hip. Perhaps Sharpe could not run. So run now, he told himself, and then the flat of the claymore's blade struck him hard across the scalp. He yelped, then went still as the sword point pricked at his throat.

'You sold me to Jama, didn't you?' Sharpe said. 'But that was a mistake, Obadiah, because I beat his *jettis* into pulp. I'll do that to you now. But take your clothes off first.'

'You can't do this to me!' Hakeswill shouted, hoping to attract attention. His face twitched. 'You can't do this! 'Gainst regulations, it is!'

'Strip, Obadiah,' Sharpe said.

'There are rules! Regulations! Says so in the scriptures!'

The claymore's point jabbed at Hakeswill's throat, drawing blood from the scar that had been left when they had tried to hang the young Obadiah. The pain quietened the Sergeant, and Sharpe smiled. 'I half beat Captain Morris to death, Sergeant, so do you think it worries me that there are rules which say I mustn't touch you? Now you've got a choice. You can strip naked, or you can let me strip your corpse naked. I don't care which it is. I don't care if they bloody hang me for your murder. It'd be worth it. So shut the hell up, and get your bloody clothes off.'

Hakeswill looked for help, but there was none in sight, and the sword point twisted in his broken skin and he gabbled that he was undressing himself, and he scrabbled at the rope belt on his trousers, and tore the buttons out of his shirt. 'Don't kill me!' he shouted. 'I can't be killed! I can't die!' He pulled off the shirt, tugged off his boots and pulled down his trousers.

'Now the foot cloths,' Sharpe said.

Hakeswill sat and unwrapped the filthy strips and so was left white and naked under the terrible sun. Sharpe used the sword's tip to pull the clothes into a pile. He would search them, extract the gems, then leave them.

'On your feet now, Obadiah,' he said, encouraging the naked man with the sword's reddened tip.

'I can't die, Sharpie!' Hakeswill pleaded, his face racked by twitches. 'I can't! You tried! The tigers wouldn't eat me and the elephant wouldn't kill me. You know why? Because I can't die! I've got an angel, I do, my own soul's angel and she looks after me.' He shouted the words, and all the while he was being pressed backwards by the sword tip, and he danced on the rocks because they were so hot and his feet were bare. 'You can't kill me. The angel looks after me. It's Mother, Sharpie, that's who the angel is, it's Mother all white and shiny. No, Sharpie, no! I can't die!' And the sword stabbed at his belly and Hakeswill jumped back, and jumped back again when the tip slashed at his scrawny ribs. 'They tried to hang me but they couldn't!' he declared. 'I dangled and I danced, and the rope wouldn't kill me, and here I am! I cannot die!' And then he screamed, because the sword had stabbed one last time and Hakeswill had stepped back to avoid the lunge, only this time there was no rock behind him, only a void, and he screamed as he fell into the shadows of the snake pit.

He screamed again as he hit the stone floor with a thump. 'I can't die!' he shouted triumphantly, and stared up at the black shape of his enemy. 'I can't die!' Hakeswill called again, then something sinuous and shadowy flickered to his left and he had no time to worry about Sharpe. He screamed, because the snakes were staring at him with hard flat eyes. 'Sharpie!' he shouted. 'Sharpie!'

But Sharpe had gone to collect the pile of rags.

And Hakeswill was alone with the serpents.

Wellesley heard the distant cheers, but could not tell whether it was his own men who celebrated or the enemy who was making the noise. The smoke cloud that had hung so thick and constant beyond the fortress faded.

He waited.

The defenders on the south wall still fought. They fired their cannon at the 74th's skirmish line which, because it was well spread out and sheltered by the rocks on the steep hillside, survived the sporadic cannonade. The smoke of the guns hung by the walls. Wellesley looked at his watch. Four o'clock. If the fort had not fallen, then it would soon be too late. Night would come and he would have to retreat ignominiously to the plain below. The intermittent crackle of muskets from the north told him that something was still happening, but whether it was men looting, or the sound of the defenders firing at defeated attackers, he could not tell.

Then the guns on the south wall fell silent. Their smoke lingered, then drifted away in the hot wind. Wellesley waited, expecting the cannon to fire again, but they remained quiet. 'Maybe they've run,' he said. The green and gold flag still hung over the gate-tower, but Wellesley could see no defenders there.

'If the fortress has fallen, sir,' Wallace pointed out, 'then why aren't they running out of this gate?'

'Because they know we're here,' Wellesley said, and took out his telescope. By mistake he had brought the new glass, the one he intended to give to Sharpe which had been engraved with the date of Assaye, and he put it to his eye and examined the southern wall. The embrasures were empty. The guns were still there, their blackened muzzles just showing, but no men. 'I think we shall advance, Wallace,' Wellesley said, snapping the glass shut.

'It could be a trap, sir.'

'We shall advance,' Wellesley said firmly.

The 74th marched with colours flying, drummers beating and pipers playing. A battalion of sepoys followed, and the two regiments made a brave sight as they climbed the last stretch of the steep road, but still the great Southern Gate of Gawilghur was closed before them. Wellesley spurred ahead, half expecting the defenders to spring a surprise and appear on the ramparts, but instead it was a redcoat who suddenly showed there and Wellesley's heart leaped with relief. He could sail home to England with another victory in his pocket.

The redcoat on the wall slashed at the flag's halyard and Wellesley watched as the green and gold banner fluttered down. Then the redcoat turned and shouted to someone inside the fortress.

Wellesley spurred his horse. Just as he and his aides came into the shadow of the gatehouse, the great gates began to open, hauled back by dirty-looking redcoats with stained faces and broad grins. An officer stood just beyond the arch and, as the General rode into sight, the officer brought his sword up in salute.

Wellesley returned the salute. The officer was drenched in blood, and the General hoped that was not a reflection of the army's casualties. Then he recognized the man. 'Mister Sharpe?' He sounded puzzled.

'Welcome to Gawilghur, sir,' Sharpe said.

'I thought you'd been captured?'

'I escaped, sir. Managed to join the attack.'

'So I see.' Wellesley glanced ahead. The fort seethed with jubilant redcoats and he knew it would take till nightfall to restore order. 'You should see a surgeon, Mister Sharpe. I fear you're going to carry a scar on your face.' He remembered the telescope, but decided he would give it to Sharpe later and so, with a curt nod, he rode on.

Sharpe stood and watched the 74th march in. They had not wanted him, because he was not a gentleman. But, by God, he was a soldier, and he had opened the fort for them. He caught Urquhart's eye, and Urquhart looked at the blood on Sharpe's face and at the crusting scabs on Sharpe's sword, then looked away. 'Good afternoon, Urquhart,' Sharpe said loudly.

Urquhart spurred his horse.

'Good afternoon, Sergeant Colquhoun,' Sharpe said.

Colquhoun marched doggedly on.

Sharpe smiled. He had proved whatever he had set out to prove, and what was that? That he was a soldier, but he had always known that. He was a soldier, and he would stay a soldier, and if that meant wearing a green jacket instead of a red, then so be it. But he was a soldier, and he had proved it in the heat and blood of Gawilghur. It was the fastness in the sky, the stronghold that could not fall, and now it was Sharpe's fortress.

Historical Note

I have done the 94th, sometimes known as the Scotch Brigade, and their Light Company which was led by Captain Campbell, a great disservice, for it was they, and not Sharpe, who found the route up the side of the ravine and then across the Inner Fort's wall at Gawilghur, and who then assailed the gatehouse from the inside and, by opening the succession of gates, allowed the rest of the attacking force into the fortress. Fictional heroes steal other men's thunder, and I trust the Scots will forgive Sharpe. The Captain Campbell whose initiative broke Gawilghur's defence was not the same Campbell who was one of Wellesley's aides (and who had been the hero at Ahmednuggur).

The 33rd's Light Company was not at Gawilghur; indeed the only British infantry there were Scottish regiments, the same Scotsmen who shocked Scindia's army into rout at Assaye and took the brunt of the Arab attack at Argaum. Wellesley's war against the Mahrattas, which ended in complete victory at Gawilghur, was thus won by Madrassi sepoys and Scottish Highlanders, and it was an extraordinary victory.

The battle of Assaye, described in *Sharpe's Triumph*, was the engagement which destroyed the cohesion of the Mahratta Confederation. Scindia, the most powerful of the princes, was so shocked by the defeat that he sued for peace, while the Rajah of Berar's troops, deserted by their allies, fought on. Undoubtedly their best strategy would have been an immediate retreat to Gawilghur, but Manu Bappoo must have decided that he could stop the British and so decided to make his stand at Argaum. The battle happened much as described in this novel; it began with an apparent Mahratta advantage when the sepoys on the right of Wellesley's line panicked, but the General calmed them, brought them back, then launched his line to victory. The Scots, just as they had been at Assaye, were his shock troops, and they destroyed the Arab regiment that was the best of Bappoo's infantry. There were no Cobras in Bappoo's army, and though William Dodd existed, and was a renegade fugitive from the East India Company army, there is no record of his having served Berar. The survivors of Argaum retreated north to Gawilghur.

Gawilghur is still a mightily impressive fortress, sprawling over its vast headland high above the Deccan Plain. It is deserted now, and was never again to be used as a stronghold after the storming on 15 December 1803. The fort was returned to the Mahrattas after they made peace with the British, and they never repaired the breaches which are still there, and, though much overgrown, capable of being climbed. No such breaches remain in Europe, and it was instructive to discover just how steep they are, and how difficult to negotiate, even unencumbered by a musket or sword. The great iron gun which killed five of the attackers with a single shot still lies on its emplacement in the Inner Fort, though its carriage has long decayed and the barrel is disfigured with graffiti. Most of the buildings in the Inner Fort have vanished, or else are so overgrown as to be invisible. There is, alas, no snake pit there. The major gatehouses are still intact, without their gates, and a visitor can only marvel at the suicidal bravery of the men who climbed from the ravine to enter the twisting deathtrap of the Inner Fort's northern gate. Defeat would surely have been their reward, had not Campbell and his Light Company found a way up the side of the ravine and, with the help of a ladder, scaled the wall and so attacked the gates from the inside. By then Beny Singh, the Killadar, had already poisoned his wives, lovers and daughters. He died, like Manu Bappoo, with his sword in his hand. Manu Bappoo almost certainly died in the breaches and not, as the novel says, in the ravine, though that was where most of his men died, trapped between the attackers who had captured the Outer Fort and the 78th who were climbing the road from the plain. They should have found refuge within the Inner Fort, and bolstered its defences, but for reasons that have never been explained, the Inner Fort's gates were fast shut against the survivors of the Outer Fort's garrison.

Elizabeth Longford, in *Wellington, The Years of the Sword*, quotes the late Jac Weller as saying of Gawilghur, 'three reasonably effective troops of Boy Scouts armed with rocks could have kept out several times their number of professional soldiers'. It is difficult to disagree.

Manu Bappoo and Beny Singh made no effort to protect the Outer Fort's walls with a glacis, which was their primary mistake, but their real stronghold was the Inner Fort, and it fell far too swiftly. The supposition is that the defenders were thoroughly demoralized, and the few British casualties (about 150), most of them killed or wounded in the assault on the gatehouse, testify to the swiftness of the victory. A hundred and fifty sounds like a small 'butcher's bill', and so it is, but that should not hide the horror of the fight for the Inner Fort's gatehouse where Kenny died. That fight occurred in a very small space and, for a brief while, must have been as ghastly as, say, the struggle for Badajoz's breaches nine years later. Campbell's escalade up the precipice saved an enormous number of lives and cut a nasty fight blessedly short. Indeed, the victory was so quick, and so cheaply gained, that a recent biography of the Duke of Wellington (in 1803 he was still Sir Arthur Wellesley) accords the siege less than three lines, yet to the redcoat who was sweating up the hill to the plateau and who was expected to carry his firelock and bayonet across the rocky isthmus to the breaches in the double walls it was a significant place and his victory remarkable.

The real significance of Gawilghur lay in the future. Sir Arthur Wellesley had now witnessed the assault of the breach at Seringapatam, had escaladed the walls of Ahmednuggur and swept over the great defences of Gawilghur. In Portugal and Spain, confronted by even greater defences manned by determined French soldiers, it is claimed that he underestimated the difficulties of siege work, having been lulled into complacency by the ease of his Indian victories. There may be truth in that, and at Ciudad Rodrigo, Badajoz, Burgos and San Sebastian he took dreadful casualties. My own suspicion is that he did not so much underestimate the ability of defences to withstand him, as overestimate the capacity of British troops to get through those defences and, astonishingly, they usually lived up to his expectations. And it was Scotsmen who gave him those high expectations: the Scots who used four ladders to capture a city at Ahmednuggur and one ladder to bring down the great fortress of Gawilghur. Their bravery helped disguise the fact that sieges were terrible work, so terrible that the troops, regardless of their commander's wishes, regarded a captured stronghold as their own property, to destroy and violate as they wished. This was their revenge for the horrors that the defenders had inflicted on them, and there was undoubtedly a vast slaughter inside Gawilghur once the victory was gained. Many of the defenders must have escaped down the steep cliffs, but perhaps half of the seven or eight thousand died in an orgy of revenge.

And then the place was forgotten. The Mahrattas were defeated, and even more of India came under British rule or influence. But Sir Arthur Wellesley was done with India, it was time to sail home and look for advancement against the more dangerous and nearer enemy, France. It will be four years before he sails from England to Portugal and to the campaign that will raise him to a dukedom. Sharpe will also go home, to a green instead of a red jacket, and he too will sail to Portugal and march from there into France, but he has a snare or two waiting on his path before he reaches the peninsula. So Sharpe will march again.

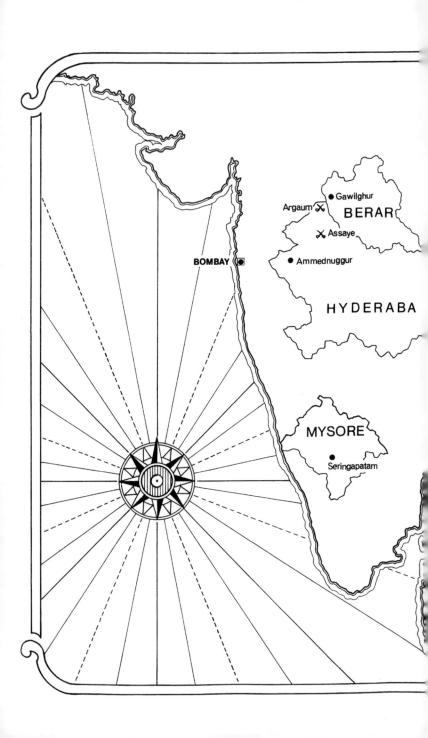